FIRECRACKER

KELLY JAMIESON

PRAISE FOR KELLY JAMIESON

"Kelly Jamieson delivers a blazing passionate read that tugs at the heartstrings!"

~ Carly Phillips, *New York Times* Bestselling Author

"seductive and bewitching from the very start... Softly romantic and wickedly provocative"

~ *RT Book Reviews* on Rule of Three

"Kelly Jamieson now has a permanent place on my keeper shelf and I can't wait to see what she writes next."

~ Joyfully Reviewed

"Ms. Jamieson once again gives the reader a richly detailed story that is brimming over with sexual tension, intoxicating desires and intriguing carnal needs that is edgy and psychologically intense..."

CHAPTER ONE

*M*oving into a fifty-five-plus seniors' complex in Fort Meyers, Florida, was about as appealing as having her hoo-haw bleached.

Hey, apparently vaginal whitening was a thing.

Arden shook her head. Never mind cosmetic procedures for rarely seen body parts. She had more important things to focus on. Like where the hell she was going to live.

She sighed and stared at her email on her laptop. It was nice of Mom and Dad to offer their spare bedroom, but it wasn't going to happen. She knew exactly how that would go down—they'd wrap her up in a blanket and hug her and feed her carbs and tell her everything was going to be okay.

That sounded pretty good, actually.

No. Arden lifted her chin. She'd handled all the crap for the last year on her own. She wasn't going to regress into the pampered princess she'd been when she last lived with her parents. She was a grown woman and she was taking charge of her life.

She was going to have to take her little brother's charity offer instead.

She rubbed her forehead where the chronic ache was worsening. She had enough money in her bank account to cover the move from Phoenix to Chicago, and a tiny cushion, but the word "tiny" when referring to her savings made her stomach cramp and panic flutter in her throat. She had to be out of the house on June 30. That gave her three weeks to pack and ship what furniture and household items she wanted to keep, sell off the rest, and get out of town.

Going home to Chicago wasn't so bad. She'd left there to go to college ten years ago and she still missed it. Phoenix was lovely, but it was different, and now it felt like a prison. She couldn't leave home without thinking people were looking at her, judging her, pitying her, or wondering how she could have been so stupid.

She was wondering that herself.

For an intelligent, educated woman, she'd fucked up epically. Now here she was, twenty-eight years old, homeless, penniless, and widowed.

Arden squeezed her eyes closed at the stab of pain. It was still hard to believe Michael was gone. She'd spent the last ten months coming to terms with that, grieving, even though she'd no longer loved him at the end—and didn't that jab of guilt just add to the pain—but he was her husband.

All their hopes and dreams, gone, in the blink of an eye.

Hell, the truth was, her hopes and dreams had been slowly dying over the last few years. While she'd watched her friends' perfect lives unfold on Facebook, she'd pretended her life was equally perfect. But it wasn't. And wasn't that a guaranteed trip to Depressionville, constantly watching the illusion of everything her friends apparently had that she didn't.

She sucked in a long breath, lifted her chin and focused on

her laptop. Fingers flying over the keyboard, she messaged her brother.

Hey, Jamie! I've given it a lot of thought and decided to take you up on your offer of Apartment 4 if it's still open!

Her little brother the tech geek had become a multimillionaire with his business StatTrakker, and had been buying properties in Chicago, including the four-unit building in Lincoln Park where he lived. He rented out two other units to friends, and one was currently vacant.

His reply came quickly. *Great! When are you arriving? We'll try to get it habitable before you get here.*

Eeek. Habitable? That didn't sound promising.

*You sure this will work? I can go stay with Mom and Dad... *shudder**

Ha! Yes, it will work. We're in the process of renovating that unit—the last one to be done. So you'll have to put up with Tyler doing some work, that's all.

Tyler was Jamie's long-time best buddy. She remembered him hanging around with Jamie when they'd been younger. Nice kid, though he and Jamie had been equally gangly, awkward, and goofy. Tyler'd been tall and skinny with major orthodontic work. The two boys had been sixteen when she'd left for college.

Sure, that's fine, she typed back. *Beggars can't be choosers.* Then she added a smiley face, even though it was a sad truth. *I'll let you know my flight details as soon as I book it.*

She looked around the nearly empty ranch-style house she'd shared with Michael the last four years of their five-year marriage, filled with brilliant Arizona sun. She loved this house and giving it up was hard. But in a way, it was for the best. There were painful memories here that she wanted to leave behind. She'd start over in Chicago.

The uncertainty of her life filled her with churning dread.

But it would be okay. *She* was okay. The last year had been a nightmare, but it was done now, and it was time to move on.

She couldn't book a flight online because she had no credit cards anymore, so she had to go to a travel agent where she could write a check. She'd already sold their two vehicles, so she had to walk to the bus stop, which wasn't exactly close. In the hundred-degree afternoon heat, she was soon wilted and sweaty.

When she'd accomplished that errand, she had one more stop to make. She paused in front of the shop, eyeing the sign that said "Diamond Joe's." She sucked briefly on her bottom lip, then entered.

The small store was lined with glass display counters full of gold, silver, and gems that glittered in the fluorescent lights. She crossed to the back counter where a man was inspecting a piece of jewelry with a loupe. He looked up at her and smiled, his round face creasing. He was round everywhere...the top of his bald head, his face, his belly in a strained white shirt. "Hello," he greeted her. "How can I help you?"

She bent her head to look at the diamond wedding set on her left hand. She'd loved these rings so much. She couldn't help but remember the day Michael had proposed to her, how giddy and in love they'd been—probably too young to get married but with stars in their eyes as bright as the diamonds on the engagement ring, they'd imagined a perfect life together.

An ache of loss and regret bloomed inside her.

She'd sold nearly everything else of value they had. She'd resisted selling the rings, even though she had no daughter to pass them on to and her marriage had been a shell, because at one time they had meant something. They'd meant so very much.

Her throat thickened as she slowly pulled the rings off. "I'd like to sell these."

Two weeks later, she stood in the kitchen surveying the boxes of household items, trying to decide what to pack and what to get rid of. It was painful to contemplate giving up the Lagostina cookware, Henkel knives, and KitchenAid mixer. Even more than it had been to decide which designer shoes to keep and which to send to consignment.

The doorbell rang.

Her head jerked around. Who could that be? Frowning, she headed to the front door to see her mother standing on the doorstep.

She threw open the door. "Mom! What are you doing here?"

Mom smiled and opened her arms for a hug. "I came to help."

Arden moved into her mom's embrace, and as her mother's arms closed around her, emotion surged into her throat painfully. She hugged her mom back, and they stood together for a moment. Then she drew in a shaky breath and pulled back.

"I told you not to come."

"I know you did."

Arden stepped back, and Mom picked up her small suitcase and followed her inside. "Nice and cool in here," Mom said, fanning herself. "I had to come, honey. You're all on your own, trying to pack up things in this huge house all by yourself."

"I can handle it." She'd been determined to be strong and self-reliant, but now her mom was here, she was actually... grateful. She'd been feeling overwhelmed. She still wasn't sleeping well, tired both physically and mentally, and that didn't help.

"I know you can." Mom touched her cheek. "But you don't have to. That's what family is for."

Arden wanted to cry but fought back the tears. "You're right," she managed to choke out. Her brother was taking her in and helping out, and now her mom was here to help and even though she wanted to be a grown-up and take responsibility for everything…she was so glad she had family. She'd do the same if they needed help.

She met her mom's eyes. "Thanks, Mom."

Mom clasped her upper arms gently and held her gaze. "You're going to be fine. You *are* fine. This will be a good change for you."

Arden nodded. "A new start. I agree." She smiled. "Jamie's been great, letting me stay at his place."

"Of course. I'd be giving him hell if he didn't." She smiled ruefully. "You two…" She shook her head. "I don't know what happened to you."

"What do you mean?" Arden strolled to the kitchen, ready to make her mom a cup of coffee or iced tea. She paused at the big granite island and set her hands on the cool stone, facing her mom as she followed.

"You both lead such different lives…it kind of blows my mind."

Arden laughed. "What?"

"Well, look at Jamie…making so much money he doesn't know what to do with it, buying real estate and renovating it, and making even more money. And you…married to a famous football player, hobnobbing with celebrities, hosting fancy dinner parties…" She chuckles. "That's not how you grew up. That's not who your father and I are. We're just regular mid-westerners—"

"Who retired to Florida."

"Well, yes, but we're not living in some super luxurious

retirement resort. We wanted to give you both a good life and encourage you to be the best you can be, but we sure as heck never envisioned what you've both done. Your worlds are so different than ours."

"Not anymore," Arden muttered, aware that she hadn't really done anything with her life. "Would you like coffee? Or something cold?"

"A cold drink would be wonderful."

Arden opened the fridge and grabbed a pitcher of tea, then poured two glasses.

"So, where should I start?" Mom looked around the kitchen. "You know I love organizing things."

She really did. More gratitude flooded through Arden, a little of the weight lifting off her shoulders. "Thank you, Mom."

A week later, Arden arrived at O'Hare. Jamie was there to meet her, and when she saw him, sudden emotion swamped her. She'd felt lonely in Phoenix, abandoned by the people she'd thought were friends, until Mom showed up.

"Hey!" He threw his arms around her in a big bear hug. "You're here."

She nodded against his broad chest. He may be her younger brother, but he sure wasn't little anymore, now over six feet tall, still lean but broad-shouldered. She hugged him back. "I'm here."

"I'm glad. We've been worried about you. It'll be good to have you here where I can keep an eye on you."

Her head jerked back, and she frowned up at him. "Jamie. I don't need a babysitter. I'm fine."

He grinned. His mop of dark curls still fell over his forehead and ears, and he still wore dark-framed glasses, but now had a layer of dark stubble on his jaw. "I know, I know. Humor me. It's been hard being so far away from you, knowing what you're going through."

She'd tried to downplay the disaster her life had been after Michael's death, but eventually had to tell her family everything. They'd been there for Michael's funeral, but she'd insisted she could deal with things on her own after that.

"It's done," she said. "Finally."

"Good." His smile faded and he studied her face. "You sure you're okay? You look like you've lost weight."

"Yay."

He rolled his eyes. "As if you needed to."

"Ten pounds. I always wanted to lose ten pounds." She smiled.

They headed toward the baggage carousel for her flight, Jamie's arm slung around her shoulders. "So, is the apartment 'habitable'?" she asked.

He laughed. "Yeah, it's habitable. We worked on the kitchen first, so you have a nice new kitchen, but there's still a lot to be done in the rest of the place."

"When you say 'we worked,' you mean Tyler worked."

"Hey." He frowned in affront. "I do help. I've been learning from him."

She lifted her eyebrows. "Really?"

"Well. Some. Mostly I'm just his gopher. I tried to use some crazy huge power saw once and nearly cut my hand off. But I have other talents."

"That you do." Even though Jamie's success made her feel even more like a loser, she was proud of her geeky little brother. He'd started his business when he was in his senior year of high school and holy fuckbuckets, look at him now.

Literally, look at him now. Because all the other women

around them were definitely looking. Jesus. She squinted at him.

"What? Why are you looking at me like that?"

She elbowed him in the ribs. "Those girls are checking you out."

He smiled.

"I'm trying to figure out why." She put on a mystified expression.

Jamie scowled. "Thanks."

She grinned. Teasing her baby brother was making her world all better.

Eventually her bags arrived. "Holy shit," Jamie said as he hauled one off the conveyor belt. "What the hell did you bring?"

"All my worldly possessions. In two suitcases, FYI."

"Not quite all your worldly possessions. The stuff you shipped is in the apartment."

"Oh, good."

They each took one suitcase and started toward the exit to the parking garage. Arden's shoulders were burning by the time they arrived at his vehicle, a gleaming new Jeep. "Nice ride."

"Thanks." Despite his earlier complaints, he lifted her heavy suitcases into the back of the Jeep with ease and she shoved her carry-on in there too. Soon they were zipping along I-90. She watched familiar scenery slide by as Jamie talked about his business and baffled her with techy bullshit.

When they exited and Jamie eventually turned onto North Hudson, she gazed around her new neighborhood, smiling. Mature trees lined the narrow street and provided leafy green shade to the late nineteenth century stone and brick row houses, and at the base of the trees, wrought iron fences surrounded beds full of ivy and begonias. Jamie parked in front of a red brick building with ivy climbing up and around the arched windows and a pretty green courtyard in front. A wrought iron fence edged the courtyard, bordered by green shrubs on each side. Jamie unlocked the gate and as they walked up the sidewalk, she eyed the neatly trimmed patch of grass, the entrance with its substantial wooden door, and above it the name THE TRIUMPH carved into stone.

"Did you plant that?" She gestured at a big black pot on the front steps overflowing with bright red and orange impatiens, lime green sweet potato vines, and multicolored coleus.

"Nah. Mila did."

"Figures. It's nice."

He laughed.

Arden had yet to meet Mila, though she'd heard about her. Mila and Jamie had gone to college together, and now she lived with him. Well, not *with* him, not *that* way. But in the same building. Arden had teased Jamie once about Mila being his girlfriend, and he'd been horrified. "Christ no!" He'd waved his hands like an umpire calling someone safe on base. "We're friends. That's all."

Apparently it was, because Jamie was constantly out with women, and Mila had a boyfriend.

As they entered, Arden took stock of the building, having never been there. The hardwood floors had been beautifully refinished, as well as the tall baseboards. She admired the original stained glass windows, the ornate ceiling medallion and crystal chandelier hanging above, and elegant sconces on the walls now fitted with electric lights. Mahogany doors on either side of the hall wore big brass numbers *1* and *2*, and a grand mahogany staircase climbed to the second floor.

"Wow, this is gorgeous, Jamie."

"Thanks. The place needed a lot of work, so I got a good deal, but it's coming along."

She could only imagine how much a building like this—in

this neighborhood—cost, even if it did need work. She set a hand on the big carved newel post. "Up?"

"Yeah. Leave that case, I'll come back and get it."

The door of apartment two swung open and a woman popped out into the hall. "Hiiiii! You must be Arden!"

Arden smiled tentatively. "And you must be Mila."

"Yes! I'm so happy to meet you! It's going to be awesome to have another woman in the building!"

Mila was stunning…shiny dark hair cut in one of those bobs that was short in the back and longer at the front, curving around her perfect oval face. The tilted-up corners of her eyes gave her a mischievous look. Her full lips and high cheekbones had Arden blinking in awe of her beauty.

And her enthusiastic greeting was…nice. Arden's smile widened. "Yeah, you don't want to be outnumbered."

"Hell no. The testosterone around here sometimes is suffocating. And annoying." But she grinned. "Welcome back to Chicago."

"Thank you." Mila obviously knew her story, but there was no awkwardness as she stepped forward to hug her.

"You've been through a rough time," Mila said, her tone gentler. "So we're going to have some fun."

Dammit, tears stung Arden's eyes again. She didn't want pity, but someone being nice to her was enough to make her cry. "I'd like to have some fun."

"We'll get you settled in." Mila reached for a suitcase.

"You can't carry that upstairs," Jamie told her.

She frowned. "Yes, I can. I've been working out."

He snorted. "With five-pound weights."

She bugged her eyes out at him. "I'm up to eight pounds now." She raised one slender arm and flexed, and tiny biceps appeared.

Arden rolled her lips in to keep from laughing.

"I've never had good upper body strength," Mila said to Arden. "A while back, I lost an arm wrestling match against your brother, and I vowed that would never happen again."

Arden widened her eyes. "Jamie beat a girl at arm wrestling?" she asked in a shocked tone.

Jamie gave the back of her head a gentle smack. "Hey now. Enough of this. Up." He jerked his chin at the stairs.

Mila and Arden exchanged smiles, and Arden started up with her carry-on.

The second floor was similar to the first, with a small hall and a door on each side, this time obviously numbered *3* and *4*.

Mila entered first, the door unlocked, and Arden followed, Jamie bringing up the rear with a suitcase. "Tyler's working, or he'd be here to welcome you too."

Arden walked to the middle of the living room. "You unpacked my stuff."

"Yeah." Jamie dragged the big suitcase into the bedroom and reappeared. "Tyler and Mila helped me get things arranged."

"You guys." Arden's bottom lip quivered yet again. "You didn't have to do that."

Mila shrugged. "It was no trouble, really. You don't have a lot of stuff." She said it in such a matter-of-fact tone that Arden decided right then that she loved her.

"Nope, I don't." There'd been a time in her life when having the new car, the big house, designer clothes, and beautiful furniture had mattered. Now, she knew stuff didn't matter at all.

While Jamie clomped down the stairs and back up with the other suitcase that Mila had apparently changed her mind about carrying up, Arden looked around the small apartment. The hardwood floor had been refinished up here too, the golden oak gleaming in the afternoon sun that flooded in the two arched windows overlooking the street. The walls on the other hand…were a mess. All the trim had been removed and there were big holes here and there in the plaster, the paint chipped and peeling.

"I love the fireplace," she murmured, moving toward it to inspect the old brick and the oak mantel.

"We all have one," Mila said. "It's definitely a great feature of this building. They're going to clean up the brick and refinish the mantel. And you can see some of the work that's in progress." She waved a hand. "But come see the kitchen! It's gorgeous."

Arden moved to the kitchen, separated from the living space by a granite counter. "It *is* beautiful." She contrasted it to the huge gourmet kitchen she'd had in Phoenix. She loved to cook and had taken a bunch of cooking classes over the years. But even though this space was tiny, it had decent counter space and was fitted with new stainless steel appliances among the dark wood cupboards. She could see herself cooking there. Maybe not the big dinner parties she and Michael used to host, but even cooking for just herself, it was a nice space.

"I love it." She smiled at Jamie. "You did good."

He grinned. "It was a team effort."

"As in Tyler did all the work." Mila wrinkled her nose at Jamie.

"Bullshit. Also, you helped." He pointed at Mila. "She picked out the cabinets and appliances."

Arden slid open a drawer and found her cutlery already there. When she opened a cupboard, she discovered the set of dishes she'd elected to keep, about half of her bright Fiestaware collection. "Thank you," she said again, touched by how they'd helped.

"I picked up a few basics at the store." Mila gestured at the fridge. "So you won't have to go out shopping right away.

There's coffee and milk, bread…cheese and crackers. But we'll take you out for dinner tonight."

"You don't have to do that."

"Sure we do! We want to show you around the neighborhood and help you settle in. And anyway, we have to eat, and neither Jamie nor I are very good in the kitchen."

"Okay, thank you. That sounds nice." She couldn't help but think Mila and Jamie sounded like a couple. But just friends…okay.

Mila and Jamie showed her the rest of the apartment. The bathroom was functional but had dated fixtures and ugly wall tiles. Her king-size bed had been set up and was made with the bedding she'd shipped, and her only dresser sat against one wall. Boxes of books and clothing sat stacked in the corner for her to deal with.

"We'll let you explore a bit and unpack," Jamie said.

"You might want to move things around from the way we arranged them," Mila added. "If you need any help just come on down."

They arranged a time to go out for dinner, and then she was alone. She looked around, pressing a hand to her heart. Okay. This was it. Her new home and her new life.

She was terrified.

CHAPTER TWO

*T*yler rolled out of bed at the crack of noon on Sunday.

Hey, he'd just come off a twenty-four-hour shift. He'd only had a few hours' sleep due to not one but *three* drug overdoses they'd had to respond to…typical Saturday night. He'd crawled into bed when he got home at eight thirty to grab a few more z's.

He yawned and stretched as he walked naked to the bathroom to crank on the shower. After that and a pot of coffee, he'd be good to go.

Two full days off stretched ahead of him. A gorgeous summer Sunday, judging from the bright sunlight streaming in the bathroom window. He'd see what Jamie and Mila were up to; maybe they'd hit the beach or something.

After a shower and a rub of a towel to his hair, he started coffee then returned to the bedroom to pull on a pair of loose athletic shorts and a faded navy CHICAGO FIRE DEPARTMENT T-shirt. He looked at the mail that had arrived yesterday while he'd been at work. Nothing interesting.

He poured coffee into a travel mug and headed downstairs to find Jamie, but paused outside his apartment door. He needed to get bathroom measurements from Apartment Four so he could go to Home Depot and pick up some stuff. Maybe he should do that now.

He ducked back inside his apartment to grab a tape measure and a notepad. He shoved a pencil behind his ear. Juggling his coffee and the other things, he crossed the hall. But when he tried the knob, it was locked. Huh.

They hardly ever locked their doors in the building, since it was just the three friends, and the exterior doors were always locked. But he had a key, so he retrieved it then let himself into the apartment.

He'd helped Mila and Jamie unpack Arden's things a couple of days ago. They hadn't touched the really personal stuff, but unpacking her sheets and pillows had felt weird. Even weirder because it was *Arden's* sheets and pillows. The girl who'd starred in every single one of his teenage fantasies.

The apartment even smelled different now…must be because of her things being there…an exotic fruity floral scent. He strode purposefully to the bathroom and yanked open the door.

The female scream that split the silence nearly ripped his eardrums open.

"Jesus Christ!" The items he was carrying flew out of his startled hands, the tape measure and the mug clattering to the floor, the note pad skidding down the hall. As he staggered back, he caught a glimpse of naked woman.

Smooth, tanned skin. Long dark hair. The sweep of a hip and—sweet mother of God— the curve of a breast tipped with a dark nipple. And wide, horrified eyes as she grabbed a towel and held it in front of herself.

"Get out!" she shrieked then let out another piercing scream. "Aaaaah! Help! Jamie! Help!"

Jesus, fuck, it was Arden. Tyler held up his hands. "Hey! Hey! Calm down."

She made some frightened noises.

"It's me, Tyler! Remember...Tyler Ramirez? Jamie's friend?"

She gaped at him, the little blue towel she clutched not covering much. Now *he* wanted to whimper. She was fucking gorgeous.

Still.

"I am so sorry." He kept his eyes firmly on her face, smiling tentatively. "When did you get here?"

"Um." She looked like she was having a heart attack. Good thing he was a trained EMT. "Yesterday."

"Shit." He grimaced. "I could've sworn Jamie said you were arriving Monday."

"No." She swallowed. "Are you really Tyler?"

He frowned. She didn't even recognize him? "Yeah."

"Oh. Okay. Um...could we continue this conversation when I'm dressed?"

He smacked his forehead and turned around. "Yeah. Of course. Dumbass," he muttered under his breath. "I'll, uh, wait in the living room."

He picked up his things, rubbing at the hardwood floor he'd just refinished weeks ago, hoping like hell the travel mug hadn't scratched the new finish. Looked okay. Then he strode back to the living room where they'd arranged her furniture. He was going to fucking kill Jamie.

He set his things down on the granite counter and pressed the heels of his palms to his eyes. Christ, that vision was seared into his retinas for the rest of eternity. Naked Arden Lennox. Holy shit.

Okay, okay, calm down, dude.

He was over that high school crush. Way the fuck over it.

She was here and he was an idiot.

He'd been trying to imagine what it would be like to see Arden again. It had been, what—eleven years since he'd seen her? Nah, he'd seen her one year at Christmas when she'd been home...so maybe nine years ago? Whatever. So he'd had a crush on her. That was a long time ago. He'd been a kid then, and she'd married someone else. She was a widow now, mind you, but still. They were different people.

And he'd just embarrassed them both.

A few minutes later, Arden appeared, now dressed in a pair of cropped black leggings and a loose tank top. And yeah, she was still just as beautiful with those big brown eyes, creamy smooth skin, and sweetly curved lips.

"Well, that was a great reintroduction, wasn't it?" Tyler said with a grin. "I really am sorry. I had no idea you were already here. I came to get some measurements so I can get started on your bathroom next week."

She still seemed shaken and annoyed. "I guess there was a miscommunication about when I was arriving."

"Yeah. I'm going to murder your brother." He frowned. "I'm surprised he didn't come running to your rescue. That scream was loud enough that everyone in Lincoln Park probably heard it."

"He's not home," she admitted. "He and Mila went out to get breakfast a little while ago. They're going to bring back something for me, so I jumped in the shower."

"What? They're not bringing *me* anything?"

"Actually, I think they are, but they didn't want to wake you up."

"Oh. Okay." He paused. "So you screamed for him even though you knew he wasn't here."

She made a face and her lips twitched. "I figured a burglar wouldn't know that."

"Quick thinking. Luckily I'm not a burglar."

"How did you get in?"

"Through the door."

Her eyebrows rose. "You have a key?"

"Yeah. Uh…is that a problem?"

"I'd kind of like to know when someone's coming into my apartment."

"Interesting concept."

She frowned, and he couldn't stop his grin. Jamie and Mila wandered at will in and out of every other apartment, and he'd learned to lock the door if he really needed privacy.

"We hardly ever lock our doors inside, since the outside doors are always locked. But we all have keys to one another's apartments just in case. I'm in this unit all the time working on it. But I'll try not to get in your way."

She nibbled her bottom lip. "Jamie told me you're still working on this place. I knew that was part of the deal."

Right, right. Apparently she'd had to sell her house. Jamie'd told him that she'd discovered after her husband had died that he hadn't exactly been in good financial shape.

She moved past him to the kitchen and reached into a cupboard for a bright yellow mug. "Would you like some coffee?"

"Got some, thanks." He picked up the travel mug that had bounced off the floor minutes ago. Luckily the lid had stayed tight.

He watched her pour coffee into the mug. "You haven't changed at all," he blurted. Maybe she had a bit—that smile she'd beamed around seemed to have dimmed a little.

Her lips curved up reluctantly and she curled her hands around the mug. "Thank you. You sure have."

He rubbed his face. "You really didn't recognize me?"

"I think you were sixteen the last time I saw you. You weren't even shaving, probably, and you had braces." Her gaze swept over him, lingering on his chest and shoulders. "And you've...filled out."

The air in the apartment thickened, and Tyler's blood heated at her perusal of his anatomy.

Then she blinked and added, "You were a pretty scrawny kid."

Okay, maybe that *hadn't* been sexual interest and a flirtatious comment. And her reminder that she'd viewed him as a kid was even more deflating. "Huh. Yeah, I guess I was. I work out a lot now; we kind of have to stay in shape to do our job." He scratched the side of his neck.

"You're a firefighter, Jamie says."

"That's right."

"That's a hard job."

"Sometimes. Sometimes it's also boring as hell." One corner of his mouth cranked up. "But I work with a great group."

"I understand I have you to thank for getting my stuff unpacked." She waved a hand.

"Partially." He grimaced. "I helped. Mila's the one you should thank. She was all concerned about you feeling comfortable when you get here. I'm afraid Jamie and I were kind of clueless males."

"Well, it did help, so thank you." She sipped her coffee.

He wanted to say something about her husband, but fuck, this was awkward. He swallowed. "I'm sorry for your loss...of your husband. Jamie told me about it." He cleared his throat. "Of course."

Yeah, he was smooth. As smooth as Lake Michigan in a winter windstorm.

"Thank you. It's been a tough year." Her mouth tightened and her eyes flickered, but she kept her head high.

"I'm sure. But you made the right decision to come home. Family's important."

She blinked at him and nodded. "That's true."

"Jamie's been worried about you."

"Aw." She rolled her eyes and lifted her mug to her lips again. "Yeah, I know. Truthfully, *I've* been worried about myself." The corners of her mouth quirked up.

Her humor in the face of adversity made his chest warm.

"But I'm fine," she added. "So…you said you needed some measurements…?"

"Right." Christ. He was distracted watching her, kind of blown away by the fact that he was standing there with Arden Lennox. Er, Arden Hughes, now. "Yeah, I can do that." He set his cup down and grabbed his other things, then booked it into the bathroom.

Here that scent was even more evident…warm and feminine and sexy, the air still slightly steamy from her shower. He paused a moment to breathe it in. Damn. Letting out a long, slow breath, he checked out the room. Yeah, it would be good to get this done. He started measuring and jotting notes, ignoring the dripping pink puffy sponge, the bottles of shampoo…his gaze fell on the body wash. Bombshell. That was the scent. Jesus Christ.

He scrubbed a hand over his face and refocused on work.

The sound of thudding feet up the stairs reached his ears, then voices in Arden's apartment as Jamie and Mila returned. He heard Jamie shout, "Hey, Ty! You up?"

"He's here," Arden told her brother. "In the bathroom. Measuring something."

Seconds later, Jamie appeared in the bathroom door. "Dude. You want waffles?"

"Hell yeah." Tyler slid the pencil back behind his ear. "I was afraid you forgot about me."

Jamie grinned. "Nah."

Tyler followed the scent of bacon back to Arden's kitchen, where Mila was making herself at home per usual, pulling out plates while Arden opened the bags of food.

"From the Waffle Shack," Mila announced. "Best waffles in town. And bacon. We don't go there *every* Sunday, but…"

"We go there a lot," Tyler said.

Arden smiled, but seemed a little bemused by the people who'd invaded her kitchen as they all filled plates with food and moved to her small dining table.

"I don't have any napkins," Arden said apologetically.

"No worries! We got some." Mila pulled paper napkins out of a bag and handed them around.

"You don't want that butter, do you?" Mila asked Jamie, reaching for his plate.

Jamie pretended to stab her hand with his fork. "Yes, I do."

Tyler handed over a small container of whipped butter. "Here you go, butterball."

"I love butter," Mila confessed to Arden. "I probably shouldn't have it, but thank you, Tyler."

"You don't *look* like someone who likes butter," Arden said.

"She eats like a goddamn elephant," Jamie said. "And yet still looks like a stickman."

"Stickman! Seriously?" Mila scowled at Jamie.

Tyler ignored their insults. "Who wants to go to the beach today? I feel like some beach volleyball."

"Sure," Mila said. "It's a nice day. I'll need to shave my legs."

"Thanks for sharing that." Jamie shook his head and forked up more waffle. "Yeah, the beach sounds great."

"Arden?" Tyler looked at her, trying to make his expression friendly and casual. "You want to come?"

She stared back at him for a moment, and he wondered what was wrong. Did he have bacon in his teeth? She nodded slowly. "Okay." Then she gave her head a shake and looked down at her plate.

"Hey, let me text Olivia and book a cabana at the Beach Ball Café." Jamie pulled out his phone.

"You'll never get a cabana at this short notice," Mila said.

"Pfft." Jamie bent his head as he texted.

Tyler's own phone buzzed in his pocket, and he pulled it out. "Norton." He made a face. "Should I invite him?"

His cousin Norton was close to their age, a couple of years younger, and hung out with them sometimes. He was a good guy, but easiest to handle in small doses.

"Sure, invite him," Mila said easily. "Arden's going to have to meet him some time."

"I apologize in advance, Arden," he said as he tapped in a text message. "He has a good heart."

Arden laughed. "Ooookay."

"And I'll see what Garth is doing." Mila turned to Arden. "Garth's my boyfriend."

"Got a cabana," Jamie announced triumphantly a moment later.

"That's so cool!" Arden looked more animated than she had all morning.

"Norton will meet us there," Tyler added.

"Perfect. Let's clean up this mess and get going."

"It's okay—" Arden started.

"Hell no, we invaded your apartment and made the mess, so we'll help clean it up." Jamie began picking up dishes.

"Maybe next weekend I can make you all waffles," Arden said. "I make pretty good waffles, if I do say so myself."

"You can cook?" Mila and Jamie both said at the same time, staring at her as if she'd just announced she'd cured cancer.

"Yeah. I like cooking."

"Me too," Tyler said. "I cook for the guys at the station all the time."

"You don't cook for *us*," Jamie complained.

"You can *definitely* make us waffles next Sunday," Mila said to Arden.

"I'll drive to the beach," Jamie offered. "There's room for all of us in my Jeep, and since you have tomorrow off, Ty, that means you can drink."

"Hey, how was your date Friday night?" Tyler asked Jamie as he too carried dishes into the kitchen.

Jamie's lips thinned and his gaze slid away. "Uh. I had fun."

Mila started choking and leaned against the counter. Was she laughing?

"Do I need to Heimlich you?" Tyler asked her.

She waved her hands and shook her head. "I'm okay," she wheezed.

"What's so funny? And why are you looking so weird?" he said to Jamie.

"The date didn't turn out like he expected," Mila said.

"You met this chick on Spark, right?" Tyler said, naming a popular dating app. "You thought she was amazing."

Mila collapsed onto the counter in a fit of giggles.

"What?" Tyler demanded, grinning too.

Arden looked back and forth among the three of them, wide-eyed. "Oh we *have* to hear this. Come on, Jamie."

"Tell them, Jamie," Mila choked out.

"Okay, okay. This chick seemed really perfect on Spark—hot, fun, a little geeky. Sounded perfect. So we met for a drink on Friday…turns out she's a drag queen."

"You mean he," Mila corrected.

"Well, he's Honey Deville onstage, but he introduced himself as Danny when I met him."

Tyler and Arden burst out laughing at the same time.

"How did that even happen?" Tyler asked.

"It was totally my bad." Jamie waved a hand. "That's the embarrassing part. I've never used Spark before, and I didn't read the whole bio or swipe through all his pictures, so I just saw the Honey picture."

"But here's the best part." Mila waved a hand at Jamie to go on.

"He was a really nice guy," Jamie said. "So I stayed, and we had a few beers. It was a fun evening." He hitched one shoulder and shut the door of the dishwasher, looking around at them all earnestly.

Tyler laughed. "Are you seeing him again?"

"Not on a date. But we might hang out and play Call of Duty sometime."

"Oh, Jamie." Arden shook her head, an affectionate smile brightening her face.

Tyler looked at her across the small room. There it was—the smile. The one that had made his knees weak and his heart stutter. It lit up her eyes and transformed her face from girl next door to glamour queen.

And goddammit…it still made his heart stutter.

CHAPTER THREE

*A*rden looked around the upscale, beachside restaurant and bar. She'd never been to this place. A group played live music on the patio at one end, and people wearing skimpy swimsuits and casual clothes lined the bar. The hostess led them past the bar and tables arranged on the outdoor deck to a white-canopied cabana. Dark wicker furniture with bright cushions formed a U-shape around a long, low table. They had a perfect view of the beach over the low railing.

"I'm impressed," she said to Jamie, dropping her tote bag on a chair. "This looks fun and way too cool for a nerd like you."

"Pfft."

Arden caught Tyler's quick grin.

Oh yeah, Tyler'd been a nerd too.

Not anymore, though. He looked like he fit right in here, wearing a pair of black board shorts and a T-shirt that hugged his broad shoulders and chest and draped over his flat abs. His thick dark hair gleamed in the sun. His sunglasses hid his eyes, and yet she had the feeling he was looking at her too. She was glad she also had sunglasses on, hoping they hid the fact that she was totally checking him out.

Other women at the bar weren't hiding that fact. Arden couldn't help but notice the looks he was getting. Although some of the looks were for Jamie, as at the airport yesterday.

She had to admit her little brother and his friend had grown up into chick magnets. What was happening in the world? "I need a drink," she announced.

"Hell, yeah." Mila nodded. "Me too."

"It's National Daiquiri Day," Arden said, picking up a menu card.

"How the hell do you know that?" Jamie asked.

Arden shrugged, studying the card. "I just do. Do they have daiquiris?"

"They have great daiquiris," Mila said. "I love the peach one."

"Perfect!"

"Is Garth coming?" Jamie asked.

Mila wrinkled her nose. "No. He's working."

"On Sunday?"

Mila looked down and plucked at her beach coverup. "Yeah. They're really busy right now."

Arden felt the faint tension emanating from Mila.

"He works all the fucking time," Jamie said with a snort.

"You're one to talk." Mila lifted her chin. "The guy who works sixteen-hour days."

Jamie shrugged. "Not every day. I like to have fun."

"Sixteen-hour days?" Arden gaped at her brother. "Jamie, that's not healthy."

"I love it," Jamie simply replied. "Work is fun for me."

"With the Fourth of July holiday coming up, Garth will take some time off," Mila said confidently.

As they ordered beers and settled into the comfortable

chairs, the breeze off the lake teased Arden's hair, and she turned her face into it, enjoying the pleasant temperatures. Unlike Phoenix, where sometimes you needed mist sprayers to sit outside, this was so pleasant. And that big expanse of blue, blue water…she'd missed that too.

With a sigh, she leaned back in the chair and crossed her legs. This was nice and relaxing. She hadn't slept well last night. She hadn't slept well for the last year.

Of course her first night in her new home, her mind wouldn't shut off, and when she did drift off to sleep she was startled into heart-pounding wakefulness by her dreams… terror-filled dreams of trying to get to Michael to save him and not being able to, over and over. She'd been having that same dream in various forms off and on for months. She probably had enormous bags under her eyes from lack of sleep, thankfully now hidden behind sunglasses.

Somehow she sensed Tyler's attention on her, even though he too lounged in a chair opposite her in a casual pose. Her skin tingled everywhere.

"So are you looking for a job, Arden?" Mila asked when they had daiquiris in hand.

"I will be." She made a face then sipped her drink through the straw. "Not sure what kind of job, though."

"Were you working in Phoenix?"

"No." She peered into her drink and stirred the ice cubes around. "I have a business degree, but when we moved to Phoenix, my husband was playing professional football. He made good money, so I didn't need to work. I did some volunteer work, though."

Mila nodded.

Arden's stomach tightened as it did whenever she thought about her financial situation and the need to find a job. Quickly. Except a business degree from six years ago with no work experience other than organizing charity events wasn't going to help much with that. She took a few deep breaths, trying to relax the tension that gripped her. She needed to just live in the moment. It was a beautiful day, and she was here with her brother and his friends sitting beside the beach drinking a delicious cocktail. She had a cute, albeit somewhat dilapidated, apartment, but it was a place to live and it was comforting to have Jamie living right in the building so she didn't feel totally alone.

"Heeeeeey!" a loud male voice cut through the conversation the others were having about the Cubs season.

Arden looked up to see a man about the same age as the rest of them, dark haired like Tyler, about five nine and stocky. He wore Ray-Ban sunglasses with neon green arms, a blue T-shirt that said Do not be alarmed, this is a kindness, and a pair of baggy board shorts.

"Hey, Norton." Tyler gave a casual wave.

Jamie reached over to bro shake Norton's hand. "Hey, buddy. Have a seat."

"Hi, Jamie. Hi, Mila."

"Hey, Norton, how's it going?"

"Good." Then Norton's gaze fell on Arden. "Hel-looooo." He pushed up his sunglasses and smiled at her.

"Norton, this is my sister, Arden. She just moved into the empty apartment in our building."

Norton frowned. "You told me you weren't renting that apartment out until you were finished renovating it."

Jamie's mouth opened and then shut. Arden felt the atmosphere around them shift to bordering on uncomfortable. "Well, uh, yeah, but Arden needed somewhere to stay right away. She just moved here from Phoenix. I warned her that it would be under construction, and she was okay with that."

Norton turned his attention back to Arden, extending a

hand. She smiled and shook it, uncertain of where the sudden tension came from. "Nice to meet you, Norton."

"Likewise." He smiled, his gaze moving over her in a way that was more awkward than creepy. But his smile seemed sincere. He dropped a backpack onto the deck and took the empty seat next to her. "So. Arden. Besides being sexy, what do you do for a living?"

Arden choked on a laugh. "Uh. Funny, we were just discussing that. I'm unemployed right now. Got any leads on a good job?"

His eyes widened. "Hell yeah. I can put a good word in for you where I work. The girls in HR are all hot for me."

She rolled her lips in briefly, trying not to look over at Tyler and Jamie seated across from them. "Where do you work, Norton?"

"At Guardian Mutual. I'm a desktop support tech."

"Oh. Cool. You and Jamie must have a lot in common." She bit her lip and now chanced a look at her brother, who grinned.

"Yeah, we're both tech dudes," Norton agreed. "Except he's rich and I'm…not. But hey, I'm working my way up the ladder."

Arden nodded.

The waitress arrived again, and Norton gave her a long up-and-down look. Arden couldn't blame him; she was lovely, wearing a tiny pair of shorts and a bikini top. The girl smiled brightly at Norton. "What can I get you, handsome?"

Norton's eyes brightened. "I'll have a piña colada, please."

The girl's eyes flickered. "Sure thing!"

Norton turned back to Arden. "Hey, Arden. Feel my T-shirt. Know what it's made of?"

She slanted a look at Tyler, then back at Norton without moving a hand. "What?"

He grinned. "Boyfriend material."

She grinned, nodding. "Good one."

"That's my *sister*, Norton," Jamie said. "Cool it."

"Right, right. So. What are we up to today?" Norton drummed his hands on the table as if playing a bongo. "Maybe some beach volleyball?"

"Sure." Tyler shoved his glasses on top of his head and sat forward. "That'd be fun. I was thinking that too."

"Let's finish our drinks," Mila said. "Except we're an odd number now."

Jamie looked around. "Pretty sure I can find one more person...oh, there she is."

Mila frowned. "Who?"

"I don't know her yet." Jamie grinned. "But I will. Be right back."

Mila snorted and watched him stand and stroll over to a blonde at the bar in a turquoise bikini.

"I guess it's easy to pick up chicks when you're loaded," Norton said, and the dejected tone of his voice tugged at Arden's heart strings.

"I doubt that was his opening line, dude," Tyler said mildly. "Pretty sure he didn't go up to her and say, 'Hey, I'm rich, wanna play beach volleyball with me?'"

Arden laughed and met Tyler's eyes. "Oh, who knows," she said. "I never thought Jamie was particularly skilled with women."

"You've obviously been away for a while." Tyler grinned at her, and holy hotness, she felt that smile all the way into her bikini bottom. She blinked and quickly sipped her daiquiri.

"Your brother's all growed up." Mila winked. "Chicks dig him."

Norton sighed. The waitress arrived with his drink, and he took it and gulped half of it down.

Arden was now realizing why they'd warned her about Norton. She could see how he could get on your nerves. But she remembered Tyler saying he had a good heart, and they apparently kept including him in their activities, and that was kind of…nice.

She relaxed a little more, grateful to Jamie for letting her stay in the apartment and for having these friends who were so welcoming to her. They were good people. She had problems in her life she had to deal with, and she would. But for now, she was going to have fun this sunny Sunday afternoon in Chicago.

"I could have called my friend Emma," she said. "Then we would have been six."

"Is she hot?" Norton asked.

Tyler shook his head but Arden grinned. "Yes. She is."

"How is Emma?" Tyler asked. "That's Emma Malone, right?"

"Right." She and Emma had been best friends in high school. Emma still *was* her best friend; Arden had stayed in touch with some friends from college, but after moving across the country, she'd drifted apart from a lot of people. Everyone else seemed to be living the dream, with great jobs, marriage, beautiful houses and families, and when Arden had been going through hard times, nobody seemed very interested in that. Everyone wanted to know the pro ballplayer's wife but didn't seem to care too much about the destitute widow. She didn't blame them. Who wanted to log onto Facebook and read someone's whiny complaints every day? Not that Arden did that. She didn't even *want* people to know how crappy things had gotten. But that had made it hard to maintain real relationships with some people.

Except for Emma. Emma was her one, true, steadfast friend, and even though they didn't see each other that often, they'd stayed in touch. Emma was the one person with whom she'd been honest about what was happening in her life, and she was so looking forward to living in the same city as her again and picking up their friendship.

"She's good, I think. I haven't seen her for quite a while, but we keep in touch online. She's a hedge fund manager. Very career oriented."

"I like a career woman," Norton said.

Tyler smiled, shaking his head. His amusement at Norton wasn't mean; it was more affectionate. And that gave Arden a warm feeling in her chest.

Jamie returned and introduced Tiffany.

Tiffany appeared to be about sixteen years old. She had to be of legal drinking age though.

"That's so cute," Mila said to Tiffany. "Your bathing suit is Tiffany blue."

"I know!" Tiffany giggled and flipped her hair. "I love Tiffany!"

Mila glanced at Arden and they shared a look of…well, Arden wasn't sure what it was, other than the feeling she was going to get along with Mila. They smiled at each other.

"Let's go play volleyball," Jamie said, and they all headed to the beach.

Out on the sand, Arden followed the others. Mila dropped her cover-up to the sand and Arden slowly pulled her loose tank-style dress over her head. Even though she'd always wanted to lose ten pounds, she'd never been motivated enough to starve herself, accepting her body the way it was. Michael had liked it. She'd been healthy and strong, and that was what mattered, right? But Jamie'd teased her about losing weight, and although the last thing she'd been worried about lately was how much she weighed or how she looked, suddenly she was self-conscious.

It didn't help that she felt Tyler's gaze on her and wanted him to like what he saw.

That was stupid. Stupid thinking. Who cared what he thought? Who cared what anyone thought? She just wanted to have fun. So she threw herself into the volleyball game.

Even though she'd been a cheerleader, she'd enjoyed sports as a kid. Not that cheerleading wasn't athletic. She'd totally defend it to anyone who criticized it. Her dance and gymnastics lessons had been so valuable when it came to cheerleading. But it was also fun to compete—spiking the ball, diving for it, slapping hands with her teammates (Jamie and Tiffany), and groaning when the other team made a great serve.

None of them were especially great players, although she couldn't help but watch Tyler as he moved. He was in great shape. When he took off his shirt, she was so distracted she let the ball land in the sand at her feet. Oops.

"Sorry!" she called to her teammates, grabbing the ball to throw it back to Tyler to serve.

Luckily it was all in fun, and after an hour they were hot and sweaty and panting.

"Who's coming in the water?" Jamie called, heading toward the lake.

"Me!" Mila followed, along with Tyler and Arden too. A dip in cool water sounded like heaven.

Tiffany and Norton elected to go back to the bar.

"Order us another round, Norton," Tyler called to him.

They waded in. Cold water swirled around Arden's calves. Children played and splashed nearby. Jamie and Tyler both ran in and dove into the water, making Mila and Arden laugh.

"Come on in, girls!" Jamie called to them, his dark hair streaming water. He disappeared into the water again.

"I'll just take my time," Arden said to Mila.

"Me too." Mila swirled her hands in the water. "What a great day."

"It's beautiful. Thank you for including me."

"Of course! Now you're here, you're one of us."

Oh hell. Arden's eyes prickled. She and Michael had had a circle of friends in Phoenix, but she'd always been aware they were Michael's friends—teammates, business associates, and their wives and girlfriends. And they'd faded away after Michael's death. Only now was she realizing how lonely she'd been.

She wasn't going to cry. So she too dove into the water, immersing herself in the coolness, letting it wash away the lone tear that escaped. She popped above the surface, laughing. "Oh wow, that's cold!"

"You'll get used to it, you baby," Jamie said. He started wading toward Mila with an intent look on his face. "Mila needs to get wet."

"No!" Mila tried to back away, but Jamie was faster, grabbing her, picking her up, and tossing her. She landed with a huge splash and a scream. When she emerged, she yelled, "You asshole!" But she was grinning.

"Watch your language. There are children nearby," Jamie said with an unrepentant grin.

They swam around for a while, then Tyler said to Jamie, "You better get back. Norton's probably putting the moves on Tiffany. You could lose out."

"Ha."

"Well, *I'm* ready for a drink," Mila said. "Let's go."

"Why didn't Norton come in the water?" Arden asked as they trudged across the warm sand.

"He can't swim," Tyler said. "He doesn't even like to get his feet wet."

"Oh."

As requested, another round of drinks sat waiting for them. Arden picked hers up and, instead of sitting, moved to lean against the railing so she was in the sun. She tipped her face up and sipped her drink, letting the sun dry her hair and warm her skin, moving a little to the music the band was playing, a cover of a Chainsmokers' song.

Tyler grabbed his beer and joined her. "Having fun?"

"Yes." She smiled. "I really am."

"You sound surprised."

"I guess it's been a while since I've had fun."

He nodded. She watched a drop of water trickle down his neck, over his collarbone, and then lower, over his still bare chest. He had a beautiful body—just enough chest hair, but smooth enough that his brown skin gleamed in the sun. His muscles shifted and flexed as he moved, his shoulders wide and powerful, his chest and abs lean and cut.

She'd been married to an athlete, and she definitely appreciated the male body. She still had a hard time reconciling this muscular man with beard stubble and chest hair with the teenage kid she'd known years ago.

She became aware of the conversation Mila and Jamie were having. "How old is Tiffany?" Mila hissed at him. "She doesn't even look legal."

Jamie shrugged. "She has to be legal. She's drinking."

"Like *you* never used a fake ID?"

"Actually I didn't. I tried once, but they laughed at me because I looked twelve."

Arden laughed. "I remember that. It was just before I went to college."

"Why are men always interested in younger women?" Mila asked. "You go on any dating site, the men are all looking for women younger than them."

"True." Jamie rubbed his chin. "I guess there is something

appealing about a younger woman. Hey, it's got to be some kind of primal instinct. Younger women are more likely to be reproductively healthy. So men are just instinctively attracted to younger women because there's a better chance of procreating and continuing the human race."

"Oh, for Chrissake," Mila said. "A thirty-year-old woman can still have children."

"Sure, make me feel old, jerk," Arden said to her brother.

"You're twenty-eight. You're not old."

She made a face. There were times lately she'd definitely felt old.

"Not *every* guy is attracted to younger women," Tyler said.

Arden's skin tingled and heated. She determinedly didn't look at him.

"Speak for yourself." Jamie shrugged. "Let's order food."

"Where did Tiffany go, anyway?" Mila asked.

"Not sure. Why are you obsessed with her?" Jamie grabbed a menu from the table.

"I'm not obsessed with her." Mila rolled her eyes.

"What's the problem with men liking younger women?" Norton asked. "Don't women like older men?"

Mila shrugged. "I guess. There's something to be said for a guy who's sexually experienced. And who has money."

"You don't need to be old for that," Jamie said. "Let's order a bunch of things to share."

"You're quiet on this subject," Tyler said to Arden.

She smiled. "I don't care about age."

"So you'd date a guy who's twenty-one?"

She choked. "Okay, maybe I care a bit. Twenty-one is pretty young. But it doesn't matter, because I'm not dating. Ever."

"Oh, come on. You don't want to spend the rest of your life alone. You're a young woman."

Arden caught the concerned glance Jamie flashed her way.

"I can't think that far ahead right now," she said lightly. "But right now, that is definitely not on my radar. And I don't know if it ever will be."

"Damn." Norton sighed.

Arden grinned.

"Because you know," Norton added, "if you were a chicken, you'd be impeccable."

She frowned. "What?"

"Im-pecc-able. Get it? Chickens peck…"

Tyler cuffed him on the back of the head. "Okay, Norton, you're done with the cheesy compliments today."

Arden laughed. "Oh my God. Yes, let's get food."

She was getting a little worried about how much this afternoon at the beachside bar was going to cost. The drinks here weren't cheap. Ah well, she'd eat ramen all week if she had to.

CHAPTER FOUR

*A*fter a trip to Home Depot Monday morning, Tyler lugged his supplies into the house and up the stairs. Eyeing Arden's door, he paused in the hall. He'd checked with her last night that it was okay for him to come in and work today, since he had one more day off, but he was a little nervous about another naked bathroom encounter.

Actually if he was being honest, he'd love another naked bathroom encounter. He'd relived that moment a thousand times last night in his restless sleep. Of course his filthy mind had embellished things and imagined shower sex scenes with a slick, soapy Arden. Then he'd relived the beach volleyball game, watching her jump around in that black bikini, tits jiggling, the tight little cheeks of her ass on display, making him think of bending her over and pressing his cock against there, filling his hands with those perfect breasts.

All day, every time he'd looked at that bikini top, he'd envisioned the perfect round globes and tight nipples he'd glimpsed in the bathroom. Christ. He'd spent the whole day at the beach with a stiffy, thankful for loose board shorts and the cold water of Lake

Michigan. Possibly the reason he'd drank too many beers and woke up late this morning with a faint headache and dry mouth.

He knocked on her door, which was weird since he was used to being in and out of this apartment at will.

It opened immediately.

Arden gazed at him, one hand on the door. "Hi."

Fuck, she was even hot as hell wearing a pair of yoga pants and a T-shirt. The yellow top hugged her breasts. "Hi," he managed to say even though his tongue weighed as much as the pail of drywall compound he'd just carried up the stairs. "Is this an okay time to do some work?"

"Of course. Come in." She stood back, and he carried in a few things and set them in the living room.

"I have a few more trips."

"Can I help?"

"No, no. I'm good. I don't want to inconvenience you." Although he felt unreasonably annoyed that he'd have to work around her for the...however long it took him to finish this goddamn reno.

Her lips quirked. "I think that's my line. I'm the one who dropped into the middle of things because I was homeless. Seriously, if I can help, I'm totally willing."

"How are you at patching drywall?"

"Um..." She bit her lip.

"Kidding. I don't expect the prom queen to know anything about construction." She'd probably hurt herself if she tried to hammer a nail.

A crease appeared between her eyebrows. "Prom queen?"

"You were, weren't you?"

"Well, yes..."

He shrugged.

"You say it like it's a bad thing."

Tyler sighed. "It's not a bad thing." It just meant she was out of his league. But then again, she was two years older than him, gorgeous and had been dating the football team's wide receiver—she was already out of his league because of those things. "I'll be back."

He made a few trips up and down with insulation and cans of paint. By the time he had everything upstairs—some of it stored in his own apartment, since now that Arden was occupying the place, he couldn't just stack boxes and piles of lumber everywhere—he was hot and sweaty. And watching her move around her small kitchen didn't help.

He fucking loved yoga pants on a woman. They were tight and stretchy and showed off a gorgeous ass perfectly. Not as well as a bikini, but as far as clothing went…only a tight pair of jeans compared. Or maybe a pencil skirt. He'd seen women wearing skirts that hugged their butt…

If anyone thought he was obsessed with female anatomy, they'd be right.

Women were amazing. Goddesses. Sometimes he found it hard to believe that such beautiful creatures existed in the same universe as him. Their soft curves and smooth skin and silky hair, the way they moved and smiled…Christ. He knew there was more to women than just the physical, and he appreciated all that too, but when faced with female beauty…he was in awe. He didn't mean to be objectifying, but readily admitted to checking women out on the street on a regular basis, just because…damn. They were beautiful.

And now he was doing it with Arden.

Of course, she was at the top of Mount Goddess, or wherever it was that goddesses hung out, and she had been since he was about fourteen.

"Okay," he said. "Here's the deal. I'm ready to start your

bathroom, but that's gonna mean you don't have a bathroom for a while."

She regarded him with wide eyes. "For how long?"

"Hard to say. Depends on my work schedule. I could get started today, but I have to work tomorrow. After that, I have four days off. So I could do some demo work today, and then be ready to really rock and roll on Wednesday. But I probably won't get it all done in four days, so it might be a couple of weeks before you can use your bathroom."

She blinked. "What am I supposed to do with no bathroom?"

"Use mine."

Her lips parted and she stared at him. "No, really."

"Really. Why not? I'm right across the hall. Even if you need to sneak in during the middle of the night, that's fine." *Don't go there, don't think about Arden sneaking into your bedroom, don't...*

She nibbled her bottom lip. "Maybe I could use Mila's bathroom."

Tyler frowned. "Well, sure, I guess you could. It's farther away though. And remember, I work twenty-four-hour shifts, so there'll be a lot of times I'm not even home."

"Oh. Right." She nodded. "You don't mind a stranger using your apartment?"

"You're not a stranger."

Her lips pursed and, fuck, that made him want to kiss them. Then she smiled. "Well, thank you. I appreciate the offer."

"Sorry you're being put out."

"No, no. I knew that was the deal when Jamie offered me a place to live. I'm grateful. I'll try to stay out of your way."

"And I'll try to make it as painless for you as I can."

"If I helped, maybe it would go faster?"

He eyed her. "Yeah, I'm still not convinced about your

construction skills. If you're like your brother, it's probably better if you don't help."

To his surprise, a smile broke out on her face. "Ha. I knew he wasn't that useful."

"He's learning."

"Well, I could learn too. I can paint. Seriously. How hard can that be?"

"Well, that'll be about the last thing we do in the bathroom."

She glanced around the living room. "This room needs painting."

"Yeah, it does, but I have a lot of repairs to do to the walls. And I have to clean the brick of the fireplace and refinish the mantel before we paint. Also, we're replacing all the baseboard and casings around the doors and windows."

He became aware of the scent of coffee and something baking in the apartment. His nose tipped up and he sniffed the air. "Is that…coffee?"

"Um, yeah. Would you like some?"

"Love some." He'd made a Starbucks stop on his way to Home Depot, but that had been hours ago. "And what are you baking?"

"Muffins."

"They smell fantastic." He followed her to the kitchen.

She opened the oven door and peeked in. "Two more minutes." She pulled a bright red mug out of a cupboard and filled it with coffee. "Do you need milk or sugar?"

"Nope. Black, black, black."

She nodded. "Here you go."

"Thank you." He took a sip of the hot elixir. "What kind of muffins are they?"

"Blueberry lemon."

"Damn."

"It's National Blueberry Muffin Day."

"What?"

"It's a thing. Really. So I made blueberry muffins. Um, are you hungry?"

He grinned. "Always. Especially for baked goods."

Her lips twitched. "I see."

"I'm a pretty good cook, but I can't bake shit."

"Well, baked shit would be pretty awful."

He barked out a surprised laugh at her joke.

"Oh, come on." She made a face. "That was a terrible joke."

"No, it was funny."

"Hopefully my muffins don't taste like baked shit." The timer on the oven beeped and she grabbed a yellow oven mitt.

"I'm sure they don't. I'm salivating at the smell of them."

"They'll need to cool for a few minutes." She set the big muffin tin on top of the stove, then moved to the fridge and pulled out a container of margarine.

"Jesus, don't let Mila see that."

"See what?" She turned big eyes to him.

"The margarine." He nodded. "She thinks it's a crime."

Arden's grin was gorgeous. "Oh right. Butter lover. I'm in trouble." She popped the lid off the container. "Do you object to margarine?"

"Hell no. That's what I buy."

"I actually prefer butter. But I don't use much of it, and it's hard to keep soft. Margarine's convenient."

"True." He paused. "Can I eat one now?"

She smiled and carefully lifted a muffin out of the tin. "It's still pretty hot, but what the heck, go ahead."

He slathered margarine on it, although it kind of fell apart because yeah, it was still really hot, but he managed to devour it in about two bites. "Damn, that's good." She

44

handed him another one, which he eagerly accepted. "Thanks."

"You're welcome."

The muffins were really excellent. He rubbed his abs, enjoying how Arden's gaze followed his hand there and lingered. Too bad his dick also took notice. "Okay, now I'm ready to work."

He left her apartment to retrieve his sledgehammer and crowbar. He'd burn off that sexual energy with some physical activity. He entered the small bathroom and stopped. "Hey, Arden!"

"What?" Her voice came immediately from behind him. She must have followed him.

"You wanna move your shit out of here?"

"My shit?"

"Yeah." He jerked his head at the towels and various bottles of female potions. There was also a hairbrush, a curling iron, and a tube of toothpaste on the vanity. "It'll get all covered with dust."

"Okay." She squeezed past him into the small space and, call him an asshole, he didn't even try to move to make room for her, enjoying the brush of her body against his. Heat sizzled in his veins.

She gathered up all her shit. He helped by picking up the blow dryer and curling iron and followed her into her bedroom.

He was in Arden Lennox's bedroom.

He almost laughed at himself. It was a thought his fourteen-year-old self would have had, and probably sprung a huge boner over. He was too old for that, way past that ridiculous crush.

Except he *had* thought it, and he couldn't help but notice her bed, where she slept, and some clothes she'd started to unpack…including a pile of lacy lingerie on the bed.

Fuuuuuuck.

He dumped the stuff onto the dresser and stalked back to the bathroom. It was now completely empty. After shutting off the power to the room, he rolled out plastic and duct taped it around the door, then stepped inside, and with vicious enjoyment, picked up his sledgehammer and slung it against one of the walls. The old plaster shattered with a satisfying crack.

He heard a little scream from the hall.

With a sigh, he turned and saw Arden staring at him with big eyes through the plastic curtain. "What?"

"What are you doing?"

"Tearing down the walls."

"Why?"

He gave her a look. "We're gutting this room and rebuilding it. I'm going to take the walls down to the studs."

"Studs." She continued to stare at him.

One corner of his mouth kicked up. "Yeah. Don't worry. Like I said, I'll leave the fixtures for later in the week so you can still use them. It'll just be ugly for a while."

"Okay."

He resumed his demolition work, slamming away at the plaster, pulling some chunks down with his gloved hands. After a while, he'd again worked up a sweat, so he yanked his T-shirt off over his head, wiped his forehead with it, then tossed it out onto the hall floor.

The physical work made him feel good, his muscles jacked, blood pumping. He got a lot of satisfaction out of his hobby, even when it involved destroying something, because he knew how good it was going to be when it was done.

He moved on to the tiles around the bathtub, smashing them with energetic violence.

"Tyler?"

He turned again at Arden's voice. The room was full of dust, and he couldn't see her well through the plastic. "Yeah?"

"I'm going out for a while."

He paused. "Where are you going?"

She frowned. "Out."

"Yeah, but where? You don't have a car. Do you need to borrow my truck?"

"Um, no. And I don't think I need to explain to you where I'm going."

"Sure you do. What if you never come back? How will we know where to look?"

She didn't say anything for a long moment, and the air around them went heavy. Shit. He shouldn't have said that. He knew exactly what she was thinking about now, and she was probably feeling sorry for him. Fuck.

"I'm just going for a walk to explore the neighborhood," she said quietly. "I'll be fine, Tyler."

He repressed a sigh. "Okay."

Okay, yeah, it worried him a little, but he had to admit she was an adult who'd been living her own life for a while, in a city far away.

"I'll be back in a while." And she disappeared.

That was probably good. He was used to working alone, most of the time anyway, unless it was an evening or weekend when Jamie was helping. He wouldn't have to worry about disturbing her.

CHAPTER FIVE

*a*rden ran lightly down the stairs and left the building. Jamie and Mila were both at work, so it was just her and Tyler there. She made sure the front door was locked, then turned left on the sidewalk and started walking toward West Armitage.

She had her phone and the map app so she wouldn't get lost. Tyler didn't need to worry about her.

His insistence on knowing where she was going had at first annoyed her, but then he asked that question. *What if you never come back?*

Memories had flooded back, things she hadn't thought about for years.

When she'd been sixteen and Tyler and Jamie fourteen, Tyler's twelve-year-old sister had gone missing. It had been a huge incident in their neighborhood, well, for the entire city. People had all joined forces to look for her, along with the police. Unfortunately, the story hadn't had a happy ending. Tara's body had been found a week later. She'd been murdered.

It was a shocking tragedy that traumatized so many of

them. With Tyler being Jamie's best friend, the Lennox family knew the Ramirez family well. They'd all been horrified and grieving. Arden's parents, like many others in the neighborhood, had gotten very protective of both Jamie and her. Arden had had nightmares for weeks, and had been nervous walking to and from school for a long time.

If *she'd* been affected that much, it had to have been much worse for Tyler.

She hadn't been close enough to him then to really know, but she did remember seeing him at the funeral, trying not to cry, and her heart had ached for him and his parents. She'd wanted so badly to go up to him and give him a hug, and had finally given in to the impulse. It had been brief, a little awkward, and had made the tears in Tyler's eyes shine even more, although he'd bravely said, "Thank you for coming." Other memories from that time were fuzzy now.

So when he'd said that…about what if she never came back…it had frozen her in place. And instead of arguing with him that where she went was none of his business, she'd tried to assure him that she'd be okay.

Was that incident still affecting Tyler?

Perhaps a person never really got over something like that.

She rubbed at the faint ache behind her breastbone that had appeared along with the memories, then pulled a long breath in and slowly let it out. She turned her face to the bright sun that filtered through the lacy canopy of old trees lining the sidewalk. Another beautiful summer day in Chicago.

She admired the houses and gardens on each side of the street. The neighborhood was old, but evidently more people like Jamie had been buying houses and apartment buildings and renovating them.

She rounded the corner onto the cracked sidewalk of West Armitage and continued walking, taking in the little shops. It was good to know what was near…a dry cleaner, a pharmacy, a bank. She noted the location of a bus stop, then paused outside a used bookstore and a lot of interesting-looking restaurants—Thai, sushi, and a few fast food chains.

She was hungry for lunch. Maybe there was somewhere she could get a sandwich, somewhere not too expensive. At the next corner, she stopped in front of a pub. The front was small but nicely kept, with red brick and dark wood, and a sign above the door that read SHENANIGANS in a gold, Celtic-looking font. There was also a sign in the window that said: HELP WANTED.

With a shrug, she pulled open the door and stepped inside. Cool darkness greeted her, along with a muted rumble of voices and laughter. There was no hostess seating people, so she walked farther inside. On her left, a long dark wooden bar lined the wall, a couple of big screen televisions mounted behind it along with shelves filled with bottles and glasses. Most stools were occupied.

The pub stretched out long and narrow, with some small tables near the bar, a fireplace with some comfy-looking couches arranged around it, then wooden booths lining both sides at the back. The ceiling was high, paneled with tin squares and dark beams.

The bar was busy.

After surveying the place, she strolled over to one of the high stools at the bar and climbed up. She picked up a tent card sitting there, listing drink specials for each day of the week and a food menu. She perused the options—fish and chips, burgers and sandwiches, but there were a few more interesting things like pub pie, fish tacos, bangers and mash, and…cottage boxty? She didn't even know what that was. Fish and chips sounded good…she'd take a chance on that. Her stomach growled in anticipation of food.

Two men on her left were watching a baseball game and

arguing about the Cubs' pitcher, and a man and woman on her right held an animated conversation about something that sounded like business, while sipping beers.

She glanced around for someone to take her order, but there appeared to be nobody working. That wasn't good. Also probably why there was a help wanted sign in the window.

Finally a man appeared through a swinging door at the end of the bar, carrying a tray of food which he served to the man and woman sitting near her. He smiled and nodded at Arden, so she knew he'd seen her.

He approached her moments later, wiping his hands on a bar towel. He wore a white apron over a striped shirt and dark pants. Probably near her age, maybe early thirties, he had messy sandy hair, and almost looked like Prince Harry. Not the type she was attracted to, but she had to admit he was good-looking with twinkling eyes and a slightly wicked grin.

"Hello, love," he said. "What can I get you?"

Oh Jesus, he had a faint Irish accent. She sighed. *That* was sexy.

"O'Hara's Irish Wheat is our beer special today." He laid down a paper coaster in front of her.

"Oh." She blinked. She hadn't been planning on ordering a drink but… "Okay, sure."

"Are you wanting lunch as well, love?" The sexy bartender pulled on a tall tap to begin filling a glass.

"Yes." She hesitated. "Is the fish and chips good?"

"Everything's good here." He set the full glass on the coaster and winked. "The fish is freshly battered halibut and the fries are hand cut."

"Oh. That sounds good. Okay, I'll have that."

"Sure look it."

She blinked again. "Uh…what does that mean?"

"Who knows?" He shrugged. "But in Ireland, it's an acceptable response to pretty much anything."

She smiled and reached for her beer. "Okay, then." She took a swallow of the smooth, fruity beverage.

She caught the eye of the two men arguing over the baseball game and they both gave her big smiles. She smiled back hesitantly. They seemed harmless. Friendly. Another man passed by on his way out and stopped to clap both men on the back and exchange pleasantries, calling them by name…Kasim and Brad.

The bartender returned with a tray of glasses he started moving to a shelf.

"Hey, Liam, can we get another round here?" Kasim called to him.

Liam. Nice.

Liam filled two more glasses and carried them over to the men, pausing to chat with them, hands on the bar, a smile on his face. He appeared to know them well. They must be regulars.

A harried-looking woman appeared behind the bar, young, pretty, with red hair and freckles. Arden looked back and forth between her and Liam and immediately knew they were brother and sister. "Liam," the woman said. "I need three more Guinness and a Bud Light."

Liam grimaced and moved away.

The girl shoved her hair off her face, darting around behind the bar to grab bundles of cutlery wrapped in paper napkins and a stack of menus, then disappeared again.

Arden turned her attention to the framed sign on the wall that read:

In all this world, why I do think
There are five reasons why we drink:

Good friends,
good wine,
lest we be dry,
and any other reason why.

She smiled and lifted her beer in a small toast, then sipped. She liked this place.

More people were leaving as the lunch crowd apparently finished up, and the place grew slightly quieter. She pulled out her phone to keep herself busy, feeling a little self-conscious by herself.

"So, *a chara*." Liam paused in front of her. "I've not seen you here before. New in the neighborhood?"

"As a matter of fact, yes." She smiled at him. "I grew up in Chicago, but I just moved back."

"And where have you been living till now?"

"Phoenix."

"Ah. A touch warmer than here. Especially in winter."

"Yes. But I can handle Chicago winters."

While he was friendly, she didn't feel he was flirting with her, so she was quite comfortable talking to him.

"I'm Liam Murphy. I own this joint." He extended a hand.

She shook it. "Oh, I didn't realize you own it. Seems like a popular place."

"That it is."

"I'm Arden. Arden Hughes. I'm living with my brother and his friends just a few blocks from here."

"Lovely to meet you, Arden."

The young waitress returned in a rush and set a hand on her hip. "Where are those drinks, Liam?"

"Oops." He flashed a wry grin. "Excuse me."

Arden nodded and watched them work together, the girl's

exasperation affectionate, both of them obviously familiar with each other and with the bar.

Moments later, Liam served her fish and chips, sliding the big plate across the polished wooden bar. It smelled amazing. "Here you are, love. Enjoy."

"Thanks."

She picked up the cutlery and dug in, and damn, he was right…this was good. The fish was firm and flaky with a crisp batter, and the fries were golden and hot. Even the coleslaw, usually added as a passing nod to veggies, was good, with a tangy dressing.

"How's everything?" Liam returned when she'd made good progress on her lunch.

"It's excellent."

He winked. "Told you so."

"Yes, you did."

"So what do you do for a living, Arden Hughes?"

She made a face, setting down her fork and picking up her beer. "Nothing at the moment."

"Ah. We're hiring, if you didn't know. Though you're probably not looking for a waitressing job."

She stared at him. She was looking for *any* kind of job. "Actually," she said slowly. "I might be."

His russet eyebrows lifted. "Yeah?"

"Yeah." She gave a firm nod. "I need a job. This seems like a nice place."

"Well, sure, I'm biased, but yeah, it's a nice place. We have a pretty regular clientele. Things can get a bit rowdy in the evenings, but it's rare that we have to eject anyone for being bollocksed."

She laughed. "Good to know."

"You'd likely do well with tips." He gave her an appreciative look.

Her cheeks heated. "Um. Thanks?"

He grinned. "Any waitressing experience, darling?"

"In high school." She pasted a bright, confident smile on. That had been ten years ago, but so what?

He nodded, eyes narrowed. "Well, we do need help…how soon could you start?"

"Tomorrow?"

He laughed. "You're hired. Sorcha!"

The young waitress called back, "What?"

"I just hired another waitress."

Sorcha appeared, green eyes big. "Seriously?"

"This is Arden. She starts tomorrow." He nodded. "My sister, Sorcha."

"Pleased to meet you, Sorcha." Arden stuck out her hand.

The girl took it, studying her. "Likewise." She didn't have an accent like Liam did.

"Easiest job interview I ever did," Liam said.

"Liam." Sorcha set her hips on her hands. "You didn't even interview her, did you? Did she fill out an application form? Did you get references? No, you didn't."

Arden bit her lip. It had been her easiest job interview ever too. Was her newfound job going to be nixed by Sorcha?

Liam made a face. "I'll deal with that stuff. Don't worry."

Sorcha sighed. "That's what you said last time, when the girl you hired cleaned out the cash register and disappeared after her first day on the job. And the one before that helped herself to the Jameson and passed out in the ladies' room."

Arden's eyebrows flew up. "That won't happen. I promise. No drinking on the job. No stealing. I'm honest."

"I'm sure you are." Liam nodded.

Sorcha frowned. "Liam."

"I'll get you to fill out an application form," Liam said. "And tax forms. I'll be back in a jiff."

Sorcha gave Arden a long look. "Well, we *do* need help. Especially this week, with the Fourth of July tomorrow."

Arden smiled. "Great!"

A few hours later, she walked back into her apartment. The place smelled dusty, and plastic tote boxes filled with debris lined the small hall. Music blasted from a smartphone in the hall—Simple Minds singing "Don't You Forget About Me." She tipped her head. Seriously? Tyler was into eighties music? Okay, that *was* a good song…

She took a step closer to look past the plastic hanging from the door frame. Tyler was sweeping the bathroom. He'd taken off his shirt.

Arden's mouth went dry seeing the muscles in his strong back flex as he swept. He sang along to the music in an off-key voice that made her smile.

For a moment, she just watched, mesmerized by the beauty of his big body.

Yep, Tyler Ramirez was definitely all grown up.

His jeans sat low on his hips, exposing twin indentations at the base of his spine. She dragged her tongue along her bottom lip, then sank her teeth into it. Her body tingled everywhere, studying the expanse of sleek skin and muscles.

This was her little brother's best friend. She should definitely not be objectifying him. Or lusting after his hot body. She took a deep breath. "Hey," she called over the music.

He started and turned to face her. His bare chest gleamed with sweat, although dust had accumulated on top of his shoulders and hair, which stood up in all directions. He'd apparently been working hard, and it looked good on him. "Oh, hey. You're back."

She nodded. "I'm back, safe and sound. And guess what?"

"What?"

"I got a job!"

His eyes widened, then he frowned. "A job? What kind of job?"

"Waitressing!"

His frown deepened. "Seriously? That's what you want to do?"

Her pleasure at her accomplishment dimmed a little. "I don't know what I want to do. But I do know I need money." She lifted one shoulder. "So this'll be fine for right now, while I figure things out."

"Where's the job?"

"A cute little place called Shenanigans."

His eyes widened again. "Shit. Really? We hang out there all the time."

"You do?"

"Yeah." He leaned on the broom handle with both hands. "You met Liam, then?"

"Yes! He's very nice."

"He's a good guy. But...damn, Arden. I can't picture you hauling around trays of beers and cleaning sticky tables."

"Why not?" She lifted her chin. "I worked as a waitress in high school. For a while."

"You sucked at it."

"I did not!"

"Didn't you set the kitchen on fire?"

"That was an accident! I slipped on some grease and knocked over a pan."

"What about the eggs you dumped into Mrs. Biletsky's cleavage?"

He *had* to remember that. "It was my first day on the job. I leaned over too much with the tray. I learned from that."

Tyler shook his head, still frowning. "How much are they paying you?"

"I, uh, don't know."

"What?"

She made a face. "I forgot to ask that. But they have to pay me minimum wage, right? Plus I'll make tips." And *any* money coming in was better than *no* money.

"Jesus, Arden. And what kind of shifts will you be working? That place is open until midnight during the week, one o'clock Fridays and Saturdays."

"Well, tomorrow, I work four to midnight."

"Fuck that."

"What?" She frowned at him and crossed her arms. "That's a normal eight-hour shift."

"You're going to be walking home all alone at midnight?"

"I told you I'm a grown woman! I can handle this."

Once again she remembered his past, but that was nothing like this. She wasn't a twelve-year-old girl, she was an adult who'd been on her own for a long time.

And why did he have to look that good while pissing her off? It was hard to be angry when he was standing in front of her shirtless and all she could think about was licking the ridges of his abs. "Thank you for your concern. But I'll be fine."

He sighed. "Well, at least we know the place, and we know Liam's a decent boss, even if he is a little scattered. He won't sexually harass you or steal your tips."

"Good to know." She lifted her chin. "I *am* a pretty good judge of character."

Her failed marriage immediately taunted her about that comment. The man she'd married hadn't turned out to be whom she'd thought he was. But she didn't have to share that with Tyler.

He narrowed his eyes at her. "You got lucky." Then he

laughed. "Or maybe not. I guess we'll see how long you last serving beers and burgers."

"It can't be that bad." She rubbed her upper arms. "I don't have a problem with working hard."

"When's the last time you actually worked?"

She gazed back at him, her throat tightening. "Ouch."

He winced. "I didn't mean it like that."

"Okay, it's been a while. That doesn't mean I'm lazy. I've held jobs. I worked hard in school and at college."

He didn't appear convinced.

She swallowed a sigh. The truth was, most things in her life had come easy to her. She'd studied as much as she had to, but got decent grades even when she didn't. Her waitressing jobs had been short-lived when she got bored with them. Her cheerleading had been fun, so she'd willingly practiced. College had been a little more work, but she'd enjoyed a busy social life for the most part. She *had* committed to the volunteer work she'd done in Phoenix, though. She wasn't a total slacker.

But life hadn't been easy the last few years. Tyler didn't know everything she'd been through. He didn't know how desperate and lost she was. He didn't know she wasn't too proud to work as a waitress, and she'd do her very best at it. He didn't know that she was stronger now because of everything she'd gone through.

She'd show him.

CHAPTER SIX

yler grabbed his phone where he'd set it and ended the music, which he'd cranked up since he was alone. Silence descended around them as he bent to sweep up the last of the dust and chunks of plaster and tile on the bathroom floor. The floor that was now stripped down to plywood, in the room that was bare studs and wires.

He'd accomplished a lot while Arden had been out. And now he was almost done cleaning up for the day.

He tucked his phone in the back pocket of his jeans, and bent to pick up one of the heavy totes. Arden's gaze tracked up and down his abs and chest, then moved over his arms and shoulders. She swallowed.

He fought back a grin. Arden liked what she saw. *Yessss.*

Other women had complimented his body. He worked out regularly at the station, as did most of the guys. Strength was important for their job.

"I'll get rid of all this stuff." He held up the tote. Her gaze dropped to his biceps and he flexed a little more than was necessary to lift the tote. "And then I'll be out of your way for a few days."

She nodded. "Thank you."

"No problem."

He carried the tote box out and down the stairs, then out the back door to the dumpster in the lane.

She'd found a job. Waitressing. At Shenanigans. Jesus.

Well, like he'd said, it could be worse. She could have gone a little farther down the road and ended up working at Cherry's. The "gentleman's club" was *not* where he (or Jamie—or her parents, for fuck's sake) would want her working.

Yes, Shenanigans was a better choice, but hell...waitressing?

He swiped sweat off his forehead with his forearm and made more trips up and down the stairs to carry out all the crap he'd ripped out of the bathroom. This was his workout for the day. It felt good.

It had also felt good when Arden had given him that look, like she'd been impressed...and maybe a little turned on.

Kind of like how he'd felt that morning he'd walked in on her in the bathroom. And that day at the beach. And...well, pretty much every time he set eyes on her.

Fuck, what was he thinking? Yeah, he'd had a crush on her. But that was a long time ago. Also she was Jamie's sister. There was no way she was going to see him as anything more than her little brother's friend, and it would make things very messy for them to get involved in any way. It couldn't happen. He needed to shut that shit down.

He returned to her apartment one last time. She was unpacking some shopping bags in her kitchen. Apparently she'd stopped to pick up groceries.

"If you want to make a bigger run to a grocery store, I can drive you."

She looked up. "Oh, thank you. But that's okay."

"No, seriously." He walked over and set his hands on the edge of the island separating them. "I like to go to Whole Foods. I'll take you next time I go. And on Saturday, the farmers' market is pretty cool."

She met his eyes. Hers were alight with interest. Ah. He'd tempted her with grocery shopping. Interesting. And yet he sensed she wanted to reject his offer.

"It's not a big deal," he said, holding her gaze.

She dropped her eyes to the big container of Greek yogurt she'd pulled out of a bag. "I'm trying to do this on my own."

"Why?" He frowned. "You're not alone. Your brother's here. We're his friends and we're here for you too."

"I just…" She bit her lip and turned to the fridge. "I made a mess of my life in Phoenix. I want to prove that I can get back on track. By myself."

He studied her slender back, her long dark hair hanging all shiny down it, her very grabbable ass displayed in snug jeans. She'd made a mess of her life? Her husband had died, so yeah, obviously she'd been having a rough time, but… "How'd you make a mess of your life?"

She didn't turn at his question, just bent to put the yogurt away. Oh man, she did that…putting that ass on display. Then she straightened and closed the fridge door. "It's a long story."

Okay, he got that message loud and clear. She didn't want to talk about it. It made curiosity burn behind his sternum, but he wasn't going to be an asshole. "Well, you ever wanna talk about it, I'm a good listener." He kept his tone casual.

"Thanks." She turned, and he caught the shadows in her eyes even though she smiled that sweet smile of hers.

"So come and see the bathroom."

"Okay."

She followed him and he pulled aside the plastic he'd used

to cover the door. He gestured for her to enter the small space, and she brushed past him, with a quick glance at his bare chest as she did so. He caught a hint of that fruity floral scent he'd banished by tearing down the walls of the room. He wanted to grab her and bury his face in her hair and breathe in the sexy scent. *Focus, man.* "So, you can't shower or have a bath now." Jesus. His throat dried up thinking about her having a bath…all naked and soapy and slippery… He gritted his teeth. "But I replaced the toilet so you can still use it for now. Sorry it's ugly, but at least it's functional."

"Yes, that's fine. I can handle ugly for a while, thank you."

"If you want to shower, just come over to my place. My door's always open. I work at eight tomorrow morning for a twenty-four-hour shift, so I'll be gone until Wednesday morning."

"Um, okay."

Yeah, thinking about her in his shower didn't help the tightening in his groin.

"Okay." The word came out gruffly and he cleared his throat. "I'll be back Wednesday to do more. Not sure what time…depends on if I get any sleep while I'm at work."

"You sleep at work?" She gazed back at him with big, beautiful dark eyes.

"If it's not busy." He made himself smile. "It's a twenty-four-hour shift. If things are quiet, I might get some sleep. If not…well, I'll be ready to crash when I get home."

She nods. "Okay. Wednesday morning. Got it."

He started back toward the door, grabbing his T-shirt from where he'd hung it on her bedroom doorknob. Then he hesitated at her door. Dammit. He didn't want to leave her alone.

She was so proud of herself for getting that job. And yet there was still an air of sadness about her. He sensed that she really felt she *was* alone, even though she was living with the three of them, and he absolutely knew Jamie would take care of her, even though she'd outright said she wanted to make it by herself.

His jaw tightened.

"What?" She stared back at him, elegant dark eyebrows lifted.

There it was. The princess look. The one that had intimidated him in high school. Now, though…he wasn't intimidated. He was seeing there was a lot behind that look.

She lifted her chin.

He smiled. "Nothing. Let me know if you need anything."

He knew she wouldn't. But at least he was right across the hall.

She gave a tiny eye roll, pursed her lips on a smile, and shook her head. "You're as bad as Jamie. I'm *fine*."

"Yeah." He studied her face…smooth skin, high cheekbones, the appealing curve of her mouth. "You are. See you later, Arden."

He left her apartment, crossed the hall to his own, and shut the door.

He paused there for a moment.

Arden Lennox—er Hughes, he had to remember that—living across the hall from him was going to kill him.

He closed his eyes briefly, then strode to his bathroom. He needed a goddamn shower. She smelled like passion fruit and orchids, and he probably stunk of sweat and dust.

He cranked on the water and stepped in, and of course was immediately assailed by images of Arden in there with him, naked, hair dripping, water running over those perfect fucking breasts he'd caught a glimpse of yesterday. He'd never, ever forget that.

Jesus. He was still fourteen, crushing over a girl. He needed to get a grip. He needed to get laid.

He also needed to have a little talk with Arden's new boss. Yeah.

He shampooed his hair, scrubbed his body clean and rinsed off, then stepped out to towel dry. It wasn't long before he was leaving his apartment, dressed in clean jeans and a T-shirt, his cell phone, keys, and wallet all accounted for.

He eyed Arden's closed door as he shut his own. Jamie and Mila were still at work, and with the kind of hours they put in, who knew when they'd be back, despite it being a holiday tomorrow. He hated leaving Arden there alone.

But he didn't need to make a fool of himself by being that guy—the needy, desperate guy. Nope.

He jogged downstairs and headed out, walking the few blocks to Shenanigans in the warm late afternoon. After the heat of the last few days, dark clouds were accumulating low in the sky. The air felt thick and heavy. Probably going to be a wicked storm tonight. Be good if it happened tonight and cleared the air before the Fourth of July festivities tomorrow.

He entered Shenanigans, which was getting busy with the happy hour crowd. Sure enough, Liam was behind the bar, laughing with a couple of regulars seated there. Tyler slid onto a stool next to the guys, Dave and Hashim, who ran a nearby business selling soccer jerseys. "Hey, guys."

They all greeted one another, and Liam slid him a Goose Island Pilsner. He grinned his thanks and picked it up.

"So I hear you hired a new waitress," he said to Liam.

Liam's eyebrows shot up. "Well, the grapevine is astonishingly efficient. How the hell did you hear that?"

"She's Jamie's sister."

"Feck clean off. Seriously?"

"Yeah."

Liam rubbed his forehead. "She has a different name."

"Yeah. She…was married."

Liam's eyebrow rose.

"He died." Tyler grimaced.

"Well, shite."

"It was a year ago."

"She said she's moved back to Chicago and is staying with her brother."

"Yeah. She's living in the vacant apartment."

"Huh." Liam shrugged. "Well, she needed a job and I needed a waitress, so…"

Tyler leaned forward. "You'll treat her well."

Liam's head jerked back, and he slapped a hand to his chest. "What the hell? You think I don't treat all my staff well?"

Tyler shook his head, smiling. "Just sayin'." He lifted his glass. "You'll also keep an eye out for her so players like these dudes don't hit on her." He jerked his head at Hashim and Dave.

"Is she hot?" Hashim grinned.

"Don't even go there," Tyler warned. "She's… Her husband just died. Leave her alone."

All three men made sympathetic and apologetic noises. "We'll *all* watch out for her," Dave said. He shrugged. "We're here enough."

"That you are." Liam grinned. "And I appreciate the business. Another pilsner, Tyler?"

"No thanks. Just having one tonight."

"If I wanted only one drink, I'd go to communion," Dave muttered.

Tyler laughed. "I have to work tomorrow."

"Don't we all."

"But I *will* have something to eat. Can I get a pulled pork sandwich?"

"You bet."

The pork came with a tangy marinade made with Guinness

that was damn good, along with the bar's excellent fries. That was dinner for tonight.

What was Arden doing for dinner on her own?

Christ, he had to stop thinking about her. Worrying about her. She wasn't his concern.

But she'd just moved back to Chicago and was living alone and…

Stop.

He forced himself to focus on the banter between the guys while he waited for his sandwich.

It arrived moments later, served by Sorcha. She smiled at him across the bar as she set the plate down. "Here you go, handsome." She turned away and grabbed a goblet, filled it with ice and water and placed it in front of him too. "Anything else I can get you?"

He gave her a vague smile and shook his head. "This looks great, thanks."

She didn't leave, watching him, still smiling at him with an idolizing look on her face.

Tyler repressed a sigh. Sorcha didn't hide how much she liked him. She'd even asked him out. Why he didn't want to go out with her, he wasn't sure. She was pretty and nice. She kept Liam in line; without her, he'd dream away his days and the bar would go all to hell. That probably wasn't entirely fair to Liam. But there was an element of truth to it.

Finally Sorcha's smile dimmed, and she moved away to look after other customers.

Damn. The young redhead just didn't interest him. There was no figuring out why; chemistry was there or it wasn't. And even though he'd already determined that he needed to get laid, it wouldn't be with her.

He looked around the bar. Maybe there was someone else here he could hook up with tonight. A group of four women sat at one of the booths, all of them attractive, apparently having a good time.

Actually that would be a shitty thing to do in front of Sorcha. He wasn't interested in her and didn't want to lead her on in any way, but picking up another chick and leaving with her in front of Sorcha was kind of asshole-ish.

Then again, maybe that was the best way to show her once and for all they weren't going to be together.

He sighed. Maybe it was time to stop hanging out at Shenanigans.

Except Arden was working here now, and he was definitely going to make sure she was okay. He couldn't be here every day, obviously. It just sucked that Sorcha made him feel uncomfortable when he really liked this place. He and Jamie liked coming here to watch baseball, football, or hockey, depending on the season, kicking back on the couches over by the fireplace, munching on chicken wings and Irish nachos.

He finished his food, pulled out his wallet, and left the money on the bar including a decent tip, then waved good night at the guys he'd been talking to. He headed out into the summer evening for the walk home. Another benefit of Shenanigans—within walking distance, so no worries about drinking and driving.

Back in the apartment building, he tried to pretend he didn't care whether Arden was behind her closed apartment door or not. He sniffed the air. Even though he'd just eaten, something smelled fantastic.

Ignoring it, he went in and closed his door. He had shit to do—laundry he hadn't put away since last week, dishes he hadn't unloaded from the dishwasher, and garbage that needed taking out. That would keep him busy until bedtime.

∼

"You know that saying…you never get a second chance to make a first impression?"

Arden nodded at Sorcha, nerves buzzing in her stomach at her first shift of her new job. She resisted the urge to twist her fingers together and tried to appear relaxed and attentive.

"That's so true in the restaurant business. Luckily, we have a lot of regulars, but still, we get new customers all the time and we want them to come back. If something happens in their first visit, they won't. No matter how good the food is, no matter how big the beer menu is, if the service is crappy, it ruins the whole experience."

Arden listened intently. She was going to rock this job.

Sorcha spent time with her showing her their standard table settings, explaining how the tables were divided into sections, and where silverware, glasses, menus, and cleaning supplies were located. She showed her the computer program they used. She let Arden shadow her as she waited tables so she could get used to greeting and seating guests. Sorcha walked her through the order-taking process, showing her how orders were called when ready and how to deliver them to tables, and told her how often she should approach diners during the meal and what to say.

"You don't want to be interrupting them constantly. So also take cues from what's happening…if they're in a deep conversation, that's not a good moment to stop and ask how things are. For tables like that, I do what I call a 'slow pass'…I walk by their table slowly so they can see I'm looking at the table, not them. I can pick up an empty plate, or fill their water glasses, and they'll know I'm aware of them and available if they need something, without interrupting."

Arden took it all in, mentally filing away the information.

"Between table visits, you can keep busy by wrapping silverware or drying glasses, refilling service stands, wiping tables, picking up crap from the floor…that kind of stuff."

So when things were quiet, she prepped linens, silverware, and glassware, filled condiments, and restocked napkins. Sorcha also had her clean tables and run plates to the kitchen, which she did without complaining.

As things got busier, Arden tried to help more by picking up orders to serve. She arrived at a booth with two meals and smiled at them. She'd been smiling since she arrived there, and her face was starting to hurt, but she knew the importance of a pleasant expression. "The turkey club?"

Both men looked at her blankly.

She blinked. "Um…turkey club and shepherd's pie?"

"Nope. Not ours, honey."

"Oh. I'm so sorry." She flashed her smile even bigger, and returned to the kitchen to check the order. Had the kitchen screwed up?

"What's wrong?" Sorcha asked.

"Um, they didn't order this."

"Table twelve," Sorcha snapped. "You got the wrong table."

"I thought that *was* table twelve." She swallowed a sigh of frustration.

"Great. Just remember…your screw-ups affect *my* tips."

Arden swallowed and nodded. "I'm sorry. I apologized."

"Get table twelve their meals, now."

She hurried to the right table. She needed to go over the seating again and make sure she'd memorized everything.

As she carried a tray of plates back to the kitchen, a man at table two near the bar flagged her down. "Excuse me. What's that martini called that has a cocktail onion?"

She gaped at him. She had no clue. "Um. A martini?"

He frowned. "No, it's got a different name. Anyway, we'll each have one of those."

She hesitated. "Okay, sure."

Probably better to take their order, even though she had no idea what they wanted, than to tell them she wasn't waiting tables yet. She paused at the bar and waved to Liam.

He moved toward her with a smile. "Yeah, love?"

"Table, um, two wants two martinis with pickled onions."

His eyebrows rose.

"What's that called? A martini with a pickled onion."

"That's a Gibson."

"Oh." She blew out a breath. "Damn."

"Yeah, we'll spend some time on the menus, don't worry, love. Is Sorcha cracking the whip?"

"Oh, no, no." The last thing she was going to do was complain to the boss about her trainer. Especially when she was the boss's sister. "She's great. Teaching me a lot."

"I'll get the drinks to them. You take those dishes to the kitchen."

She nodded and picked up the tray again. The kitchen was sweltering chaos because things were so busy tonight with people off celebrating the Fourth. Her entire body was hot, sweat trickled between her breasts, and her feet hurt, and she hated screwing up.

Maybe taking this job had been a mistake.

CHAPTER SEVEN

*A*rden slowly opened the door of Tyler's apartment the next morning. She poked her head in and called softly, "Hello?"

Silence greeted her.

Tyler had finished work at eight, so she expected he was sleeping. She didn't want to disturb him as she used his bathroom. She carried a bundle of towels, shampoo, conditioner, body wash, shaving cream and a razor, a loofah sponge dangling from one of her fingers.

She could easily use Mila or Jamie's apartment, but Tyler was right, this was closer. She edged into the apartment and paused to look around. Curiosity about where Tyler lived danced in her belly.

She tiptoed into his living room. The apartment layout was similar, but instead of an island separating his kitchen from the living room, he had a small dining table. She took in the details of the renovations that had been done...similar shiny hardwood floors to her apartment, the walls painted a nice taupe color with deep, white baseboards and casings around doors and windows. The fireplace was beautiful, the brick painted white with a heavy oak mantel, his kitchen stunning with black cabinets and white counters.

For a bachelor apartment, it was pretty clean and tidy. A bowl of fruit rested on the counter along with a newspaper and what appeared to be some mail. A squarish taupe sectional sat in the corner of the living room facing the fireplace, which was topped with a big screen TV. The square table in front of it held an empty bowl with crumbs of what appeared to be potato chips, the remote control, some magazines and—she had to smile—a hammer.

She turned to a long low bookcase that was stuffed with all kinds of things…electronics, video games, and books, of course. She took in the titles—lots of science fiction and fantasy and…holy shit. She peered closer. A bunch of books by one of her favorite authors, Lora Leigh. It was the shape-shifter series she herself hadn't read, although she'd read many of the author's other books. But all Lora Leigh books were super sexy. She smiled. *That* was interesting.

A little guilt poked her at how she was snooping around. She glanced over her shoulder as if expecting to see Tyler watching her. But hey, she wasn't opening cupboards and drawers or anything. She didn't look at the mail to see if his bills were past due or if his bank statements showed a negative balance. She was just observing.

She headed to the bathroom, pausing for a peek into the second bedroom across from it. The room held a black desk and leather chair, a small couch that probably folded down to a bed, a bike, and a bunch of exercise equipment.

Stop, Arden. Shaking her head, she turned to the bathroom.

And sighed with pleasure.

Was this what her bathroom would look like when finished?

A big soaker tub occupied a lot of space, but there was still room for a separate glassed-in shower stall, a toilet, and a double sink vanity. The floor was gray and white hexagon-shaped tile, the vanity a charcoal gray, the walls a lighter gray, and the tiles in the shower a mix of various shades of gray and white.

She eyed the tub with longing. Her intent had been to jump in and out of the shower and get out of Tyler's place. But her feet and lower back were still aching from her shift at Shenanigans last night, and the idea of soaking in steaming hot water was so enticing…she couldn't resist. Biting her lip, she set down her things on the marble counter and started filling the tub. She hesitated, then locked the bathroom door. Tyler was sleeping, but just in case…she didn't want a repeat of him walking in on her naked in the bathroom. Nope, that hadn't been embarrassing at all. Gah.

She eyed Tyler's bath products…a masculine sponge hanging in the shower with black bottles of men's shampoo and body wash. Pretty minimal. Although there were several hair products, a hairbrush and an electric shaver/beard trimmer sitting on the vanity. If she snooped, would she find prescriptions drugs? Guyliner?

She laughed at herself as she stripped off her clothes, then squirted a generous amount of her Bombshell body wash beneath the faucet to create some bubbles. Heaven.

Soon, she was submerged in steamy, soapy water up to her chin. This tub was amazing. She sighed, closing her eyes and wiggling her toes. Long baths were a guilty pleasure of hers that she hadn't indulged in for too long. She'd been busy packing, traveling, and now living in an apartment with no tub or shower.

Tyler was going to regret offering his bathroom to her, because she was going to be in here every chance she got.

Well, not if he was home. Probably. Maybe.

She wished she'd brought her e-reader (which she tucked into a Ziploc bag when she had a bath), but she hadn't planned on this. Damn. She could have borrowed one of Tyler's Lora Leigh books...but she wasn't going to get out of the tub and trek naked through his apartment to get one. So she relaxed and let her mind wander, reliving her long shift yesterday and the various humiliations she'd endured.

For a moment, she let herself indulge in a little pity party for one. When she'd trudged home late last night with burning feet, sore legs, and an aching back, feeling like an idiot, she'd questioned her sanity. Maybe she should have waited and looked for a nice office job where she could sit and answer phones or something.

She sighed. There was nothing stopping her from looking for a job like that while she worked at Shenanigans. Other than the fact that answering phones all day didn't sound a hell of a lot better than waiting tables.

She wasn't going to feel sorry for herself. Waitressing was hard work, but it was work. To her surprise, she'd left with a share of tips in her purse even though she hadn't waited on any tables herself. Liam seemed like a good boss, although he was a little slapdash about rules and policies and procedures. It appeared that Sorcha stayed on him about those things, while he kept staff and customers alike charmed and happy.

After her bath, she was going to study the online menu of Shenanigans. She'd had another embarrassing moment when a table had flagged her down and asked which she'd recommend between the pork tacos and the fish tacos. Her response had been brilliant: "Well, the pork tacos are made with pork, so if you like pork, you should definitely have those, but the fish tacos are made with fish so they're really good if you like, um...fish."

They'd all stared at her while her cheeks flamed.

Now she closed her eyes, held her breath, and slid down until the water closed over her head.

Dammit. She wasn't going to let shit like that happen again. She at least could have made up some bullshit about fish tacos being lighter, even if she had no idea what was in those dishes.

She pushed up out of the water and ran her hands over her eyes.

Liam was going to give her a lesson in beer and cocktails. That should be fun. She was *so* not a beer girl.

Didn't matter. This was her livelihood now, and she was going to kick ass at it if it killed her.

She reached for her can of passion fruit-scented shaving foam and her razor, and took care of defuzzing underarms and legs. She scrubbed up with her sponge, then shampooed and rinsed her hair using the handheld attachment.

Out of the bath, she combed through her wet hair as the tub drained, then considerately cleaned out the tub. It was nice of Tyler to let her use his place; she didn't want to leave it in a mess. She wiped down the vanity too, then dressed and gathered up all her things to leave.

It still seemed weird that they all left their doors unlocked, but they were friends and trusted one another. That was kind of comforting, actually, to know she was living among people who had one another's back.

She wouldn't see much of Jamie and Mila when she was working late shifts, but now she had a schedule for the next week, and there were some days she'd work earlier. She'd been chatting online with her friend Emma, who also worked a nine-to-five type job, though it sounded like Emma too worked long hours. They'd been trying to figure out a time to get together with Arden now back in Chicago, and now that Arden knew her schedule, they could arrange something. She was excited to see her best friend again.

She opened the bathroom door and poked her head out. The hall was empty, so she stepped out, all her things rolled up in damp towels.

"Hey."

She jumped, nearly throwing her bottles of shampoo and conditioner down the hall. She turned to see Tyler coming out of his bedroom, wearing a pair of athletic shorts sitting sinfully low on his hips, his hair all mussed. "Jesus! You scared me. I thought you were sleeping."

He gave her a slow, slumberous smile, his eyelids heavy. "I think you might want to cut back on the caffeine. You're as jumpy as peas on a hot griddle."

She couldn't stop the laugh that bubbled up. He was right, though. She'd been on edge for a long time, and the stress of picking up and moving across the country hadn't helped that. "I guess that long bath I just had didn't help me relax much."

"You had a bath?" One eyebrow rose and his eyes took on an interested gleam.

"Yes. I hope that was okay."

"Yeah, that was okay. I told you, you can use my bathroom any time."

"That tub is amazing. I love it."

"Hmmm."

She blinked.

"Well, good. I need coffee. You need coffee?" He moved toward her down the hall.

"You just told me to cut back on caffeine."

He brushed past her with a smile. "How many cups of coffee have you had today?"

"None."

"Then you're good. Come on."

"I should go..." She had wet hair dripping down the back of her T-shirt and no makeup on.

"Have a cup of coffee."

"Did I wake you up?" She followed him slowly to his kitchen, watching the muscles in his back, the shorts so low she could almost see the shadow of his butt cleft. She swallowed. They really had to stop meeting like this...

"Nope." He grabbed a package of Tassimo cartridges and checked the machine for water. "Just woke up. I only needed a nap, since things were quiet last night."

"Oh. That's good."

"It was good. Busy day yesterday."

"Did you rescue any cats from trees?"

He laughed as he started the coffee maker. "Is that what you think I do?"

"It's the stereotype, I know. Have you ever rescued a cat?"

"No. We don't do that."

"What? You just leave them up there?"

He turned and leaned against the counter, an amused expression on his face. "Have you ever seen a skeleton of a cat in a tree?"

She frowned at him, then burst out laughing. "Good point."

"I did rescue a dog, though."

Her eyes widened. "You rescued a dog from a fire?"

"No." He grimaced. "He ran under a parked car and got stuck in the engine compartment."

"Oh. Really?"

"Really. We had to lift the car and get underneath."

"He's okay?"

"He's fine. Back with his family. Crazy mutt." He shook his head, but smiled.

"You like dogs?"

"Love 'em."

"Would Jamie let you have one?"

"Probably. We don't have much of a yard though, with

parking behind the building. I think I'd rather wait until I can buy my own house someday." He rolled his eyes. "Which could be in fifty years, and I'll be too old to look after a dog."

"Buying a house is hard."

"Unless you're Jamie Lennox."

She sighed and accepted the cup of coffee he handed her. "True." She eyed him. "Am I sensing I'm not the only one who's a little envious of Jamie?"

"Nah." He started making another cup. "Jamie deserves everything he has. He's worked his ass off for it since he was seventeen."

"True."

"And I'm exaggerating on the home buying thing. I've got some decent savings, thanks in large part to living here. Jamie and I have a deal so the work I do comes off my rent, and that's really helped me put some money away."

She found the idea that he might move away...unsettling. Even though she'd just arrived here and had no idea how long she'd stay. "I guess I'm in a similar boat. Jamie's letting me live here rent-free because the apartment is still under construction."

"Well, think of it this way. He can't rent it to someone else; nobody would pay to live in an apartment that's still being renovated. And it could take a while, since I just do it part-time."

"What about Norton?"

"Huh?" He squinted at her.

"Sunday at the beach...he seemed upset that Jamie had given me the apartment. Was it promised to him?"

"No." Tyler's lips twisted and he shook his head. "Norton wants to live here. But he couldn't afford the rent if Jamie charged him regular price. Norton still lives with his parents."

She nodded. "That's not unusual these days."

"Especially for Puerto Rican families. My grandma lives with them too. Norton's my cousin on my dad's side, obviously. Multiple generations tend to live together. Norton would like to get out, but he can't afford it anyway, and nobody promised him anything about this apartment."

"Well, hell. I feel bad. I feel like I took that away from him."

"You didn't," he said firmly. "If Norton really wanted to live on his own, he'd find a way."

"It's not easy."

"I know. Hey, I don't make that much money. It might seem like I'm getting some kind of deal from Jamie, but I work for it. So *I* found a way."

"True. Um…why don't you still live with your mom?"

He grimaced. "I offered. With Dad gone, I thought she might want me there to help out. But my mom's not Puerto Rican, and she thinks a guy my age needs to live on his own, not with his mother."

"Ah." She recalled that Tyler's dad had passed away around the time she'd graduated from college, from a heart attack that had taken him way too soon.

"Hey, how'd your new job go last night?" He picked up his own mug of steaming coffee.

"Oh. Um. It was great!" She beamed a smile before taking another sip of coffee.

He tilted his head. "Really?"

She wasn't about to share all her missteps last night. Not right now, anyway. Maybe someday they'd be funny stories, but she wasn't quite ready to laugh at herself. She wanted everyone to think she had her shit together and was moving on with her life and doing just fine. "Really!"

He eyed her and she held his gaze for a long moment. The warmth in his eyes made something inside her crumble. "Not really." She dropped her head forward. "It was exhausting. I have so much to learn. And being on my feet all that time tired me out. That's why the bath felt so good. Although I do love a nice, long bubble bath." She lifted her head to give him a wry smile.

His eyes darkened and his mouth firmed. He swallowed. "Well, good. You can use my bathtub any time."

"Thanks." She sighed. "I made a bunch of stupid mistakes. I don't know anything."

"Hey." He moved closer, his dark eyes fastened on her. "It was your first day. Don't be so hard on yourself."

"I don't like making mistakes or feeling stupid."

"Nobody does. Most people mess up from time to time." He paused, holding up a hand. "But…wait…are you seriously telling me you're not perfect?"

Her forehead tightened. "Of course I'm not perfect."

"Well, hell. You're destroying my illusions. I always thought Arden Lennox was perfect. Gorgeous. Smart. Fun. Kind."

"Kind?" She tipped her head to one side.

"Sure. You may have had an annoying little brother, but you were always nice to his geeky friend. After Tara died…"

"Oh." She swallowed. He did remember that.

"I also remember that day in high school when a bunch of kids were making fun of Barry Wong because he tripped and fell in the hall and broke his glasses and couldn't find them. And you gave him his glasses and told them to shut up and leave him alone. And they listened to you. Because you were Arden Lennox."

Something expanded in her chest, stealing her breath. She couldn't even speak.

"I guess it's true. Nobody's perfect." He shook his head with a sad expression. "Everybody's ass has a crack."

A surprised laugh shot out of her. "Oh my God!"

He grinned back at her. "Actually it's good to know you're not perfect."

"Oh yeah? Why's that?"

His face changed, his eyes dropping. He shrugged. "Just good to know."

She didn't think that was the real answer, but despite her curiosity, she didn't push.

"So, what are you going to do about it?" he asked.

"About the fact that I'm not perfect?"

"About the fact that you don't know everything about your new job on day one."

"Ah." She didn't tell him she'd thought about quitting. "Well, I've given myself some homework. I need to study the menu. And make sure I've memorized the table sections."

"There you go." His voice softened. "That's all you can do, beautiful. Learn from your mistakes."

That soft warmth in her chest expanded even bigger and suddenly all her stupid mistakes didn't seem so bad. "Right. You're right."

"I usually am. Except about you being perfect, sadly."

She shook her head. "You're crazy."

"Could be." He paused. "Did you tell Jamie about the new job?"

"Yeah."

"And what did he think about you working at Shenanigans?"

She made a face. "Kind of the same as you."

Tyler nodded. "I won't say I told you so."

"You just did."

He grinned, a flash of white teeth that was incredibly charming. "It kind of sucked you had to start work on the Fourth of July."

"Whatever. It's not like I had big plans. You had to work yesterday too."

"Yeah." He shrugged. "No big deal. Someone has to do it. I'm used to working holidays. And now I'm off for four days."

"That's nice."

"That's why I need a hobby like helping Jamie renovate this place. Keeps me busy."

"You must do other things besides that." She paused. "You don't have a girlfriend?"

"Nah. Not right now. I was seeing someone for a while...we broke up about six months ago."

"Oh." She wasn't sure if she should express sympathy.

"I play baseball once a week in the summer, when I can, with the guys from the station, and in the winter I play for the CFD hockey team. I help out my mom, when she lets me. And I do some community work."

"What kind of community work?"

He shrugged. "My buddy Tremon and another guy—a cop —and I started a nonprofit organization a couple of years ago. We raise money for victims of fires. People's lives are destroyed in an instant; they get injured or lose a family member, their homes are demolished. We saw how people suffered after a disaster, and we decided to try to do something to help."

"Oh. Wow."

"We do different fundraisers throughout the year and some outreach programs."

She nodded, intrigued by knowing this about Tyler. "That's awesome. I used to volunteer with a women's shelter in Phoenix. I enjoyed contributing to something...meaningful."

"Yeah."

"Does the nonprofit have many volunteers?"

"Oh yeah. Couldn't do it without them."

She nodded thoughtfully. "Well, I need to go dry my hair. And do my homework." She picked up her bundle of toiletries.

"You can leave your stuff here." He nodded at it. "Just leave it in my bathroom. It'll be a while before you can use your own, and it won't get in my way."

"You sure?"

"Hell yeah. And you can have a bath any time. I hardly ever take baths."

Her lips twitched and opened her mouth to make the joke.

He laughed, reading her mind. "Don't worry, I *do* shower. I'll be over to your place in a while to do more work. Just gonna grab some breakfast."

"Right. Okay." She returned to the bathroom, set her bottles and shaver on the shelf above the bathtub and hung her sponge from the faucet. This was kind of weird. Another funny little intimacy for a couple who barely knew each other.

But she was getting to know Tyler Ramirez. Grown-up Tyler Ramirez. And she really liked him.

CHAPTER EIGHT

*H*e needed a shower.

Tyler grinned, remembering his earlier conversation with Arden. Yeah, bubble baths weren't his thing, although he could be persuaded if Arden asked him to join her.

He let out a low groan. Keeping her firmly in the friend zone was getting harder and harder the more they hung out. He hadn't offered her his bathtub to feed his spank bank with hot fantasies about wet, soapy Arden, but that's what was happening, dammit.

It was now nearly seven and he'd been working most of the day, stopping for a sandwich midafternoon. He was dirty and sweaty again but felt a sense of accomplishment. He was also starving.

Until she left for work, Arden had been curled up with her laptop in the living room—when she wasn't hovering around the bathroom asking if she could help.

That was cute.

He pulled his T-shirt off over his head as he crossed the hall between their apartments.

He heard noises in the foyer at the bottom of the stairs and moved to peer down at Jamie and Mila coming in. "Hey, guys! You eat yet?"

They both looked up at him. Mila grinned. "Tyler. You have no shirt on. Come down here so I can objectify your gorgeous body."

He laughed.

Jamie shook his head. "Haven't eaten."

"I was gonna order pizza. Want in?"

"Yeah. That'd be good."

"Can't," Mila said. "Going over to Garth's place."

"Order something, Jamie," Tyler called. "I need a quick shower. Be down in ten."

"Bring beer!"

He flashed a thumbs-up and headed back to his place.

Forty minutes later, he and Jamie had each consumed two beers and now had pizza. As they loaded plates up, Mila walked in. She'd changed into a short baby doll dress with a jean jacket over it. "That smells great."

She wandered over and helped herself to a piece of the Italian special.

"Hey." Jamie frowned at her. "I thought you were going over to Garth's."

"I am." She took a big bite.

Jamie shook his head and headed to his couch. "There's a ball game on. Let's watch it."

"No, let's watch *Keeping Up with the Kardashians*." Mila sank down beside him.

"You're going out!"

"And I am *not* watching that show," Tyler added.

Mila pouted. "I need someone to watch with me. Maybe Arden will. When she's not working."

"Maybe." Jamie found the Cubs game on TV, who were winning five-two.

Mila finished off the piece of pizza, jumped up and washed her hands at his kitchen sink, then walked to the door. "Okay, guys, see you later."

"Have fun."

When the door had closed behind her, Tyler said, "Have you noticed she and Garth aren't seeing each other as much?"

Jamie gave him a blank look. "No."

Tyler shrugged. He picked up his pizza. "He was too busy working on Sunday to come to the beach. I can't remember the last time I saw him, actually. And she didn't seem in a big hurry to get to his place."

"Of course not. There's free pizza here."

Tyler snorted. Maybe he was imagining things.

"How'd you do upstairs today?" Jamie picked up his beer.

Tyler filled him in on the progress he'd made with Arden's bathroom.

Already it was "Arden's bathroom." A few days ago it was Apartment Four.

When the baseball game ended, they played Call of Duty until about eleven, then Jamie shut things down to go to bed. Tyler headed back upstairs to his place. He was physically tired from the work he'd done today, but considering he'd napped after getting off work, he wasn't ready for sleep.

He reached for the remote for his TV, then paused. Arden worked until midnight. He didn't like the idea of her walking home alone at that time of night, although she'd done it last night without incident. He'd been thinking about it at work though.

What the hell.

He grabbed his keys and jogged back downstairs. He exited the building into the mild night air, the street quiet and dark.

He soon entered Shenanigans, greeted by voices and music. He peered around, slowly walking toward the bar, keeping an eye out for Arden. There she was, loading up plates onto a big tray, dressed in a pair of narrow black pants and a white shirt that was fitted to her curves. The back booths had mostly cleared out, although the tables near the bar were about half occupied, and a group of people sat on the big couches by the fireplace.

He paused at the far end of the bar, watching Arden hoist the heavy tray and head to the kitchen. A strand of hair hung in her face, which was flushed and shiny. His heart shifted in his chest.

She was really doing this.

"Tyler, my man," Liam greeted him. "What can I get you? The usual?"

"Yeah, thanks."

Liam grabbed a Blue Line Pilsner and set it on the bar in front of him. "What's new, man?"

He made small talk with Liam while keeping an eye out for Arden to return. She walked out carrying an empty tray and paused beside one of the booths. Four men were sitting there, and she leaned in, apparently listening and smiling. Then she shook her head and said something, and all four guys roared with laughter.

Tyler frowned.

With a grin, Arden headed to the back of the bar, checked the booths, and then turned back. As she approached the bar, she spotted him. Her eyes widened and her head tilted.

She walked closer to him. "What are you doing here?"

"Getting a manicure. What does it look like I'm doing?" He lifted the bottle.

Her lips twitched, but she lifted her eyebrows and gave him a long look.

"I told you we hang out here a lot."

"He's not lying, love," Liam said with a wink.

"Okay." She shrugged. "How did things go in the bathroom?"

Liam snorted. "Jaysus, man, you can't be talking about your bowel issues with lovely Arden here."

Tyler met Arden's eyes, and they both burst out laughing. Arden had to lean on the bar she was laughing so hard.

"Oh my God." She wiped an eye. "Liam!"

Liam grinned. "What? That's not what you meant?"

"You know that's not what I meant!"

Tyler shook his head, still chuckling. "Christ, Liam."

The four guys she'd been talking to passed by on their way out, calling, "Night, Arden!"

"See you soon, beautiful," another added.

"Good night, guys!" She waved.

"Making friends already?" Tyler asked, his jaw tight.

She grinned. "Sure. Welp, must get back to work."

The booths had cleared out now. While he sipped his beer and watched another baseball game on one of the TVs, he glanced at her occasionally as she cleared the tables and wiped them down. Every once in a while, she'd look up and catch him watching her, as if she felt his gaze on her.

He couldn't stop, though.

This was crazy.

Every time he was around her, his body vibrated with tension. He was mesmerized by her—by her beauty, yes; by her appealing curves too; but also by the sad hope in her eyes, by the determined optimism in her smile, and by her unassuming rejection of all those amazing qualities that had made her the perfect prom queen.

Now, watching her interact with customers and with Liam, who all appeared to be as entranced with her as he was, something unfurled in his chest.

Christ. He gulped a mouthful of beer. That crush he'd had on her all those years ago apparently hadn't died. How could that be?

It seemed as if getting to know her better made her even hotter. Even more beautiful. Even more…special.

They were both different people now. Looking back at the geeky kid he'd been, tongue-tied and wide-eyed in her presence, feeling completely out of her league, he almost felt sorry for himself. But he wasn't that kid anymore. He was a man now, a man who'd had relationships with women, a man with the confidence to go after what he wanted in life.

He wanted her.

He let out a short exhalation and bent his head briefly. Okay, he'd admitted it. He wanted her.

But there were problems with that. She still saw him as her little brother's friend. Or maybe not…he was pretty sure she felt those sparks that sizzled around them. Or she felt *something*. Maybe.

The other problem was that her husband had just died. Fuck. He hated thinking about her in love with another man. Was she still in love with him? Was she heartbroken and grieving?

It had been a year. That was enough time for someone to move on. Wasn't it?

Or maybe the guy had been the love of her life and she'd *never* get over him. Fuck.

All these questions backed up in his brain.

He looked up at her as she said good night to more customers with that luminous smile. The bar was empty now, other than Liam, Sorcha, and Arden, and whoever was left cleaning up in the kitchen. And him.

"Okay, gorgeous, you can head on home," Liam said.

"Thanks," Sorcha said with a smirk.

Liam snorted. "I was talking to Arden."

"I know." Sorcha rolled her eyes. "When have you ever called *me* gorgeous?"

Arden came back a few minutes later with her purse and a sweater over her white shirt, tucking her tips into her purse.

"I'll walk home with you." Tyler slid off the stool.

She gave him a look, then said good night to Liam and Sorcha.

Outside the bar, in the soft summer darkness, they turned toward home.

"Is this why you came here tonight?" Arden asked.

She was a smart woman. She might have fretted over not being as smart as Jamie, but there was no doubt she was bright. He lied anyway. "No."

"Bullshit." She sighed. "Tyler. You didn't need to do this."

"I wanted a beer."

"And you have none at home?"

He grinned. "Okay, fine. I don't like you walking home alone late at night."

"I told you, I'll be fine."

"Humor me."

She shook her head but didn't protest.

"Did tonight go better? It looked like the customers all love you."

"It did go better. But not all the customers love me. There was a couple in tonight who apparently hated everything, including their food, their drinks, and possibly each other."

Tyler laughed.

"They even hated Sorcha. But she got back at them."

"Uh-oh…did she spit in their food?"

"No. She told the man his credit card was declined." Arden laughed softly. "I thought his head was going to explode."

"Guess they won't be back."

"Nope. I think Liam will be okay though."

"Yeah. Also, I don't know how worried Liam is about making money."

"He should be worried about it! Isn't that why you have a business?"

"Sure. And I think he does fine. But he's not trying to become a millionaire or a big restaurant chain owner. He just loves what he does."

"And that's awesome. That's how life should be." She glanced sideways at him. "That's how you are."

"Well, I'm not gonna lie. I want to work my way up in the fire department." He'd passed his lieutenant's exam. Now it was a matter of waiting, since promotions were based on seniority, and there were a lot of people ahead of him.

"Do you want to be fire commissioner one day?"

"Eh, don't know about that. That'd be a dreaded office job. Then again, maybe when I'm older, I'll *want* an office job."

They turned the corner onto their street and kept walking. The leafy trees formed an arched canopy above them, shifting gently in the breeze. Arden let out a soft sigh.

"Are you tired?"

"Oh yeah." She flashed a wry smile. "My feet and legs are killing me."

"Shit."

"I can handle it." She lifted her chin.

"I know you can."

After a beat, she said in a quiet voice, "Thanks."

"Want me to carry you?" He would. He'd pick her up and carry her all the fucking way home.

She choked on a laugh. "Um, no."

"You work tomorrow night again?"

"Yes, but earlier. Eleven till seven."

"Ah." He nodded.

"Emma is coming over tomorrow night, after I get off work."

"Cool."

"I'm so excited to see her again!" She actually gave a little hop, despite her fatigue.

"That'll be nice. She never left Chicago?"

"No. She went to college here and then started working at Hutter Golding." He recognized the name of the big asset management firm. "We kept in touch of course, and she came to visit me in Phoenix a couple of times."

They walked up the short sidewalk to the dark house.

"Wonder if Mila's home. She was going over to her boyfriend's place earlier." He frowned, remembering his convo with Jamie and his concerns about Mila. But Jamie'd brushed it off, so he was probably just being an old lady.

"I have to meet him."

"Yeah, I'm sure you will."

He let Arden go up the stairs ahead of him, locking the front door behind them, then following her. He allowed himself to watch her ass in those snug black pants. She couldn't tell he was ogling her from behind her. And her ass was definitely worthy of ogling.

In the upstairs hallway, the motion-sensitive light came on and they stood there outside their apartments.

"Well, thanks for walking me home. Even though you didn't need to."

They were about a foot apart. Her hair was pulled back into a ponytail, with a few strands loose around her face, and it gleamed in the overhead light. The opening of her shirt was modest but revealed a hint of cleavage, the white cotton fitted to her breasts. Those sparks he always felt around her prickled and heated his skin. Awareness shimmered between them. Her eyes darkened and her lips parted. She felt it too. She *did*.

God*damn*, need for her burned inside him in a searing blast. He wanted to taste that pretty mouth, feel her soft lips under his, pull her hair out of that ponytail and run his fingers through it. Desire throbbed inside him, a nearly overpowering urge to reach for her and…

She took a step back, her breath hitching. "G-good night, Tyler."

He gave a jerky nod. "Yeah. See you tomorrow."

"Oh. Right." She blinked rapidly, then reached for the doorknob behind her and opened her door. "See you tomorrow."

She disappeared inside her apartment and the door closed.

Tyler pressed his lips together and closed his eyes, his body still aching for her. Fuck.

He turned and shoved into his own place, giving the door a firm push to shut it. He pulled a long breath into his lungs. Okay.

He was frustrated. But that was okay. Because the good thing was…*she felt it.*

He wasn't going to push too hard, or too fast. Christ, patience had never been a strength of his, but he learned it over the years. She'd just arrived a few days ago. She was in the middle of a huge upheaval in her life. It wouldn't be fair for him to be too aggressive. He'd take his time. Show her it was okay.

In the meantime, he needed to rub one out. Spank the monkey. Arm wrestle with his one-eyed vessel. Yeah.

CHAPTER NINE

*A*rden hurried home from work. She'd left fifteen minutes late because Elena, one of the other servers, had taken an extra long break, and Emma was going to be at her place soon. She hadn't had a lot of time to prepare for Emma's visit after a late shift last night and working earlier today, and that annoyed her.

She enjoyed being a hostess. She and Michael had entertained a lot, and she'd taken pride in having the perfect party—mostly the food, because she enjoyed cooking, but also decorations, music, ambience.

Today, she had no decorations, not even a vase of fresh flowers. The music would be a playlist from her phone, and the food was a bunch of nibbles she'd picked up—nothing fancy.

But the important thing was seeing Emma!

She raced up the stairs and into her apartment, feeling sweaty and gross as usual after a shift. She'd planned to shower after work, but she skidded to a halt in her hall facing the demolished bathroom.

Oh right. She had to shower at Tyler's.

At least her things were still there. With a quick glance at her watch, she turned and bolted across the hall. She knocked on the door.

Tyler opened it. "Hi." His face lit up at seeing her, that gorgeous smile spreading wide to reveal perfect white teeth. Damn. That smile reached down inside her and made her girl parts squeeze.

"Can I have a real quick shower?"

He blinked. "Sure."

She pushed past him and headed straight to the bathroom. "My friend Emma is coming over."

"Right. You said that last night."

"I was late leaving work and I need to clean up quickly."

"Go for it."

After a rapid shower and shampoo, she grabbed her clothes. Ugh. She didn't want to put them back on. She needed to invest in a nice thick terry robe for crossing the hall. She sighed and wrapped a towel around her, tucking it in at her breasts to hold it in place. She twisted another towel around her hair in a turban.

She peeked out of the bathroom. Could she make a run for the door and leave without encountering Tyler?

Clothes clutched in her hands, she made a move, scurrying on bare feet over his shiny hardwood floor.

"Done already?" He appeared in front of her.

She sighed and halted. "Yes. Thank you."

His gaze swept up and down her body, leaving a wake of tingles on her skin. "Nice outfit."

"Sorry. Just wanted to get home and get clean clothes on."

His eyes gleamed. "Don't apologize. This is the highlight of my day." His admiring gaze lingered on her bare shoulders.

Heat slid up from her chest into her face.

She shook her head and exited the apartment, coming face to face with Emma in the hall. "Hey!"

Emma blinked at her, her mouth open. "Um, hi." Her eyes flickered to Tyler standing behind Arden, then back to Arden.

Arden gave a strained laugh. "Oh my God, I'm sorry! I'm running late and needed a quick shower." She gave Emma a one-armed hug. "Let me get dressed so I can hug you properly."

"Sure." Emma's wide eyes went back to Tyler. Her head tilted. "Tyler Ramirez, right?"

"Right." He grinned, leaning against the doorframe, arms crossed. "Good to see you again, Emma."

"Uh…you too." She blinked again, and Arden caught the appreciation in her friend's eyes as she took in Tyler's sexy smile, shadow of beard stubble, broad shoulders, and bulging biceps.

"I'll look after Emma while you get dressed," Tyler said to Arden. "Go on."

She stared at him, and he met her eyes with a small smile. Then she whirled and pulled open the door to her apartment. "Come on in."

She dashed to her bedroom, quickly discarded the damp towels and dressed in jeans and a tank top. She brushed her hair out and aimed the blow dryer at it until it was half dry, then took one extra minute to brush on some eye shadow and mascara, although Emma wouldn't care about that.

I'll look after Emma.

What the hell was that about?

Annoyance at this added to her haste to get back to them. She found them in her kitchen, leaning on the counter laughing together, Emma with a glass of the Chardonnay she'd had in her fridge, Tyler with a beer.

Huh.

"Sorry!" She beamed a smile at Emma and moved toward her with open arms.

They hugged for a long moment, then drew apart. Emma smiled at her. "Don't apologize, I understand. No big deal."

"It's so good to see you."

"You too. You look great."

"No, I don't. I look frazzled and my hair's a mess, but whatever." Arden waved a hand.

Tyler handed her a glass of wine. "Here."

She cocked her head and gave him a long look. "Thank you."

"I better head downstairs. Jamie's got some guys coming over to play this new game that just came out."

"Oh." Arden made a face. "Sounds like fun."

Tyler grinned. "I'll let you ladies get caught up. I'm sure I'll see you again, Emma."

"You bet." She winked at him.

Hmm.

Tyler waved as he left, leaving her apartment door ajar.

Arden and Emma both watched him then turned to each other.

"What is going on here?" Emma demanded.

Arden gulped her wine. "Nothing."

"I don't think so! You were at his place—naked! Are you two…?"

"No! My bathroom is being renovated." She waved a hand toward it. "It's pretty much gutted right now. So Tyler's letting me use his bathroom to shower. Since it's right across the hall."

"I can't believe that's Tyler Ramirez."

"I know, right? I didn't recognize him the first time I saw him." When she'd been naked. She shook her head.

"He's all grown up, and wow!"

Arden didn't want to get into a lengthy discussion about

Tyler's hotness, because she was trying not to notice that. "He's a firefighter."

"Oh God, that's even hotter." Emma sighed. "How's Jamie?"

"Good." Arden moved to her stove and turned it on, then opened the fridge to take out some of the food she prepared earlier. She set out a bowl of mixed olives, another of cubed feta cheese marinated with herbs, and some sliced Italian salami.

"Yum." Emma popped an olive into her mouth.

"Jamie's business is going well, apparently." Arden set slices of bread onto a baking sheet to toast them. "He's been buying properties like this one and renovating them. Lucky for me, since I have no money to pay rent."

"Oh." Emma's eyes shadowed. "I can't believe what happened, Arden."

"I know. Me either." She gave her friend a wry smile. "But it happened, and I'm dealing with it. I have a job!"

She told Emma about Shenanigans while she finished making bruschetta, and they nibbled and drank wine. They fell right away into easy conversation, moving the food to the coffee table in the living room so they could curl up on the couch with their glasses of wine.

It was so easy being with Emma. It was like they'd never been apart.

"I have to admit, I'm a little disappointed there's nothing going on between you and Tyler," Emma said much later.

"What? Why?"

"Because he's gorgeous. And you deserve some hot, sweaty sex with a gorgeous man."

Arden laughed.

"Seriously. You need to get back out there. I'd fix you up

with someone, except I'm not that good at it since I can't even find a guy for myself."

"I'm sure you could." Emma was beautiful, wicked smart, and fun to be around.

"I don't have much time for dating." Emma sighed. "I work such long hours, I don't have time for anything."

"That's not good for you."

"I know, but that's the nature of the business. Up early to check the London market, then New York, then when the markets close at four, it's time for meetings to review portfolio holdings and talk about ideas for potential opportunities the next day." She smiled. "I love it."

A female voice spoke from the door. "Hey, Arden, are you...oh."

Arden and Emma turned to see Mila at the door. "Hi, Mila." Arden smiled and gestured. "Come in."

Mila entered. "Sorry to interrupt. The guys are all into some video game, so I came up to see if you were busy. I see you are."

"This is my friend Emma. Emma, this is Mila. She lives downstairs and works with Jamie."

Emma and Mila shook hands.

"Sorry," Mila said again, holding up her hands. "I'll let you get back to your visit."

"No, stay. Have a glass of wine with us."

"Sure?"

"Yes, of course." Arden rose and moved to the kitchen. Luckily she had a couple of bottles, because the first one was nearly empty. She filled another glass and handed it to Mila where she sat on the loveseat.

"I met Arden's hot neighbor earlier," Emma told Mila. "I was just saying that Arden should climb his fire pole."

Mila laughed. "I guess he *is* good looking. Hard for me to

imagine banging him when I see him as a brother."

Emma nodded with satisfaction. "Okay, good. I wondered if there was competition for him."

"Emma! You're crazy." Arden shook her head. "He's my little brother's friend."

"Okay, first of all, Tyler is *not* little. Second, who cares if he's your brother's friend?"

"Well, it would be awkward. Since we all live here."

"I suppose. Also, I have to say that your little brother is looking pretty hot himself these days."

Arden frowned. "You've seen him?"

"He let me in when I got here. Also I ran into him at a club a while back."

"Oh."

"He's all grown up too, and I like the hipster glasses and beard stubble."

Mila frowned. "You're talking about Jamie?"

"Yes, I am." Emma grinned. "Don't worry, Mila, I'm not interested in him that way."

Mila's eyebrows shot up. "Me? Worried? Ha! Jamie's a pain-in-my-ass friend. Besides, I have a boyfriend."

"Oh." Emma tilted her head. "Okay."

"Hey." Mila straightened. "I don't suppose you two girls would like to come to pole dancing lessons with me?"

Arden choked on her wine. "Um, what? Pole dancing?"

Emma grinned.

"Yes. I signed up for a class. It's supposed to be a great workout."

Arden blinked. "I don't even know what to say to that."

"When is it?" Emma leaned forward.

"Sunday afternoon."

"I'm off Sunday," Arden said slowly.

"Perfect!"

"I'm in," Emma agreed.

Mila helped herself to some Soprasetta and olives, and they all chatted, Emma and Mila getting to know each other and discovering a mutual love of *Keeping Up with the Kardashians*.

"I don't even know why I love it," Emma said with a laugh. "It's crazy."

"I know, right? We should get together next week and all watch it together. How about here?"

"Depends if I work." Arden wrinkled her nose. "Damn job is going to interfere with my social life."

The others laughed. "Yeah, working for a living does put a crimp in fun. Okay, we can DVR it and watch it together when we can all do it. With lots of wine. We'll make a date."

"Sounds good."

A knock sounded on the door of the apartment, and the three women turned to see Tyler.

"Hi, Tyler!" Mila called. "Are you geeks getting tired of gaming?"

Tyler grinned. "Never. Okay, maybe a little. We thought you might want to come down and join us…" His eyes fell on the food spread out on the coffee table. "Or maybe we'll come up here…you have better food than we do."

Arden smiled. "Sure. Come on up. I'll make more bruschetta." She'd added pita chips and hummus to the spread, and she could whip up her famous five-ingredient dip and put out some crackers with it.

Tyler disappeared but came back moments later with Jamie and two other guys he introduced as Danny and Asher. Jamie and Emma greeted each other with friendly ease, and Arden watched Tyler make more introductions from her kitchen where she stirred together mayonnaise, bacon bits, slivered almonds, cheddar cheese, and green onions.

Jamie set a case of beer on the island and started handing

them out. Tyler leaned on the island. "Anything I can help with?"

Oh hell yeah, he could help with something. He could help with that ache low down inside her that appeared when she was around him. Or when she thought about him. When he smiled that easy, sexy smile and his eyes crinkled up. When she watched his big strong hands with a crowbar or a hammer and thought about his hands on her, and how he could definitely help her…

She pushed a box of crackers and a plate toward him, clearing her throat. "You could put some crackers on this plate."

"What are you making? It has bacon in it. I love bacon."

"It's a dip for the crackers." She set the bowl onto the plate.

Tyler picked up a cracker and scooped up dip with it. "Goddamn. That is *good*."

Arden smiled, a lightness filling her.

Look at her—in her new apartment that was now noisy and full of people, and she was serving them food and making them happy.

At that moment, she felt…maybe her life was going to be okay.

A swelling feeling of gratitude rose inside her. She looked over at her brother, talking to Emma and Danny. Yeah, she could see that women would find him good looking, with his shaggy dark curls and beard stubble, and tall, lean build.

Family was important. Thanks to him, she had a place to live, and all these new friends. She swallowed away the thickness in her throat.

"You okay?" Tyler's eyes were watchful.

She smiled and nodded. "I'm great. You can take that plate over there."

Tyler carried it and set it on the now-crowded coffee table.

"Try this dip, Jamie. It's fucking fantastic."

Everyone reached for crackers, and Arden watched in pleasure as they enjoyed the food.

Arden's attention caught on Mila, who was watching Jamie and Emma with a notch between her eyebrows. Jamie laughed at something Emma said, and Mila's eyebrows drew down even more.

Hmmm.

Arden went over and sat beside Mila on the sofa, between her and Asher. "Well, this turned into a party."

Mila smiled. "Are you okay with that? We all kind of barged in on you and Emma."

"It's fine. Now I'm living here again, Emma and I will have lots of time to get together. Hey, Jamie—Mila, Emma, and I are going to take pole dancing lessons."

Arden felt Tyler's heated gaze land on her. "Pole dancing?"

"Yeah. Isn't that fun?"

"Jesus." He rubbed his mouth. "Okay."

"Is there a recital at the end of the class we can come watch?" Jamie asked, which was met with laughter.

"No way you're watching," Arden said.

"I can pole dance," Danny spoke up. "I'm pretty good at it, actually."

Arden smiled at the man. He was around their age, mid-twenties, not as tall as Jamie and Tyler, probably about five-eight, with a slim build. His features indicated an Asian background, his dark hair cut very short. Small gold hoops glinted in each ear, and he wore jeans, a T-shirt, and multiple leather bracelets on both wrists.

"Oh yeah," Mila said. "Danny is who Jamie went out on a date with last week."

Emma's eyebrows lifted.

Danny grinned.

Arden bit her lip. "Oh. Right. I forgot about that. Do you perform, Danny?"

"I do, yeah. At the Firefly Lounge and Supper Club."

"Danny's a drag queen," Mila explained to Emma, whose expression changed to one of interest. "We should go see you perform sometime!" Mila clapped her hands together. "That would be so fun!"

"Sure." Danny smiled. He was cute. "I'm Honey Deville."

"We are totally planning a night out when everyone can go. I'll arrange it."

Arden hoped her job didn't interfere with the plans. She was super curious about the Firefly Lounge and Supper Club. Between watching the Kardashians, pole dancing lessons, and now this, her social life was filling up.

She checked out the other guys in the room to see how they were reacting to Danny's talk about pole dancing and being a female impersonator. Jamie obviously must have been okay with it, or he wouldn't have invited Danny over again. Tyler seemed unfazed, and Asher, who she didn't know at all, wasn't bothered by it either.

Cool.

"This dip is amazing." Mila picked up another cracker. "Jamie, you did good letting Arden stay here." She paused. "But don't think we just love you for your food, Arden. We like you too."

"Gee, thanks." Arden met Mila's teasing eyes and melted a little inside.

"I'm expecting waffles this weekend," Tyler reminded her. "Saturday, though. I have to work Sunday morning."

"I can do that." She'd have to make sure she had time to go shopping again before then. Crap—had she packed her waffle iron? She didn't remember seeing it…but she was pretty sure she had.

"Perfect," Mila said. "Saturday morning waffles. Should I bring the butter?"

Arden laughed. "Um, maybe. Tyler pointed out that you wouldn't approve of my use of margarine."

"Hell no!" Mila's face contorted.

"I actually prefer butter too," Arden assured her. "Don't worry, I'll get some."

"I certainly hope so."

Arden had to laugh. "Emma, you want to come for waffles on Saturday?"

Emma looked bemused by all this banter. "Um, sure. Sounds good."

Eventually, people started talking about leaving. It was a slow process, but a while later, her apartment was empty and quiet…except for her and Tyler. He was loading dishes into the dishwasher.

"You don't have to do that."

He looked up. "It's not a problem. Just helping out. We all invaded your home, and you fed us. Thank you."

"It was fun." She paused, looking down at the counter.

Tyler moved closer to her, and she startled, feeling his warmth, breathing his scent. God. He was so damn attractive. She wanted to see if his T-shirt felt as soft as it looked, and whether the muscles beneath it were as hard.

"You seem a little sad."

She shook her head, surprised at his perception. "No. I'm not sad. I mean…maybe a little. This isn't how I pictured my life. But…life is still pretty damn good."

"Yeah."

She met his eyes. Heat shimmered around them. This was crazy. She was a widow. She'd been betrayed by her husband. She wanted nothing to do with men. And it was *Tyler*… Why was she feeling like this about him?

CHAPTER TEN

$\mathcal{A}$rden worked four to midnight at Shenanigans on Saturday night, so Tyler offered to take her to the farmers' market and Whole Foods early Saturday afternoon—after she made waffles for all of them in the morning, which turned out to be a big hit.

"You guys want to come with us?" Tyler asked Jamie, Mila, and Emma as they sat in Arden's kitchen drinking coffee, bellies full of waffles and bacon. Bacon. Mmm. He loved bacon.

"Nah, I'm good," Jamie said.

"I'm going over to Garth's place," Mila said.

"And I have to go into the office for a while," Emma said.

Okay. It was just the two of them. Fine with him.

"How's the bathroom coming?" Jamie asked him.

"Not bad. Wanna see?"

"Sure." Jamie stood and Tyler followed him to the bathroom, which was still a disaster.

"It always takes longer than I think it will," he said to Jamie. "Especially when I'm waiting for someone else. I need Brent to come and do the wiring."

They had an electrician and a plumber they liked to use, but those guys were both really busy.

Also, he'd clued in to the fact that the longer it took to get Arden's bathroom functional, the longer she'd be coming over to his place to shower. And he really enjoyed those times. Especially when she left with just a towel wrapped around her, water drops on her shoulders from wet hair, her legs bare…

He shook his head, trying to refocus. "The plumbing work is minimal, since we're not moving the location of the fixtures, so that's good."

"What's your schedule like this week?" Jamie asked. "Anything else we can start on while we're waiting for Brent?"

"Twenty-four on starting tomorrow, forty-eight off, twenty-four on. Maybe Monday I can start working on the walls, or the fireplace. No—fireplace first."

"Or you could take a day off for yourself." Jamie faced him. "You don't need to spend every minute of your days off working here."

Jamie'd told him that before. "I know."

"You'll be off all weekend, right? I can help with some things then."

"Okay, sounds good."

They wandered back to the kitchen where Mila was helping Arden clean up. "Okay, I'm outta here." Mila tucked a dish towel over the rack inside the cabinet door. "See you guys tomorrow. At least…I'll see you, Arden, for pole dancing. One o'clock. Be ready." She pointed.

Oh yeah, that wasn't distracting at all—imagining Arden spinning around a pole in sexy moves. "What do you guys wear for pole dancing?" He kept his tone casual. "Sequined g-strings?"

Mila laughed. "Um, no. I'll be wearing leggings and a tank top."

"Good to know," Arden said. "I would have been so embarrassed showing up in my thong and pasties."

Jamie choked.

Grinning, Tyler slapped him on the back.

Mila and Jamie left and clomped down the stairs to their apartments.

"Does Garth ever come over here?" Arden asked, rinsing a sponge in the sink.

"Not much. Especially lately. Maybe he hates us."

"I doubt that."

"It's possible. Even though Mila's been going out with him for a while, I don't feel like I know him that well."

"Huh. You guys are so much fun to hang out with, I would've thought he'd be here all the time."

"Really? You think we're fun?"

"No. I was just being polite."

He snorted. "Come on!"

She smiled. "Okay, fine, you're fun. I'm ready to go, just let me get my purse."

"I'm gonna pop back to my place and grab some grocery bags."

They met up in the hall, and he followed her down the stairs, taking in the short shorts that hugged her cute ass and left her legs bare. Her long hair bounced against her back as she ran down the stairs.

"We'll walk to the farmers' market first," Tyler said. "It's not far, and it's hard to find parking that's much closer than we are. Then we can leave our stuff at home and drive to Whole Foods. Plus the market's only open until one o'clock."

"Sure, make me walk. As if I don't do enough of that at my job."

He paused and eyed her.

"I'm kidding." She rolled her eyes and kept walking. "I know you think I'm a princess, but I can walk a few blocks."

"What's wrong with being a princess?"

She slanted him a look as they walked along the sidewalk. "Someone who's so pampered, spoiled, and sheltered that she has no idea about the real world?"

"That's not you."

She sighed. "That's exactly me. I mean, it used to be."

"A princess can also be someone who uses her status to help others."

"I suppose."

"Sure. Like Princess Diana. She did a lot of humanitarian work."

Arden said nothing.

"And I'm sure I remember reading that she had a way about her that made people feel special. Because she was genuinely interested in them." And that totally described Arden too. The other night at her place, she'd opened her door to people she didn't even know and made them all feel welcome— no, more than just welcome…she fussed over them with food and drinks and took an interest in them.

"I am *not* like Princess Diana. And I can't believe you know so much about her."

He laughed. "I'm just saying, being a princess doesn't have to be negative, if you don't want it to be."

Once again she fell silent, clearly thinking.

The farmers' market was busy, as usual on a sunny Saturday. They wandered among the tents set up with all their different wares, taking in baked goods, produce, flowers. He watched Arden's face light up as she studied heirloom tomatoes, bunches of Swiss chard, and crusty ciabatta. She lingered over a tent with gorgeous potted plants and colorful flowers.

"I don't know what to buy." She met his eyes with a look of

longing in hers that made his heart kick against his ribs. "I want everything."

"I know."

He caught her checking her wallet and got the feeling money was tight for her, which sucked, because he wanted her to have everything she wanted.

She ended up with some tomatoes, bread, cherries, raspberries, and a bunch of fresh carrots. She'd lingered over flowers, then turned away. Then they found the tea tent, and she picked up some Tranquil Dreams tea.

Tyler stopped at a tent selling meats and sausages. As he picked out andouille sausage and Canadian bacon, Arden studied the sign. They also sold eggs and butter.

"I'll take a pound of butter," she told the man behind the table when Tyler had paid for his goods.

Tyler lifted an eyebrow at her eight-dollar purchase.

"For Mila. I bet it's really good."

"It is," the man behind the table said with a smile.

Tyler's heart turned over in his chest. That was nice of Arden, thinking of Mila, especially since she'd clearly held back from buying things she wanted herself.

They picked up more veggies—beans, chard, onions, and mushrooms, as well as honey.

Arden sighed and smiled as they left, some of the booths starting to close down. "That was awesome. I love food."

"Hold on." He paused at a flower tent and picked out a bunch. He didn't know what they were, but they were pretty—tall stems with multiple small flowers in shades of pink, yellow, and orange. An elderly woman was about to pay for a bunch of sunflowers, and he waited behind her.

"Oh no!" The woman dug through her purse. "I've lost my wallet!"

Tyler met Arden's eyes and they both grimaced. Arden bit her lip.

"I can't believe it!" The lady sounded near tears. "I just had it!"

"When did you have it, ma'am?" Tyler stepped up beside her.

"I just bought this bread…"

He recognized the paper bag and knew exactly where she'd bought it. "Hang on." He handed Arden his flowers and took off jogging toward the tent. They were almost closed down when he skidded to a halt. "Hey, there was a woman here who just bought some bread…white hair, pink sweater…she left her wallet here. Did you happen to find it?"

"Yes!" The dude's eyes widened. "I was going to try to get hold of her."

"Oh great. She was pretty upset."

"I'll get it." The guy pulled it out of a bag. "Here it is."

"Thank you! She'll be so relieved."

It struck him that he must look honest for the guy to turn the wallet over to him. He hiked back to the flower tent. Arden comforted the woman, who had tears running down her face, Arden's arm around her shoulders.

He held up the wallet.

"Oh, thank you!" The woman took it and clasped it to her, pale blue eyes beaming at him. "You're a sweet young man."

He bit the inside of his lip, then smiled at her. "Happy to help."

She opened the worn wallet and pulled out a bill. She handed it to the man selling the flowers. "I'll pay for his flowers too."

"No, no." Tyler held up a hand. She didn't look like she had a lot of money. "You don't have to do that."

"I want to thank you," she said firmly. "It's nothing. Please let me."

He still hesitated, then gave in. "Thank you."

"You're a lucky girl," the lady said to Arden with a smile. "Hold on to him."

"Oh, um…" Arden's eyes went big as they met his. Then she smiled. And he smiled back.

The moment stretched out for an hour, or maybe a few seconds, while he admired her glowing face, the sparkle of her eyes, the curve of her mouth. Desire punched through his stomach.

Then they both blinked and stepped apart.

"Okay," Arden said breathlessly. "Thanks for bringing me here. This was great. I love food."

"Me too. Mostly eating it."

She laughed.

The afternoon was heating up, but the big old trees shaded them as they walked home.

"You're carrying all the stuff." Arden reached for a bag. "Let me carry something."

"I got it. But here, you can take these." He handed her the big bundle of flowers.

"They're so pretty. I love snapdragons."

"Is that what they are?"

"Yeah. Didn't you ever play with them when you were a kid?"

"Uh, no."

"Look." She plucked one of the blossoms off the stem and pinched it between her thumb and forefinger. "It's a dragon mouth…see?" The flower opened and closed with the pressure of her fingers, indeed like a little mouth.

"Learn something every day. Although I wouldn't say it looks like a dragon."

She bumped him with her elbow. "Don't mock me. It's a nice childhood memory."

"Wasn't mocking you, princess."

"Argh!"

He laughed.

When they got upstairs outside their apartments, he followed her into hers to unload her purchases. "I'll just go put my stuff away, and then we can head out again."

"Here." She thrust her arms out. "Don't forget your flowers."

"No, those are for you."

She tilted her head and pursed her lips, looking like she was going to argue with him. She glanced at the flowers, then her mouth softened. "Thank you. They're beautiful."

"Be right back."

He quickly put his own things away, then returned to her place. "Let's shake it, babe. You have to work at four."

"We're not going to spend two hours at Whole Foods!"

"Yeah, you're right. Much as I love food, and don't even mind shopping for it, I can't handle that much. In and out. Let's rock and roll."

They ended up being at the store longer than he planned. Arden walked around with big, bright eyes, smiling and exclaiming over the olive bar, the baked goods, the huge selection of wines and produce and chocolate. "Oh God, I've missed shopping here." She sighed, clutching a wedge of cloth-bound cheddar cheese. "I have to try this."

Again, she was careful in her purchases, and a lot of the things she bought were snacks and appetizers like she'd served the other night, as if she expected to feed people again. It seemed like she loved doing that.

Usually, he was happy to buy what he needed and get out, but watching Arden drool over prepared salads and pizzas and unique crackers was enough to keep him entertained for hours. He ended up driving Arden to work since they'd run out of time, plus she'd done a lot of walking and would be on her feet all night.

"I'll pick you up when you get off," he said as he pulled up in front of Shenanigans.

She blew out a breath and turned to him. "No. You won't. You work in the morning. And…and…"

"What?"

"Tyler." She bit her lip and met his eyes. "I don't… you're…*aw, shit.*"

"Spit it out, princess. What are you trying to say?"

"I just…"

Wow, she was really stumbling. He cocked his head and waited.

"My husband died," she said in a near whisper.

His head jerked back. "I know."

"I'm not interested in…in anything…in dating…you know."

He kept his face neutral despite the feeling of being punched in the gut. But hadn't he already thought that? Wasn't he supposed to be taking things slow, showing her that they could be good together?

Had he pushed too fucking hard today? It was the flowers. Had to be the flowers. "Okay."

But he wasn't giving up that easy.

"You don't have to look after me all the time. You don't have to drive me to work and pick me up. I'm a grown woman and I'm trying…I'm trying t-to…" She stalled out. "I have to do this on my own. It's…important."

"Arden. I know you're a grown woman. Believe me." Oh hell. That probably wasn't the right thing to say. "Okay, let me be frank here. I don't like playing games. I'm attracted to you."

She stared back at him.

"And I have the feeling it's mutual."

She swallowed.

"I get that you're maybe not in a place to explore that right now. So I'm not gonna push it." He held her gaze. "But I'm not giving up either."

Her eyes remained big and unblinking. Then she hopped out of his SUV and disappeared into the pub.

Shit.

~

Arden rushed into Shenanigans, her face hot, her hands shaking.

What the hell was that?

She couldn't believe what Tyler had just said.

I'm attracted to you.

She hurried into the staff room where she stored her purse in a locker, and set her hands on her face. Okay, okay, it's not like that was a huge shocker. Yes, she'd felt it too. But it was out of the question for them to act on it.

She'd brought up the issue of Michael's death, but that wasn't really the problem. She'd fallen out of love with Michael before he'd died; he'd changed so much. Nonetheless, she *had* grieved his death, of course she had. She'd also grieved the loss of so many other things…the life she'd thought she had, the future she'd thought she would have, the friends she'd thought she had, her home. Not to mention the loss of her innocence. Maybe innocence wasn't the right word for it…naiveté? She didn't like to think she was stupid, but she'd certainly been blind to what had been going on.

And *that* was the problem. She'd been an oblivious idiot. Michael may have not been a model husband, but as his wife and partner, she'd failed him. Never again would she risk doing that to someone else.

It had been a long time since she'd had sex, and damn Tyler for making her feel that hot, achy knot of need low down inside her. For making her imagine his big naked body moving against her…inside her…his hands on her skin…*gah.*

She sucked in a long breath and let it out, then straightened her shoulders. She was stronger than that. She could ignore those thoughts, those feelings. She could be around Tyler and remember the geeky, tongue-tied kid who'd hung out at their home. Not the sexy firefighter with big muscles who saved dogs and ran to find a little old lady's lost wallet.

She headed out to start her shift, focusing on the things she needed to remember…menu items, table sections, what was in the Irish Breakfast.

"Liam hired another waitress," Sorcha told her as they stood next to each other at a counter in the kitchen.

"Oh, that's good."

"Yeah. Maybe now I can have a day off." Sorcha grimaced.

"I guess you'll need to train her."

"Yes." She sighed and picked up a stack of menus. "Hopefully she catches on as quickly as you did." She disappeared.

Arden blinked. She'd caught on quickly? She still felt like a bumbling fool most of the time.

Was there anything she could do to help Sorcha?

As everything was quiet at the moment, she walked over to the bar where Liam was. "Hey, I heard the good news. When does the new waitress start?"

"Not until next week."

"You know what would be good?"

"What?"

"A service manual."

"A what?"

"A service manual. Some kind of guidelines in writing. Service goals, steps of service, performance expectations."

Liam gaped at her. "Well, sure and good, but where am I going to get something like that?"

She sighed. "I don't know. Sorcha is the one who knows the most—"

"Hey. This is *my* place."

"I know." She smiled at him. "You know a lot too, but she's the one who trains new waitresses."

"Yes."

"But she's so busy working and training new people, I'm sure she doesn't have time to work on something like that. The thing is, if you had a service manual, it would make training new people so much easier for her. I can tell you, it would have helped me when I was starting."

"This would be your business degree coming out."

She laughed. "I guess so."

"I'll consider it. Maybe you could help her?"

"I don't think I know enough."

"You're a smart lass."

"Thanks. Well, I better check my tables." She walked away, warmth spreading through her middle. Two compliments in one night! Maybe this job wasn't so bad.

CHAPTER ELEVEN

*T*yler arrived for his shift Sunday morning, early as always. After the morning briefing, he readied his bunker gear, then worked with the rest of the crew on maintenance things, stocking medications, checking the equipment on the trucks—air masks, EMS kits—to ensure it was all operational before the shift got going.

He was on rotation with dipshit Evan Crenshaw. He'd never liked the dude, who was one of those assholes who talked like he knew everything but really didn't. Tyler's low opinion of the guy had been reinforced on one of their first calls together when Tyler had first started at Engine 25 as a firefighter candidate. Crenshaw had a year of experience on him.

They'd been called to a home in Ravenswood where a thirty-five-year-old man had had a seizure. They'd gotten his legs and waist strapped to the gurney when the dude had punched Crenshaw in the mouth. To Tyler's horror, Crenshaw had punched him back, calling him a "fucking retard."

He still felt a knot in his gut every time he thought of that. He'd stopped Crenshaw from hitting the guy again, and later, after they'd left the man at the hospital, back at the station when they were alone, he'd laid into him about it, despite the other man's seniority.

"I was subduing him!" Crenshaw had said. "What the fuck, man, he punched me!"

"He was having a seizure! I should report you for that."

"Try it."

And why hadn't he? Crenshaw's dad was the Chief of Battalion 5, and possibly next in line to be a deputy fire chief.

The CFD was an insular organization, with many family members working there, sons and even daughters often following in their parents' footsteps. Tyler hadn't had any family or other connections; he'd worked his ass off to get where he was. And it pissed him off that Crenshaw got away with bullshit like that because of who his old man was.

Even worse? They'd both taken the last lieutenant examination. They'd both passed, although Tyler knew he'd gotten a better score on the exam. But Crenshaw would likely get there first because of seniority, despite the fact that Tyler knew he was way fucking better at his job than Crenshaw was.

This morning, Tyler and Crenshaw checked all the tools and equipment while Tyler's buddy, engineer Tremon Jones, checked the truck/engine and Lieutenant Cliff Murkowsky checked the MDC—mobile data computer, the onboard laptop that linked to dispatch.

He made himself act professional around Crenshaw, but man, the asshole made it a challenge sometimes. Like now… Crenshaw was hanging around paramedic Ronda Norris as she washed windows, one of the regular chores that had to be done. He wasn't helping, he was just being a jerk, pointing out the window she'd just finished wasn't clean. Crenshaw pressed his hand to it as if showing her, of course leaving a fucking smear on the glass.

Ronda glared at him. "Jesus, Crenshaw, what the fuck?" She tossed her cleaning rag at him. "Here. You fucking clean it."

"Hey, hey." Crenshaw caught the cloth. "What's the matter? You on your period? You're supposed to let us know when that is so we can be prepared."

Ronda gritted her teeth. "Fuck you."

"Shut up, Crenshaw." Tyler walked up behind them. "Either help her or find something else to do."

"Who put you in charge?" Crenshaw glared at him.

Tyler rolled his eyes. "Don't be a douche."

Crenshaw stalked off.

"Thank, Ty," Ronda said quietly. "But I can handle him myself, you know."

"I know." Taken aback, he set a hand on his chest. "I do know that. I was just trying to help."

She smiled wryly, shaking her head. "You always are."

Shit, wasn't that a good thing?

He headed to the kitchen, debating whether to cook pancakes for everyone, or make a run to Sabroso, a nearby Mexican restaurant that made fantastic breakfast burritos.

He was the one who mostly did the cooking on his shifts. He remembered one of his instructors telling them that whoever did the cooking was the most popular crew member. He didn't set out to be the most popular, but he liked food and liked finding ways to put it together, so he'd just kind of slipped into it. Which also meant he did the supermarket runs to pick up shit to cook.

After inspecting the contents of the fridge and cupboards, breakfast burritos won out. A short time later, over soft tortillas wrapped around scrambled eggs, sausage, peppers, and cheese, they discussed plans for the day and what other chores needed to be done.

He managed to get in a workout before they got called to a structure fire. Over the radio, they learned that cops were already on the scene and reported smoke coming from the garage of the home.

There were about five cop cars parked on the street in front of the house. Tyler jumped off the truck as soon as the air brake was set and started toward the back of the property.

"I don't see any smoke," Tremon stated.

"Me neither."

"Pair of underwear burning in the garage," one of the cops told them.

"Oh, for fuck's sake." Tyler shook his head and made his way into the cluttered garage. Sure enough, there was a pair of men's underwear smoldering away. He glanced around, found a rake, and used it to lift the garment. He showed it to Captain Maxwell.

"Great," he said, one corner of his mouth lifting. "Use the thermal imager to make sure there's nothing else burning in there."

Turned out that one of the cops had showed up at the house to arrest a parolee for not checking in. The dude had been in the garage and lit the tighty whities on fire in an attempt to get away. When he ran out of the garage, another cop had been there, waiting for him. So much for that great escape.

That evening, Tyler made dinner, a big pot of chili, which he served with garlic cheese buns. His chili was one of his more popular menu offerings, and he made lots so they could stash it in the fridge, and the shift tomorrow could have some.

As they sat around the scarred wooden table eating, Tremon said, "Holy shit, this is spicy chili."

"It's not that spicy," Tyler objected. He tasted another mouthful. Maybe a little more heat than usual.

"Hot enough to set your underwear on fire," Cliff said, and they all busted out laughing.

Tyler went over to his mom's place the next evening. She'd invited him for dinner, and he hadn't been there for a while, plus he loved her roast beef. Despite the disappointment she never hid, he loved his mom and knew there would be things at the house that needed taken care of.

He pulled up on the street in front of the red brick house in North Center where he'd grown up. The house was bigger than his mom needed now she was alone, but she refused to sell. It was a solid house, a decent neighborhood, and it was all paid for thanks to insurance on the mortgage, but it was too much for Mom to look after.

"What's new with you?" Mom asked as Tyler set the table and she filled a platter with slices of roast beef. "Are you seeing anyone?"

"No." He wanted to be. But he wasn't going to tell Mom that.

"I still miss Claire."

"Sorry, Mom." Just another way he'd let Mom down. "It just wasn't working for us."

"She was such a smart girl. She's probably going to be a partner in that law firm she works at."

"I'm sure she is."

Claire was just the kind of woman his mom wanted for him —smart, together, with a high-powered career that was on track to make her lots of money and prestige. In fact, that was what Mom wanted for *him*.

Mom set the platter of beef next to him and he loaded up his plate, snitching a piece to pop in his mouth. Then she brought out a bowl of mashed potatoes, along with a salad and a bowl of green beans—the kind with butter and almonds that Tyler loved—and some carrots.

"This is a lot of food for two people, Mom."

"I know." She sighed. "I can never get it right."

They sat, Mom said a quick prayer, and they began passing the food back and forth, filling their plates.

"You know, Rachel Bronstein just broke up with her fiancé," Mom said, referring to the daughter of one of her friends.

Tyler repressed a sigh. "I'm not interested in Rachel, Mom."

"She'd be perfect for you!"

He had to get the subject off his love life. Too bad Mom wasn't interested in his job at all. "Remember Arden Lennox?"

Shit, why had he brought up Arden? He cut a piece of roast beef with his knife and fork.

"Yes…Jamie's sister. Didn't her husband die?"

"Yeah. She just moved back to Chicago. She moved into the empty apartment in our building."

"Oh, that's nice. How is she doing? What a sad thing, to be a widow so young."

"She's doing okay. I think Jamie's glad that she's closer now so he can help out."

"Jamie's a smart boy."

"Yep."

Mom admired Jamie and the success he'd made of his business. "Maybe Jamie can convince you to go back to college. Look how he's done."

Tyler's chest tightened. They'd had this discussion so many times. "I'm not going back to college. Not full-time anyway. I took some courses to help me do better on the lieutenant's exam."

Mom *had* been happy he'd obtained top marks on the exam. "I just think you could be doing something better with your life. Something with more of a future."

"I want a future with the fire department, Mom. Everyone I work with is dedicated to this profession. Willing to risk our lives to help others." He met her eyes.

Her face tightened and she dropped her gaze. "I know."

"And like I said, I plan to move up. Also, I'm not into a nine-to-five kind of job. I like the flexibility."

She was never going to get it. She was never going to get that he wasn't going to be the one to live up to her hopes and dreams, the hopes and dreams that had been shattered when her daughter had died.

His parents had never blamed him for Tara's death. Not overtly, anyway. But he'd felt the survivor guilt. The feeling that if he hadn't been hanging out playing basketball after school, Tara wouldn't have been walking home alone that day.

They'd never really gotten over that, and he'd become the focus of their world. The one they pinned all their aspirations on. The one they'd pushed to do more, to do better, to get into a good college, to have a career and a beautiful, perfect girl-friend that he'd marry, and to give them beautiful, perfect grandchildren.

For years, he'd tried to be that guy. He'd tried to do everything he could to make them happy. To make up for them losing their daughter. He'd worked hard at school and did okay, but never got top marks. He'd taken courses that would get him into college. He'd won science fair awards, mostly thanks to Jamie, and basketball championships, mostly thanks to the guys who'd been the real athletes. He'd gotten into college, but when Dad had died, it had been a good reason to drop out. He needed to start making money, not spending their money on tuition for courses he hated.

But in doing that, he felt he'd let his mom down…again.

There was a saying about how people would accept any kind of check except a reality check.

Today was Arden's reality check.

She was feeling pretty good about how things were going. She had a nice place to live, she was with her brother, she had a new friend and had reconnected with an old friend. She had a job she enjoyed (mostly) and even though it didn't pay much, she'd managed to save up a little.

She also had a hot, single man who was interested in her and who wasn't giving up.

That was both gratifying and terrifying. And exciting.

She'd been thinking about Tyler and the things he'd said when he'd dropped her off at work, although she hadn't seen him since. She felt…*alive*. Aware. Energetic.

She hadn't been working out, other than the pole dancing class, which had definitely exposed her lack of fitness. Back in Phoenix, before Michael had died, she'd belonged to a fashionable gym where she'd gone five days a week to do yoga, barre, circuit training, or Exalt, a trendy new class that combined restorative movement and meditation with strength and cardio training. Sitting in front of her laptop in her little apartment researching gyms in Chicago quickly informed her that even a low-cost gym membership was outside her budget.

Okay, so no more barre classes. She could stay fit without spending a lot of money. More Google searching brought up a bunch of YouTube videos on workouts you could do at home with no equipment. And, she could run. Running just required a good pair of shoes and some shorts.

She had some workout clothes, but the other day she'd

noticed her favorite leggings had holes worn in the inner thigh seams. And the shoes she had weren't going to work for running on city sidewalks. She'd go shopping today. Also, she badly needed a haircut. Her ends were embarrassingly dry and fizzy.

This required more googling, to find a salon nearby. She really needed a good keratin treatment to tame the frizz, but that was probably out of the question. She couldn't spend four hundred dollars on her hair. So the salon on North Wabash was out of the question.

Well, she'd head down to Michigan Avenue to hit up Lululemon or Under Armour for some leggings. Maybe she'd find a hair salon there she could pop into for a cut.

It was about a twenty-minute bus ride to Michigan and Oak Street. She eyed the overcast sky and tugged her sweater closer around her to ward off the damp chill as she strolled along Michigan. First up was Lululemon. But the prices there dismayed her. Somehow, she'd never really thought of Lululemon as expensive. She fingered the fabrics and studied a cute hoodie. Ah well.

She headed south on Michigan, peering into windows as she walked. Just as she arrived at the corner of East Superior, drops of rain pelted her and it started to pour. Spying the doors of Saks, she dashed toward them and nearly fell into the foyer. She made eye contact and exchanged a sheepish smile with the big dude at the door, shaking rain off her hair. Well, might as well look around inside for a few minutes. Maybe the rain would stop.

She strolled through the perfumes and cosmetics, pausing to look at the new makeup from MAC. She did need mascara. And that highlighting powder was so beautiful. But the mascara was forty bucks, and damn, she could buy mascara for five bucks at CVS.

She rode the escalator up. She could check out workout gear here, if they had some. Maybe they had a sale. She found a sale rack of active wear and flipped through it. She pulled out a pair of leggings and sighed. Damn, those were pretty. She flicked the price tag over and sighed again, shoving the leggings back onto the rack. Reduced to a hundred fifty dollars wasn't going to cut it.

There was no point in even looking. But she couldn't help but stop at the shoe salon to drool a little over a pair of glittery Jimmy Choo stilettos and an adorable pair of leopard-print booties. She smiled wistfully as she picked up a bootie.

After hiking farther down Michigan, popping in and out of various stores to dodge the rain, she found the Under Armour shop. Inside, she fingered cute, strappy sports bras, shorts, and bright-colored tops. She wanted it all. And having pretty clothes would motivate her to run. But the whole outfit added up to over two hundred dollars. It was just stupid to spend that much money on something she didn't *really* need.

Emerging onto Michigan Avenue empty-handed, she turned her face to the sky as the sun tried to break through the clouds, and let out a long exhale. Oh well.

She spotted a hair salon on the other side of Michigan just down the side street. Carly's Cuts. It didn't look too fancy. A shampoo, cut, and blow dry would pick her up. She waited in the crowd for the lights to change, then crossed Michigan and continued down the street. Stepping inside, she eyed the price menu posted behind the counter. Sixty bucks.

She would have thought nothing of paying sixty bucks for a haircut at one time in her life. But now that too seemed… extravagant. Unnecessary.

She was changing. And that was okay.

She left the salon and walked to a bus stop to head home.

She'd seen a salon not far from Shenanigans that she would check out…one of those chain places.

Sitting on the bus as it motored north, she leaned her head against the window. How spoiled she'd been, letting Michael pay for expensive fitness classes, pricey clothes to wear to fitness classes, and lavish hair treatments. Not to mention regular manicures and pedicures, which she'd been doing herself lately. She'd been so clueless. This was her reality check. Those things didn't really matter.

She hadn't grown up in that kind of world. Her family had been comfortable, but by no means wealthy. As a teenager, she and her friends had liked to spend money they earned at part-time jobs on trendy things, but never Christian Louboutin shoes, and if they got a manicure or pedicure, it wasn't at a fancy downtown place.

She remembered one of the first times she'd gone shopping with Michael's credit cards after he'd signed his big contract with the Cardinals, how she'd thought it was obnoxious and wasteful to spend a thousand dollars on a pair of shoes. Yet somehow, she'd become accustomed to that, to having beautiful things, basically whatever she'd wanted. Deep inside, that wasn't her. This was good.

Magik Kuts' price for a shampoo, cut, and blow dry was $21.99 and they could take her in right away. Perfect.

"I'm Imani," the young woman said as she led Arden to a chair in front of a sink. Imani was probably about Arden's age, maybe mid-twenties, with perfectly smooth brown skin, high cheekbones, impeccable eye makeup, and her hair in gorgeous natural curls. "How's your day going?"

"Well." Arden sank into the chair and let Imani drape a towel around her neck. "It's been…eye-opening."

"Hmm. You don't sound happy about that."

Arden smiled. "It's a good thing."

"Better to have your eyes open, than shut." Imani started wetting down her hair.

"That is so true."

Imani shampooed her hair twice then applied conditioner, giving her scalp a lovely massage that melted her bones. It only lasted a few minutes, but it was wonderful. Then she led her to a chair in front of a big mirror on the wall and draped a plastic cape around her.

"So what are we doing today?" She ran her fingers through Arden's hair, lifting it and letting it fall. "Your hair's really thick."

"Yes. And it tends to be frizzy. I think I just want a trim and a nice blow out."

"Do you want to keep these long layers?"

"Sure."

"I'll blend them in a bit more." Imani studied her hair. "If I take about a half an inch off, that's okay? That'll get rid of these dry ends."

"Perfect."

She clipped up the top layers and started combing and snipping.

Arden spied the book sitting on the counter. "Are you reading that?" she asked Imani.

"Yes. It's so good!"

"I just finished it. I loved it."

"She's one of my favorite authors. My book club is reading it right now. We're getting together on Thursday night to talk about it." She paused. "And drink wine, of course."

Arden laughed "Of course. That's what book clubs are for."

"You belong to a book club too?" Snip, snip, snip. Hair fell to the linoleum floor.

"No, not anymore. I recently moved here from Phoenix. I used to belong to one there, though. It was fun."

"I love talking about books. And this group is really nice because they're not snobby about what we read."

"Oh, that is so important." Arden made a face. "The club I belonged to mostly read literary fiction. It was okay, but then I'd read a great romance, and I'd be dying to talk about it, but I'd never suggest that there."

"Yes, totally!"

They launched into a conversation about books and authors they both loved and read, finding much in common.

"You should come to our club." Imani unclipped a section of hair and combed through it. "Seems you'd be a good fit. We don't invite many new people."

"Do you meet in this area?"

"Yes, most of us live around here. We take turns hosting."

"Maybe you should check with the others first?" Arden bit her lip. "I mean, I don't know any of you, really."

They agreed to exchange information and Imani would be in touch with her about the book club. They continued to chat as Imani snipped away, discovering other things they had in common—both single, both had a much more successful younger sibling, and both liked trying new kinds of tea.

Imani blew out her hair, then added beachy waves with a flat iron.

Arden studied her reflection. "I love it. Thank you!"

"I'm so glad!" Imani held a hand mirror behind Arden so she could see the back, then whipped the cape off. "All done."

Arden paid up front, adding a tip for Imani, and then they exchanged phone numbers.

"I'll text you about the next book club meeting," Imani promised.

"That would be so fun, thank you."

As Arden sauntered along the sidewalk toward home, the sun now drying up puddles and creating humidity, she laughed out loud. Something settled inside her comfortably…a feeling of contentment. She'd made a new friend. Who cared that she couldn't afford Lululemon and expensive salon treatments? None of that mattered. It was the people in her life who were most important.

CHAPTER TWELVE

"What the hell is that?" Tyler regarded the pieces scattered over Mila's living room floor with a frown. Outside Mila's front window, the skies had darkened with heavy clouds. All day the air had been thick and humid.

"It's a stripper pole."

"Jesus Christ."

"Cool, huh? I bought it so Arden and I can practice between classes.

Tyler glanced at Arden, sitting on Mila's couch. He hadn't seen her since the day he'd confessed his attraction to her. Their eyes met.

Christ, she was gorgeous, even with her dark hair pulled back in a loose ponytail, no makeup, and dressed in a pair of short shorts and a snug T-shirt. He tried not to look at her perky nipples and long bare legs, but his eager dick definitely took note.

Her eyelashes fluttered and he sensed her nerves. And yet, her lips tipped up at the corners and the air around them became charged and hot as their eye contact extended. He gave her a slow smile back.

"I just need help installing it," Mila added.

Right. The pole.

Tyler rubbed the back of his neck. "Did you ask Jamie?"

Mila frowned. "No."

"I kinda think you have to. This is his building."

"No, no, I think it's okay, it's not permanent. It stays up with pressure or something."

"Let me see the directions for this thing. If it's not too hard to take down, maybe he'd be okay with it. But you really want this in the middle of your living room?"

"Not really." Mila made a face. "But Arden wouldn't agree to it being in her place."

Tyler barked out a laugh. "Attagirl, Arden."

"I wouldn't mind it," she said. "But the place isn't that big."

"Jamie wouldn't evict you," Mila added.

"He won't evict *you*," Arden chided.

"He could fire me."

Arden laughed. "He won't do that either."

Tyler read the installation instructions and looked up at the ceiling. "Okay, you can install it with friction so we aren't going to damage the floor or ceiling." He squinted. "I hope it's strong enough to hold your weight."

"What are you saying, Tyler?" Mila frowned. "Are you saying we're heavy?"

"Jesus. No, that's not what I'm saying. I'm just imagining you doing some kind of spin and the pole falls down and you fly into the wall or something."

Arden covered her smile with her hand. "No, we don't want that."

"I know!" Mila held her hands up. "You can try it out for us. If it'll take your weight, it'll take ours."

"I am *not* swinging around on a stripper pole."

"Why not? You're a firefighter. Don't you slide down poles at work?"

"No."

"What? There's no pole at the fire station?"

"Nope. Sorry. You want this here or in your spare room?"

"Let's put in the spare room. Then I can leave it up."

"Jamie should be okay with it, since it's tension mounted. But you know what you're gonna have to do."

"What?"

"Demonstrate it."

Mila and Arden laughed.

"I think it's safe to say Jamie won't want to see *me* demonstrating my moves on the pole," Arden said.

He caught her eyes, which danced with amusement. "Maybe *he* won't."

Her lips parted as she got his meaning.

"How are the classes going?" he asked.

"Well, the first one was the most humiliating experience of my life," Mila said. "Even though I've been working out, I apparently have no upper body strength whatsoever."

Arden grimaced. "My thighs are killing me."

Ungh. He didn't want to imagine Arden's thighs wrapped around the pole. "Well, this shouldn't take long." He grabbed his tool belt, and they carried the pieces into Mila's extra bedroom.

He slotted the three pieces of the pole together, then added floor and ceiling plates. He stood the pole up and unscrewed and extended it until the top plate connected with the ceiling, and did the same for the bottom plate. After shaking it to test the fit, he tightened the nuts on the bottom plate. "Okay. Let's see how strong this baby is."

He jumped and swung himself around the pole. It held tight.

Mila clapped. "Good job, Tyler!"

"Okay, show me what you learned."

"This is the only move I could do." Arden moved toward the pole.

Tyler blinked as she gripped the pole with both hands, slender arms outstretched, then extended a long, sleek leg to hook the back of one ankle around it. She pushed her ass out and fell into a slow, graceful twirl twice around the pole.

His jaw damn near hit the floor. "Holy crap." Was she trying to make him lose his mind?

She jumped up and laughed. "That's nothing! You should see our instructor."

"Why are you so good at this?" Mila asked. "I didn't invite you and Emma to come so you could show me up."

"I'm not that good. But I *was* a cheerleader." Arden shrugged. "Maybe that helped."

"We need Danny to come and give us private lessons," Mila said. "Speaking of which, we still have to plan a night to go to the Firefly Lounge and see him." She moved to the pole and tested it, then tried to position herself. "No, that's not how my arm goes," she muttered, and changed position. And again. She lifted one leg and awkwardly tried to lift herself, ending up in a heap on the floor at the base of the pole.

Arden fell into a chair, laughing.

"Okay, never mind." Mila jumped up, grinning. "I can't remember. We need to watch some YouTube videos or something."

Tyler crossed his arms, shaking his head. "You two are nuts."

"It's a good workout." Mila stuck her tongue out at him.

"What's going on in here?" Jamie appeared in the bedroom door.

"Just installed a stripper pole," Mila blurted. "Isn't it cool?"

Jamie's eyebrows flew up and he studied the pole. "Shut the fuck up."

"Seriously. You should see Arden work that pole."

Jamie's face scrunched up. "No. No thanks."

"Told you." Arden rose from the chair. "Fine. I won't show you my one and only move."

Which was fucking hot.

"Please don't tell me this is your new career goal," Jamie said.

"Hmmm." Arden tapped her chin. "I should check into how much pole dancers make. It's probably better than waitressing."

"Don't even joke about it. Waitressing at Shenanigans is bad enough."

"Oh, come on. Shenanigans is a nice place."

"Liam's keeping an eye on her," Tyler offered.

Arden slowly turned her gaze on him, her eyes narrowing into a death stare. "Oh no. Oh no, you did not."

His face heated. "What?" Fuck, he was busted.

"You told him to keep an eye on me, didn't you?"

"Uh. No. Course not."

"Oh my God. Tyler!"

Jamie laughed and slapped Tyler on the back. "Don't worry. I had a word with him too."

Arden glared at them both. Then, to Tyler's horror, her eyes actually got all shiny and her bottom lip quivered. What the fuck?

"I have to go." She whirled around. "I have buns in the oven."

Tyler met Jamie's eyes, full of as much concern as his. "Jesus, I hope not," Jamie muttered.

Mila turned to them with wide eyes. "What just happened?"

Tyler rubbed his forehead. "She doesn't want us looking after her."

Mila's forehead creased. "What? Why? And how do you know that?"

Tyler wasn't sure what to say to that.

"Because of what happened with her asshole husband," Jamie said. "Fuck."

"She hasn't really talked about it," Mila said.

Arden hadn't told Tyler much either. Why was her husband an asshole?

"I've been walking her home from work at night," Tyler said. "When I'm off."

Jamie gave him a curious look. "Yeah? Well, thanks."

Tyler shrugged. "It's late, it's dark…I just felt like I should. Even though it annoys her."

"Should I go talk to her?" Mila asked.

"Maybe I should." Jamie frowned. "It was Tyler and me who pissed her off."

"I will." Tyler strode to the door, just barely catching the bug-eyed look Mila gave Jamie. Yeah, yeah, they were probably wondering what the hell was going on. Well, nothing was going on, sadly.

He took the stairs two at a time, knocked softly on Arden's door and entered. He was greeted by the delicious yeasty scent of bread. "Hey," he called, seeing her on her couch. She turned her head, and though she wasn't crying, her eyes were pink.

He shut the door, walked over, and sat beside her. Not too close. Not as close as he wanted. Fuck, he wanted her on his lap with his arms around her. "I'm sorry."

She sighed. "I know."

"You have to believe us, princess." He winced, remembering she didn't like the nickname. But she didn't react, just regarded him with a steady gaze. "We didn't talk to Liam because we don't think you can look after yourself. He's a buddy, and you're…Jamie's sister, and you're beautiful, and we know every guy in that bar is absolutely going to hit on you."

Her lips twitched, the corners lifting. "Well. I guess you sort of made up for it with that compliment."

"Are you pissed at us?"

"Yes. And no." She pursed her lips. "I know Jamie's worried about me. Because he's my brother. So I get that he's just looking out for me, and it's nice that he cares. But you…" She met his eyes, hers wary. "I don't get why you think *you* have to look out for me."

"You don't think I should care about you."

Her eyelashes fluttered as she broke the connection and dropped her gaze. The air thickened around them. "It's not true, you know."

"What?"

"Not every guy in the place hits on me."

One side of his mouth lifted. "Hard to believe."

"And when they do, I can handle it."

"I know you can. Don't be mad. Because you know what?"

"What?"

"Liam would be watching out for you whether we asked him to or not. Because he's your boss. And because he's a good guy."

She tipped her head to one side, meeting his eyes again. "You're probably right."

"I usually am."

She huffed out a laugh. "But it still feels like you both think

I'm some helpless little female. I know I was stupid about Michael, but I've handled it. I'm doing okay."

Again, what did that mean? He didn't really want to ask, so he said, "Jamie said your husband was an asshole."

"Did he?" She wrinkled her nose. But she didn't offer anything more.

Rain drizzled down outside and the wind had picked up, pelting water at Arden's windows.

"Looks like we're in for a storm." Tyler nodded toward the windows.

"Yes. It was so muggy today."

"Well." Tyler stood, feeling like he was trying to drag himself away from a powerful magnet. "Just wanted to make sure you were okay. And apologize."

"Thank you. I guess I'm just not used to having people around who look out for me."

"Well, that fucking sucks." If that was true then hell yeah, her husband had been an asshole, because wasn't that what a husband was supposed to do?

She chuckled.

"Now you do," he added. "Get used to it."

She looked up at him, a little smile playing on her mouth. "Yes, sir."

He rolled his eyes. "Okay, good night, Arden."

"Night, Tyler."

He crossed to his own apartment.

How hard was it going to be to sleep tonight, remembering Arden spinning around that pole? And not just thinking about those legs wrapped around him, or his hands on her breasts… but also wondering what had happened with her husband.

~

Tyler had been asleep for about an hour when a ferocious crack of thunder shook the building. He jerked away, staring into the darkness. Wow. That was a good one.

He loved thunderstorms.

It was a tiny rush, a little thrill of danger, even though the risk was small. Nothing like the adrenaline rush he got from fighting a fire. Which he loved. Over the years, he'd learned to control the adrenaline rush, to keep himself safe, but he still felt it, still loved it. The stress hormones that flooded his veins could be harmful, but he'd learned ways to come down off that high. Sex was the best way.

Fuck, he was thinking about sex again.

He rolled to his back and watched the flashes of lightning out the window, waiting for more thunder. Then he heard a crash of breaking glass from the other side of the wall. The wall that separated his bedroom from Arden's.

Without thinking, he leaped out of bed, charged through his suite and across the hall. Arden's door was mercifully unlocked—good girl—and he flung it open and strode in. "Arden?"

"Wh-what?"

She opened her bedroom door, long dark hair messed, eyes huge, legs bare. She wore a strappy little black sleep shirt showing lots of pale skin in the darkness. "Tyler? What?"

"I heard something break." He frowned. "Are you okay?"

"Oh. Shit." She rubbed her face. "Yes, I'm fine. The thunder woke me up. I was startled and I knocked a glass of water off my night table."

Thunder rumbled around them.

"Did it break?" His gaze dropped to her feet.

"Yes. But—"

"And you're walking around in bare feet? Goddammit!"

She shook her head. "I'm fine, Tyler."

"You could have stepped on broken glass in the dark."

"Well, maybe if someone hadn't come barging into my apartment in the middle of the night, I would still be in bed." She crossed her arms and narrowed her eyes at him.

"Shit." He rubbed the back of his neck. "You're right."

The apartment lit up again and he tried not to drool over her skimpy attire. Then a crack of thunder had her feet leaving the floor and she let out a little shriek.

Tyler lunged toward her and closed his hands around her upper arms. Her skin was soft and warm. "Hey. It's just thunder."

"That one was loud! I felt the building shake."

"I know." He grinned. "Cool, huh?"

She frowned as he rubbed his hands up and down her arms. "You like thunderstorms?"

"Love 'em. They're fun."

"Uh…" She tipped her head to gaze up at his face in the dusky light. "What if we get struck by lightning?"

He laughed softly. "I think we're pretty safe here. I mean, you do have to be cautious in certain situations. Maybe that's why a storm is exciting, because there *is* an element of danger."

She stared at him wide-eyed. "You're crazy."

"Possibly. But life's boring without a little danger. A little risk-taking." Although he was the one who tried to keep everyone else safe, he liked a little adrenaline rush in his own life.

"Um…"

"But we're safe here," he added hastily. "Just enjoy the amazing power of it. It's really kind of fascinating, that light can create such a loud noise."

"Th-the lightning creates the noise?"

"Yeah. A bolt of lightning opens a hole in the air, and then when the light is gone the air collapses back in and makes a sound wave. That's thunder."

"Huh."

"We see the light first because light travels faster than sound."

"I knew that, at least." She rolled her eyes. "I didn't know you were a science nerd."

"Really? You didn't know that?" His voice was low and teasing. "Jamie and I won first prize in the tenth grade science fair for our project on how fast light travels in water versus in air."

"Oh."

"You don't even remember that, do you?"

"Jamie won all kinds of awards in high school. I couldn't keep track of them all."

"You weren't jealous, were you?"

"Of course not." She tossed her hair back. "Well. There may have been times I wished I was as smart as he is."

Tyler snorted. "You *are* smart."

"Eh. Not like he is."

"Maybe if you'd spent more time studying and less social butterflying…"

She jerked back, but he kept his hands curled around her arms. "What?"

"Oh, come on. You didn't care enough about getting awards to spend your whole life studying."

She blinked at him. How did he know her that well? "That's the second time you've implied I'm lazy."

"That's not what I'm saying! I'm not criticizing you. You think Jamie and I weren't envious of all your friends and the parties you went to and how easy it was for people to like you? The teachers loved you. Even the principal loved you."

She could only gaze back at him for a moment. "I guess things look different through someone else's eyes."

"And with ten years of hindsight." He smiled. "You lived life the way you wanted to. Nothing wrong with that."

Her eyes grew distant and the corners of her mouth drooped. Huh. What had he said?

The room flickered into light then darkness, and another boom of thunder vibrated the floor. Arden flinched, then laughed. "I'm okay."

"It'll pass over quickly, I think." His skin tingled every-where, as if electrified from being so close to her. Or maybe it was the electricity in the air from the storm. Yeah, right, that was why his dick was thickening in his boxers.

He released her arms and moved behind her, then gave her a little nudge. "Go make yourself some herbal tea or some-thing. I'll clean up your broken glass."

He grabbed the big broom he'd left in the hall from his work earlier and headed into her bedroom. He turned on her lamp, swept up broken glass, mopped up with a towel he found neatly stacked on her dresser, and deposited the shards into the waste basket.

When he returned to the kitchen, she'd flicked on the over-head light, had the kettle on the stove, and was pulling a tin of loose tea out of a cupboard.

"Do you want some tea?"

"Sure. All cleaned up. Dried up the water so my beautiful wood floors don't get wrecked."

"Oh." She bit her lip, her gaze dropping to his bare chest, then lifting quickly back up. "Did I do any damage?"

"Nope." He rested his hands on the counter on the other side of the island, looking down at the two cups with tea infusers sitting on top. "What are we having?"

"Honey Lullaby."

"Uh. Okay."

"Not a tea drinker?"

"Not really. I like nice strong coffee to keep me awake." He rubbed his face. "But not right now. Need sleep."

"I'm sorry."

"Hey, I didn't mean this is your fault. I was already awake from the storm."

"Enjoying the storm."

"Yeah."

She poured boiling water over the tea leaves, and the scent of honey and chamomile rose from the cups.

"That smells good."

"This is one of my favorites when I can't sleep."

She removed the tea infuser and pushed his mug across the counter to him, then fixed her own. She lifted the steaming cup, breathed in the aroma and sipped the hot beverage.

Tyler did the same and wrinkled his nose.

"You don't like it?"

"No, it's fine. Just different."

They were both standing at her island to drink the tea. "I need to get stools," She said. "It would be nice to sit here, maybe eat my meals here. Somewhere for guests to relax while I cook."

"Yeah. That would be good."

"Not in the budget right now, unfortunately. I need to make some money."

Yeah…again he wondered why she seemed so broke.

She picked up her tea. "We can sit in the living room."

Tyler followed her to the couch, his eyes lingering on her legs.

Seated there, they eyed each other. Tyler's body heated, and tension arced between them. He gulped his tea, damn near scalding his mouth.

CHAPTER THIRTEEN

*A*rden curled her legs under her, aware of how skimpily she was clothed.

As was Tyler.

Um, yeah. She was sitting in her living room in her nightie, with a man wearing a pair of boxers.

She and Tyler had seen quite a bit of each other's bare skin in the last couple of weeks. Although he'd been working a lot of the time, they had managed to run into each other—on top of that time she'd tried to sneak out wearing a towel, there was also the day she'd gotten mixed up about his shifts and walked in to find him wearing nothing but a towel around his hips. It was a good look on him, for sure.

Then there were the days he was working in her place. Despite the air conditioning, he seemed to have to take his shirt off a lot. She wasn't complaining, mind you. When he wore his tool belt low on his hips, it was jaw droppingly sexy. He was always screwing and nailing and finding studs...and it all made her think very inappropriate thoughts about her little brother's friend.

Tonight, when the lightning had flashed, she'd taken in the boxers sitting so low on his hips she could trace with her eyes the thin line of dark hair trailing from his navel, lower, lower… Then he'd been holding her, so close the heat of skin enveloped her along with a spicy, woodsy scent that was…delicious.

She took a big mouthful of her tea.

"Do you often have trouble sleeping?"

"Um, what?" She blinked at him, nudged out of her contemplation of his hot body.

"You said you like this tea when you have trouble sleeping. Just wondered if it happens a lot."

"Oh. Yeah, I do." She grimaced, cupping her tea. She'd been having nightmares and insomnia since the night the police arrived at her Phoenix home. But she didn't need to share all her shame with him. That was in the past, and she was starting over. "Do *you* have trouble sleeping?"

"Nope." He grinned. "Never. I fall asleep in seconds, and I'm usually out unless the alarm at work wakes me up."

"Or a thunderstorm."

"Yeah. At work I never know how much sleep I'm going to get, so I've trained myself to shut things down and crash fast."

"I guess that's a good skill to have in your job."

"Yeah."

"Do you like your job?"

"I love it."

"I never pictured you as a firefighter."

"No?" His mouth twisted into a wry smile. "Should I even ask what you pictured me doing?"

"I don't know. Something like Jamie, I guess."

"I'd go crazy sitting in an office all day." He dropped his gaze. "But that was what my parents wanted me to do."

She tilted her head. "They wanted you to work in an office?"

"They wanted me to go to college. 'Make something of myself.'" He held up two fingers and moved them in air quotes. "My dad and his family came here from Puerto Rico when he was a baby. He worked in construction, like his dad did. My grandma cleaned houses. They wanted me to do something more white-collar—like an accountant or something. Make lots of money."

She sighed. "Money's not everything." As she well knew.

"True. After the summer my dad died, I applied to the fire department and never went back to college. My mom was so pissed at me for that. But it's not that she's money hungry. She just wants the best for…for me."

"Well, I guess that's not that unusual. I think most parents want their children to be successful. But it's not fair if she pressures you to do something you don't want to."

"Being an educated white-collar professional was her idea of success, and a firefighter isn't that."

"You *are* a professional." She set her jaw. "Firefighting is an admirable profession." Her body tensed, thinking that his mother wasn't proud of the man he'd become, the profession he'd chosen.

He met her eyes, and his warmed. "Thank you." One corner of his mouth lifted. "I also wanted to do something that helped people."

A fist squeezed her throat. "That's great, Tyler."

"Jamie helps people too."

She blinked. "Yes, I guess he does."

"Just in a different way."

Jamie's web analytics company helped small businesses— lots of small businesses, judging by his success—by giving them detailed information about how their online sales were doing. He also helped millions of other users with trend information from his business's global statistics services. It was a bit of a stretch to compare that to running into a burning building to rescue someone. But Tyler's modesty and generosity of spirit melted her inside.

"You okay now?" He met her eyes.

"I'm fine. I was just a little nervous…it's still new here, and the storm was wild, so…"

"I get it."

He'd run into her apartment to rescue her. Admittedly it hadn't been on fire, but his intent had been the same. She shivered, her nipples tightening.

"Cold?"

"Um, a little."

Tyler set his mug down on her coffee table and reached for the throw blanket draped over the back of the couch. He shook it out and shifted closer to her to drape it around her. His hands lingered on her shoulders, and she looked up at him, his face so close. She breathed in that intoxicating scent again, studying his strong jaw and long eyelashes and…his mouth…his perfectly shaped lips…

Her breath caught in her throat and heat built between them as his lips parted and his fingers tightened on her shoulders. "Arden…"

She dragged her bottom lip between her teeth, her heart racing. White-hot desire tore through her, an undeniable, overwhelming need to feel his mouth on hers, to feel his body against hers, his arms around her. To just…give into the lust heating her insides.

Her eyelids lowered. His mouth moved closer. Only a breath apart, he paused. The silence of the room vibrated around them.

She closed her eyes and tipped her chin up so their mouths met.

A low groan rumbled in his chest and his mouth opened

against hers in a long, clinging kiss. And another kiss. Slow liquid heat pooled inside her, her breasts growing heavy. Heat radiated from his bare skin and she lifted a hand to lay it over one firm pectoral. The muscle jumped at her touch and with another groan, he tilted his head, opened his mouth wider and deepened the kiss.

Oh holy hell. Rational thought fled as heat flooded her body. She made a noise of need in her throat as he devoured her mouth with long, deep kisses. His tongue slid into her mouth and met hers in a dizzying, panty-melting caress.

Tyler knew how to kiss. Wow, did he know how to kiss. He tasted amazing, faintly of the chamomile and sexy male. His stubble grazed her jaw, so male and a little rough, and she loved it.

Lightning flashed and thunder crashed, and she was almost oblivious to it, dazed and breathless, the storm inside her more powerful than the one outside. Her head whirled, her body pulsed and ached.

"Fuck." He leaned his forehead against hers, and it thrilled her that he was panting and trembling just like she was. "Christ, Arden, your mouth…" He brushed another kiss over her lips, and she parted instinctively for him. "Never imagined you would taste so goddamn good."

She moaned. "You taste good too. Kiss me again."

This time, he hauled her right up against him, crushing her aching breasts to his chest, and it felt amazing. The blanket dropped away and his hands came up to cup her face, holding it while his mouth took hers. She kissed him back, and they both slid a little lower on the couch, one of her knees lifting up over his legs. She wanted to be closer still.

His hands slid into her hair, now holding the back of her head, his thumbs caressing her jawline, and she melted even more at the tenderness of his touch. She let her hands roam, exploring hard muscles and hot skin, smooth in some places, hair-roughened in others.

"Oh God." She let out a soft sigh as he used his thumbs to tip her head back and stroked his tongue along her throat. His lips latched onto her skin and sucked so gently. She was on fire everywhere, her nipples tingling, her inner muscles squeezing.

He kissed her mouth again and one of his hands slid over her shoulder, brushed one taut nipple straining at the thin cotton of her nightie, then swept along her waist and hip and around to her bottom. The short nightie had ridden up and, with only cheeky panties beneath it, he found bare skin and squeezed.

Her breath left her all at once, making her head swim. Tyler's big hand on her butt cheek felt amazing, a sensual wicked promise of more. He palmed her flesh, pulling her closer still until she was pressed against his muscular thigh, just where she needed it. A moan climbed up her throat as throbbing sensation built there, spreading through her body.

"You have the sweetest ass."

"Th-thank you."

His mouth teased over the side of her neck, her jaw, her cheek. He kissed each eyelid, the tip of her nose then her mouth again, his tongue licking inside in a deep, wet kiss that had every nerve ending in her body burning.

His hands moved over her, one fisting in her hair, pulling her head back, his other caressing her throat and jaw. She opened her eyes and met his, almost gasping at the desire blazing there. His fingertips brushed over her cheek and she swallowed at the intensity of the moment, their gazes locked, his hand on her vulnerable throat. Heat shimmered through her.

"You're beautiful, Arden." His voice was a rasp. "So goddamn beautiful."

Her heart swelled in her chest and she could only stare, mesmerized.

"I want to do such bad, dirty things to you. You, the perfect prom queen."

"I thought we already established that I'm not perfect."

"So you're saying you're okay with that?"

She whimpered.

"I'll worship you." He rubbed his beard stubble against her jaw, nipped at her ear lobe. "I'll pleasure this gorgeous body. I'll make you feel so good, baby. Let me."

Her eyes fell closed at the onslaught of sensations his words brought on. "This isn't really happening."

"You feel it. You want it." He licked over her bottom lip. "If I slid my hand inside those little panties, what will I find?"

She squeezed her inner thighs, knowing without a doubt what he would find.

"It's okay," he murmured, hands smoothing down her back and cupping her ass again. "Because I'm hard as a fucking fire hydrant."

She made a choked noise of amusement and lust. "Hopefully not as big."

His lips twitched as he squeezed her cheeks. "Close."

She leaned her head on his shoulder, filled with an undeniable need to laugh despite the heat that flowed through her veins. "Now you're scaring me."

With a hoarse laugh, he lifted her head, bringing her closer still, his hand pulling her thigh higher over his lap, and she felt his erection behind the thin fabric of his boxers. Hard, throbbing heat tantalized her, and she rubbed her knee against it. A growl escaped his mouth as he captured hers in another searing kiss.

They strained together, desperate, hands all over each other, mouths sliding, tongues gliding. She'd never wanted so much in her life. And she'd never *felt* so wanted—so consumed, so *craved*. It was as fierce and beautiful as the storm outside, sensation spiraling through her, light, heat, sparks, and crashing pleasure. It twisted higher inside her as she rubbed herself against him.

He cupped her breast through her nightie, and pleasure jolted through her. She pushed into his palm in yearning supplication. He found her nipple with thumb and fingertips and pinched. She felt that deep inside her, and the coiling pleasure shot up. "Oh God," she gasped, her entire body clenching, sparks shooting from her core to her toes and fingertips. She shuddered against him.

"Christ, Arden." He held her as she pulsed and pulsed, helpless noises falling from her lips.

"Oh my God." She dropped her head to his chest, quivering.

He rubbed her back in circles as she caught her breath. Her face burning, she kept her eyes squeezed closed. She couldn't believe that had just happened.

"I'm sorry," she said weakly a moment later.

"For what? For having an orgasm?"

"Yes."

He lifted her face with the same motions he had earlier—hands cupping her face, thumbs brushing her lips. "An orgasm is nothing to apologize for. I wanted you to feel good. I wanted you to have that. I might have done it differently, mind you…I want to use my fingers on you. Or my tongue, so I can taste you and feel you come on my face."

"Oh God." She wanted to slide into a pool of lust and misery on the floor at his feet.

"What?" He slid his thumb inside her mouth briefly, his eyes fastened on hers. Her belly did a warm flip. "What's wrong with telling you what I want?"

"We aren't…we can't…this is crazy."

"Why?" His eyebrows pulled together. "Just tell me why."

"Because…" She stopped. It all sounded so feeble. Tyler was in no way the boy he'd been when she'd last known him. He was a man, there was no doubt about that—a man who knew how to kiss, a man who knew how to touch her in ways that lit her on fire and melted her inside…a man who wanted her.

She swallowed. "You're Jamie's friend."

"This has nothing to do with Jamie."

She couldn't argue with that.

His eyebrows notched together even more. "Are you still in love with your husband?"

She sucked in a breath, staring at him, her eyes going wide at his blunt question. She considered how to answer that. If she told him she was, he would end this. She didn't know him well, but somehow she knew he was honorable that way—he would never force her to do something she wasn't ready for.

But that would be a lie. And a man like Tyler deserved honesty.

"No," she finally said.

His frown eased into a look of puzzlement. Then he lifted her away from him and sat back.

She pushed her hair off her face, not taking her eyes off his. "What?"

"You're not ready."

"I am," she said. "I'm so ready." She squeezed her thighs together.

Again his lips twitched. "That's not what I meant."

"Oh." She blinked. Then she sighed. "It's not that I'm not ready. It's that…I don't want to get into a relationship again. I'm not good at that."

Tyler's forehead pulled into a perplexed crease. For a moment he didn't speak. Then he said, "Why would you say that? I mean, I know your husband died, but Jamie said *he* was an asshole."

She swallowed. "It's a long, ugly story." She peered at him through her eyelashes. "He committed suicide."

Tyler's eyes flew open. "Jesus. No."

"Yes." She closed her eyes. This was the last thing she wanted to talk about when all she really wanted to do was jump back into Tyler's lap and do the wild thing.

"I'm sorry," he said quietly. "I didn't know that."

"Jamie didn't tell you?"

"No. He hinted that things weren't great for you, even apart from your husband dying, but he didn't share the details."

She bent her head, letting her hair fall over her face. "It's a long, painful, humiliating story."

"You don't have to talk about it. But if you want to, I'm here."

This wasn't a story she wanted to tell anyone, but for some reason the words started pouring out of her. "Michael played football for the Cardinals."

"Yeah."

"We lived big, enjoying his money. His fame. We hung out with other players and their wives and girlfriends, and other celebrities in Phoenix. We went to expensive restaurants and clubs. We bought a big, beautiful house with a pool. We had parties and entertained a lot. I sort of wanted to work, but Michael made a lot of money, so I didn't have to. I did some volunteer work that made me feel a little useful."

Tyler picked up the throw from the floor and once more wrapped it around her, pulling her back into his arms.

She snuggled in, head still bent. "Michael got injured a few years into his career. He couldn't play football anymore. He was lost at first, but then he found a job selling real estate. He enjoyed it, and he made some money, but…we kept living the same lifestyle we always had. Ugh. This is the embarrassing part. I had no idea we didn't have as much money as we used to. He acted like he was making tons of sales, and money wasn't an issue. I had no idea he was going into debt so we could keep the house and the cars and the trips. I didn't know he hadn't filed our taxes for years."

"Fuck."

"Yeah." She pulled in a breath and let it out slowly, resting her cheek on Tyler's strong chest. "I found out when they were apparently going to arrest him for tax evasion. He…that was when he took his own life."

"Oh Christ, Arden." His arms squeezed her tighter. "Jesus Christ.

She gave a tiny nod. "That was bad enough, of course, losing my husband like that. I didn't find him, if you're wondering that. He drove himself out into the desert and did it. Put a gun in his mouth." Her heart quivered at the thought. She'd spent months imagining what he'd been going through to take that final, fatal step. Images of Michael's last hours haunted her dreams and kept her awake at night, while guilt and grief, anger and self-hatred twisted in her belly.

"The police came and told me. Then I found out even more about how bad things were financially. The money we owed. There was no way to keep the house, even if I got a job. I had to sell it to pay off the debts. It took a year to get everything settled, with lawyers involved. Then of course they took a fuck-ton of money in legal fees. With what little was left, I packed up and moved here."

"I don't even know what to say." He rubbed his jaw over her hair. "I'm so sorry, Arden."

"Thank you. It was a rough time." That was a major understatement, but she wasn't going for pity here. "There was more than that, of course. Being a widow was bad. The money issues were horrible. I discovered what a spoiled princess I really was."

"Fuck. I'm sorry…when I called you that I had no idea…"

"I know." She sighed. "I know. It just hit close to home. I had no idea what to do, how to deal with things. Michael handled all our finances, paid all the bills. All I did was go shopping with his credit card. I was such a fool."

"He kept things from you. He lied to you. You're not a fool."

"I should have known. We should have been partners in our marriage. I should have pushed harder for that. I should have contributed something."

He made a low, rough sound in his throat. "You can spout out shoulda woulda couldas forever and a day. They don't change anything, and it's just beating yourself up about things you can't change. And it doesn't let him off the hook. *He* was the one who didn't make you a partner. He didn't tell you the truth about what was going on."

"I had my head in the sand, and don't try to tell me I didn't because it's true. There were a lot of reasons I liked our life. But deep down inside…I wasn't really happy. Michael was… different than the guy I fell in love with in college."

"Oh fuck no, don't tell me he cheated on you too."

"I don't think so. But he changed. We used to have fun together. When he first got signed and we moved to Phoenix, we were both just laughing all the time at the crazy money they paid him and how we ended up in that kind of life. But he got really into that world. After he couldn't play anymore, it seemed like the money and the lifestyle were more important to him than I was. He worked long hours. Actually it turned out he was busy gambling, desperately trying to make back some money, I presume. I found out about that afterward too, from some friends who let it slip." She blew out a frustrated breath.

"Too bad they didn't care enough to tell me *before* he committed suicide, when maybe there'd been a chance of getting him some help. But that was another thing I discovered…our friends weren't really 'friends.' They all disappeared pretty quick."

He made a growling sound.

"Michael and I had grown apart. He loved the good life… the fancy restaurants and parties, hanging out with rich, famous people, driving expensive cars, living in a beautiful house. He wanted me to look the part too, so he never minded that I shopped for clothes and shoes, and decorated the house, and went for lunches, manicures and pedicures. I went shopping with friends and belonged to a gym where all the other players' wives went. It all felt silly and frivolous sometimes, but then…" She closed her eyes. "That was how I filled the emptiness in my life. It was all I had. Michael and I didn't talk, and that's partly my fault too. It was awful when he died, of course. There are no words…I was in shock. Numb. In denial. But…" She lifted her head and met Tyler's eyes. "I didn't love him anymore."

CHAPTER FOURTEEN

*T*yler's heart banged against his ribs. Dismay tightened his gut at the terrible story Arden had just told him. And yet…

I didn't love him.

It was fucking bizarre how happy he was to hear that.

He wasn't competing with a dead guy. That was something. If she was still in love with her husband, he would have to back the fuck off, and he was so goddamn glad he didn't have to do that.

Whatever else was making her hesitate, much as he fucking hated what she'd gone through—he could deal with it.

He was also struck by how strong she was to have dealt with all that. Sure, he teased her about being a princess, and she admitted she'd been a little spoiled and sheltered. But being lied to and betrayed by her husband, who then took his own life rather than deal with the consequences of what he'd done, had to have been devastating for her. Then she'd been the one left to clean up the mess that hadn't been her making. The mess that had left her homeless and pretty much broke.

It sure as hell didn't seem fair. But she wasn't crying and whining about it. She hadn't run home to her parents and asked them to bail her out. She hadn't asked her brother, who had a fuck-ton of money and could easily have helped. Other than she'd taken his offer to live in this apartment that was a fucking mess. And now she was working as a goddamn waitress without a complaint, happy to have a job and go to work every day.

This all gave him a weird ache in his chest, along with a fierce desire to take care of her and make things better for her.

"I'm sorry, Arden. So damn sorry. You've been through hell." He stroked her hair.

"I'm okay. I know I'm kind of taking advantage of Jamie by living here rent-free, but I *am* going to pay him rent. I have a job now."

He didn't want to tell her that the money she made from her waitressing job probably wouldn't cover the rent Jamie should charge for an apartment like this. She didn't need that kind of reality check right now. She was trying to make a life for herself.

"This is why it's so important for me to do this on my own." She lifted her head and gazed at him, her eyes bright. "I need to prove I can do it. That I can be a grown-up and handle my own life and not screw it up."

He wanted to assure her that she was definitely a grown-up and that he knew she could do it. But somehow he knew whatever he said would sound patronizing to her. And he got why she was pushing back at his attempt to help her. He could see how important it was to her.

"And I'm definitely not looking for a relationship." She bit her lip.

Right. That was how they'd gotten into this discussion.

She'd said they shouldn't be doing this. But at least now he knew it wasn't because she was still in love with her husband.

He smiled.

Her eyes widened.

"That's great," he said casually. "Neither am I. And since we agree that this has nothing to do with Jamie…" He bent his head and found her mouth again.

She made a little noise, but she kissed him back. The blanket slid off her shoulders, and he set his hands on her skin there, so soft, so warm. She lifted her arms and twined them around his neck as he deepened the kiss, that heat between them flaring up again.

She was here, in his arms, practically on his lap, and he was kissing her. Arden.

Fuck yeah.

He pushed the blanket away, set his hands on her waist, and lifted her so she was straddling him. She gasped, her hands gripping his shoulders. Wide-eyed, she stared at him. "You're strong."

She made him feel like he could crush bricks with his bare hands. "I have to be." He slid his hands down to her ass and pulled her closer, so his throbbing erection was pressed right to her warm, damp center. He lifted the hem of her nightie and found skin again.

Christ. When he'd filled his palms with her taut little cheeks, he'd damn near come. He squeezed the firm flesh and let out a groan. "Damn, Arden."

"Tyler…"

The strappy little garment had to go. He slid his hands along her back, pushing it up, slowly, anticipation tightening his lungs, blood surging to his groin. He held her gaze as he eased the fabric up…and up…and she didn't stop him. His fingers skimmed over her ribcage, thumbs brushing the undersides of her breasts, and then she lifted her arms so he could draw it over her head and off.

His head spun as he took in nearly naked Arden, perfection right in front of him. "Jesus," he muttered. "Look at you, gorgeous girl."

Her hands drifted down to rest on his shoulders again. He studied her avidly, and then he cupped her breasts, another groan rumbling up from his chest. Her head fell back, her back arched, pushing her softness into his palms. "Oh…"

Her nipples hardened and more heat flooded to his groin.

Christ, she was perfect, sweet, addicting…better than any of the fantasies he'd had about her in his teenage bed when he jerked off thinking about her—after watching her bounce around on the sidelines in her little cheerleader skirt; after seeing her in a tank top with no bra one day; or another summer day he'd glimpsed her lying in the sun in a bikini in their backyard. So much better…now he could breathe in her scent, taste her mouth, fill his hands with her softness…he felt like he'd waited his whole life for this. For her.

He hadn't thought of her *every* minute for the last ten years. He'd been with other women. But now *this* was happening… that all fell away, like smoke clearing.

He felt the weight of her breasts as she made breathy little noises and squirmed against him, which only made him harder. He skimmed his hands down to her waist, which he could easily span, and dipped his head to taste her.

Her hair tickled his hands, flowing down her back. "Oh God."

"Mmm." He sucked, enjoying the feel of her hands smoothing across his shoulders, her fingers brushing the nape of his neck, then sliding up into his hair. Tingles slid down his spine and pooled in his low back. "That's it, baby. Give me these…they're fucking perfect." A buzzing in his groin was building in intensity, but he wanted to draw this out, to enjoy every second of it, every breathy moan, the feel of her on his tongue, her hands tugging at his hair. His entire body was lit up, combusting.

She rubbed her palms over his chest, setting even more nerve endings on fire. He tangled a hand in her hair and brought her mouth to his for another hot, lush kiss. She rocked her pelvis against him, and damn near made him lose it.

Panting, they broke apart and stared at each other. He rubbed his nose alongside hers and murmured, "Are we doing this?"

"Oh please. Please, yes."

"Thank Christ." He gripped her ass and stood. She let out a little squeal and held onto his shoulders as he started toward her bedroom. Her legs wrapped around him as he'd imagined a few or maybe a million times.

He couldn't make her whole life better. At least not right now. But for the next few hours, he could make her feel pretty damn good.

He carried her into her bedroom and set her in the middle of the bed, then leaned down, fists planted in the mattress and kissed her again. He lowered one knee to the bed between her legs, then the other, slowly rolling her down to her back so he was lying in the cradle of her thighs. One of her hands caressed his face, the other gliding up and down his bare back. Her hips rolled, pressing her core against his straining hardness, and he matched her rhythm so they were slowly rocking together in an exquisite, brilliant cadence.

He pushed up onto straight arms again, watching her face…her eyes shadowy, her lips parted. He lowered his head and kissed her lower belly, then slowly drew his tongue up over her stomach. She moaned as he licked higher.

Her body twitched hard and her hands tightened on his

arms. Still taking his time, he opened his mouth over the nipple and drew it into his mouth in a long, slow pull.

"Oh God." Her hips bucked up against his. "Oh God, that feels good."

"Mmmm." He sucked harder, pressing his whole mouth into her plump flesh, then moved to the other breast. He feasted...long, delicious draws, circling the tip with his tongue, then sucking again.

Her soft whimpers teased his ears, making him even harder, almost unbearably primed. He kissed his way back down her abdomen, aware that she was watching him, then sat back on his heels and tugged her up to sitting and leaned in for more long, deep kisses. She sighed into his mouth and he pulled back. "Jesus. You're so goddamn hot. I want to make you come again."

She whimpered.

"Want you to come on my tongue." He kissed her again. "Want to make you lose your mind."

"Oh God." The words eased between her lips on a shaky breath.

He cupped her breasts with both hands and gently squeezed, admiring the shape and weight of her, then he lost patience. His dick was a throbbing spike in his boxers, leaking with the urgent need to come. He hauled Arden up on to his lap, her legs around his hips, her arms encircling his neck, and kissed her again and again, both of them now making frantic, fraught sounds, hands grabbing and clutching at each other.

He urged her down to her back again and, a smile curving her lips, she reached for his boxers and palmed him through the thin cotton. He let out a low groan, closing his eyes, letting her tug the elastic waistband down, lower, freeing his heavy cock.

"Oh." Her eyes lit up and she let out a soft sigh of pleasure, curling her fingers around him to stroke. "Wow. You're, um, big."

Okay, there was no bigger turn-on than a woman looking like *that* at his dick. Like she wanted to worship it. Like she couldn't wait to have it. Call it primal, but his manhood was definitely tied to his dick, and if he already wasn't crazy about Arden, he was now.

"Fuuuuuck, that feels good." He dragged his eyes open to see her watching her hand fondle his shaft and balls. Sharp need built inside him, fierce and throbbing. Then he shifted back and set his hands on her knees, pushing them open. She was still wearing the little black cheeky panties.

He bent and kissed her inner thigh, working his way closer to her center. She smelled insanely good, musky and feminine, obviously aroused. Then he opened his mouth over the fabric of her panties.

"Oh God." She bent an arm behind her head to raise it and watch him, her eyes heavy lidded, her chest flushing a pretty pink. "That's so hot."

He licked and kissed her through her panties, inhaling the scent, getting a faint taste of her. Eager for more, he tugged the fabric aside and revealed the most goddamn gorgeous pink lips he'd ever seen, completely bare and smooth with a neat triangle of dark hair on her mound. He wanted to weep. "Jesus, Arden. You have the prettiest pussy." With a groan, his eyes drifted closed and he lowered his mouth there and swiped his tongue over smooth, smooth flesh.

Her body twitched and she gasped, her head falling back and her back arching, pushing those perfect tits up. He pulled her soft skin into his mouth in tiny sucks, swirled his tongue up and down, sinking it deeper to taste her more fully.

"So damn wet. Look at you." He slid his fingers through her slit. "That's for me. Right, baby?"

"Yes. For you…"

He tasted her again. "Christ. Could eat you like this forever."

Her hips rolled against his mouth, faster, and he tongued her clit. She reached for his hand and he twined his fingers through hers, holding on tight as she gave a soft cry. He moved his tongue faster too, her body quivering and tightening as she came in another exquisite orgasm, her pussy getting even slicker. He kissed her thighs again, eyes on her face, drawing back to lift her legs straight up.

"Jesus, look at you." Her plump folds pouted between her thighs. "Fucking gorgeous."

He pulled her panties up her legs and off and tossed them aside, then shucked his boxers too. Then he froze, hands on her thighs. "Fuck."

"What?"

"I need a condom."

"Oh." She swallowed. "Right." She bit her lip. "I don't have any."

His lips quirked. "Luckily I live nearby. Be right back."

He jogged naked in the darkness to his apartment, snatched up a couple of condoms, and sprinted back. He ripped open one and had it on before he made it to the bed, and was rewarded by her sleepy, sexy smile as he crawled up over her.

He returned the smile, mesmerized by her, lost in the moment, then he bent his head to kiss her. She cupped his face with both hands, her knees coming up to his sides. He found her entrance, his body tensing.

"Tight," he muttered, easing in. "So goddamn tight. And hot."

"Mmm." Her fingers curved over his shoulders, digging in. "Okay?"

"Yes. Oh God, yes…do it. Please."

He *loved* hearing her say that, the perfect princess begging him. "Oh, hell yeah."

She held onto him, staring up at him. Arms pressed into the bed, he held eye contact as he slowly moved his hips, rolling them against her. His skin tingled everywhere at the connection between them, at the intensity of their linked gazes. Sensation skittered up his spine, pressure building, fire burning beneath his skin.

"Not gonna take me long." He brushed his mouth over hers. "Want you to come again though."

"No. It's okay…I don't know if I can."

He'd always liked a challenge. Not to be cocky, but he prided himself in his ability to make a woman come. Making a woman orgasm made him feel powerful. And he fucking loved that feeling. Loved giving that to her.

He slipped a hand between them. She bucked against his hand with a gasp. "There?"

"Yes…oh…" It didn't take long and she shuddered against him, her face contracting. "Oh my God…"

He kissed her mouth, still moving inside her.

"Harder." She gripped his shoulders.

Oh yeah. Harder. Faster. Her soft cries cheered him on, inflaming his senses. Now he was the one making noises, helpless guttural noises that came from deep inside him. He buried his face in the side of her neck, her knees at his ribs, her heels on his ass, gripped by a nearly paralyzing bliss.

Sweaty and sticky, breathing hard and heart pounding, he lay on top of her, taking as much weight as he could on his arms, feeling like he'd just been caught in a flashover. He was blistered and fatigued and so incredibly satisfied, his brains scrambled, overloaded on sensation.

Her hands roamed up and down his back, her mouth opening on his shoulder in a long, wet kiss.

Arden.

He was with Arden. He'd just defiled the prom queen.

A smile tugged at his lips. Because she'd loved it. Again, not to be cocky, but he'd made her come three times, and there was no way that wasn't good for her. Not to mention, she'd begged for more.

He couldn't wait to do it again.

CHAPTER FIFTEEN

*A*nother thunderstorm was passing over, but this time Arden was so relaxed and content, it didn't bother her at all. It helped that there was a big, strong man in her bed, and she snuggled closer into him. His arms wrapped around her, their bodies fitted together in a way that was particularly satisfying. She rubbed her calf against his and breathed in Tyler's unique scent, that delicious clean and spicy scent.

After a huge crack of thunder, Tyler said, "That was a good one. Are you still nervous?"

"Nope. Not even a little."

Maybe she was drunk or something…high from breathing in his scent, intoxicated by the flood of hormones several orgasms had released. She knew this was probably a very bad idea, and yet…right now it didn't seem all that bad. In fact, it seemed pretty damn good.

She wouldn't think about tomorrow or the next day or what was going to happen between her and Tyler, and whether they would pretend this never happened, or…no, she wouldn't think about that stuff. She'd just drift on this cloud of contentment for a while longer, enjoying the threat of danger from the violent storm outside while feeling safe and protected in Tyler's arms.

"Thanks for telling me about what happened." Tyler's hand smoothed over her shoulder. "With your husband. I had no idea what a rough time you've been through."

"There've been times I felt sorry for myself," she admitted. "But I'm not a victim. I want to own my part in what happened and hopefully learn something from it." But would she ever learn how to really love someone?

"Good for you."

"This isn't what I thought my life would be. Not the money part! I mean, when I was a kid, my parents always told me I could do anything, be anything I wanted to be. I always believed that. Then I married Michael, and I had everything I wanted. Except…it wasn't because *I'd* accomplished anything. My own goals and ambitions got…forgotten. And here I am, a widow, twenty-eight years old, and I have nothing to show for myself."

"I don't know if that's necessarily true," he said quietly. "You've proved how strong and resilient you are."

She was silent, absorbing that. "I guess that's true."

"My parents told me I could be anything I wanted, too. But turned out that really meant I should do what they wanted." He grimaced.

Ugh. She hated that.

"But you know what I've learned?" he continued. "We all figure things out differently. Jamie knew what he wanted to do when he was seventeen, but some of us take longer. Mila had about ten different jobs before she ended up working for Jamie. I didn't know what I wanted to do when I started college. I spent that year all frustrated. Like I said, my parents were pushing me to go into business or law school…" He paused.

"When you said this isn't how you thought your life would be, well, this isn't how I thought mine would be either. I thought I'd end up in some white-collar profession, but...I didn't know what. I like computers, but not the way Jamie does. Then when I saw something about applying to be a firefighter, it caught my attention. It was what I wanted to do, and I'd never really considered that."

"That's so good you found it."

"My mom's never been happy about it."

"Yeah, you said that. That sucks." She paused. Again, she hated that his mom didn't appreciate what he did. "*I'm* proud of what you do." Uh...maybe she shouldn't have said that. "Not that that means a whole lot."

He squeezed his arms tighter around her. "You know what? It means a lot."

"I just don't like the idea that your job is dangerous."

"There can be danger," he agreed. "But we're trained to deal with it. And honestly, there aren't that many big fires that require rescue."

"Have you ever had to do it? Go into a burning building?"

"Yeah. Not gonna lie, it's scary. We're weighed down with equipment, facing a wall of heat and smoke. We have breathing tanks, but it's awkward and we don't have that much time. I went in, and of course it was totally unfamiliar. When it's dark like that, we don't know our way around, we don't know what kind of hazards there are. We didn't know if there was anyone in the house, so we had to check...basically crawling through the heat and dark, feeling our way around and trying not to get lost in the smoke and end up trapped ourselves."

"Oh God. Was there someone?"

"No. Turned out the house was empty. We got the fuck out of there just before the whole roof collapsed."

Her heart bumped, and she rubbed his shoulder. "That's scary."

"I was fine. I'll do it again if needed."

Something expanded in her chest—warmth, admiration, maybe pride. He was brave and strong. She wanted to be brave and strong like that.

She *would* be brave and strong like that. Sure, her life wasn't what she'd thought it would be. Neither was Tyler's…but he was doing what he wanted to do and had made a good life. It was up to her to make her life good. And maybe that even included having hot sex with a hot guy. Why the hell not?

She rolled toward him, pushing him onto his back and wriggling herself on top of him.

"Whoa." His big hands clasped her hips.

"I want you."

His smile was white in the dark room. He'd turned off the lamp a while ago. "I like that."

She lowered her head and laid a string of kisses across his chest, then down the middle. She heard his sharp intake of breath as she wiggled lower, licking down the center of his chest, then lower over the rippled muscles of his abs.

God, she loved his abs.

Every time she saw him working without a shirt on, her mouth went dry while her panties dampened.

Now, she was up close and touching those abs, licking them, leaving lingering, open-mouthed kisses on them as she worked her way to his navel…and then the tender skin below that.

His groan rumbled up from his chest and his fingers threaded through her hair, tugging it back from her face so gently. "Arden…"

"Mmm." She positioned herself between his thighs, curling her fingers around him again, as she had earlier, marveling at the soft skin over hardness. It had been a long time since she'd done this. She's always enjoyed this part of a man's anatomy, enjoyed giving him pleasure and reveling in the sensuality of it herself, but being perfectly honest, she hadn't been enthusiastic about it when her relationship with Michael had started to deteriorate.

Now, excitement filled her with buzzing anticipation, her core clenching, her mouth watering. She glanced up at Tyler and found him watching her, eyes blazing. "Oh Christ." His fingers tightened in her hair, clasping it back off her face.

Holding his gaze, she opened her mouth.

Moments later, she crawled up beside him, draping one arm and leg across his body.

He panted, eyes closed, finding her hip with one hand. "I think I just saw Jesus."

She smiled. "Me too. He was here earlier."

He chuckled and squeezed her hip. "I fucking love blow jobs. And that was amazing."

A little shiver of delight worked over her. "Thank you."

"You know what makes it so good?"

"Um, what?"

"You were so into it. You looked like you loved it."

"That's because I did love it."

"And that makes it extra hot." He shifted and pulled her into his arms. "I'm about to crash. Give me an hour and we can go again."

"Ha." Feeling sleepy herself, she let her eyes drift closed. "You need that long?"

"Just need…sleep." His voice had gone thick, and she felt his body relaxing against hers. And she slept too.

They didn't wake up an hour later. They woke up six hours later, at nine in the morning. Tyler was still off for another day, but Arden had to work at eleven.

"Lots of time," Tyler murmured as he rolled her onto her back and moved over her.

"Don't kiss me."

He cocked his head. "Why not?"

"I need to brush my teeth."

He pursed his lips. "Hmm. I guess I'll allow that."

"Pfft."

He moved off her and she slid out of bed. She grabbed the black knit robe that matched the nightie now lying on her living room floor and slipped her arms into it. She'd start keeping a toothbrush and toothpaste in her kitchen, so she didn't have to go over to Tyler's apartment just to brush her teeth, since she now had no bathroom sink. The renovation seemed to be taking a lot longer than expected.

Tyler followed her, big and naked, which made her inner muscles squeeze. "Guess I better be minty fresh for you too," he said before disappearing out the door, presumably to his place. Apparently walking around naked didn't bother him. Hopefully Jamie or Mila didn't happen to be around as he crossed the hall with all his impressive man parts on display.

She scrunched up her face and squeezed Crest onto her toothbrush. She hoped she hadn't killed the mood, because her body was surprisingly aching to be filled with him again. She wanted another one of those orgasms he delivered with expert ease.

He was back just as she rinsed her toothbrush under the tap. She dropped it into the cup and turned. He tilted his head toward the bedroom. "Get that sweet ass back in there."

Her belly flip-flopped at his command. She shouldn't like that. She did, though. A lot. "Just so you know…I only like to be told what to do in the bedroom."

One eyebrow arched. "I think it counts if you're in the kitchen and I'm telling you to get in the bedroom."

She tried not to smile and tossed her hair back. "Okay. I'll let it go this time."

Oh my God, this was so fun. She scooted past him, but not before he got his hands on her and gave her ass a little tap. That was also something she shouldn't like…but totally did. Excitement flared low in her belly as she raced to her bedroom and jumped onto the bed, followed closely by Tyler who flipped her to her back, held her hands and pressed them into the pillow next to her head while he kissed her.

God, she wanted him again. His body was heavy on hers and she arched against him. His tongue slid into her mouth and liquid heat pooled in her core. His strength and weight thrilled her.

"Minty fresh," she panted when he lifted his mouth from hers.

He smiled. "Good. Wouldn't want to offend you."

"Mmm. Be quick, I have to go to work." She said it teasingly.

"Oh yeah, that's a turn-on when a woman just wants to get it over with."

Her lips lifted into a smile. "That's not what I meant and you know it. I want another one of those stupendous orgasms you're so good at."

"Greedy girl."

"I'll own that."

He kissed her cheek and her jaw. "I'm glad you recognize my skill."

"Oh, I do. I definitely do…"

～

"I slept with Tyler."

Two pairs of female eyes flew open wide and Arden's apartment fell silent.

Emma's mouth dropped open. "Shut up!"

"What?" Mila said.

Arden paused as she scooped ice cream into bowls in her kitchen.

It was Thursday evening and since she had a night off, she'd invited Emma and Mila over to her place. Because it was National Hot Fudge Sundae Day, she'd picked up ice cream and made her own hot fudge sauce with cocoa, vanilla, butter, and cream, and it was to die for if she said so herself.

Last Thursday had been National Root Beer Float Day, and everybody had come up to her place for root beer floats and snacks.

"It's true."

"Oh my God." Mila gaped at her from the other side of the counter.

Emma's mouth now stretched into a grin. "Good for you."

"Was it good?" Mila leaned forward.

"Good. Oh my God. So good." Arden closed her eyes briefly, her belly doing a lusty little flip. Which it had been doing every time she thought about Tyler.

She hadn't meant to say anything, but she was bursting to talk about it to someone. "Nuts or sprinkles?" she asked brightly.

"Sprinkles," Emma said.

"Nuts," Mila replied. "And speaking of nuts…how is Tyler, um, endowed?"

"Very well." She scooped up a spoonful of chopped

peanuts and dumped it over Mila's sundae. "And that's all I'm saying."

"How did this happen?" Emma blinked long eyelashes at her.

"Well, remember that thunderstorm the other night?" She told them how Tyler had come rushing into her apartment to rescue her.

"I had a feeling about this." Mila dug her spoon into the ice cream. "He watches you all the time."

Arden's belly did another flutter. "He does?" Hell, she knew that, because she watched him too, and often caught him looking at her.

"How many orgasms?" Emma asked.

Arden burst out laughing. "Plural? Really?"

"I'm hoping."

"Okay, um, in total, four. He stayed overnight," she added in a rush. "So we had morning sex too."

Emma made a sound like she was weeping as she lifted her spoon of ice cream to her mouth. Then she paused. "Holy shit, Arden. This hot fudge sauce is amazing."

"Thank you. And there are no calories whatsoever, obviously."

Mila snorted. "It tastes like sin. Unbelievable."

"Speaking of orgasms, I think I'm having one from eating this sundae." Emma sighed.

"I want to hear more about Arden's orgasms. Apparently Tyler is generous. This doesn't surprise me, actually."

"He's very generous. And his head game is…oh my God." She closed her eyes briefly.

"Meanwhile, my vagina is a sexual wasteland," Emma said morosely.

"You and me both." Mila stared at her sundae.

"Wait, what? What about Garth?" Arden gazed at Mila in concern.

"We haven't had sex in weeks." The corners of Mila's mouth drooped. "I don't know what's going on."

Arden met Emma's eyes, which were also concerned.

"Have you talked to him?" Arden asked.

"No. I hardly ever see him. We both work long hours, but lately it seems like he's always busy. And when we do get together, he's tired, or distracted…" She sighed.

"Do you think…he's seeing someone else?" Emma asked carefully.

Mila shrugged. "I don't know. It makes me wonder. But why would he do that? Why not just tell me?"

"Good question."

"Well, I'm probably not the one to give advice…seeing as my own marriage was a total failure…but if I learned anything, it's better to speak up if you're worried about something than to ignore it or pretend there's nothing wrong."

Mila lifted her head to meet her eyes. "Your marriage was a total failure?"

Arden spooned more ice cream into her mouth and nodded. "Yeah. It was. And it was partly my fault."

Even though Tyler had tried to convince her that Michael was the one responsible for his actions, she knew she had responsibility too. Sure, she wasn't responsible for Michael's actions, but maybe if she'd handled things differently instead of floating obliviously along Denial, which wasn't just a river in Egypt, it wouldn't have turned out the way it did.

"It wasn't your fault," Emma said quietly. "I've told you that many times."

Clearly Mila wanted to know what had happened, and Arden wanted to include her. She hadn't known Mila long, but the three of them had bonded over pole dancing and the Kardashians. And now homemade hot fudge sauce.

So she gave Mila a condensed version, with Emma contributing additional helpful information such as "he was such a douche dick" and "what a jack hole."

Arden hadn't wanted everyone to know that when she'd moved back to Chicago. She'd wanted to leave that behind. She'd wanted to pretend that her life had been perfect and beautiful, other than the fact she was a widow at twenty-eight. But real connections weren't made with people over fake perfection—connections were made over shared struggles, with honesty. And since Mila had been honest about the problems she and Garth were having, it felt right to open up and admit that her perfect life had been a sham.

"I'm so sorry." Mila's eyes filled with compassion. "I can't even imagine."

"Thanks."

"And not to speak ill of the dead, but yeah, he was a knobhead."

Arden huffed. "I'll never understand what happened with him. It makes me feel like I never really knew him. He got so into the money, the lifestyle…the prestige. And then he couldn't…do without it, I guess. He must have been so messed up. Losing his football career was so traumatic for him. That was his whole identity, and when he didn't have that, he must have been lost. And then when his new career wasn't doing well, he must have been so desperate to try to make it seem like it was…" She shook her head. *I should have known.*

"You're amazingly understanding," Emma said quietly. "But I still think a real man would have been honest with you."

"Well, my whole point in the story is to say that I was oblivious to what was going on, mostly, but when he started to get distant and pull away from me, I…didn't do anything. It worried me a little…I shouldn't have ignored it. I should have confronted him and made him talk to me. So you should talk to Garth." She gave Mila a stern look.

Mila scrunched up her face. "Yeah. You're right. I will." She sighed. "You know, I'm trying to tick off all the boxes— good job, fabulous apartment, lots of friends, great boyfriend. I thought I was finally getting there. I got this great job at Jamie's company, and the beautiful apartment. But this is, like, the eighth job I've had since college. Garth is the sixth boyfriend. I've had five roommates. Some of my friends have disappeared, and I'm still paying off student loans. Now I'm going to lose the great boyfriend."

"Well, maybe he's not so great," Emma said carefully. "Not that I've ever met him."

"I haven't either." Arden frowned. "And that's not right. I want a chance to judge him on whether he's good enough for you."

Mila laughed. "You know what? I think I love both of you."

Arden's heart expanded hot in her chest. "I think I love you too." She pointed her spoon at Emma. "*You* already know I love you."

"Back atcha, babe." Emma winked. "Mila, we're here for you, whatever happens."

"Thanks, bishes. You're gonna make me cry."

"See, I was just talking to Tyler about that," Arden said.

"After the third or fourth orgasm?" Emma made a face.

"Ha. I mean, I feel the same…this wasn't supposed to be how my life is. I'm a widow at twenty-eight, broke, I'd be homeless if it weren't for my brother—or living with my parents, God forbid. When are we ever going to get there?"

"When is my vagina ever going to get some action?" Emma asked.

"You work too much. That's your problem."

Emma shrugged. "I love my job."

Arden sighed. "See, *that* I'm envious of."

"You'll find what you love."

"Well. You know what I'm happy about?" Arden looked around. "I'm happy I have you. Oh, damn."

"What?" They both spoke at once, frowning.

"I might cry. Sorry. This was so hard, coming here with nothing, my entire life in shreds. And you both have made it so easier."

"Aw." Emma smiled. "Of course, hon. I'm always here for you."

"Me too." Mila dropped her spoon into her empty bowl. "I'm so glad Jamie's sister turned out to be a kindred spirit."

Arden's heart quivered.

"Also, I'm glad you can cook," Mila added. "It's been awesome."

The air in the room lightened and Arden choked on a laugh.

"And, let's not forget what else is here for you."

"What?"

"Tyler's magnificent wang."

CHAPTER SIXTEEN

"*I* know right away when I'm attracted to a woman." Jamie shrugged. "It's there or it's not."

Tyler nodded. "Yeah. I agree." He leaned back on the couch at Shenanigans, half his attention on the conversation, the other half on the ball game on TV. No, check that, part of his attention was also on Arden, waiting on a table of four guys who were all drooling over her. He tried not to scowl.

Mila frowned. "Seriously? What about getting to know someone? Getting to know her personality. It can't just all be superficial."

"I guess it is." Jamie looked around Shenanigans, where they were gathered Saturday night, possibly looking for a woman he'd feel that instant attraction to.

Tyler grinned. "Men *are* superficial assholes."

"It's different for women," Emma said. "Sometimes you meet a guy and you think he's okay—"

"Or you even think 'no way,'" Mila interjected.

"True." Emma nodded. "But then you get to know him

better, and he's got a great sense of humor, and you find your-self starting to find him more and more attractive."

"That happens to me all the time," Norton said.

Everyone looked at him.

"You mean…you find women more and more attractive as you get to know them?" Mila asked.

"No. Women find *me* more attractive as they get to know me." He lifted one shoulder and picked up his drink.

"Um. Okay."

"So you just take your time, Emma." Norton winked. "You'll come around. You're gonna want me in no time."

Tyler tried not to laugh at the expression on Emma's face, who clearly had no idea how to respond to that without hurting Norton's feelings. This was Emma's first time meeting Norton.

Norton, Norton. They had to find a woman for him.

It sure as hell wasn't going to be Arden. Probably not Emma either. Norton had been flirting like crazy with both of them since they'd arrived at Shenanigans. Luckily Emma had laughed when Norton told her she reminded him of an overdue library book because she had "fine" written all over her.

"But it's true about men," Norton added. "I know in three seconds if I'm attracted to someone."

"You're attracted to every woman, Norton," Jamie said.

Norton frowned and thought about that.

Arden approached their table, still smiling from her conver-sation with that table full of ass monkeys. "How's it going here?"

Holding an empty tray, she planted her butt on the arm of the big comfy chair Emma sat in.

"Good." Emma reached over and squeezed Arden's knee, which had Tyler's full attention. He usually saw Arden wearing black pants and a white shirt, the "uniform" of Shenanigans, but tonight she was wearing a short black skirt. Tyler caught Norton's open-mouthed gaze on Emma's hand on Arden's knee. He sighed.

"Need another round?" Arden tilted her head and met his eyes.

Heat punched through his gut at the eye contact. Jesus.

They'd been dancing around each other since Tuesday night when they'd fucked each other stupid. She'd left for work the next day while he stayed at her place, pretending to work on her bathroom. There *had* been legit delays with getting the plumber they knew to squeeze them in between jobs, but truthfully? He'd been dragging it out because he liked having her in his apartment naked. That night, he'd gone to Shenanigans to walk her home, as he had any night he wasn't working. Even though it pissed her off, she'd gradually accepted that he was going to be there when he could. When they'd got back to her place, he'd paused outside her apartment, then kissed her forehead and said good night.

He'd sensed that puzzled her.

Then he'd had to work the next morning and hadn't seen her much until tonight.

"I'll have another Fuzzy Navel." Norton held up his empty glass.

Arden smiled. "Sure."

"Why the hell are you drinking those?" Jamie asked. "That's a girly drink."

The sharply sucked-in breath of the three women was audible even in the noisy bar.

"What did you just say?" Mila asked.

Jamie blinked. "Uh…"

"What does that even mean?" Emma said. "What is a girly drink exactly? And why does a drink have to be gender specific? Why can't men drink whatever they want?"

"And women," Arden added.

Jamie held his hands up. "Sorry."

"I'm secure in my masculinity," Norton said.

"Good to know," Jamie said dryly. "I'll have another beer."

"Same," Tyler added, though he hated Arden waiting on him. It just felt wrong. He wanted to be the one looking after her. But planting her ass on this couch while he went and got drinks would definitely be weird.

"You drink whatever you like, Norton," Arden said, squeezing his shoulder.

Norton shot her a look of near adoration.

Arden was always so kind and respectful to Norton, despite his idiosyncrasies.

Just as she was leaving to get their drinks, Danny arrived.

He was greeted with enthusiasm, except for Norton who hadn't met him yet. Jamie made introductions, and Danny sat in the empty spot next to Norton on the couch opposite Tyler.

"What can I bring you to drink, Danny?" Arden asked.

"Jack and Coke, please."

"You got it."

"So, Danny," Norton said. "We were just talking. What do you think...how long does it take you to know you're attracted to a woman?"

Danny smiled. "Long. Very long. In fact, never."

"Huh?"

"I'm gay. I'm not attracted to women."

Norton's mouth fell open. "Oh."

Tyler grinned. "Okay, how about men?"

Danny cocked his head. "I dunno...maybe a minute. Or less."

Norton shot Danny a suspicious look and shifted away from him on the couch. Tyler winced and shook his head.

"Don't worry, Norton. I'm not attracted to you." Danny patted Norton's knee and Norton nearly leaped off the couch.

Everyone else laughed.

"*That* guy," Danny said, nodding toward the bar. "Now *he's* attractive."

They all turned to look at Liam.

As if sensing their interest, Liam looked up and gave them one of his usual cocky smiles. He handed Arden the last of their drinks, which she loaded onto the tray. When she started toward them, Liam followed her.

"Hello, mates," Liam said. "Is lovely Arden here looking after you well?"

"Absolutely."

"Yeah."

They were all enthusiastic in their praise of Arden to her boss. Her cheeks flushed as she set their drinks on the table. Tyler studied her legs, her skirt riding higher as she bent over. He wanted to slide his hands up the backs of her thighs... Yeah, he was a perv. He got annoyed at Norton, yet he was just as bad. Maybe not quite as inappropriate as Norton.

"We haven't met," Liam said to Danny, eyeing him with as much interest as Danny had showed in him.

Apparently the attraction was mutual.

Arden blinked, clutching her tray, watching her boss.

"Hey, Liam, this is Danny," Jamie said. "Danny, Liam. Liam owns this place."

"That I do. Pleased to meet you, Danny."

Danny smiled. "Anyone ever tell you that you look like Prince Harry?"

"Never." Liam winked.

"You're Irish," Danny said.

"That I am."

"But he has that Irish curse," Jamie said, smirking.

Liam frowned.

"What Irish curse?" Danny asked.

"You haven't heard of the Irish curse?" Jamie grinned. "Irish men are cursed with very small penises."

Smiles and chuckles broke out all around. Liam tossed his head. "I've offered to prove that's false many times." He shrugged. "Step into the men's room."

"No, thanks." Jamie still grinned.

Liam didn't give up. "As a matter of fact, my dick's so big, it's against the law to fuck me without protective headgear."

Laughter rose around them.

"It's so big, I entered a big dick contest and came in first. And second. And third."

Tyler caught the look of interest mingled with amusement on Danny's face.

"Oh my God," Mila said. "You guys and your biggest dick competitions." She turned to Danny. "We still haven't come to see your show at the supper club. I've been trying to plan something, but it's hard with everyone's schedules."

"That's okay," he said. "It'll work out some time."

Liam leaned on the back of an armchair. "What show is that?"

"Danny's a…an entertainer," Tyler said.

Liam pursed his lips. "A singer?"

"Dancer." Danny's eyes gleamed. "I sing a little too."

"Cool."

"You need to give Arden a night off," Mila said with a cheeky grin for Liam. "And maybe you could even join us."

Liam tilted his head. "Arden gets two days off a week."

"But the supper club is closed Mondays."

"Maybe I could work an early shift one Friday?" Arden eyed her boss hopefully.

"We could do that."

"Yay!" Mila pumped a fist. "I'll make a reservation for Friday. Who's in?"

They were all in, even Liam. He pushed away from the armchair. "Well. Best be back to work. You kids have fun."

Tyler grinned. He knew Liam was nearly forty, but the dude didn't look it. He didn't act it either. He was tons of fun.

Tyler watched Danny's gaze follow Liam back to the bar. Then he looked at Arden, saw her watching them too, before she met his eyes again. He grinned at her bemused expression.

Sorcha stopped next to Arden. "Arden…table five is still waiting for their drinks."

"Oh. Right. Sorry." She broke the connection and hurried away.

"Hi, Tyler." Sorcha smiled at him.

"Hey, Sorcha. How's it going?"

"Good." Now it was her turn to perch on the arm of his chair. "Busy, but it helps with a few new waitresses. Hopefully they'll stick around longer than some have. How's the fire-fighting business? Save any lives lately?"

"Every day."

"You must work out a lot to stay in such great shape."

"Uh. Yeah." He glanced at Arden who stood at the bar watching them with an expressionless face. Then she turned back to Liam who was handing her several cocktails that she set on her tray.

Sorcha was leaning in with a flirty smile, and he knew Arden had noticed.

He wasn't the kind of guy to play games, and he'd never lead Sorcha on, knowing it would go nowhere, but hey, maybe it was good for Arden to see that another woman liked him. So he smiled back at her. "We all work out," he said. "It's part of the job."

Her gaze lingered on his biceps. "I guess it is. Carrying those big hoses…"

He nearly choked. "Yeah, among other things."

She sighed. Then she turned, catching a customer at a booth waving at her. She rose with a regretful expression. "Sorry. I have to get back to work."

Tyler turned his attention back to his friends, who were now talking about how women had better hearing than men.

"It's true," Mila insisted. "Studies have proven it."

"See, my last girlfriend didn't believe me when I told her that," Jamie said with a grin. "She kept accusing me of not listening to her. I just didn't hear her."

"Much as I hate to support you on that, there is science behind it," Mila agreed. "Testosterone affects the development of the auditory system, so it blocks out unwanted, repetitious noise."

"That's why my brain was blocking her out. She was definitely repetitious." One corner of his mouth lifted.

"Well, she probably *had* to be, to get you to listen," Mila said. "But she did have a very annoying voice."

"Yeah, you never liked Ashley." Jamie frowned. "Come to think of it, you never like any of my girlfriends."

Mila snorted. "That's not true. And anyway, most of them aren't around long enough for me to like."

Tyler's forehead tightened, listening to their exchange. Mila seemed…edgy tonight.

"I need another beer," she announced, looking around. "Where's Arden?"

"I'll get it for you." Tyler already knew Arden was in the kitchen. He rose. "Anyone else?"

Everyone else was good, so he headed to the bar and slid onto an empty stool. Liam noticed him right away and he ordered Mila's Pilsner and another IPA for himself.

As he waited, he watched Arden come out of the kitchen with a tray of food for another table. She served them with her bright smile, getting more smiles in return.

"Jaysus, man, stop making glad eyes at her."

Tyler turned to Liam, frowning. "What?"

"You can't take your eyes off her." Liam nodded at Arden. "What is up with that?"

Shit. Was it obvious to everyone? Tyler rubbed his forehead.

"You're here to walk her home nearly every night," Liam added. "I'm still surprised she lets you."

Tyler barked out a laugh. "It pisses her off, but she lets me."

Liam nodded. "Does Jamie know?"

"Know what?"

"That you're hot for his sister."

"Jesus. No." He wanted to tell Liam it wasn't one-sided, that Arden was just as hot for him, but even though he was as happy as the next guy to brag about his sexual conquests, it didn't feel right when it was Arden. Also, there was no way in hell he was telling Jamie.

He grabbed the drinks and headed back to the table.

Had Arden said anything to Jamie?

Nah, not possible. Jamie would have mentioned it. Or punched him in the nose.

But it was none of Jamie's business.

Okay, Arden was Jamie's sister, so it sort of *was* his business. But then, she probably didn't go around telling Jamie about every guy she slept with.

He pretended to be interested in the conversation, but when this round of drinks was done, everyone started making noises about going home. He cast another glance Arden's way. She'd probably be here another half hour.

He held up his beer, which was only half-done. "I'm gonna hang a bit longer. You guys go on."

"I'll stay too," Norton said, his "fear of missing out" always there. Tyler sighed, but Norton's FOMO was probably easier to deal with than Jamie.

They watched a rerun of a NASCAR race on TV while they sat there. Tyler finished his beer but still made no move to leave while Arden cleared the last few tables until the place was empty.

Finally Norton gave up, giving Tyler a look laced with what-the-fuck-dude as he left money for his tab and headed out. Not before checking into plans for next weekend, though.

Arden was finally done, pushing her arms into a sweater and pulling her hair out from it. "Tyler. Why are you still here?"

"I had to finish my beer."

"Bullshit." But her tone was mild, and her lips quirked into a smile even as she shook her head.

They left together and walked through the cool night air home.

"Why did you tell Jamie you weren't leaving?" she asked.

"I told him I had to finish my beer."

She snorted. "Tyler."

"Did you tell him about us?"

"God, no! What would I tell him? 'I slept with your best friend'?"

"I wasn't sure."

"So you haven't said anything either?"

"No. But I want to."

"What? Why?"

"I don't like lying to people."

In a very soft voice, so quiet he almost couldn't hear her,

she said, "Of course you don't." She let out a short sigh. "But…what would you tell him, Tyler?"

I'm crazy about your sister. I always have been. I want more of her. I want all of her.

He didn't say those things out loud. Fuck no. No way in hell was she ready for that. "Uh…"

"I mean…it's not like we're dating."

"We could date. Let's do that. Let's go out on a date."

She turned confused eyes on him. "Really?"

"Why not?"

Her pretty mouth twisted up as she contemplated that. "Because neither of us wants a relationship."

Oh yeah. He'd said that. "Oh, come on. We have fun together. We can go out and just have fun. When's your next day off?"

"Tomorrow."

"Shit. I work at eight." He thought. "But then I'm off Monday morning for four days."

"My next day off is Thursday again."

"Okay! That'll work. Thursday night."

They walked up to their building. Tyler used his key to open the front door and let her go in ahead of him, making sure the door was locked behind them. He followed her up the stairs, both of them treading lightly so as not to disturb Jamie or Mila. In the hall between their apartments, he paused. The air around them crackled with anticipation. Arousal. He longed to pull her into his arms. Feel her soft curves against him. Carry her into his apartment and do dirty things to her all goddamn night. He willed his dick to calm the fuck down and took a deep breath. "Okay. Thursday night. I'll see you then."

A faint crease appeared briefly between her eyebrows and her eyes flickered. "Okay." She hesitated. "I'm still not sure it's a good idea, but…okay."

He leaned down and brushed his mouth over hers in a quick kiss. Any more and he wouldn't be able to stop himself, and the magnetism shimmering around them told him she felt the same and was puzzled by his restraint. "Good night, princess."

Her lips quirked. "Night, Tyler."

Letting her go home without him was so fucking hard. But he wanted this to be about more than sex. And he wanted *her* to want more than that too. Watching her walk into her apartment and softly close the door, he squeezed his eyes shut, hands in fists against the urge to touch her, then turned and entered his own apartment.

CHAPTER SEVENTEEN

"So I have to do this thing."

Arden smiled at Jamie where he sat at her kitchen counter on one of the stools she'd purchased from a yard sale, eating the dinner she'd cooked for them Sunday evening. "Thing?"

"Yeah. A breakfast thing." He grimaced. "With some clients. We don't want to go to a restaurant, so I was going to get it catered, but I have no clue who to call."

"You might find Google helpful. Also, don't you have an assistant who can organize things like that for you?"

"Yeah. But I had this idea...that maybe you would do it."

"Organize it for you?"

"Well, yeah, sort of. I thought you could do the food."

Arden frowned. "What?"

"You love cooking. It would be a way for you to make some extra cash."

She narrowed her eyes at him. "Are you just doing this because you feel sorry for me?"

"Hell no." He gaped at her. "I really need to do this. And you love stuff like that."

She considered it. That was…true. "How many people?"

"Twelve."

She pursed her lips. That sounded…doable. "What kind of food did you have in mind?"

"I got nothin'." He shrugged and picked up a piece of chicken tikka masala with his fork. "This is really good, by the way."

"Thanks."

"It just has to be breakfast. You can get creative."

"Where's it being held?"

"At our office."

She nodded. "But how would I get the food there? I don't have a car."

"You can use mine. I usually take the 'L.'"

He did. It was amusing, since he was probably rich enough to have a chauffeur drive him to the office.

Arden tapped her fingers on the counter. Ideas were already popping into her head…frittatas, muffins, cheesy hash browns, fruit…

"Breakfast won't interfere with your job," Jamie added.

"What day is this breakfast?"

"Not for another few weeks." He gave her the date. "Eight o'clock."

She nodded. "Okay. I guess I could do that."

Jamie's smile beamed. "Awesome. Thank you."

She smiled too. This was something fun to plan and look forward to. And yeah…she could use the extra money. "How much are you paying me?"

"Hell, I have no idea. Figure out what you need to charge to cover the food and your time, and make a profit."

"I have a few questions. Like…do you want this served on

actual dishes and cutlery, or paper plates? Any theme? Any food allergies with people? Vegetarians? Vegans?"

"Jesus. I don't know."

Arden grabbed a note pad and they spent the rest of the meal talking through the plan. Jamie truly hadn't thought much about it, but that meant Arden had lots of freedom to do what she wanted, which was cool.

"So…" She set her cutlery down on her empty plate a while later. "I have a question for you about something else."

"Okay…"

"How would you feel about…" She hesitated. "About me going out with Tyler?"

"Going out where?" He stood. "Can I have more chicken?"

"Sure." She watched him move over to the stove and help himself. "Have more rice too. I mean, go out…like, on a date."

He went still, his hand holding a spoon poised over the pan. "You want to go out on a date with Tyler?"

"Um, yeah."

He turned and eyed her. "*Why?*"

His baffled expression made her laugh. "Don't make me explain it to you. Please."

"Ugh." He shook his head and loaded his plate up with more chicken and basmati rice. "Why are you asking me this? Is this hypothetical?"

"We're going out Thursday night." She didn't tell him they'd already slept together. So they'd done things backwards; Jamie didn't need to know that.

He sat back down at the counter and met her eyes. "Again, I say…why are you asking me this? What if I don't want you dating him?"

"I'm not asking your permission." She held his gaze. "I'm trying to be open about it. And I do care about how you feel…but…"

"But you're going out with him anyway."

She bit her lip. "Do you really think it's a bad idea?"

"Jesus. I don't know. I don't even know *what* I think about it." He eyed her. "Are you ready to start dating again?"

"It's just a date. I'm definitely not interested in a relationship."

"Okay, whoa, whoa." He held up a hand. "Hold the fuck up."

"What?" She widened her eyes at him.

"Tyler's a good guy."

"I know."

"You may not be interested in a relationship, but he's a relationship kind of guy."

She frowned. Her heart sank. Despite what Tyler claimed about not wanting that, Jamie was right. She dropped her gaze to her plate.

"I don't want you to screw him over," Jamie added.

Her insides squeezed up like a fist. "I wouldn't."

He rubbed his forehead. "I know you wouldn't do it intentionally. But…"

She swallowed, her throat constricted. "You're right. It probably is a bad idea."

"I didn't say that."

"I get it, though. Really." She forced a smile. "Forget I ever mentioned it."

"What are you going to do? Cancel on him?"

"Yes."

"Shit." He looked away. "Did *he* ask you out?"

"Yes."

"Shit."

"I'm sorry, Jamie." She slumped on her stool. "I didn't mean to come here and mess things up. I'm grateful to you for letting me stay here."

"You haven't messed anything up."

"I have. And I'm sorry. I love having your friends as my friends and hanging out with all of you and…and…even though I haven't figured everything out yet, I will. I definitely don't want to cause problems between all of you. Damn." Her eyes stung a little in the corners, but she determinedly blinked away tears.

"Look, it's none of my business, really," Jamie said. "You and Tyler are adults."

She nodded. She knew what she had to do. "Yes, we are." She smiled at her brother again. "Don't worry, it's all good, Jamie. No big deal. Do you have room for dessert?"

"Hell yeah."

"Good. I picked up raspberries at the market yesterday; they're so good. And I made little meringues." While Jamie cleared away their dishes, she set the meringues onto plates and topped them with berries and whipped cream.

They were just finishing when someone knocked on her door. They both turned as the door opened and Mila's head poked in. She'd been out with Garth. "Oh hey. You're both here."

"Come on in." Arden waved a hand. "Want some dessert?"

Mila walked in and instantly Arden knew something was wrong. Mila's usual smile was absent, and she shook her head at the offer of dessert. "No thanks."

"What's wrong?" Arden asked.

Jamie frowned, apparently not picking up on Mila's mood.

"Nothing." Mila took a seat on another stool. She pointed at the bottle of Chardonnay sitting on the counter. "I'll have a glass of that, though."

Arden slid a sideways glance at Jamie, then back to Mila. "Sure." She slipped off her stool and grabbed a glass from a cupboard. "Here you go."

Mila emptied the bottle into her glass, nearly overflowing it, then took a big gulp.

Arden bit her lip. "Something's definitely wrong."

Mila's head dropped forward. "Garth and I broke up."

Arden sucked in a sharp breath. "Oh no."

"What?" Jamie's eyebrows flew up. "You broke up?"

"Yeah." Mila sniffed, then squared her shoulders, lifted her head, and chugged back more wine. "But it's fine."

"Are you okay, hon?" Arden reached out to cover Mila's hand with hers.

"Yeah. I'm good."

"Why'd you break up with him?" Jamie asked, a perplexed pleat between his eyebrows.

"*He* broke up with *me*." Mila shook back her hair. "He's met someone else."

"Motherfucker," Jamie growled. "He was cheating on you?"

"I don't know. He says he wasn't, but I'm pretty sure this has been going on for a while."

"Asshole."

"I never even got to meet him so I could decide that first-hand," Arden said. "But yeah, I agree."

A tear slid out of Mila's eye and down her smooth cheek. Arden's heart clenched in sympathy.

Jamie pulled in a breath and his head jerked back. "Hell, Mila…don't cry." He looked like he wanted to bolt.

Arden took pity on him. "You can take off, if you want. I'll take care of her."

Mila just nodded glumly.

Jamie's mouth twisted into a conflicted expression. Arden read his concern for Mila, mingled with discomfort. "You sure? I, uh, can stay…"

Mila waved a hand. "S'okay, Jamie. Don't worry. I'll be fine. I'll be at work tomorrow."

"Jesus. Take a day off, if you need." He stood, rubbing the back of his neck. "I'm not worried about that." He edged toward the door.

Arden would have laughed if she hadn't been hurting for her new friend.

"You want me to go find him?" Jamie paused at the door. "Take him down?"

Mila snorted. "You're not exactly a big bruiser."

"Hey." Jamie frowned and squared his shoulders. "I could do it."

Mila tilted her head and gave him a sad smile. "Thank you. But it's okay. Really. I signed him up for a bunch of newsletters about erectile dysfunction and penis enlargement. Also some gay porn sites."

Arden choked on her wine.

Jamie grinned. "Attagirl. We could hack into his Facebook and Snapchat too, if you want."

Mila's head tilted the other way. "I'll consider it." Her smile warmed. "You're a good friend, Jamie."

"Yeah."

Arden grinned at his agreement. "But not good enough to stick around to dry her tears."

"I hate crying," Jamie muttered. "But I *am* here for you."

"I know." Mila waved him out.

When he'd gone, Mila turned back to the counter and slumped on it. "Damn."

"I'm so sorry."

"Do you have any more wine?"

"I do." Arden retrieved another bottle from the fridge, this one a nice pinot grigio.

"Can I get drunk?"

"I think in this situation, you absolutely *must* get drunk. And probably eat some junk food."

"What've you got?"

Arden wrinkled her nose. "Not much that's junky. Vanilla ice cream. Cheese and crackers."

"That's not good enough. I need potato chips. A *huge* bag of chips. And possibly peanut butter cup ice cream. That's my favorite."

"You want me to go out and get some?"

"No. Course not. You're a good friend too, but I don't need junk food. Wine is good."

"I also have Jägermeister."

Mila's eyes widened. "Even better!"

Arden opened the wine. She'd look after Mila. Sure, she'd serve her a couple of shots, but she'd make sure she didn't overdo it, and she'd make sure she made it safely home. All the way downstairs. She smiled. "Want to tell me about it?"

Mila sighed and drank again. "I don't know. It's done. Things weren't great for a long time. You know that."

"Yeah."

"I kind of felt it was coming." Mila moved the base of her wine glass in a circle on the granite counter. "It's just…well, I told you and Emma…it's just one more thing on my list I thought I'd checked off, and now it's over."

"You don't need a man, you know."

Mila straightened. "I know that. Don't think I'm one of those women who thinks she's not worthy unless she has a man. It's not that."

"Then what is it?"

"I'm not sure." Her shoulders slumped again. "I just always pictured my life *with* someone."

"Yeah. I get it."

Mila's bottom lip pushed out. "I'm sorry. This must seem really trivial to you after what you went through."

"Of course not. Heartbreak is never trivial."

Mila nodded. "The thing is…I don't think I'm really heart-broken. Guess I didn't care as much about Garth as I did about the idea of having a boyfriend."

"Well, that's pretty insightful for someone who just guzzled down half a bottle of wine."

"You exaggerate. That wasn't half. Maybe a third." She pushed her empty glass across the counter and Arden filled it up. "Where's that Jägermeister?"

"I can't go out with you tonight."

Tyler frowned as he carried a sheet of drywall into Arden's apartment on Thursday. "What? Why?"

"It's just not a good idea." She twisted her hands together, her stomach knotted. "I talked to Jamie about it—"

"Jesus."

"He's my brother. Anyway, he made me realize it's not a good idea."

"What the fuck?" Tyler dropped the drywall sheet to the drop cloth laid out on the floor, propping it against a wall. "Seriously? He talked you out of it?"

"No! No, he didn't. It's just that…I told you before…I'm not ready for a relationship."

"I told you, I'm not looking for a relationship either."

"Tyler. You said you don't lie."

His mouth tightened, then relaxed. He shook his head in mild exasperation. "It's one date, Arden."

When he put it that way…it did make it seem like she was being a little ridiculous. She nibbled her bottom lip. Tyler held her gaze steadily. "Okay," she finally said. "Fine. We'll go out tonight. Just one date."

"Don't sound so enthusiastic."

"I'm sorry." She closed her eyes and sighed. "I don't know how to do this. I haven't been on a date in almost ten years."

Tyler made a rough noise. "Yeah."

"I didn't mean to be insulting."

"Okay. Well. Good. I made a dinner reservation for seven o'clock."

"Okay. What should I wear? I mean, is it a fancy place?"

"Not super fancy. A little bistro not far from here."

"Okay." She hesitated. "Do you need help today?"

He paused. "I do, actually. I was going to wait for Jamie to help on the weekend, but you might be able to hold the drywall in place while I screw it to the studs."

She blinked. Hearing Tyler talking about screwing and studs sounded sexual. She caught the gleam in his eyes. Her lips twitched. "Okay. I can do that. Screwing studs is always fun."

"Oh, baby." He grinned, and his tense shoulders relaxed. "Just wait."

Her body tingled everywhere as she followed him to the bathroom. It had been over a week since she and Tyler had slept together, and although they'd seen each other several times, he hadn't initiated anything more than a few kisses. They'd been amazing, melt-her-insides kisses. She'd spent a lot of time daydreaming about Tyler and the things he'd done to her, the way he'd made her feel, the things she wanted to do to him. She had to be honest and admit that she hoped their date was going to lead to more action of a sexual nature. Because she really, really wanted him.

She'd started to doubt that he wanted her though, except he still seemed to want to take her out for dinner, so…hell, like she'd admitted to him, she didn't know how to do this.

She'd just go with the flow.

Tyler directed her on what to do in the small space of her bathroom. Finally it seemed they were getting somewhere, now that the plumber had been there. Twice. The first time he'd apparently cut out and removed water lines and plugged up the open drain lines to keep sewer gas out. Tyler had then worked on framing the walls of the bathroom, and the plumber had come back to do more work. Now Tyler was ready to drywall. He pulled out a drill and began noisily driving screws into the drywall piece that she was helping hold in place against the wall.

"Why is it green?" she asked. "Is the bathroom going to be green?"

"No. It's green because it's a special water-resistant drywall for bathrooms."

"Oh. What color is the bathroom going to be?"

He smiled. "You want to pick?"

"Can I?"

"Sure. I doubt if Jamie cares."

"How about pink?"

Tyler choked. "Yeah, he might care about that. Probably something neutral is better, in case you ever move out."

"I was kidding."

"Good." He continued working, measuring, cutting drywall, hauling it in, and fastening it into place. She admired how he worked—not just his strong hands and arms, but his competence, measuring carefully, cutting precisely, taking care with every drywall screw. Competence porn was definitely a thing.

She focused on following his directions, helping him fit the boards and hold them in place. "How did you learn to do all this?"

"I guess I mostly learned from a buddy at work. He did renovations on the side, and I offered to help out. I learned a lot from him. He retired last year, but we still help each other sometimes if we need extra hands."

"It looks like you enjoy it."

"Yeah. It's fun doing something hands-on."

"You're good at it."

He eyed her, and her belly did a little flip at his intense expression. "Thanks."

"It's lunch time. Should I make us a sandwich?"

"That would be great."

She left him to head into her kitchen, where she put together two toasted bacon, tomato, and avocado sandwiches. Then she made one more sandwich, with the feeling that Tyler probably had a bigger appetite than she did. "Okay," she called to him. "Lunch is ready."

He emerged and strode to her kitchen sink to wash up. "Do I smell bacon?"

"Yeah."

He groaned. "I love bacon."

"I think you mentioned that a time or two." In fact, she'd remembered that he loved bacon, and had picked up a package at the store with that in mind, not sure when she'd get to feed him but wanting to make something he'd like.

He sat on a stool at her counter, took a big bite, and chewed. He closed his eyes. "This is so good."

"Thanks." She slid onto the stool beside him and picked up her own sandwich. "I like your bathroom, with the gray and white. I think that would be nice. Maybe with some black."

He nodded. "Gray tiles too?"

"Maybe." She pursed her lips. "I should look on Pinterest for some ideas."

"Or come with me to the tile store. You might see something you love there."

"I guess I could do that." She grinned. "Especially since Jamie's paying for it."

He smiled back at her. "Yeah. Not very often you get to

decorate your place for free."

She wrinkled her nose and looked down at her sandwich. "I feel a little guilty about that."

"Hey, we talked about this before. He was renovating this apartment anyway, right? And you'll pay rent when you can."

"Oh hey, guess what? Jamie offered me a job catering a business meeting for him."

"No shit?" Tyler cocked his head.

She told him about the plan.

"That's really cool. And it's something you enjoy."

She ducked her chin and looked up at him through her eyelashes. He knew that about her? Warmth filled her chest. "Yes," she agreed. "I do enjoy it."

"What are we going to celebrate next?" He picked up a piece of bacon that had fallen from his sandwich and popped it into his mouth. "National Lemon Meringue Pie Day?"

She grinned. "No, that's in May. I'm not sure what today is." She picked up her phone and scrolled to the app she had. "National Chili Dog Day." She lifted her gaze to meet his. "I think we're going to have to give that one a miss. Unless the place we're going to tonight has chili dogs."

His teeth flashed white. "Nope, pretty sure that's not on the menu at Bistro Noir."

Their eyes met and held, the warmth of amusement sliding into something hotter…crackling sparks and a low-down kick of lust. His smile faded and she couldn't help but stare at his mouth, those perfect, sculpted lips that knew how to kiss so well…and do other things so well.

Heat rose up around her and her lungs stopped working. Her own lips parted and the distance between them shortened as they slowly leaned in closer. Her eyelashes fluttered closed and her lips tingled in anticipation of Tyler's touching them.

When his firm mouth met hers, a jolt of electricity pulsated through her, straight to her core. She leaned in more, and his big hand came up to cup the side of her neck, his thumb rubbing her jaw. A little moan mounted her throat and leaked into his mouth, and he deepened the kiss, tilting his head, opening wider over her.

She set a hand on his thigh, feeling the heat of his skin through the denim of his jeans, the muscle there hard. Her insides lit up, hot and quivering.

He drew back slowly, his tongue lingering on her bottom lip, his eyes dark and hazy. "Wow. Every time I kiss you, it blows my mind."

She stared at him, her breath coming in jerky pants, her skin burning. "Yeah?"

"Yeah." He rubbed his thumb over her wet lip. "Let's ditch the bathroom remodel and spend the afternoon in bed."

Her eyes widened. Oh God. That sounded so good. So decadent and hedonistic. "Wow."

The corners of his mouth lifted. "Kidding."

Disappointment deflated her. "Oh."

One thick eyebrow lifted. "You really want to do that?"

She closed her eyes and drew in a long breath. "It sounded very tempting. But not very practical."

"True. And I'd totally say fuck practical, but…I have plans for later for your bed."

She swallowed. "Y-you do?"

"Oh yeah."

She smiled. "What if I don't put out after one date?"

His smile went wry. "Then I'll be pissed at myself for going with delayed gratification instead of carrying your sweet little ass into the bedroom right now."

He had nothing to worry about. She wanted him now, and she'd want him even more later. But she didn't need to tell him that. Let him work for it. "All right, then. Back to work."

CHAPTER EIGHTEEN

"This place is beautiful."

Tyler held Arden's chair as she took her seat and gazed around the patio of Bistro Noir, then moved around the small table covered in a white cloth to his chair. He looked around too. It had been a while since he'd been there—this wasn't the kind of place to hang with the guys and drink beer.

Old brick walls bordered the patio on two sides, and a wooden fence topped with a trellis laced with flowering vines ran along the other two sides. A couple of Japanese maples created a leafy canopy, and little white lights lined the walls and twinkled in shrubs. Pots of flowers added color and a fresh scent to the warm evening air, soft jazz music floating around them.

He turned his gaze back to Arden, and she smiled. "I love it."

"Wait till you try the food."

A server approached them to fill water goblets while they opened their menus. "Would you like to pick a bottle of wine?" Tyler asked her. "I think you know more than I do."

"Sure. Would you like red or white?"

"I like red, if that's okay."

"Of course." She skimmed through the selections and ordered a bottle of pinot noir. Then she turned her attention to the food menu. "Wow. How am I going to decide?"

"I think we should get an appetizer," Tyler said.

"I want one of everything," she murmured, eyes still on the menu.

He studied her face—she was wearing a little more makeup than usual, her eyes shadowy and lips shiny. Her hair hung long and loose, and she'd dressed up in a black dress, sheer and floaty, with multiple little straps on bare shoulders. When she'd opened her apartment door a short time ago as he arrived to pick her up for their date, he'd been rendered speechless at seeing her in such a sexy dress. His gaze had followed her bare legs from the above-the-knee hem down to the strappy black sandals with killer heels that immediately had him imagining them over his shoulders.

This whole delayed gratification thing was worth it just to sit across from her and stare at her.

Eh, maybe not. If he didn't get her under him, if he didn't get inside her tonight, he was probably going to cry like a baby.

He swallowed a sigh and refocused. "I thought you'd like this place because most of the food is organic, and they try to buy from local farmers at this time of year."

She nodded. "I see that." She looked up from the menu and tilted her head, her dark hair falling over one shoulder. "You knew that's important to me?"

"Um, yeah, I kinda got that from when we were at the farmers' market and Whole Foods."

"It's important. We have to look after this world."

"I guess so, yeah." Truthfully, while he knew sustainable agriculture was important, and he did enjoy buying local foods at the market, it wasn't something he thought about a lot. "I have to admit I'm kind of surprised you feel that way."

Her eyebrows rose. "Because I'm a princess?"

Heat rose from the open collar of his dress shirt into his face. "Hell. I guess so."

"You must have forgotten I was on the Environment Committee in high school."

"I don't think I even knew there *was* an Environment Committee."

She laughed. "Princesses can be concerned about the planet too."

"Yeah, of course. In fact, it makes total sense."

"I like supporting local businesses too. Oh! I had the best idea today!"

He grinned. "What?"

"The breakfast I'm catering for Jamie...I was trying to figure out a way to make it special, and I was thinking about all the vendors at the farmers' market...I could use all local products. Jams and honeys...breads...cheeses..."

He watched her eyes light up talking about it. "That *is* a great idea."

"I've wanted to buy all that stuff, and support those people and try their products, but I can't afford to myself. But for this...it would be perfect!"

"Yeah." It really was a good idea. "You're amazing, Arden."

She shook her head, smiling, dropping her gaze back to the menu. "How about escargots? Or mussels? Or...yum, this caramelized onion strudel sounds good too."

"Let's get two appetizers and share them."

The more he got to know about Arden, the more he realized how superficial the crush he'd had on her back in the day was. Okay, not totally superficial; he knew she was more than a pretty face. But the intelligence and caring and strength he was seeing now made her even more beautiful in his eyes.

He was so fucked.

Letting out a short sigh, he too turned his attention to the menu, although he already knew he was going to order the steak frites. The steak which was sustainably raised beef.

"This place is pricey," Arden whispered to him.

He shrugged. "Don't worry about it." He could afford a nice meal out once in a while.

She bit her lip, looking conflicted, then nodded, reminding him of her money situation.

The server arrived with their wine, pouring a little for Arden to taste. She gave a nod of approval, and the server filled their glasses, then disappeared again while Arden continued to peruse the food selections. Finally she decided and closed the menu, setting it aside. Picking up her wine, she leaned forward and lifted her glass in a toast. "Thank you for this."

He touched his glass to hers with a gentle clink. "You're welcome."

She sipped her wine, glancing around. The best word to describe the patio was "romantic," which was totally what he'd been going for, but he could see the wariness in her eyes.

He tasted the wine. "This is really good."

"It is."

They made some small talk until the server came to take their order. For her meal, Arden requested the salmon.

"So have you talked to Mila?" she asked him, picking up her glass again.

"Not really. Jamie told me about her and Garth breaking up. Can't say I'm surprised."

"No?" She lifted an eyebrow.

He shook his head. "I've been wondering about things

between them for a while now." He related some of the incidents he'd noticed.

"That's very perceptive of you."

He shrugged. "Just observant. Is Mila okay?"

"Yes. We got drunk together and talked it all out. She'll be fine."

"Jamie and I are gonna go see Garth and beat him up."

She laughed. "You are not."

"Okay, maybe not beat him up. But for sure I'm gonna have a little chat with him."

She bit her lip. "I don't know if you should interfere."

He shrugged. "She's a friend. We look out for each other. Don't look like that. It'll be fine."

"Ooookay." She paused. "Jamie was so funny the night she came up and told us."

"Funny how?"

"He was obviously very uncomfortable because she was upset, but he almost looked…upset too."

"They've been friends for a long time."

"True. Anyway, we're going have a girls' night some time. Go to a club and dance and flirt with a bunch of men."

Tyler frowned. "You're going to flirt with a bunch of men?"

"Shhh." Her eyes darted around, and he realized he'd nearly shouted.

"Sorry." He lowered his voice. "But seriously…?"

She smiled. "What's wrong with a little flirting?"

How the hell did he even answer that question? There was *everything* wrong with a little flirting, unless the man she was flirting with was *him*.

He pulled in a long slow breath, working for control. He'd gotten her here, on this dinner date, in this romantic restaurant, but she didn't think she was ready for a relationship, so he had to keep things casual and light. But the possessiveness inside him was growing, the powerful, protective need to claim her as his, to look after her and make her life as perfect as he could. It was making it damn hard to keep his hands off her, to keep from forbidding her to flirt with any other man. Hell, she shouldn't be *smiling* at any other man. And it was making it damn hard to keep from telling her exactly how he felt about her.

Too soon.

Their appetizers arrived, and they continued to talk as they shared the small dishes—about his job, the upcoming beer festival being held in Oz Park, and the plan to go to the Firefly Supper Club Friday night. She shared more of her ideas about the breakfast she was catering, how she'd collected business cards last weekend and had already made a few calls to some of the vendors, and she told him about something she was working on at Shenanigans—a service manual, she called it, which Liam hadn't asked her to do but which she'd taken on herself after seeing a need for it when she'd been hired.

"I'm sure he'll appreciate that." Tyler held a mussel shell in one hand and a small fork in the other. "It sounds like it'll make training new staff easier, and that helps everyone."

"Including the customer. They apparently have a lot of staff turnover." She scrunched up her face. "Why is that, do you think?"

"No idea." Tyler popped the mussel into his mouth.

"It's not that Liam's a bad guy to work for. And Sorcha is great too, although she's a little stern at times."

"I think she has to be, because Liam's such a pushover."

"He kind of is. I love him, though." She tilted her head. "What's with you and Sorcha?"

He went still and dropped his gaze. "What? Nothing."

"Yes, there is. I saw the way she was talking to you last

weekend. Oh my God." Her mouth dropped open. "She's not your ex-girlfriend, is she?"

"No! Christ no. We've never gone out. But…"

"What?"

"I think she has a crush on me." He shifted on his chair. "She doesn't really hide it."

"Oh." She blinked. "You're not…interested? She's lovely."

He lifted his head to meet her eyes, moving his head from side to side. "No. Not interested in her. Not even a little."

The moment stretched out, the air around them growing hot, as if a bubble surrounded their table, capturing them inside it together, the rest of the world on the outside. He didn't try to hide his feelings, and knew she could read his face.

The only one I'm interested in is you.

He wanted so damn badly to say it out loud. He didn't. But she knew.

Her lips parted and her tongue came out to wet her bottom lip. Watching it, his groin tightened and heat gathered in his core. Fuck, he wanted her.

"Stop looking at me like that," she choked out.

"Like what?"

"Like…like you want to jump me."

"I do." His disclosure made the air around them buzz even more with tension. He leaned across the table and lowered his voice. "I want to do you right here on this table."

She made another small sound in her throat, and he hardened even more. A flush rose on her cheeks. He kept staring at her, and heat built between them as they eyed each other.

Finally she broke the connection, picked up her fork, and stabbed at the onion strudel on her plate. "Okay! So. If you could make one rule that everyone had to follow, what would it be?"

He stared at her with the abrupt shift in conversation. "What?"

She repeated the question with a nervous smile, picking up her wine glass.

"Um, okay." He thought about it. "I would say...no biting during oral."

She choked on her wine and took a few seconds to recover. "Really? One rule and that would be it?"

He grinned. "You were thinking bigger picture? Like, everyone should always be on time?"

She smiled too. "If punctuality is important to you, then yes."

"I thought you were talking about sex rules."

"Why would you think that?"

"I dunno. I just think about sex a lot, I guess." *Sex with you.* "Also, if you have to spit, don't do it in front of the guy."

She fell back in her chair, laughing. Thank God she had a sense of humor. "What is it about spitting that offends men?"

"How would you feel if a guy went down on you and then ran straight to the bathroom to rinse his mouth out?"

"Um, okay, I see your point."

"I'm not offended by it, per se, but it's just nice if a woman doesn't act like she's disgusted by it, that's all. There are lots of ways around it, if she doesn't want to swallow."

"Um...much as I can't believe we're talking about this as our romantic dinner conversation...like what?"

"Like, direct it onto her, uh..." He glanced around and leaned forward again to whisper. "Onto her chest. Or some-where else."

"Ah." She shifted in her chair, her long eyelashes lowering.

"But I don't need to ask your personal preferences about that." He gave her an evil leer.

"I guess you don't." She met his gaze steadily, but her lips twitched. "Wow, I was just trying to start a get-to-know-each-other conversation and I can't believe we jumped right into a discussion about oral sex."

"You're welcome."

The smile tugged the corners of her lips higher, and she shook her head.

"Okay, if this is about getting to know each other better, what sex rules do *you* have?"

Another laugh slipped from her lips. "Oh my God. Well... number one rule...foreplay is *not* optional."

He grinned and leaned back in his chair. "Good one."

"Also, since we're talking about oral...don't expect to receive if you aren't willing to give."

He smiled with a slow wink. "I think we already know I'm a giver that way."

Arden's cheeks grew pink again. "Um, yes. That's true. And..." She hesitated, then said, "And you're very good at it."

His lungs expanded with pride. "Thank you."

"Maybe this is a good time to ask you about those Lora Leigh books."

He hoisted an eyebrow. "You were checking out my books?"

"I happened to notice. I like her books too."

"She writes great sex."

"Are you telling me you learned about sex from reading romance novels?"

"They're not romance. They're fantasy."

"They're romance."

"Okay whatever." He shrugged. "I may have picked up a few tips. But mostly, I just like doing it, so..."

She let out a strangled-sounding sigh.

He knew just how she felt. "Yeah, I know, we haven't even gotten our main courses yet, and I'm ready to throw you over my shoulder and take you home."

Heat flared in her eyes, lust mingling with amusement. "I'm ready for that too."

He let out a low groan. "Christ. Now we're both going to be in agony."

"Maybe we should stop talking about sex. That might help."

"Yeah. Okay." He cast around in his mind for a new topic. "How are your parents?"

"Yeah, that'll do it." Arden wrinkled her nose. "They're good. They love living in Florida now. It's so weird. My grandma has lived there for years, and they used to make jokes about the retirement community, and now they're part of it. They don't seem old enough for that."

"They did retire young."

"But my dad hasn't totally retired. He still does some consulting work."

"Right. Do you visit them there?"

"I have a couple of times. They have a great place with a pool, so it's a nice place to relax. Not wild and exciting." She wrinkled her nose, smiling. "But relaxing."

"You like to travel?"

"I love to, but haven't done much. Michael never wanted to. You?"

"Yeah, I love it too. Jamie and I make a point of taking a week trip somewhere hot every winter. Claire and I went to England last year."

"That's your ex-girlfriend?"

"Yeah." He enjoyed the way her eyes narrowed at that.

"And what about your mom? Is she still working?"

"Yeah. She's still at the hospital." He paused. "She wants to fix me up with her friend's daughter."

Arden blinked. "Oh."

He shrugged. "I told Mom I'm not interested in her."

"So she wants you to be an accountant, and she wants you to get married."

He rolled his eyes. "Pretty much, yeah. And don't forget the grandchildren. Jesus. I'm not ready for that."

"But some day you want kids."

He shrugged. "Sure. Some day."

She nodded. "She wants a lot for you."

"I guess all parents do, but…for her it's hard because she was supposed to have two kids to pin all her hopes on. Now it's just me." He shrugged, trying to look nonchalant even though this topic made his insides clench. "I've tried, but I can't be everything to her."

She stared across the table at him, her eyes warm. "You put way too much pressure on yourself."

He frowned. It wasn't him putting pressure on himself. It had been his parents, now just his mom, putting pressure on him…wasn't it?

"No child can be everything to his or her parents. If your mom really wants that, then that's just wrong. You need to be your own person and live the life you want to live."

He didn't answer right away, letting her words sink in. "But I'm disappointing her. Don't you want your parents to be proud of you? Oh wait, I forgot I'm talking to the prom queen who could do no wrong."

She tilted her head to one side, studying him. Her scrutiny made him shift in his chair and drop his gaze. She seemed to recognize that this time the prom queen reference came out as more envious than teasing. And to recognize that it really bothered him that he'd disappointed his parents.

"You don't think *I've* felt like I let my parents down over the last few years?" she asked softly. "Living in a marriage that was a sham, letting myself get into such a huge financial mess, letting my husband down to the point that he felt helpless and took his own life?"

"That *wasn't your fault.*" He'd already told her that.

"I know," she said quietly. "I do. But still…I feel like a huge failure at life. I know they've been worried about me, and I hate that."

They had something in common there. Even though he'd found what he wanted to do, even though Arden hadn't figured it all out yet, they both felt like they were letting people down.

He reached across the table and closed his fingers around her hand. She met his eyes, and he gave her hand a squeeze. "Maybe we both need to ease up on ourselves."

She curled her fingers around his, holding his gaze. "Yeah. Maybe you're right."

They managed to keep the conversation off sex, mostly, during their delicious dinner, but even so, having Arden sitting across from him in this romantic setting looking so goddamn gorgeous kept his dick at half-mast most of the time.

He had to say, though, he was having fun. Even talking about nonsexual topics with Arden was entertaining…discovering they shared political views, had similar feelings about the importance of community and giving back, and both hated when people talked about everything wrong in the world being because of millennials, and stereotypes about them.

"We're not all the same," Arden said with an eye roll. "Some of us actually do want secure jobs we can stay at for the rest of our lives."

"Like me."

"Yeah."

"Is that what you want?"

She huffed. "I don't know what I want. But I'm envious of you."

Once again, he had that fierce protective instinct, a feeling of wanting to look after her. Which he knew was not the way to go with her while she was finding her way. So he kept quiet about that, while vowing to do anything he could to make life easier for her and keep her safe.

He signed off on the credit card slip for their meal, adding a tip, then slipped his card into his wallet. They'd finished the bottle of wine and that arousal was still a low-grade buzz inside him.

"Okay," he said. "Let's get out of here. It's time."

She blinked and reached for her purse. "Okay. Time for what?"

He rose from his chair and moved around to pull hers back for her. When she stood, he leaned in and whispered, "Foreplay, baby."

CHAPTER NINETEEN

"My place." Tyler shoved open the door and pushed into his apartment, tugging Arden in with him. He slammed the door shut and yanked her up against him, her back to his front.

Excitement heated her blood, her belly doing a pirouette at being the object of Tyler's intense, nearly rough desire. She felt how hard he was, pressing into her back, and a small whimper escaped her lips.

"Yeah," he said on a low growl, nuzzling the side of her neck. He slid one arm around her front, the other moving her hair aside so he could suck on her skin at the juncture of her neck and shoulder.

Her breathing quickened. Her body quivered.

He slid the narrow straps of her dress off her shoulder and glided his tongue across her skin there. His other hand gathered up the sheer fabric of her dress and lifted it higher on her thigh. He pressed his erection against her lower back, and she pushed back against his thighs. Electricity sparked over every nerve ending in her body. "Tyler," she gasped.

"Yeah." He closed his teeth over her skin, gently, but still… it was a possessive, dominant gesture, and she shivered. "That was so goddamn hot sitting on that patio, people all around us while we were talking about me eating you."

"Oh God." Thick liquid heat pooled down low inside her, remembering their dirty conversation.

"Right?"

"Y-yes. It was hot." So hot. He'd shocked her a little, but she'd been so turned on…

He now had her dress high enough that he could slip his hand over the front of her panties and then between her thighs. "Your panties are soaked, you sexy girl. I love that."

A helpless moan leaked from her lips.

"Were you wet like this all during dinner?"

"Yes." Her thighs clenched on his hand as he cupped her over her panties.

"Good. Because I was this hard." He titled his pelvis, nudging her even more with his erection. "You make me this hard all the fucking time, Arden." He rubbed his beard stubble against the soft skin of her neck, and she shivered again. "Thinking about you in my shower…seeing you leave wearing nothing but a towel…knowing you're sleeping right across the hall from me in that sexy little nightie…or maybe naked…*fuck*."

She moaned. "Oh God, Tyler. I think about you too. I dream about you."

"Yeah?"

She pulled in a shaky breath. Her confession poured from her lips as he rubbed her. "Sex dreams." She panted as he kissed her neck then sucked on her earlobe. She pulsed against his hand.

"I like to hear that." His voice rasped near her ear. "Do you touch yourself?"

"Yes. A couple of times…I nearly came in my sleep. I woke up and I was so turned on…so close…and I touched myself."

"Jesus." He spun her around and stepped her backwards until her back met the wall forcefully. "That's enough to make me come too."

He crushed her up against the wall and their mouths crashed together. He consumed her, nipped at her bottom lip, licked over it with his tongue, then slid his tongue into her mouth. The bold stroke of his tongue against hers rendered her boneless, and she sagged between his hard body and the wall.

He licked inside her mouth, softly bit at her lips, then pushed her lips farther apart with a desperate hunger. She gasped but kissed him back. He found her hands and lifted them, pinning them to the wall above her head while he dipped his knees and flexed his hips, pushing against her soft core.

"Feel that?" His lips moved against hers. "That's for you, baby. You make me hard enough to drill through concrete." He nipped her bottom lip. "That gorgeous body of yours and your hot mouth make me lose my mind."

Her head thunked back against the wall as his lips cruised over her cheek and neck and his cock rubbed against her. Desire swirled and heated inside her, her inner muscles squeezing, her breasts swelling. She caught his face in her palms and held it to kiss him again. He cupped her ass, bringing her closer to his erection.

He released one of her hands and hiked her dress up again, rough fingertips brushing over her thigh and hip until he found her thong. He curled his fingers around the string and gave a sharp tug, and it snapped.

She whimpered again.

He dropped her panties, grabbed her hands again and lifted them over his shoulders. "Hang on, baby."

"Condom," she gasped, a faint voice of reason tricking into her consciousness.

"Shit." He groaned. "Got it." He pulled his wallet out of his sagging pants and found the small package.

She cried out when he pushed inside. Delicious tension throbbed in her body at the intrusion, clamping around him.

"Fuck yeah."

"Oh God, Tyler, that feels so good."

She gasped and he kissed her, sucking her tongue as he filled her. Sensation burned and twisted inside her. It was dirty and wicked and so hot she thought she might burst into flames. And then she did burst into flames—a bright, burning conflagration.

Moments later, both of them breathing hard and slumped against the wall, she attempted to speak. "Wow. I've never been banged up against the wall before."

He groaned. "I'm sorry."

"Don't apologize." She met his eyes. "I loved it. Although you did promise me foreplay."

He choked on a laugh. "What? The drive home wasn't enough foreplay?"

"The whole dinner was foreplay." She smiled ruefully and pushed his hair off his forehead.

And it hadn't been just the sexy talk. Layers of feelings for him kept building the more time she spent with him. Hearing him talk about his mom and how he felt he was letting her down had made something inside her soften and warm. Yes, she was attracted to him. Yes, she liked him. But getting a glimpse of his vulnerabilities caused a feeling of warm tenderness, a desire to soothe him and reassure him that he was a strong, amazing man who had no reason to feel lacking. Even if his mom wasn't proud of him—and Arden seriously doubted that—*she* was proud of him. And it made wanting him so much more intense. Almost scary intense.

"True that. Christ, I can't believe we didn't even make it to the bedroom."

She smiled and rubbed her lips over his. "Take me there now."

"Not sure if I can walk yet." But he stepped back, readjusting his hold on her ass, Arden lifting her legs to cling to him.

"Gonna trip on my pants," he muttered as he staggered down the dark hall to his bedroom.

"Don't drop me."

"Never." The rough, vehement tone of his voice made her feel...secure. As if she could count on this man to be there for her always. For anything.

But she knew from experience that wasn't the case. She couldn't rely on a man to protect her or make her feel safe and secure. She had to do that for herself.

She pushed away those qualms. Because Tyler had just given her another one of those amazing orgasms he seemed so good at, and, call her greedy, but she wanted more.

She got more.

"Does it still count as foreplay if we've already boned?" Tyler stretched out beside her on the bed on his side, one hand between her legs, the other under her neck.

"It does if we're going to bone again."

"That's the plan, baby." His fingers slid through her slick heat. Her chin lifted, eyes falling closed, parting her thighs wider to give him access.

Buzzing pleasure started, a moan climbed in her throat,

and she reached for him, clasping his strong hip bone. The sweetness of his fingers and mouth on her was so deliciously erotic, turning her body liquid. She lost herself in it.

"Wanted to taste this sweetness again," he murmured. "You're addicting, Arden. I can never get enough of this."

His words made her belly flip with lust. She started to quiver, her insides tightening, sensation twisting up hard and tight, higher and higher. She cried out, her hips lifting to his mouth as it rocked through her.

"Beautiful," he said, licking her tenderly.

Consumed with the naughty, erotic pleasure of it all, she shifted down the bed, ran a hand over one of his butt cheeks, so firm and muscular, and took him in her mouth. And she answered his question about her preferences, keeping him in her mouth, relishing every groan and pulse until he finished, and then she let him slowly pull out with a last swipe of her tongue.

He collapsed onto the bed beside her, flat on his back, his head at her feet. His hand came out to rest on her lower belly, over her curls in a sweetly intimate gesture that made her heart flutter. "Wow."

"Mmmm."

After long moments, he sat up, using impressive abdominal strength, and rearranged them both under the covers with her tucked in against him, his arms around her.

"So you do put out on the first date," he mumbled.

She smiled. A strange happiness bubbled inside her, along with a luscious languor that settled in her limbs. "It was a good dinner."

He snorted, his arms tightening around her.

"Seriously, it was. Thank you. And I had fun."

"Me too." He paused. "Does that mean you'll go out with me again?"

Her skin prickled. "Tyler…"

He closed a hand over one breast.

"That won't work."

He smiled against her shoulder. "You're on to me."

"Oh yeah."

"It's okay, Arden. Just go with it, okay? We both had a good time tonight. Better than good. There's nothing wrong with that."

"I know. I know." She *did* know that. But Jamie's words about how Tyler was a relationship kind of guy floated back to her, and she squeezed her eyes shut. If he got serious and she didn't, she'd be causing a whole lot of trouble.

And if she got serious too…God. She couldn't let that happen. She had to be careful here. Tyler made her feel so good, and she really, really liked him, and damn, he could turn her on so easily and make her come so hard…even when she was just dreaming about him. Which was all great, but also seemed kind of dangerous, when she was trying to make a new life for herself and show everyone she wasn't just a spoiled prom queen.

"I guess we're sort of going out again tomorrow night," she finally said.

"Right." He gave her breast a squeeze, and dammit, tingles started building again. "To see Danny's show."

"It should be fun."

"If you say so."

She twisted her head around. "You don't want to go?"

He kissed her shoulder. "Not sure about the whole drag queen thing."

"You like Danny."

"Sure. That's why I'm going. I'm keeping an open mind."

"You *are* open-minded. I like that about you."

"Hmm."

Her eyes drifted closed. It was getting late. Along with a few glasses of wine with dinner and a couple of mind-scrambling orgasms, being held all warm and safe in Tyler's bed was making her sleepy.

"Arden?"

"Mmm?"

"Why do you celebrate all those days…like National Muffin Day, or whatever?"

For some reason, she didn't hesitate to tell him the truth, even though it probably sounded pathetic. "I started doing that when…when I wasn't so happy."

"After Michael died?"

"Before, actually. I wanted to remind myself that…no matter how bad things are, there's always something to celebrate."

His arm tightened around her again and his breathing changed. She heard him swallow. She relaxed into his body and his embrace.

A moment later, he asked quietly, "Are you going to sleep?"

"Maybe…?" Then her eyes popped open wide. "Oh. Do you want me to go home?"

"Jesus, no." He kissed her again and pulled her back against him. "Night, Arden. Go to sleep. Right here."

"'Kay." She relaxed again.

"Where you belong," she thought she heard him murmur as she drifted off.

CHAPTER TWENTY

"*W*hat the hell did you do?"

Arden's eyes swiveled to Mila as she marched into Jamie's living room. She, Jamie, and Tyler were waiting for Mila before heading to the supper club to watch Danny perform.

"What's up, hon?" Arden asked tentatively, taking in Mila's tense posture and flashing eyes.

"You." Mila pointed at Tyler.

Tyler's eyebrows rose and a flush spread over his cheekbones. "What?"

"You went to see Garth." Mila advanced on him. "Why did you do that?"

He lifted his chin. "Because he fucked with you, that's why."

"Argh." Mila closed her eyes briefly, her fingers curling into her palms.

Arden's gaze flicked back and forth between them. Tyler'd said he was going to have a chat with Garth, and she'd told him that wasn't a good idea, but… "What happened?" she asked quietly.

"Now he wants to get back together!" Mila planted her hands on her hips and glared at Tyler.

"Isn't that what you wanted?" He met her stare head-on.

"No! He was in love with someone else!"

"He wasn't," Tyler protested. "He realized he'd made a mistake."

"I don't care!" Mila's voice rose.

Arden jumped up and moved over to her, setting a hand on her back and rubbing. "It's okay," she whispered. "Calm down."

Mila sucked in a long breath. "He's an asshole, okay? He treated me like crap, and I don't care if he made a mistake. He thought he was in love with someone else, and that's it. We're done. And anyway, he doesn't like ladyhead, so why would I want him back?"

"Uh…" Tyler's mouth fell open and Jamie coughed.

Arden tried not to laugh. "Good point." She turned an I-told-you-so glare on Tyler, eyebrows raised.

He grimaced and rubbed a hand over his face. "Sorry, Mila. You were hurt, and I thought…I just wanted to make things better for you."

Arden felt the tension exit Mila's body, her hand still on her back.

"Shit," Mila muttered. She crossed the room and dropped into an empty chair, exhaling a long breath. "Okay, I get it. But you shouldn't have done that."

"I'm sorry." Tyler set his hand on his chest. "I had good intentions."

"You *always* have good intentions," Mila muttered. "But sometimes you need to stay out of other people's business."

Tyler's face fell.

Arden's heart softened. He did mean well. He cared about people. But yeah, he couldn't fix everything for everybody. She returned to the couch where she'd been sitting next to him, and now she set her hand on *his* back, leaning her head against his shoulder.

"Are we ready to go?" Jamie asked brightly.

"I am," Arden answered.

"Yeah." Mila stood, her mouth still in an unhappy line.

Tyler stood too and faced Mila. "We good?"

One corner of her mouth kicked up. "Yeah. We're good. You know what?"

"What?" Tyler's face relaxed.

"It kind of felt good having Garth want to get back with me. And me telling him to fuck right off."

Tyler grinned.

"This is not what I expected." Arden took in the supper club with wide eyes and a breathless smile.

"Me either," Mila said, taking a seat at the table for six she'd reserved at the Firefly Lounge and Supper Club.

"It's very upscale," Emma added, setting her small clutch purse on the table. "I'm glad we dressed up."

Tyler had to agree. Nearly every table in the elegant club was full of men in suits, women in party dresses, couples and groups of all ages. He hadn't wanted to pre-judge, but he'd kind of been expecting something tacky. The décor was sort of old Hollywood glamour, with glittery chandeliers, white table-cloths, and leopard print upholstery on all the chairs. Screens on one wall had multicolored images swirling.

"It's a prix fixe menu." Mila picked up a martini menu.

"We get a martini, a salad, and an entrée for one price. And they have, like, two hundred kinds of cocktails."

"Where's the stage?" Emma asked.

"I think they perform right here on the floor," Mila said. "Oh, this sounds good! The Firefly Martini—vodka and passion fruit purée."

"That does sound good," Emma agreed.

"Think I'll stick with a dirty martini," Liam said.

A waitress in a curve-hugging black dress arrived to take their drink orders. "The shows run every twenty minutes," she told them. "The next one starts in five minutes."

They all ordered drinks, and Jamie and Tyler decided to order coconut shrimp and calamari appetizers to share, even though that was over and above the prix fixe menu.

The place hummed with music and chatter and energy. They'd just been served their martinis when the lights dimmed and the music changed to "Danza Kuduro" by Don Omar. The crowd started clapping as shimmery curtains at the far end of the club opened and a woman stepped through them.

She was gorgeous, Tyler had to admit. A silvery, swingy skirt and a matching low-cut top barely covered slender curves and long legs, and she started dancing to the sexy Latin beat.

The crowd quieted, people turning in their seats to watch.

"Wow," said Arden next to him, eyes wide watching the sexy dance moves.

"That's Danny!" Emma clapped her hands together.

"No, it's not." Jamie frowned. "Oh wait…it is."

"Jesus." Tyler stared in amazement.

Long dark hair swung in time with the slender hips.

"I love his shoes!" Mila grabbed Arden's arm. "We have to get him to take us shoe shopping!"

Tyler choked on a laugh.

Danny, er Honey Deville, shook her hips, the silvery skirt

swinging. Tyler couldn't take his eyes off the sexy dancer, even knowing it was a guy. It was hard to believe Honey was really Danny.

Her face was made up with shiny red lips that smiled enticingly and deeply shadowed eyes with long eyelashes. And...that cleavage was incredible.

"Holy shit," Liam said, also apparently unable to look away, his gaze following Honey as she danced down the long aisle of the supper club toward them.

Tyler met Jamie's eyes and grinned.

At their table, Honey paused and gave them all a sultry smile and a wink, shaking her body, arms in the air. The girls all laughed with delight and clapped.

Honey danced on past them, swinging her hair, pausing to twerk her ass.

Tyler shook his head and rubbed his face.

"How does he move like that?" Arden asked.

The girls were grooving in their chairs to the catchy tune, watching with big smiles. Tyler glanced at Liam, taking in his dumbstruck look.

Then Honey dropped it low, and everyone in the club hooted and clapped.

Honey danced around the tables, pausing here and there to shimmy or do salsa dance steps to the immense enjoyment of the crowd. At one point, she brushed up against a man wearing a suit and a sheepish expression, then kissed his cheek. The man's companions laughed and clapped.

When Honey finished, standing back near the curtain, the room erupted into cheers and applause. She waved and disappeared.

Another entertainer appeared through the curtain, holding a microphone. "That was our very own Honey Deville!" she said, resulting in more clapping. "Isn't she amazing? Welcome to the Firefly Lounge and Supper Club! We are Chicago's top supper club featuring the city's most talented divas! I'm Candy Dish and I'm your hostess tonight! Let's go hard!"

She set down the mic and began lip syncing and dancing to Kesha's "We R Who We R." She too was gorgeous, with long blond hair and killer curves in a short sequined purple dress.

The crowd once again was totally into the music and entertainment.

Tyler shook his head, grinning, and turned to look at Arden.

She met his eyes, hers full of laughter, still chair dancing. "This is so fun!"

"I can't believe we're doing this."

She clasped his biceps in both hands and squeezed, leaning closer, and he wanted to bend his head, close the distance and kiss her. Aware of their friends around them, he didn't, though he caught Jamie's lifted eyebrows at Arden's affectionate touch.

Yeah, he was gonna have some explaining to do to his buddy later.

When that show ended, they ordered dinner. Then Danny appeared, dressed in a different outfit, this one a sequined red dress. "Hey, everyone. Thanks for coming."

"Dan—uh, Honey, you're *amazing*!" Mila cried.

Danny smiled. "Thanks."

"Honey's one of our most popular girls," the waitress said with a smile before leaving.

Danny grabbed an empty chair and pulled it up to their table. "I can join you for a few minutes before the next show."

"You are so coming shoe shopping with us," Emma said. "Also those are awesome eyelashes."

Danny laughed.

"I gotta give you credit," Jamie said. "I don't know how the hell you can even *walk* in heels like that, let alone dance."

"Practice," Danny said with a wink. He looked at Liam, who stared at him with a stony expression. "Hey, Liam. Glad you could make it."

"Yeah." Liam cleared his throat. "Uh…"

The air around them became charged as Liam and Danny locked eyes.

Tyler wasn't sure what was happening. There'd seemed to be a mutual attraction between the two guys at Shenanigans that night. Now, Liam seemed almost…angry.

"Danny," Mila whispered and leaned in closer. "Can I ask you a crazy question?"

"Sure." He dragged his gaze away from Liam to smile at Mila.

"How do you get that…" She waved a hand at his chest. "That cleavage?"

Danny grinned. "Mega pushup bra. And some creative contouring."

"Shut up! Really? You look amazing. What kind of bra?"

Tyler and Jamie exchanged another look of amused disbelief.

Their dinners arrived as another show began. Singing and dancing wasn't usually Tyler's thing, but the food and the martinis were good, and it was a fun atmosphere. The second show ended with an ensemble number of three drag queens dancing and lip syncing to "It's Raining Men."

After the second show, Emma, Arden, and Mila went to the bar for more drinks.

"Wow, this is crazy," Jamie said.

Tyler lifted his nearly empty beer glass. One martini had been enough for him. "Hey, you're the one who went on a date with Danny."

Liam's eyebrows pulled together and he glared at Jamie. "You went on a date with him?"

Jamie gave Liam a long, level look. "Dude. You know I'm straight."

Liam's forehead creased. "Yeah."

"I thought it was a date. I totally screwed up on the dating app and thought he was a chick. Turned out he's not. We had a good time, but we're just friends."

"Oh." Liam grimaced into his martini glass.

Tyler's attention shifted across the room to Arden, standing at the bar with her friends. Surrounded by men. What the fuck?

She laughed at something one of the men said as he leaned in closer. As the bartender set her drink down, the guy reached for his wallet. Arden waved him off with a smile. Clearly the dickhead was trying to buy her a drink. Jesus.

He narrowed his eyes and watched Arden pay for her martini, pick it up, and sip it, while apparently listening intently to the guy. What the fuck was he saying to her? Then Arden was talking animatedly, waving a hand, and smiling.

Tyler surged up out of his chair and stalked toward Arden, his gaze fixed on her. "Hi," he gritted out as he arrived at her side.

She smiled up at him. "Hi. Need another drink?"

The dude gave him a wary glance, no doubt sensing his displeasure.

"Yeah. And you need to get back to the table."

"Um, why?" She blinked at him.

"Because…because the next show's going to start."

She gave him a slitty-eyed look. "In ten minutes. I was just telling Brannon that we know Honey Deville."

Brannon. For fuck's sake. She knew his name.

Tyler edged closer to Arden and leveled a cold look at Brannon. "Yeah. We do. Friend of ours."

Arden sighed. "Okay, let's go back to the table. Nice to meet you, Brannon."

"You too." The dude's face wore a disappointed expression, clearly thwarted in his pick-up attempt.

"What the hell, Tyler?" Arden whispered at him as they made their way through tables.

"What?"

"I was just talking to that guy."

"He wanted to buy you a drink."

"He offered, yeah, but I said no thanks."

"He wanted more than a drink."

She stopped and turned to face him. "So?"

His hands curled into fists in frustration. He searched for the right words. "You can't...I don't..."

Her eyebrows rose, her mouth a thin line. "What?"

"I'm just looking out for you."

Her face tightened even more. "Jesus, Tyler. I was *talking* to him. That's it." She whirled around and zipped back to the table. He followed her more slowly, dropping into the chair beside her. She ignored him, talking to Jamie and Liam.

Shit.

"What's with you and Arden?"

There was a two-hour time limit on tables at the supper club on weekends, so after saying goodbye to Danny who had more shows that night, they'd moved elsewhere, a rooftop bar above a hotel near the park. The girls were all in the ladies' room, leaving Jamie, Liam, and Tyler alone at the table.

Tyler met Jamie's eyes steadily. "We went out for dinner last night."

"Shit."

Tyler hoisted his eyebrows. "That's a problem?"

Jamie rubbed his forehead. "I don't know. It's just weird. She's my big sister."

"She's two years older. Not a big deal."

"I guess not. But…her husband just died. He screwed her around, bad."

"I know."

Jamie cocked his head. "She told you about it?"

"Yeah." He sighed. "This didn't start last night. We…well, there's something there between us. I don't know what it is, right now. But…"

"I can't believe this." Jamie stared at him. "You never got over that crush on her?"

Tyler's face heated. "What crush?"

"Come on, man, you were obsessed with her back in high school."

"I was not!" That was a lie. "I mean, okay, maybe I had a little crush." He paused. "I didn't think you knew about it."

Liam grinned. "This is interesting."

"Sure, reliving my teenage humiliation is fascinating." Tyler grimaced.

"Everyone knew about it," Jamie said.

"Shut the fuck up!"

Jamie laughed. "Okay, not everyone."

Terror seized Tyler's insides in a tight grip. "Arden didn't know, did she?"

"Nah. Don't think so anyway. Honestly, I don't think she paid much attention to you," Jamie said, busting his balls with honesty.

"Thanks," Tyler muttered. "Good to know."

"Look, she told me that you'd asked her out. I thought she'd changed her mind, though, because she didn't want to mess things up with all of us if things didn't work out."

"She did change her mind. I convinced her one dinner together wasn't going to mess things up."

Jamie gave him a long look. "Well. She's an adult. I guess it's up to her."

Arden, Mila, and Emma arrived back at the table with fresh lip gloss and fluffed hair. Arden took a seat opposite him instead of next to him, lifting her chin at him.

She was still pissed.

Had she really been interested in that dude? Was that why she was pissed—because he'd interfered with her flirtation?

Fuck that.

Okay, now he was pissed too. They'd had a great dinner last night. They'd talked and laughed, and then they'd had amazing sex. Had that all been nothing to her?

They eyed each other across the table while others talked.

He'd have his chance when they got home. She couldn't get away from him there.

"Good night, Tyler."

He followed her uninvited into her apartment.

"Hey—"

"We need to talk."

She frowned and crossed her arms. "Yeah?"

"Yeah." He shut the door. "We do. Were you seriously interested in that dude…Brendan?"

"Brannon."

"Whatever."

"Maybe."

"What?" He stared at her.

"Okay, no, I wasn't. But you pissed me off, interfering like that."

Okay, that was good. She hadn't been interested in him.

"I'm sorry." He gritted his teeth and met her eyes. "Like I said, I was looking out for you."

"I don't need to be looked after. I'm a grown woman."

Right, right. He'd heard this before. How she was determined to prove she could do this adulting shit on her own. He studied her face, the firm set of her chin, the flash in her eyes. This was important to her.

He closed his eyes briefly. "I screwed up. I know you can look after yourself. I just…well, the truth is, I was jealous."

Her eyebrows rose. "Jealous."

"Yeah." He blew out a breath. "I guess I have no right to be. I mean, we went out once. So…I'm sorry."

Her face softened. "Thank you."

They eyed each other, still standing just inside the door of her apartment, the light above them creating an illuminated circle. Christ, he wanted to touch her. His palms tingled and his muscles twitched. The air around them hummed.

He didn't know who moved first, but somehow she was in his arms and his mouth was on hers. Heat exploded inside him, obliterating thought, and he crushed her to him, kissing her as deeply as he could. Her fingers slid into his hair, her soft breasts pressed against him. She tasted so goddamn good, spice and sweetness. He stroked his tongue over hers, lifting her higher against him, pressure building in his groin.

"I want you," he breathed. "Right now, yeah, but…more than that."

"Tyler. I want you too. But I can't…I can't make promises."

"Promise me I can fuck you right now."

She huffed out a laugh. "Okay. I can promise you that."

He bent his knees, picked her up, and threw her over his shoulder. She squealed and he set a hand on her ass as he carried her into her bedroom. Somewhere along the way, her shoes fell off.

He tossed her onto the bed and she bounced, her hair falling all over her face, but a smile on her lips. He knelt at the foot of the bed, hands on her ankles. "That dress is sexy as hell."

"You said that last night too."

"I did? Okay, correction. *You're* sexy as hell. Whatever you're wearing."

CHAPTER TWENTY-ONE

S ince Arden didn't have to work until later that night, they spent a leisurely morning in bed, even eating breakfast there—coffee, juice, and banana nut muffins Arden had made yesterday. She watched Tyler devour three of them, his enjoyment of them pleasing her.

"Are we celebrating anything today?" he asked with a smirk.

She grinned. "Ha. You're going to like this one."

He lifted an eyebrow, licking butter off his thumb.

"It's National Grab Some Nuts Day." And she shoved her hand under the covers.

He choked out a laugh as her hand closed over his junk. "Seriously?"

"Seriously."

It didn't take much to get him hard again, and they enjoyed another delicious round of sizzling hot sex.

A while later, Arden slid out of bed to carry their coffee mugs and plates to the kitchen. She didn't bother putting anything on. As she set the dishes on the counter above the dishwasher, Tyler followed, also naked, stretching his gorgeous body with his arms above his head.

She ogled him. She fully admitted it. She could look at him for hours…his broad shoulders, heavy biceps, and sculpted chest and abs. Even his legs were worth looking at.

Her apartment door opened, and Mila appeared.

Arden froze. Tyler dropped his arms and froze. Mila's eyes darted from naked Arden in the kitchen to naked Tyler at the island facing away from her, then shot open wide. "Oh shit."

Arden slapped both hands over her mouth, squeezing her arms together over her breasts. For some reason, she just wanted to laugh. The expressions on both Tyler's and Mila's faces were comical.

"I'll go! Sorry!" Mila backed out and slammed the door shut.

Tyler's eyes were closed. "Tell me that didn't just happen."

"It happened."

"Jesus."

Arden did laugh now. "It's not the end of the world. She got a view of your world-class ass, that's all."

"You think my ass is world-class?"

"Without a doubt." She moved closer, leaned across the island, and kissed him. "She knows we're sleeping together."

He opened his eyes and stared into hers, his blazing hot. "Yeah?"

"Yeah."

"I talked to Jamie last night. About us."

"You did?"

He nodded. "He's not sure about us, but he says you're an adult."

"Okay. Well. I guess it's out there, then."

Tyler nodded. "Probably also time for all of us to make a

rule about walking into one another's apartments unannounced."

She winced. "I guess so."

Rather than upsetting her, the fact that Jamie and Mila both knew what was going on between her and Tyler actually felt like a relief. Even though she wasn't exactly sure herself what was going on between them.

They went to the farmers' market again, and Arden paused to talk to more of the vendors, getting business cards and telling them about the breakfast meeting she was catering and that she was including some of their products. She got into a lengthy chat with a young woman who made specialty mustards using locally sourced ingredients, not sure if she could use mustard in any of her breakfast plans, but hoping she could somehow support the business. She smiled when Tyler ended up buying a jar of the beer chipotle mustard.

They stopped for lunch on the way home at a small café with an outdoor patio, then returned to their separate apartments to unpack their purchases. Although the flowers Tyler bought ended up in her place again. She arranged them in a vase with a smile and a fizzy, warm feeling in her chest.

Tyler walked in a while later, now dressed in a pair of ripped, faded jeans and an old T-shirt she recognized as one of his work shirts. "What are you working on today?" she asked him.

"Hoping to finish up the drywall."

It was a slow process, with letting the mud dry and sanding it, then repeating it. She was seeing what a perfectionist Tyler was when it came to the work he did.

"Here. I picked up this for you today."

She took the small jar from him with a faint frown. "What is it?"

"Lavender and lemon balm. You rub it on your temples when you go to bed, and it supposedly helps you sleep better."

She gazed at the product with hot eyes, that fizzy feeling in her chest intensifying. She hadn't noticed him pick this up, and it was so thoughtful it almost made her cry. She blinked a few times. "Thank you. I'll definitely try it."

She had no trouble sleeping when Tyler was in bed with her. Other than the fact that all the sex interfered with her sleep. Though it made her feel so good, and so relaxed, she slept like crazy afterward, so it seemed like a worthwhile trade-off. Other nights, even though the nightmares had diminished, she still spent too much time ruminating. Worries that she could set aside during the day—like how to make more money, how to afford to pay Jamie rent, what to do with her life—consumed her when lying in bed at night. But it was getting better. She felt herself settling in to her new life and most of the time felt optimistic that things would all work out.

"Next week, we need to find a day to take you to Home Depot," he said. "We're just about ready to tile and paint. And we need to pick out fixtures. Jamie'll come too, since he's paying the bill."

"Okay. Good. I'm off Thursday again."

"Mmm...yeah, that'll work for me. Maybe we can convince Jamie to play hooky from work to come with us during the day."

She puttered around her kitchen, cleaning and whipping up a coffee cake that filled the apartment with a delicious cinnamon scent. While that was baking, she ran down to Mila's apartment.

Mila was in her spare bedroom practicing some moves on the pole.

"You're getting so much better!" Arden said.

"Thanks." Mila released the pole and straightened. "So. Sorry about earlier."

"Don't worry." One corner of Arden's mouth lifted. "That wasn't as mortifying as the day I met Tyler."

She'd told Mila and Emma the story one night over wine.

Mila grinned. "Not sure if Tyler would agree. And don't take this the wrong way, but he has a great ass. Couldn't help but notice."

"I can't blame you. I agree." She grinned.

"So…you two are…?" Mila waved a hand.

"I don't know what we are. Obviously we're sleeping together. We went out for dinner the other night. Today he took me to the market and bought me flowers, and he b-bought me…" She stumbled. "Lavender lemon balm to help me sleep." Her bottom lip quivered.

"You know he's a keeper," Mila said quietly.

"I know." She met her friend's eyes. "And it terrifies me."

"Why? What are you afraid of?" Mila's face softened.

"I'm afraid…oh God." Arden tipped her head back. "I'm afraid I'll lose myself again. Like I did with Michael. I'm not sure I've even *found* myself again. And then what happens if…if…"

"If things don't work out?"

She nodded, misery lodging like a rock in her stomach. "Yes. What if I'm so self-centered I can't really have a relationship?"

Mila's jaw dropped. "What?"

Arden twisted her fingers together. "I'm afraid…" She stopped.

"What?"

"I was too busy being a pampered princess to realize my marriage was in trouble. I'm afraid I'm not good at relationships."

"I don't think that's true. I wish I were smart about shit like this, but I can't even figure out my own love life. But I don't think you're too self-centered for a relationship. You *care* about people, Arden."

Arden pressed her lips together, her throat aching. "I also came here to find myself. To figure out who I am and what I want from life. And if I get involved with someone right away, maybe I never will."

"I understand."

"Tyler and I had a fight last night. Because he butted in when I was talking to that guy at the supper club. He was jealous."

Mila's lips quirked. "Wow."

"It annoyed me. But he made me talk about it, and he apologized."

"That's worth a lot."

"Yeah. But he does that stuff all the time. He's a little over-protective."

"You know why, though, right?"

"I do. I get it."

"And it's because he cares too."

Arden puffed out a breath. "I know. But it's one more reason I feel like I could lose myself. I want to make my own decisions. About where I work and how I get home and who I talk to."

"I get it."

Arden sucked in a breath. "Okay. I'm just going to try to live in the moment. Enjoy whatever this is and not drive myself crazy trying to analyze it and name it."

"Sounds like a good plan for now. And for what it's worth… you two are awfully cute together."

Arden wrinkled her nose. "Cute?"

"Yeah." Mila grinned.

"Really?"

"Really. I could tell from the first day you were here that he has a thing for you. Watches you all the time. Does nice things for you. Gives you multiple orgasms."

Arden gave a strangled laugh. "Right."

"I'm serious. And you've admitted you like him too. And you like his hot body."

"I do." She sighed. She squeezed her eyes closed briefly. "This is crazy."

"Love *is* crazy."

"We're not in love!"

Mila lifted her eyebrows into skeptical arches.

Arden's head went spinny and she slumped against the doorjamb. "We aren't. We can't be. I hardly know him."

"You've known him for years."

"Yeah, but not really…we were kids." She drew in a shaky breath then bolted straight up. "Oh! I have to go get my coffee cake out of the oven."

"Coffee cake?"

"Yes. Want to come for breakfast in the morning? Tyler works tomorrow, so no worries about walking in on us again."

Mila laughed. "Sounds good. I'll tell Jamie too."

"Great."

She ran back upstairs, her mind churning.

Mila thought they were cute together. She thought Tyler had a thing for her.

Could this really be happening?

Tyler was working in the bathroom, his phone playing Journey's "Don't Stop Believin'" loud enough that he probably didn't hear her. She checked her coffee cake, her hands shaking a little as she pushed a wooden pick into the batter. Yep, it was done. She pulled it out of the oven and set it on a rack.

She laid her hands on her cheeks and stared across the apartment.

All kinds of feelings swirled inside her. Yes, she liked being with Tyler. A lot. And not just for the orgasms, although they were remarkable. She also liked giving *him* orgasms. She liked laughing with him. Going to the farmers' market. Walking home from work and telling him how her day had been. Hearing about his job.

She thought about him a lot. She missed him the days he was at work, and looked forward to seeing him. More than she probably should.

She checked the time. She had to get ready for work.

She walked down the hall toward the bathroom, peering through the plastic curtain Tyler had taped around the door. Once again, he'd taken off his shirt, and while she couldn't see him clearly, she could make out the shift and bulge of muscles as he sanded the drywall. He glanced over and saw her and stopped.

He moved over and pulled the plastic aside. His hair was snowy with drywall dust, some even on his eyelashes and cheeks. "Hey." He grinned at her.

"Hey. How's it going?"

"Good."

"I made a coffee cake. Help yourself to some when you want a break. I'm going to work now."

"Okay. See you later." He leaned over and smooched her mouth, and she continued into her bedroom to change with fingertips pressed to her lips.

Shenanigans was busy that night. Liam seemed distracted and

grumpy. She was at the bar when he knocked a glass off that shattered on the floor.

"Jaysus suffering fuck," he yelled.

"Chill, Liam," she said calmly. "It's just a glass."

He grumbled as he retrieved the broom and began to sweep up the pieces.

"What's wrong with you tonight?" she asked, patiently waiting for a round of drinks.

"Nothing's wrong with me tonight," he snapped. "I'm totally boxed off."

"Well, I have no idea what that means, but I beg to differ." Although he was her boss, they'd become friends too. "Did you drink too much last night? Geez, you've had a whole day to recover."

Now that she thought about it, he'd been kind of quiet last night too, after they'd left the supper club. She'd been all wrapped up in her anger at Tyler for being such a jerk, but thinking back, Liam hadn't exactly been the life of the party. In fact, he'd sat there staring into a glass of Jameson the rest of the evening.

"I didn't drink *enough* last night," he muttered, disposing of the broken glass into the trash.

"You didn't enjoy the show?" She followed him down the bar. "I thought it was so fun."

"Sure. Fun."

She eyed him. "Mmmkay. If you say so. Still need the gimlet, the mai tai, and two Guinness."

"Coming right the feck up."

When the pub finally closed, Arden was happy about the large bundle of bills she stuffed into her purse. Tips had been great all evening. She was even getting more used to being on her feet.

Tyler hadn't shown up at the bar, as he usually did when he

wasn't working. She stepped out into the cool night air. Clouds covered the sky and the wind had picked up, tossing tree branches. She looked around for Tyler's truck, thinking he might be parked outside waiting. But he wasn't there.

She frowned a little, shrugged, and started walking. The air felt like rain was coming. Maybe a thunderstorm? Tyler would like that.

If he was home.

Maybe he'd gone out somewhere with other friends. He did get together sometimes with coworkers, like their baseball games or going out for beers.

She turned down the side street and trudged along the side-walk. A man walked toward her, shadowy in the darkness. Was Tyler coming to meet her? But no…she could tell from the man's gait and size it wasn't Tyler. The street was deserted otherwise. She tightened her grip on her purse, aware of the sizeable amount of cash she was carrying. Her gaze darted around, and she debated crossing to the other side of the street as she and the man neared each other.

It was fine. Just a guy in the neighborhood. She'd walked home alone numerous times the nights that Tyler was working.

The man passed by her without incident and she let out her breath. Geez. She was the one who kept telling Tyler she was a grown woman and could look after herself. Why was she so fearful?

Because she wasn't stupid. She could talk all she wanted about being a grown woman responsible for herself, but she knew shit happened, and part of being a grown woman was making sure she didn't get herself into foolish situations.

Maybe part of being an independent woman was taking some kind of self-defense course. It wouldn't hurt. And she didn't want to rely on Tyler or anyone to look after her. She'd check into that tomorrow.

She quickened her steps the last few blocks to home, letting herself into the wrought iron gate with relief.

Inside the building, she paused outside her apartment door. Light gleamed beneath Tyler's door and she heard the faint sounds of a TV show. Why hadn't he come to get her? Was he alone?

Why did she care? Straightening her shoulders, she let herself into her apartment and quietly closed the door. She dropped her keys into the basket on the kitchen counter, ran a glass of water and drank it, then dragged her weary butt down the hall to fall into bed.

Thursday's shopping trip was a success. Arden enjoyed helping pick out the new toilet, tub, shower, and vanity, along with taps, faucets, and the shower attachment. She pored over tile samples, paint chips, and options for the vanity top—marble, granite, tile. Neither Jamie nor Tyler seemed to care that much about the choices, tapping their fingers as she deliberated, shrugging when she debated shaker gray versus gray pinstripe.

"I'd go with white and white," Jamie said.

Arden shook her head. Clearly, Mila must have had a hand in the décor of the other apartments.

She ended up picking out hexagon-shaped floor tiles similar to Tyler's except a more speckled gray color, white subway tiles for the walls, and a deep gray paint color.

That was the fun stuff. Then she had to cool her heels while they picked up grout and underlay and other boring stuff she didn't know anything about.

Eventually they left with Tyler's truck loaded up and Jamie's credit card smoking as he tucked it back into his wallet. Ha.

Luckily her second bedroom was mostly empty and they

could store things in there. She helped carry as much as she could, but Jamie and Tyler had to deal with the heavier items.

"This is so exciting!" she said when they were done and Jamie had left. "I can't wait to see it."

"Still gonna be a while," Tyler cautioned her. "Remember this is a part-time gig for me."

"I know. Don't worry, I can be patient. By the way, can I use your bathroom to get ready to go out tonight?"

"Of course. Where are you going?"

"It's our girls' night out. Remember? We're going to take Mila out to a club to dance and flirt with guys and get drunk now she's single again."

"Oh, right."

She waited for him to say more, remembering that he hadn't been thrilled when she'd talked about going out and flirting with guys.

He slid a hand around the back of her neck, leaned in, and kissed her forehead. "You have fun. I'm gonna go see what Jamie's doing for dinner."

He left and she heard his footsteps thudding down the stairs.

She stared at the open door. Huh.

Slowly, she gathered up what she needed to get ready and headed across to Tyler's apartment. As she twirled some waves in her hair with the flat iron and redid her makeup, she thought about last night…about how Tyler hadn't come to pick her up after work even though he could have. How they hadn't spent the night together. And how he didn't mind at all that she was going out with Mila and Emma tonight.

Was he losing interest in her?

Her insides squeezed uncomfortably.

Just when she was getting used to the idea that she and Tyler might be able to do this…might be able to have something…maybe it didn't really mean as much to him as she'd thought. Maybe she was the one who was getting all caught up in romantic ideas about falling in love when all he wanted was convenient, across-the-hall sex.

She had to guard her heart, or she was going to end up broken again.

CHAPTER TWENTY-TWO

"Ugh." Emma lowered her phone with a grimace. "That dude I went out with last week just sent me a dick pic."

"Let me see." Mila attempted to grab Emma's phone, but missed. No doubt the result of the many pomegranate margaritas she'd consumed.

Arden shook her head, the three of them standing at the bar at Prophecy, a hot dance club on West Hubbard. Music pumped around them, the dance floor a mass of shifting bodies, the lights changing from red to blue to purple. "Why do guys do that?"

"No idea." Mila now had Emma's phone and studied the picture. "What I want to know is why unsolicited dick pics aren't called junk mail."

Emma and Arden burst out laughing.

Mila was swiping away at Emma's phone, her forehead furrowed in concentration.

"What are you doing?" Emma asked. "You're not replying to him, are you?"

"Yep." Mila's grin held a hint of evil. "Hang on." She gave one final tap to the screen and handed it back to Emma.

Emma's eyes widened. "Oh my God!" Then she collapsed against the bar, laughing.

Arden reached out for the phone to see what Mila had done. She saw the reply to the junk mail—a picture of an obscenely huge penis. "Aaaah! Where did you get that?"

"I just searched in your browser and saved it. Gimmee." She wiggled her fingers.

Emma handed the phone back.

The reply from the dude came quickly. *WTF?*

Grinning, Mila sent another message, then held the phone up to show the second picture she'd sent. Arden and Emma winced, but Arden had to smile.

Nasty! Was the reply. *Why? I was nice!*

Mila tapped in a response. *If sending dick pics is nice, I'm being nice too.* She quickly sent three more pictures.

STOP. Just leave me alone.

Arden's abs hurt from laughing.

"There. He won't bother you again." Mila handed the phone back.

"Um, Mila?" Emma lifted an eyebrow.

"Yeah?"

"What if I liked that guy?"

Mila stared at Emma, her mouth open. "No!"

"Kidding!" Emma collapsed into giggles.

"Oh, you bitch. You scared the shit out of me for a second there." Mila grabbed Emma and hugged her. "Well, that was the most fun I've had all night."

"You're not having fun with us?" Arden stared at her in dismay.

"Of course I am. And the dancing was fun. But I thought I

was going to pick up some random guy for hot meaningless sex. And nobody's interested."

"That's not true. You're the one who's not interested." A couple of guys had tried to talk to Mila and asked her dance, and she'd rebuffed them all.

"I'm not good at this." Mila set her elbow on the bar and rested her head on her hand. "I don't know how to have meaningless sex. I've spent my whole life looking for a boyfriend."

"You'll find another boyfriend," Emma said.

"I don't want another boyfriend. I'm done with relationships. I give up on that. I'm taking it off my checklist."

Arden and Emma exchanged glances.

"Okay," Arden said. "Then you're going to have to be open to sleeping with guys who approach you."

"I can't sleep with just anyone. There has to be *some* attraction there."

Arden swallowed a sigh, because she understood Mila only too well. She wasn't interested in any of the men who'd flirted with her either. Because she kept thinking of Tyler. And wouldn't you know it, on a night when she had zero interest in hooking up, she'd been approached by one man after another. "I'm with you," she said. "No relationships. Just hot sex."

"Yeah, but you've got Tyler for that. I've got no one."

Okay maybe getting Mila drunk hadn't been such a good idea. She seemed to be sliding into depression, when the whole point of the evening was supposed to be to cheer her up with a little fun and flirting. "We should have gone to a comedy club."

"The Punch Line's not far from here," Emma said.

"Let's do it. We can still catch a late show." Mila nodded eagerly.

"Really? That's what you'd rather do?"

"Actually, I'd rather go home to bed."

"That's not happening," Arden said firmly. "Fine. Let's go listen to some jokes."

"I was so ready for sex tonight," Mila grumbled, out on the sidewalk as they headed down West Hubbard toward LaSalle. "I even took some of that stuff. Honey Pot."

"What?" Arden and Emma said together, heads whipping around to stare at Mila walking between them. "What is honey pot? Some kind of marijuana?"

"No!" Mila laughed. "Honey Pot. It's a supplement that gives your, um, secretions a fruity taste and a nice smell."

"You have got to be kidding me." Arden's jaw slackened.

"Why?" Emma demanded.

Mila shrugged, and to Arden's horror, a tear trickled out of her eye and tracked down her cheek. "Garth didn't like going down on me."

"You think it was because…of how you taste?" Emma asked, her tone laced with disbelief.

"He sort of implied that." Mila swiped at her face.

"Sweet Jesus in the lap of Mary. Change of plans." Emma stopped walking.

"What?" Arden and Mila came to a halt too.

"We're going to Garth's place, and the three of us are going to beat the ever-loving shit out of that motherfucker." Emma's jaw set.

"Much as I love the idea…no." Arden linked arms with Mila and started walking again.

"I want to," Emma muttered. "Jesus Christ."

"I hear you," Arden said. "Mila, you have to know that was *his* problem, not yours."

"It made me self-conscious," Mila said in an uncharacteristically small voice.

Arden's heart squeezed. "He's a douchenoggin." Of course, now she *had* to think about Tyler going down on her…how into it he'd been, how he'd told her he loved her taste, her smell, how he'd lingered there and made sure she came. God. Gratitude and appreciation swelled inside her. And a little heat gathered in her core, remembering how good it had been…

"Women are scared of their vaginas," Emma announced.

Arden nodded. "I think that's true. A while back I read about vaginal bleaching. Oh my God."

"Women are even having surgery to look better down there! Labiaplasty!"

"It's because of porn. Now not only do we need perfect breasts and a perfect ass, we need a perfect lady garden."

Mila snorted with laughter. "Lady garden! Ha! Also, guys apparently aren't at all worried about their junk. As evidenced by the dick pics."

"See, that's true!" Arden nodded. "And it probably has something to do with the fact that women still feel ashamed of being sexual."

"I'm not ashamed," Mila protested.

"Maybe it's a subconscious thing," Emma offered. "There still is a double standard for men and women when it comes to sex."

"The vagina is something we should be proud of," Arden said. "It gives us so much pleasure, on top of the miracle of procreation. It's…it's the essence of our femininity."

"Right?" Mila nodded.

"Women's bodies are amazing!" Emma said.

"Let's love our vaginas!" Mila shouted, attracting the attention of a group of people passing them on the sidewalk, three men and two women.

"Yeah!" One of the women in the group stopped to high-five them. "Love your vaginas, ladies!"

"I'm enthusiastically pro-vagina!" one of the men declared.

Amid laughter, they all cheered on vaginas, including the

men, then Arden, Mila, and Emma continued on to the comedy club.

~

"Where's my whisk? I can't find my whisk. Jesus, who took my goddamn whisk?"

Tyler wrapped his arms around Arden from behind in her small kitchen. "Shhh. Nobody took your whisk. What's going on?"

It was the night before the breakfast she was catering for Jamie, and she was bouncing around her kitchen like she was the ball in a pinball machine.

"I can't find my whisk! How the hell am I supposed to make the eggs without a whisk?"

"We'll find it." He released her and calmly opened the drawer where she kept her utensils. Moving aside a few spatulas, he located the whisk and handed it to her.

She dropped her head forward. "Thank you."

"C'mere." He pulled her into his arms again and pressed her face to his shoulder. "You okay?"

"Yes. No. I'm a mess. I'm freaking out."

"It's going to be fine."

"I'm terrified. Something's going to go wrong. I'm going to be totally humiliated and I'll embarrass Jamie and his whole company." Her voice quivered as she talked.

Tyler rubbed slow circles on her back. "You have a plan," he reminded her.

"I know."

"What's left to do? Can I help?"

"The list is on the counter." She gestured vaguely, not lifting her head. "I'm so nervous!"

"I know. It's okay. Nervous is good. We get nervous every

time we go into a fire. You have to use that energy the right way."

"I don't know how to do that."

"Sure you do. Let's go through your plan."

"I probably forgot ten things." She drew back and faced him.

"Probably not. But let's see."

The next morning, Arden's alarm went off for a painfully early wake-up call. Bleary-eyed and foggy-headed, she didn't bother getting dressed, stumbling out to her kitchen to start coffee. That was the first thing.

As it brewed, she tied her unbrushed hair back in a pony-tail, then got to work on the food. She'd done as much as she could the night before, but some things had to wait until morning.

Her kitchen was bursting with food, her fridge barely big enough to hold everything, her counters covered with platters of wrapped baked goods.

She gulped coffee as she worked, packing things into big insulated bags. Luckily, Jamie had given her a deposit, which had enabled her to purchase some supplies and the food without depleting her meager savings. She'd protested the deposit, but he'd convinced her by telling her most businesses wouldn't do anything without some kind of deposit. What if she went out and bought a bunch of things and then he cancelled on her? She needed something to protect herself.

Not that she was running a business, but that was true.

She leaned against the counter with her coffee mug in hand, surveying things. Okay. Time to get herself ready. She needed to look professional when she took this all into Jamie's office.

Her apartment door opened and Tyler appeared.

Her jaw dropped at seeing him.

He was dressed in his work uniform—navy pants and a crisp, short-sleeved navy shirt.

Why had she never seen him in uniform before?

Sweet baby Jesus, he was gorgeous at the best of times, but now looking all authoritative and confident, he was panty melt-ingly hot.

"Hey. How's it going? Need any more help?"

Holding her mug in two hands, she stared at him as he walked toward her.

"Are you okay, babe?" He brushed a strand of hair off her face.

She tried to gather her thoughts and ignore the clenching of her inner muscles. "Fine," she croaked.

His gaze dropped and lingered on her breasts. She was still wearing the ribbed tank top and cheeky panties she'd slept in, and her nipples were doing their best to push through the cotton. His eyes darkened. "Jesus," he muttered. "You better not be going out like that."

She snorted softly, liking that she had an effect on him, because he had just destroyed some of her brain cells. "Nope. I was about to go get ready."

"Did you do this?" He held up the banana she hadn't noticed he was carrying, a smirk on his lips.

She grinned. "Yeah." The other day, she'd taken a black Sharpie and printed on the banana: *You put this banana to shame.*

He shook his head, still smirking. "You're nuts."

"Maybe so."

"Want me to carry some of this stuff down?"

"That's okay. I don't want to make you late for work."

He took the mug from her hands and gulped down some of her coffee. "Sure?"

"I'm sure."

He eyed her as if he wanted to argue, but he didn't. He swallowed another mouthful of coffee and handed the mug back. He leaned in to kiss her forehead. "Good luck, Arden. It'll be great. See you tomorrow."

Last night he'd totally busted her for being a nervous wreck. He'd calmly talked her down, making her go through her preparations to reassure herself that she'd thought of everything and had a solid plan.

In her bedroom, she paused. Seeing him dressed in his uniform made her anxieties about this job seem trivial. He was about to go to work, where he could be called out at any time to a dangerous situation, a situation where he wouldn't hesitate to put his own life on the line to save someone else.

The uniform was sexy because it was a symbol of the courage and integrity Tyler possessed...his commitment to his career, his valor and strength. He was a superhero.

And she was serving people breakfast.

She wasn't demeaning herself. All kinds of work were important. And she was proud of what she was doing. But it did help put things in perspective. What was the worst thing that could go wrong, for heaven's sake?

Well, she could kill someone with food poisoning...

No! She was not going to think like that.

She tugged her tank top off over her head and tossed it onto the bed, then shimmied out of her panties, smiling. It was all going to be fine.

She dressed in narrow black pants and a white shirt, similar to what she wore to work at Shenanigans. It was boring, but she wasn't being judged on her fashion sense for this job.

It took several trips to load everything into Jamie's car, and she had to crank the air conditioning up full blast as she drove to his office building to cool the perspiration that dampened her skin. Luckily she'd pulled her hair up into a bun.

It was a bit of a drive to the building where Jamie's offices were, off South Michigan and Van Buren. She had to make one stop on the way there, and that was at Screamin' Beans, the micro-roaster she'd discovered at the farmers' market. They imported fair trade coffee beans, roasted them in small batches, and ground them, and she wanted to show off the local business's delicious coffee.

She texted Jamie when she parked in the loading zone, and he and a few other people came down to help her carry the food and beverages up to the meeting room. The building was old, with scarred hardwood floors and exposed ducts in the ceiling, but had newly renovated offices with lots of glass and dark metal, and funky furnishings. The meeting room was bright and airy, with a wooden trestle table and black leather chairs, trendy suspended lights and big framed black-and-white photographs of Chicago architecture on the old brick wall. A credenza along another wall was ready for her to set up.

"Hey, Arden." Mila appeared. "This looks great!"

"Thanks."

"Jamie," Mila said. "We need to talk. BMN is on the phone again."

Jamie scowled. "Again? Jesus."

Arden's eyebrows rose.

"They're persistent," Mila said. "I think you need to meet with them."

"I'm not interested," Jamie said. "We've talked about this."

"You haven't heard their pitch."

Arden had no idea who BMN was and what they were pitching, but this was obviously a source of tension between Jamie and Mila. Come to think of it, Jamie had seemed stressed lately, which was unusual. Was he having some kind of problem with the business?

Jamie blew out a breath and shoved a hand into his dark curls. "Fine, let me talk to them."

He and Mila disappeared out of the meeting room.

"What can I do to help?" Jamie's assistant Destiny asked.

Happy to have extra hands, Arden gave Destiny directions about unwrapping and setting out food, coffee, and juices.

"This looks fantastic," Destiny said as she helped. "And smells great too. I'm dying here."

"Take a muffin," Arden urged her. "Or whatever. There are lots."

"Thank you." Destiny's heartfelt gratitude amused Arden.

Jamie strolled back in looking at his phone. "All set?"

"Yep. I'll come back at ten to clean up."

He lifted his head and sniffed the air. "Smells good. And looks good too."

She smiled. She was proud of her presentation. Jamie had said it was fine to use disposable plates and cups, but she'd scouted out some really nice ones in black and white to match the StatTrakker logo, and she matched serving platters, chafing dishes, and utensils to them. Not required, but she'd also included a small black vase with a few stems of white phalaenopsis orchids at one end of the table.

It did look nice.

Now, she had a little over two hours to kill. She could go all the way back home. Or maybe do a little sightseeing, since she was so close to Millennium Park and some shops…not that she could afford to shop.

Hell. She was pretty sure there was a DSW nearby. She could at least *look* at some shoes…

～

"This so outclassed any other caterer we've ever used."

Arden smiled at Destiny a couple of hours later, back to pick up the things she needed to keep and clean up, although Destiny had pretty much taken care of that. "Thanks."

"People were raving about the food," Jamie confirmed, strolling into the meeting room. "You did good, sis."

She beamed. "I'm so glad. And relieved."

"And people loved that it's mostly local, sustainably grown food," Destiny added. "That's an excellent branding strategy, especially for this demographic."

Arden felt like she'd grown an inch taller. "Thanks!"

"You're good at it," Jamie added. "You love shit like this."

Shit like this. She grinned. "Thank you. I do love it."

"You should have had business cards." Destiny added the last of the leftover plates to a stack. "People were asking."

Arden's mouth dropped open. "Really? Shit. I never thought of that."

"Really. I took their names and email addresses and said I'd send them your information. So, give me your email address and phone number and I'll pass it on."

"Oh my God. I can't believe that." She pressed her hands to her face. Would this really lead to more business? And if it did, could she even do that? It had been a big undertaking, and her little kitchen wasn't really equipped for much more.

She gave Destiny the information to pass on nonetheless. If something came of it, she'd deal with it. Probably she'd never hear anything.

She carried the chafing dishes and leftover supplies home, made an attempt to clean up the disaster in her kitchen, then got ready for work.

"Hello, Arden darling," Liam greeted her when she walked into Shenanigans. His mood seemed to have recovered since their outing to the Firefly Supper Club. "How did your breakfast go?"

"It went great!" She filled him in on it, and shared the feedback she'd gotten from Destiny. "I don't know how I'd manage much more than breakfast or maybe a cocktail party with my small kitchen. But I'm sure nothing will come of it anyway."

"You could use the kitchen here."

She blinked at him. "What? Really?"

"Sure." He hitched one broad shoulder. "The only times we're really busy is lunch and dinner. In between, things are quiet, and the kitchen's bigger than what we need for the size of this place anyway."

Wow. That would…solve a lot of problems. Refrigerator space. Counter space. Ovens.

But still. She shook her head. She'd done one favor for her brother, and yeah, it had gone well, but nobody else was going to call her.

What if…what if she actually sought out jobs like that, though? Small catering jobs. Not big dinners or fancy parties. Business breakfasts or lunches. Cocktail parties. There were all kinds of things…

Excitement curled in her belly at the thought.

"Better look after table two," Sorcha said, passing by with a tray full of food.

Right. She had a job to do. She'd daydream about possibilities later.

CHAPTER TWENTY-THREE

"*J* love my vagina."

Tyler choked. Arden rubbed up against him, both of them naked in his bed. "Um, good. I love it too."

"I believe you."

"Why wouldn't you believe it?"

"Some guys are assholes. Like Garth."

Garth? What the fuck? What did Garth have to do with... "Okay, just stop right there. Wherever this is going, I don't want to hear it."

Arden smiled. "I just want you to know that I appreciate your appreciation of my vagina."

"Babe. I more than appreciate it." He flipped her onto her back and moved over her. He met her eyes. "I worship your vagina."

Her lips parted and her eyes darkened. "Oh."

"I'm not that crazy about the word vagina, though." He started kissing his way down between her breasts. "Too clinical. I like—"

"I know what you like."

He snorted out a laugh, now kissing her lower abdomen. Her breathing had shifted. "Let me show you how much I like it."

"Just so you know…that's not why I said that…" Her fingers slid into his hair.

"No?" He spread her thighs with his hands and kissed the inside of one.

"If I wanted you to lick me, I'd just ask." Her voice had gone low and smoky. "But if you want to show me…I'm fine with that…"

"Wanna come over tonight and watch a movie?"

"I…can't."

Tyler was finishing the work on the fireplace in Arden's apartment, wiping his hand on a rag. "Oh."

"I'm going to a book club meeting. I think." She caught her bottom lip between her teeth.

"What do you mean, you think?"

"I'm nervous. I don't know any of these women. Other than Imani, who did my hair."

"Well, you don't have to go."

"I want to."

He bit back a smile. "But you're nervous."

"Just a little. But Imani was really nice, and we like the same kinds of books, and I want to make new friends, so I want to go."

"Want me to drive you there? And I can pick you up after. Just call me."

She worried her poor pretty bottom lip again. "Would you do that?"

"Of course." He slid a hand around the back of her neck—

thankfully a clean hand now—and kissed her forehead. "I'm sure it'll be fun. What book are you reading?"

"It's called *Love Shop* by Meg Masters. I really enjoyed it."

"See, you've read the book, it'll be fine. And I bet they drink wine."

She laughed. "Yes, Imani promised me there'd be wine."

"What time?"

"It starts at seven." She showed him the address on her phone.

"That's not far from here. Just knock when you're ready to go. I'm going to go shower."

"Okay." She grabbed his arm as he moved away and he looked into her eyes. "Thank you."

"I got another job!"

Tyler looked up from his phone, a smile breaking out on his face. "No shit?"

"No shit!" Arden bounded across his apartment to stand in front of him, holding her own phone. "Just now! One of the men at Jamie's meeting loved the food, and he wants me to cater a meeting for his business!"

"That's fantastic, babe." He set down his phone and stood, wrapping her in a hug big enough to lift her off her feet. This was fantastic news.

She laughed breathlessly. "I can't believe it!"

"I'm not surprised." He smooched her mouth. "You're amazing."

"No, I'm not." But she grinned.

"Okay, let's make a plan. Sit down."

She blinked as he released her. "Um, what?"

He reached for his laptop sitting on the kitchen counter.

"We'll make a plan. The menu. The shopping list. I'll take you shopping to get what you need. When is this? Jeez, I hope it's not a day I work again."

She covered his hands with hers, stopping him from typing on the keyboard. "Whoa."

"What?" He looked up at her. "You know, we should really sit down and do a whole business plan for you."

"Wait. This is *my* job."

His eyebrows pulled down. "I know."

She slowly moved her head from side to side. "You don't have to jump in and do everything for me. I can handle it."

"I know you can."

"Okay, then."

"But—"

"Tyler. I don't help you fight fires."

He rolled his eyes. "Not the same. Come on, I'm just trying to help."

"I need to do this on my own."

He fell silent. He remembered their argument that night at the supper club when he'd been er, jealous, of that other guy and she'd been upset because she could take care of herself. He *knew* she could take care of herself. Yeah, he wanted to look after her, but...hell. She needed to do this on her own, like she said.

He smiled wryly. "Okay. But if you need help, ask. There's nothing wrong with that."

She beamed a relieved smile at him that told him he was doing the right thing. "Okay."

"Guns versus hoses."

Arden's forehead furrowed, then cleared as she laughed. "Oh my God. Seriously?"

Tyler grinned. "Yeah. We play each other every year. Firefighters versus police. Guns versus hoses."

They were on their way to his baseball game. He pulled into the parking lot near the baseball diamond, and they both jumped out. From the back of his truck, he grabbed the duffel bag holding bats and balls, then led the way to the diamond.

Because she didn't know anyone there, he took her around and introduced her to the guys (and a couple of women firefighters) already there, who in turn introduced her to their partners who were there to watch the annual event. Everyone was friendly to her, and Arden was soon seated in the bleachers, chatting away.

He greeted his friend Dody, who was one of his partners in FPCF (Firefighters and Policy Charity Foundation), and some of the cops he knew from previous years with some good-natured trash talk about the game.

It was a beautiful evening, the cool air holding hints of autumn.

It was cool having Arden there watching. It made him want to show off a bit. He hadn't been a bad ballplayer back in high school, and he'd kept playing since, so when it was his first time to bat, he readied his stance and focused on the pitcher for the "Guns" team. The ball whizzed toward him and he swung. The bat met the speeding ball with a satisfying crack, sending it soaring into the clear blue sky. He dropped the bat and sprinted to first, keeping an eye on the ball as the outfielders ran for it... but it was over the fence. Yeah! He pumped a fist in the air and jogged the rest of the bases, arriving at home plate to high fives from his teammates.

Good start to the game.

He caught Arden's beaming smile and vigorous clapping, and he inhaled a long, satisfied breath.

She was so pretty. The low sunlight gleamed on her long dark hair, and her smile flashed. She leaned over to listen to something Tremon's wife said to her, nodding her agreement. Then she caught him looking at her and waved.

He couldn't stop the big grin that tugged at his mouth. Yeah. He liked having her there.

Over the last couple of months, she'd helped him paint her apartment, and she'd made him laugh when she'd swiped her paintbrush on his nose, so he'd had to retaliate, which had turned into an attempt to cover each other in as much paint as possible, followed by a shower together to get it all off. They'd shopped together, cooked together, eaten together, shared a bunch of fun times with their friends together.

He knew she was scared about getting too involved. He got it. He'd been trying so hard not to push things…to let her make her own decisions and lead her life. He'd stopped showing up at Shenanigans every night, because he knew how important it was to her to be independent, even though he worried about her. He didn't flip out when she went out with the girls, for the same reason, even though he wanted to be there and make sure no assholes said anything offensive or tried anything handsy.

Something had grown between them, something big and powerful, also intimate and beautiful. His crush had deepened, and as he got to know her better, as they became closer and closer both sexually and platonically, and he learned more about her, he was falling for her. Hard.

And it was getting harder and harder not to tell her how he felt.

Playing second base, he made a nice catch to tag one of the "Guns" out and quickly threw the ball to first, so Tremon had Dody out. Three out and they were up to bat again.

It was a close game, ending up six-five for the "Hoses." After the game, they all went to a nearby tavern for beers and more trash talk.

"You know what they say about cops and firefighters," one of the cops said to Arden.

"What?"

"The reason they made police is so firefighters could have heroes too."

"Ha ha." She smiled as she sipped her beer. "Funny."

Dody grinned too. "Firefighters are the guys who couldn't pass the police exam."

"Hold on," Ronda said. "Not just guys."

Everyone laughed. "Okay men *and women* who couldn't pass the police exam," Dody replied.

"Well," Tremon said. "Everyone knows police are the people too out of shape to be firefighters."

"What do cops and firefighters have in common?" Tyler asked. "They both want to be firefighters."

More laugher rose around them and Arden leaned into him. He slid an arm around her waist and pulled her closer still.

"I have to stop at my mom's place on the way home," he told Arden when they were in the truck again. Her cheeks were pink from sitting in the fresh air, her eyes sparkling. "Her toilet won't stop running, and I need to have a look at it."

"Sure, no problem."

He drove to North Center and parked in front of the house. Arden made no move to get out of the truck when he opened her door. "Coming in?"

"I thought I'd just wait here."

"Come in. I won't be long, but you may as well say hi."

She hesitated, but slid out. "Okay."

"You've met my mom, right?"

"Oh yeah. Long time ago, though."

He used his key to open the door and stepped in. Mom appeared from the living room. "That you, Tyler?"

"It's me, Mom. Me and Arden." He drew her forward. "You remember Arden Lennox, right?" He knew that wasn't her name now, but Lennox was how Mom would remember her.

"Of course! Hello Arden, how are you?" Tyler read the interest and curiosity on Mom's face. Uh-oh.

"Very well, thanks. It's so nice to see you again."

"Come in. I was just watching a Netflix show." She led the way into the living room. "Have a seat. Who'd like something to drink? Coffee? Iced tea? Beer or wine?"

"We just had a couple of beers so I better not have more," Tyler said. "We're good. Won't stay long. I'm just gonna have a look at the toilet."

"I already called a plumber," Mom said. "He's coming tomorrow."

"What?" he frowned. "I told you I'd come by."

"You had a baseball game. I know you're busy."

"Mom." He swallowed his frustration. "I can do things like this for you."

"You have your own life," she protested, as she always did.

He wanted to look after her. She was his mom and she was on her own now. "Well, I might as well look at it while I'm here." He blew out a breath as he turned away.

As he left, Mom said to Arden, "I'm sorry he dragged you here."

"It's fine!" Arden protested.

Damn. He *had* dragged Arden here, and it turned out he probably didn't even have to come.

He jogged upstairs to the bathroom, lifted the lid of the tank and peered in, then flushed the toilet. Water spilled into the overflow tube. Should be easy to fix. He just needed a screwdriver.

He ran down two flights of stairs to his dad's old tool bench in the basement and grabbed one, hearing the muted conversation from the living room. Hopefully Mom wasn't interrogating Arden.

He adjusted the fill level in the tank, flushed again, and boom, fixed.

He washed his hands and returned the screwdriver before heading into the living room. "All fixed," he announced.

"Thank you!" Mom shook her head, but smiled. "I appreciate it. Now I don't have to pay a plumber."

"No problem." He sat beside Arden on the love seat. "I don't mind helping, Mom."

"I know. Are you enjoying being back in Chicago?" Mom asked Arden.

"I really am. I love Chicago. I didn't even realize how much I missed it until I was back. It's nice to be around family and friends again. Although the only family here is Jamie."

"Well, if you need a mom-cooked meal or help with anything, you just come on over," Mom said.

"Oh, that's so sweet of you. Thank you."

"We were just at a baseball game," Tyler said. "Our annual Guns versus Hoses game."

"The Hoses won," Arden added. "Tyler got two home runs." She turned and met his eyes. "You played great."

Pleasure expanded in his chest. He shrugged modestly. "It was a team effort."

Mom's avid gaze darted back and forth between them.

Hopefully she wasn't going to start talking about grandchildren. "Guns versus hoses."

"It's so funny, the rivalry between the firefighters and the police." Arden chuckled. "Both such admirable professions, but they pretend to hate one another."

"Not sure it's all pretend," Tyler muttered. "I think those guys really do believe we just sit around watching TV all day."

Arden's laugh was low and musical. "And you think they spend their day driving around and stopping for donuts."

He grinned.

"You do pretend to hate each other," she said. "But I also heard that you and Tremon and Dody started your charity organization together."

"Ah. Tremon's wife was talking to you."

"Yes. So apparently the police and firefighters do work together as a team when there's a need."

Tyler snorted. "The only reason cops are allowed on scenes is because the firefighters are busy, and someone needs to direct traffic."

She laughed. "I love all these jokes. But you know what? When it comes to popularity, firefighters always win. Lots of people hate cops, but nobody hates firefighters."

He met her eyes and his heartbeat quickened. "Eh, it's true. Despite the rivalry, we do work together when shit hits the fan. We all respect one another."

Mom's forehead creased and she watched them with a weird expression. "I keep hoping Tyler will change his mind about going back to college and do something else."

Arden's head tilted. "Why would you want that? He loves what he does so much."

"Um. Well. Firefighters don't earn that much money."

"I think it's more important to do something you love,"

Arden said quietly, leaning into him so her shoulder pushed against his. "And Tyler really does love his job."

Mom's face tightened. "I guess he does."

"He's good at it too," Arden added. "His coworkers and his superiors really respect him."

"How do you know that?" He looked down at her with amusement and surprise.

"I heard lots of stories about you tonight."

"Oh, great." He rolled his eyes, but apparently they hadn't been all bad.

"He's a very smart firefighter," she added. "And brave."

Mom's face wore a look of worried confusion. Like she'd never realized that he was smart and brave. Christ.

"So what do you do for a living, Arden?"

"Well, right now I'm working as a waitress at a pub."

Mom blinked. If she said one goddamn word that was insulting to Arden, he'd lose his shit. Protectiveness surged through him.

"It's not what I want to do forever, but I was in kind of a bad financial situation when I moved back, so I needed to find a job right away. Turns out, I enjoy it. And I've just started doing a little catering."

"Catering," Mom repeated, nodding, her face expressionless.

Tyler's gut tightened.

"Yes." Excitement lit up Arden's eyes. "I love entertaining and cooking and baking. Basically I like feeding people." She laughed. "I never thought of making a career out of it, but I'm thinking of giving it a shot."

She told Mom about her ideas for using local vendors, her enthusiasm contagious. Pride expanded in his chest as she talked.

"Well, that sounds really promising," Mom said with a smile.

Arden lifted a shoulder, smiling. "We'll see, I guess. But it's nice to have a sense of direction. After my husband died, everything felt a little…aimless."

"I'm sorry for your loss," Mom said quietly. "So tragic to lose your husband at such a young age."

Arden nodded. "Thank you. It was really difficult."

Tyler wished he could tell his mom the whole story so she'd know how amazing Arden was, but that was her story to tell, if or when she wanted.

"Well," he said. "We should get going." He and Arden stood, and Mom rose too.

"Come again, please." Mom touched Arden's arm. "Maybe for Sunday dinner one weekend when Ty's not working."

She liked Arden.

Fuck yeah.

This wasn't why he'd brought Arden here with him. Or maybe it was. Maybe he hadn't even realized that he'd wanted his mom to meet Arden. That he'd wanted her to like her. And now he knew she did…

"That would be so nice, thank you," Arden said, though he sensed her hesitance. "Hopefully we can work that out."

Noncommittal.

Enough of this. He was losing patience. He'd tried to back off a little, so she'd have time to accept what was happening between them. He wasn't some kind of woo-woo guy, but it almost felt like this was meant to be…from the time they were teenagers and he'd crushed on her…no other woman he'd dated or had a relationship with had ever been right. It had all been leading to this. To this woman. To right now.

He drove through the dark streets to their home, trying to figure out how he was going to do this. Where. What to say.

"You're so quiet." Arden reached over and curled his fingers around one of his hands.

He glanced at her and smiled. "Is that unusual?"

"No." She rubbed her thumb over his hand. "You're not a loudmouth."

He barked out a laugh. "Gee, thanks."

"It's one of the things I like about you. You talk when you have something to say, not just to fill the void or hear yourself talk."

Oh, he had something to say all right. He was practically vibrating with it.

His insides twisted up. How was she going to take this? She had to feel something too. The way things had been going between them…easy and comfortable, yet still lots of smoking hot sparks. Nights he was off, they spent together, either in her bed or his. They were in and out of each other's apartments all the time, even though her bathroom was now fully functional. He brought her her favorite organic wine, and she made him muffins.

He parked behind the house, and they entered through the rear door, then climbed the stairs. As usual he let her go in front of him, partly out of chivalry, partly because he enjoyed watching her ass in her snug jeans.

"You have to work in the morning?" she murmured at the top of the stairs.

If he worked, they usually went to her place so he could sneak out early and she could get more sleep. "Nope."

"Your place or mine?"

"Mine," he said gruffly.

"Okay."

He led her into his apartment, rubbing his hands together. Christ, his palms were sweating. "Let's make out," he blurted, the first thing that came to mind.

She flicked on a lamp and smiled at him over her shoulder. "Thought you'd never ask."

He grinned, his nerves easing slightly. She was fucking perfect.

He slid a hand over her ass and squeezed, then grabbed her and pulled her down onto the couch onto his lap. He lifted her legs across his, cupped her face with one hand and kissed her. Her mouth opened to him soft and warm, her taste as always was like a drug, shooting through his veins and making him high. His dick thickened and he shifted their bodies around, fitting her to him. His hand slid down, fingertips trailing over her throat, then he found her breast. That lush softness made him crazy. He hardened, heat pouring through him.

"Mmm." She slid her mouth along his stubbled jaw. "Such a good kisser."

"Yes, you are."

She smiled, rubbing his chest. "Watching you play baseball made me hot."

"Seriously?" He kissed the corner of her mouth.

"Totally. You were all muscular and sweaty out there, hitting home runs and sliding into first base." She breathed in, as if inhaling him. "Almost as sexy as fighting fires."

"You've never seen me fight a fire." His voice came out strangled as she slid her hand to his groin and pressed.

"No. But I've seen you in your uniform. *That's* hot too."

"Arden. Christ, Arden…I have to tell you…" Was this how he'd planned it? He couldn't even remember. His mind was shot, she had him all hot and bothered. "I have to tell you…I love you."

She went very still against him. He moved in for another kiss, but she turned her head. "Tyler…"

"Don't say anything. I know it's soon. I've been trying to

take things slow, because I know you weren't ready for another relationship so soon—"

"Not ever!" She pushed back and he tried to focus on her. She stared at him wide-eyed. "I don't want a relationship ever!"

He tried to keep his face neutral, but knew he'd failed when she squeezed her face up and said, "Oh shit. Shit."

He sucked in a breath.

"I'm handling this really badly," she muttered. "I'm sorry."

"Look, you don't have to say it back." Fuck he sounded desperate. Desperate and pathetic. This was not how he wanted to come across. "I know you feel something, Arden. I know it." He lifted her hand and pressed it to his chest. His heart. Which was crashing against his sternum. "We've got something great here, baby. Just admit that. Just go with it. I want us to…I just want you to know how I feel. I love you."

"Oh God. Oh my God."

Yeah, that didn't really sound good.

Arden closed her eyes, her face looking like someone was pulling out her fingernails. "You can't. You can't love me."

His heart dropped like a stone. "Talk to me, Arden. What's going on?"

"Shit, Tyler. I told you before…" She pushed away from him, scrambling off his lap and back into the corner of his sectional like a cornered animal. "I'm trying to get my life together. Figure out who I am. What I want to do."

"So do it. What's stopping you?"

"You!" She pressed her lips together and gazed at him. "You," she said more quietly. "You're stopping me. I can't lose myself again."

He felt like someone had just plunged a jagged blade into his chest and twisted it. He stared at her. "That's fucking bull-shit. I love you. I want to look after you. I want to walk you home and make sure Liam is treating you right and help you set up your business and—"

"Don't you see that *I need to do that for myself?*" She twisted her fingers together. "I don't need a hero. I need to be my own hero. I've said that to you, and you keep not listening. You're always trying to jump in and fix things for people. You know what happened to me. You know how important it is to me to stand on my own two feet and get my life together."

"Is that really what you think? That I'm the one who's stopping you from doing that?" He lifted his chin, his jaw set. "You think you're the only one trying to figure things out? You're not. We all are. You're just not being honest."

CHAPTER TWENTY-FOUR

*A*rden glared at Tyler, actual spots flashing in front of her eyes. Her breath had all left her body and her chest strained. For a moment she couldn't even speak.

She tried to swallow, tried to breathe. Her hands curled into fists. "That's not true," she whispered. "I am honest. I'm not lying."

"Arden..." His face contracted and he reached out a hand.

She couldn't let him touch her. Her chest now burned like a hot knife was slicing through it. But she didn't want him to know that. She didn't want him to know how much his words hurt her.

She'd tried so hard not to feel sorry for herself, not to dwell on the negatives, not to let her past drag her down. She'd told herself over and over again that life was good and precious, and she was strong enough to get through it all and one day she'd figure out where she was going. Lately she'd started to feel like she was getting there.

So for him to say that to her...that she wasn't being honest...that hurt. "You're the one who's full of shit." She tossed her hair back, straightened her legs and slid off the couch. "I'm sorry if you thought there was more between us than there is. I'm sorry I gave you the wrong impression. But don't make me feel like crap because...because..." She couldn't say it. "Don't blame me. I've blamed myself for enough stuff. But I've never lied to you."

"Arden." His voice was low and rough, his face drawn into tight lines. "I never said you lied to me."

She shook her head, sliding her hands into her hair. "Fuck! I knew we shouldn't have done this." She sucked in a shaky breath. "I'm sorry. For everything."

She'd just told him not to blame her, and yet she was apologizing. On some level she recognized that this was fucked up. Whatever.

"I didn't want things to be messed up for all of us," she choked out as she stumbled toward the door. "For Jamie and Mila. I-I'll figure out something..." Her voice was going shaky and thin as tears threatened. She had to hold it together.

"Arden."

She stopped and leaned her head against the wall next to the door, her hand on the doorknob.

"You need to be honest with *yourself*."

She squeezed her eyes shut. What the hell did that mean? "Sure." What the hell was she supposed to say now? *Goodbye?* There was going to be no avoiding each other, living right across the hall from each other. *Thanks for the memories. And the great sex.* She finally settled on, "Good night, Tyler."

She wrenched open the door, shut it, and staggered across to her own place. Inside, it was blessedly dark and quiet. He wouldn't follow her, would he?

She turned the deadbolt lock on the door—something she hadn't done since she'd first moved in.

Probably not needed. Why would he follow her? She'd just

crushed him. He'd told her he loved her, and she'd rejected him. What could be worse than that?

She closed her eyes again as pain washed down through her in a river of heat.

He didn't really love her. He couldn't. He'd be fine.

Wait…another slice of pain burned through her. Or maybe that was shame. Was that what he meant about being honest with herself? Was she telling herself lies to make herself feel better about hurting him?

Oh God, she was a terrible person. A terrible, awful person. She hadn't been able to keep a marriage together, and now she couldn't even have a fling without it becoming a complete goat fuck.

Her face wet with tears, she made her way into the bedroom through the dark, a hand on the wall. She didn't want light. She wanted her bed, covers pulled over her head, while she tried to figure out how she was going to put her life back together…again.

She slept like crap, tossing and turning and having the same dream over and over. She couldn't even remember what the dream was, but it had been disturbing. In the morning, she dragged herself out of bed and into the bathroom.

God, she looked like crap too, mascara smeared around her eyes, which were red and swollen. Her nose was pink, her lips puffy. It all could've been from a night of wild sex, except that the slope of her eyebrows and the downward tilt of her lips radiated sadness.

She washed her face, finishing with cold water, her heart like a stone in her chest, her stomach tight. She had to work at noon today, a nice early shift she'd usually be glad for because it meant she'd have an evening off to do something with Tyler or with her friends.

How could she face any of them after what she'd done to Tyler? Jamie was going to be so pissed at her. Probably they all would be. And she totally deserved it.

Once again, she was falling into that blame game. What she'd told Tyler was true…she *had* been honest with him. She'd told him she wasn't ready for a relationship. She'd let him talk her into going on that date…and then everything had just kept going. *He* was the one who hadn't been honest. He'd told her he didn't want a relationship either, but clearly he did. And now everything was fucked up.

So why did she feel so guilty?

Because it wasn't his fault. It was her fault for letting things progress to the point he wanted more than she could give.

She wanted coffee, but couldn't stomach eating anything before dressing for her shift at Shenanigans, trying to hide puffy eyes with dark eye shadow and loads of concealer. Bright blusher and some shiny lip gloss would help too.

Liam eyed her as she walked into the empty Shenanigans. "Jaysus. You look like you've got a bad case of the Irish flu."

Or maybe not.

She fluffed her hair. "Gee, thanks."

"Rough night, love?" His forehead creased as he studied her face.

"Wasn't the best." She sucked in a breath and squared her shoulders. "I'm afraid I have to give my notice."

"Notice of what?"

"Of quitting. I have to quit. I don't know how much notice you need, but it would be great if today could be my last day."

"What the fuck are you going on about?" Liam's jaw jutted. "You can't quit."

"Who's quitting?" Sorcha appeared. "Just when we hired a

bunch of new people, someone quits. Of *course*, we can never get ahead of things."

"I'm quitting," Arden said quietly. "I'm sorry."

Sorcha's mouth fell open wide enough to see her molars. "What? Why?"

"I'm going to Florida."

Brother and sister now both gaped at her. "Florida?" Sorcha finally said.

"*Today*?" Liam added.

"No." She tried for a breezy smile, showing her teeth. "Tomorrow."

"Ah."

"You can't quit," Sorcha said. "You're the best waitress we've ever had. Besides me, obviously."

"Obviously."

"This seems a little rash," Liam said. "Something is clearly arseways."

One corner of Arden's mouth kicked up. "I love you, Liam."

"Then why the fuck are you quitting?" he yelled.

"Don't yell at me!"

"I'm not yelling!"

"You're both yelling," Sorcha shouted.

Arden clamped her mouth shut, her bottom lip quivering. Dense silence filled the bar. "I have to go," she finally said. "I messed up. I got involved with Tyler. I should have known better."

Waves of displeasure radiated off Sorcha, who gave her a slitty-eyed, thin-lipped look, arms crossed.

Arden rested her forehead into her shaking hand.

"*A chara*." Liam came around from behind the bar, slid his arm behind her shoulders, and led her to a table. He eased her down into a chair and pulled one up for himself. "Talk to me."

She laid her head down on her arms on the table and rolled her forehead back and forth. "I just told you what happened."

"You told me nothing. I already knew you and Tyler were involved. What's the problem with that?"

She had no clue what to say that, acutely aware of Sorcha's simmering presence nearby. "Let's just say we ended things. It's super awkward living right across the hall from him. He's my brother's best friend. I knew that, I knew I shouldn't have gotten involved with him."

Liam rubbed her back. "I'm sorry."

"Thanks."

"So that's why I have to quit. Because this is his hangout place. I can't be here."

"Shit."

Arden's head jerked up to look at Sorcha.

"I should be happy," Sorcha said. "You're leaving. Tyler's single again. Why am I not happy?"

"Because you know you never had a chance with him, *a leanbh.*" Liam rubbed another circle on Arden's back. "And you care about both him and Arden."

Sorcha huffed. "Maybe."

The door opened and their first customers of the day walked in.

"Time to get to work." Sorcha jerked her head. "If this is your last day, make it good."

Arden's heart squeezed. Dammit, she was going to miss Sorcha and Liam as much as anyone.

Not as much as she was going to miss Tyler.

Arden leaned back into the lounge chair next to the pool at her parents' retirement complex. The fronds of a nearby palm tree tossed in the gentle breeze. An elderly couple on the opposite side of the pool were holding hands and kissing and laughing. Gah.

She tossed down the magazine she'd borrowed from Mom, unable to focus on anything. Closing her eyes, she let the hot sun warm her, trying to let the heat melt away her sadness. And pain. And guilt.

Her parents had been surprised when she'd shown up there, happily surprised at first, before clueing in that Arden was not okay. She kept telling them she was, but clearly she wasn't putting on a good enough act.

She'd run away without saying goodbye or telling anyone. When she'd arrived at Mom and Dad's, she'd texted Jamie to let him know where she was. He'd replied with a barrage of messages, mostly questions, which she'd ignored, then a bunch of phone calls she hadn't picked up.

She couldn't stay here forever, but she needed a plan. She hadn't had enough time to save any substantial amount of money. She had no home. No job. She was right back where she'd started months ago when she was leaving Phoenix. In fact, she was even worse off. This time, she actually had awesome people in her life she cared about, and she was losing them too. She'd taken the generous opportunity Jamie had given her to live in his building, the job Liam had given her, and the friendship they'd all offered her, and she'd completely fucked it all up.

"Arden." Mom took the lounge chair next to her. "Jamie just called."

"Oh."

"He's worried about you. You're not answering his texts."

"Did you tell him I'm fine?"

"No, dear." Mom's tone was dry. "Because you're not. Please. You have to talk to me. We're all worried about you."

A tear trickled from one eye and slid down her face and into her ear. "Don't worry about me."

"Jamie says you and Tyler have been seeing each other."

"Seeing each other." She gave a short laugh. "Yes. It was hard to avoid seeing each other, living across the hall from each other. And when he was renovating the apartment I was living in."

"You know what I mean. And what do you mean the apartment you *were* living in? Are you not planning on going back?"

Shit. "I can't."

"What happened, sweetie? Something with Tyler?" Mom's voice sharpened. "I know you were devastated by what Michael did...Tyler hasn't...hurt you, has he?"

"No." The word came out on a sob.

"Good. Because if any other man hurts you again, I'll have to kick his ass."

She sniffled out a laugh. "Thanks, Mom. But he didn't. It was me. I'm the one who was an asshole."

After a beat, Mom said quietly, "How so?"

"After what happened with Michael, I didn't want to get involved with someone again."

"I guess I can understand that you'd need time for that. And that you might be afraid of getting hurt again."

"It's not that I'm afraid of getting hurt again. I mean, maybe I am, a little, but...I trust Tyler."

"Then what's the problem?"

"He shouldn't trust *me*. I don't trust myself."

Mom's eyebrows knitted and she waited patiently for Arden to go on.

"I never realized how unhappy Michael was." She twisted her fingers together and stared at them. "He must have been so miserable. So desperate. We were married, and I never even noticed how unhappy he was."

Mom closed her eyes briefly, her lips thinning.

Arden pulled in a slow breath. "I should have known. I should have known how bad things were. I should have made him talk to me and tell me what was going on. I could have helped him, and I could have stopped him…from…" Her throat closed up.

"You don't know that, Arden." Mom's low, steady voice eased her tension. A little. "You can never really know what's going on in someone's head. You can't take responsibility for what happened."

"But I do! I let him down! I should have been there for him, and I wasn't. And now I hurt Tyler too. I was just letting things go on, not even realizing he was falling in love with me. I *am* a spoiled, selfish princess, just like he said."

Mom's eyebrows flew up. "He said that?"

"No. *I* said that. I mean, he did call me princess, but in a nice way. I'm the one who felt spoiled and selfish. When Michael died, I lost everything. And I realized I just coasted through life, letting other people look after me. I didn't even have a job. I felt like I was…nobody."

"Oh, sweetie."

"I wanted to take charge of my life. I wanted to prove I could do it. Be a grown-up. And…and I failed." Her voice cracked.

"I didn't realize how much you were blaming yourself," Mom said quietly.

Arden squeezed her eyes shut and nodded.

"Obviously, Michael was very unhappy with his life."

"I didn't see it."

Mom reached for her hands and squeezed them. "That's because he didn't want you to. Dad and I were there, two months before he died. We didn't see it either. But loving someone doesn't mean you can keep them from ever being unhappy. If that's what you think, you'll never have a healthy, happy relationship."

"Love is wanting the person you love to always be happy."

Mom cast her a shrewd look. "Yes, of course you want that. Since the day you were born, that's all I wanted for you. But realistically as a mother, I knew that wasn't possible. What kind of relationship would we have had—what kind of life would *you* have had—if all I'd ever done was try to keep you happy?"

Arden thought about that. Maybe her life had been easy compared to some, but she'd had her share of hardships. Mom was right…there was no way she could prevent those from happening to her. And she shouldn't.

"Love is encouraging the one you love to live their best life. But you don't have control if he chooses to live his life in a way that's unhealthy and destructive."

Arden's heart contracted so painfully she couldn't breathe. Mom's words played over in her head.

Love is encouraging the one you love to live their best life.

"You've been so strong through all of this. I know how hard it's been."

Arden couldn't talk. She pressed her trembling lips together.

"But the whole time you held your head up and did what you had to do. I guess I didn't tell you how much I admired you."

Arden's mouth fell open. "Admired me?"

"Yes." Mom stroked her hair. "Dad and I talked a lot about how strong you were. But running away isn't the way to be a grown-up."

Ouch.

"I don't know what you're running from…other than maybe yourself."

Arden flinched at that. Because Tyler had said something similar—that she wasn't being honest with herself.

"But I do know that you're strong enough to handle pretty much anything, after what you've been through."

"I don't know if I am."

"If you learn from your mistakes, you are." Mom added, "I also know you can't stay here forever."

Arden laughed. "Gee thanks, Mom."

Mom smiled. "But you can stay as long as you need."

Arden's heart swelled as Mom pulled her in for a hug. "Thank you."

Tyler was cooking bacon for sandwiches for supper when the tones alerted them to a structure fire. With a resigned sigh—he was really looking forward to bacon—he turned off the stove and set the pan on a rear burner, then headed out to the apparatus bay to step into his bunker boots and pants. It was dinnertime and probably a false alarm. Residential fire alarms were almost always the result of someone overcooking food, so this could be as benign as burned toast.

He threw on his jacket and then he, Cliff, Tremon, and Evan jumped on the rig. Cliff let dispatch know they were en route, and they listened for other information coming in. They heard from dispatch that it was a working structure fire, and they'd started the clock to time the fire. The radio crackled. "Single-story single-family dwelling. Multiple callers. Heavy smoke coming from, uh…heavy smoke and fire coming from the front door."

This meant another engine would be added to the call. It also told them it probably wasn't burned toast. Adrenaline spiked through Tyler's veins as they turned a corner and sped down the street, lights and siren going. Ahead, they could see the column of thick black smoke. Their mobile display terminal showed information about the structure and hydrants.

When they arrived, police were already there and told them there was a possible occupant trapped inside. Shit.

Cliff took control of the incident.

"Go meet with the captain from twenty-two," Cliff told Tyler and Evan. "Stretch a line between the homes in case there's a rescue."

Tyler nodded and as the two captains talked, he pulled the preconnected hose line and stretched it to the front door of the house. Then he started donning his mask while the rest of the crew joined him.

Masked up, he opened the bail to expel any air in the hose line and adjusted the nozzle to a straight stream. Tyler advanced the hose line to the door, Crenshaw behind him, backing him up. "Let's go, hit it!"

He, Cliff, and Crenshaw moved into the house. Inside, they discovered the fire had self-ventilated, having burned a hole in the roof, and they could see right through the rooms on the main floor to a back bedroom.

Jesus Christ.

Everything in the room was on fire—the wall, the clothes in the closet, the bed was a pile of flaming ash, and flames crawled around the door. It was quite a sight.

Adrenaline flowed through Tyler's veins, making his limbs tingle and his heart beat faster.

He opened the line up. The fire roared and the water hissed. Clouds of smoke billowed. He made his way forward, putting out flames. In the bedroom, flames lit up the smoke.

Behind him, Cliff said, "I'm gonna go past you. Work on the fire."

Tyler did that, Cliff moving into the smoke. Seconds later, Cliff shouted, "Evan! Give me a hand!"

Tyler's gaze landed on the body on the floor. Fuck.

Tyler covered Cliff with the nozzle as he crouched. Jesus. Jesus fucking Christ. The body, a man judging by the size of it, was black. Tyler swallowed the bile that rose in his throat. His face, his body...was it just covered in soot?

Evan stood there, frozen, staring.

"Help him!" Tyler yelled at Evan, dividing his attention between the hose, the fire, and Cliff struggling to get the body up. "For Chrissakes, help him, we have to get him out of here!"

Evan still didn't move.

"Fuck!" Anger flashed through Tyler at Evan. What the fuck was wrong with him?

Then he realized—there *was* something wrong with him. He was paralyzed with fear. Thoughts blazed through Tyler's mind as he weighed options. Acting largely on instinct, he shoved the hose at Evan. "Here! Take this. Cover us."

Thankfully Evan grabbed the nozzle. Hoping to hell he was with it enough to protect them, Tyler leaped over to help Cliff lift the body. "I'm here."

"Thanks. Right here...grab his feet," Cliff said. "Let's drag him."

"Okay."

They shifted the weight and Tyler shuffled backward through the smoke and water and debris, breathing through his mask.

"Keep going, Tyler," Cliff encouraged.

Outside, the smoke lighter, the air cooler, they laid him on the grass. They both dropped to their knees next to him. Once again, Tyler's stomach roiled but he started chest compressions.

"This is Engine 25. We have one victim," Cliff announced.

Ronda and Cam rushed up, Ronda dropping to take over the compressions, Cam going to the victim's head.

"No," Cliff said, sitting back on his heels. He looked up at Tyler with sad resignation, shaking his head.

Tyler stood, almost ready to vomit, but he swallowed. "I need to get back in there. Crenshaw's not doing so good."

He strode back into the house where Evan stood like a zombie, still holding the hose.

"The attic!" Tremon yelled.

Again, Crenshaw didn't respond, standing knee-deep in coals. His feet were going to burn. Tyler took control. He grabbed the hose and hosed down Crenshaw's feet, listening to the chatter through his earpiece about the victim and other crews arriving, their instructions. "Get out of here!" he yelled.

Crenshaw turned eerily blank eyes on him.

Christ. Crenshaw wasn't exactly his favorite person, but Tyler felt sick seeing him like this.

Tyler turned the hose on the fire in the attic, but the longer he stood there in red hot coals trying to get Crenshaw to go, the hotter his own feet were getting, and he had to take a second to hose them down and drench them.

The other crew that had arrived pulled the ceiling for them while he and Tremon chased the fire around the attic. They were making progress, but Crenshaw was still there, now shaking. He was going to have to physically get him out of the house.

He grabbed Crenshaw and shoved him forward, both of them stumbling. Finally he wrestled him outside.

Tyler re-entered the structure. As turned the hose back on the attic, with no warning the floor moved under his feet. Shit!

The last thing he heard was Tremon yelling, "Mayday! Mayday! Mayday!"

CHAPTER TWENTY-FIVE

*A*rden slid a tray of chocolate chip cookies into the oven. Because it was National Chocolate Chip Cookie Day. And no matter how shitty things were, there was always something to celebrate.

Sure.

The last few days she'd made a couple of cakes, some lemon bars, banana bread, and now cookies. It was a comfort baking frenzy.

It also gave her time to think.

Love is encouraging the one you love to live their best life.

Tyler did that for her. He encouraged her. He cared enough about her to let her walk home alone, even though he wanted to protect her. He encouraged her to try her new business. He encouraged her to make new friends and go to the book club meeting. He supported her in so many ways, small ones and the most important ones.

Maybe he tended to butt in a lot, but he did it with good intentions. With a good heart. The best heart.

She'd overreacted about him trying to help her. And Tyler

had been right—that wasn't the *real* reason she was afraid of getting involved with him.

She was terrified of messing up again. Of letting someone down in the worst way.

Was Mom right? She didn't have control over how Michael had lived his life. She could only encourage him and support him. And honestly? Tyler didn't have control over her life. He encouraged her and supported her…but he didn't control her.

She moved about the kitchen, washing the bowls she'd used to make the cookie dough, loading the dishwasher, wiping the counter, her mind working.

Tyler wanted to be a firefighter against his mom's wishes. Arden had encouraged him in that. If it was what he wanted, she wanted that for him, and she'd do anything to help him achieve his goals.

Because she loved him.

And he'd do anything to help her achieve her goals. Because he loved her.

She pressed her fingers to her mouth and froze in the middle of the kitchen.

Holy hell. She'd gone and done what she hadn't wanted to happen. She'd fallen in love with him. And then she'd screwed things up so badly.

He loved his job so much. He was so brave. She wanted him to be happy. To have everything in life he wanted.

Because she loved him.

And maybe…that was why he was such a pain. Because he loved her. And he wanted those same things for her.

Mom was right about something else—she *had* run away. And that wasn't acting like an adult. Mom's words had stung, but she had to admit the truth in them. She'd screwed up again. But Mom had also said, if she learned from her mistakes, she was strong enough to do anything.

Wasn't that exactly what she'd wanted? A new life? A chance to start over? A chance to learn from her mistakes and be a better person?

She plopped her butt onto a stool at the counter. Mom and Dad were sitting outside on the patio. She stared across the room blindly.

When things had gotten tough, she'd been scared and she'd run away. Instead of dealing with them like an adult, which she hadn't done with Michael either.

That wasn't learning from her mistakes. She hung her head, shame burning her insides.

She *was* strong. She'd been through hell. She'd survived. She could do anything.

She lifted her chin.

But could she do what she had to do to make things better with Tyler?

She pulled in a slow breath through her nose, her hands flat on the cool granite.

Yes. She had to try. She had to try to be the woman she'd wanted to become—brave, honest, strong.

She jumped off the stool and skidded across the shiny floor to the sliding doors. She flung one aside and stepped out. "Mom!"

Mom looked up from the magazine she was reading, startled.

"I need to book a flight and pack."

Mom's slow smile made Arden's heart squeeze. She set down her magazine. "I'll help."

She hadn't told Jamie or anyone she was coming back to Chicago. She felt like an idiot now, quitting her job at Shenanigans, running out on the new life she'd built. She would fix things. She would do better.

She took the train and then the bus home. *Home.*

The air in her apartment felt a little stale, but the scent of her favorite honeysuckle candles lingered. She looked around, remembering the day she'd arrived. Since then, she had a new bathroom, a beautifully refinished fireplace, and perfect painted walls. Baseboards and door casings hadn't been added, but the apartment was almost finished. Thanks to Tyler.

She remembered cooking together in her kitchen, trying new recipes using the things they'd shopped for, feeding each other tastes, him complaining about how messy she was, her telling him culinary creativity couldn't be stifled by orderliness, arguing over whether they'd used too much salt or not enough. Then the fun and laughter they'd shared with their friends and Jamie while eating what they'd cooked.

It was everything she'd lost. Friendship, companionship…love.

She unpacked her suitcase, then crossed the hall to Tyler's place. She paused, listening, but heard nothing, so she turned the doorknob and entered. Inside, she padded down the hall and peered into Tyler's bedroom. Bed neatly made as always before he went to work. A pair of jeans draped over the arm of a chair, a pair of socks on the floor next to the hamper. She shook her head, smiling faintly. She'd bugged him about why he couldn't put his socks into the hamper instead of on the floor near it. She picked up the socks and dropped them in.

She sucked on her bottom lip as she meandered through the silent apartment. The whole place smelled faintly like Tyler, like the spicy clean body wash and shave balm he used. She pressed her fingers to her eyes.

She thought she'd lost a lot when Michael had died. Now, she felt she'd lost so much more. But at least she would have the courage to stand up and admit how she felt. To tell the truth. To be honest not just with herself, but with the man she loved.

In the kitchen, she checked the dishwasher. It was full, but everything was clean, so she unloaded it and then moved a couple of glasses, a bowl, and a spoon from the sink to the dishwasher. She grabbed a sponge and wet it and wiped off the counters, then polished up the stainless steel taps and faucet.

She knew who she was. Maybe she didn't know where she was going, but she wasn't alone in that. Jamie'd told her that. Mila and Emma had told her that.

She'd already learned a lot about herself. Sure, she'd freaked out about Tyler. Maybe he couldn't forgive her for that. She'd hurt him. She understood that and it broke her own heart knowing it. But if she'd learned anything the past year, it was that forgiving herself for her screwups was the first step.

"Mom, I'm going to be fine." Tyler wasn't sure of that himself just then, but his mom was so distraught he felt a need to reassure her. "Really."

Mom couldn't stop crying, holding his hand, sitting in the chair beside his hospital bed. "Th-this is wh-why I don't want you to d-do this," she sobbed.

Tyler's forehead tightened. "Because I might get hurt?"

"Y-yes." She gave a huge, unladylike sniff. Tyler handed her some tissues from the box. Hospital issue, they were thin and sandpapery, but it was all they had. She swiped at her nose. "Every day I worry about you. If something happens to you…I can't…" She broke down again.

Christ. His jaw dropped. *This* was what her disappointment in his career was all about? She was actually terrified something would happen to him?

She tried to get control of her emotions, wiping at her eyes and nose. "I can't lose you," she whispered. "I can't lose another child. You're all I have left."

After losing one child...and then his dad... He closed his eyes, his chest tight, his thinking still muddled. "Jesus, Mom. I'm sorry." He reached out his good hand to awkwardly squeeze hers. "I'm fine," he said again. "I mean, I will be."

His injuries weren't life threatening. He'd recover from the concussion, broken wrist, bruises, and minor burns.

It might take longer to recover from seeing that body...that corpse. His mind kept going there, filled with guilt and grief.

"Please. I don't want you to do this. This just shows why you shouldn't. You should be working in an office somewhere..."

Tyler's eyes burned. "I'm sorry, Mom."

She laid her head down on the bed and wept.

His belly knotted. "I'm sorry," he said again. "I didn't do this to make you miserable. I did it so I could help people. So I could make a difference."

"I know," Mom sobbed. "I *am* proud of you, Ty."

Emotion swelled inside him and his throat constricted. "Thanks, Mom."

She stayed a while longer, hovering around his bed, asking if he needed anything. He closed his eyes. His entire body throbbed, mostly his head. His stomach roiled and the room spun around him. Fuck. He hated feeling like this, like a weak, puking baby.

He wasn't sure, but he might have slept for a while. Something made him pry his eyes open, and he saw Jamie and Mila standing beside his bed, Mila holding a huge bunch of flowers, Jamie a Nintendo Switch. Mom was gone.

"Jesus Christ, Tyler," Jamie said. "What the fuck, man?"

Tyler tried for a smile. "Are you gonna freak out too?"

Mila set the flowers on the windowsill and turned to face him. She looked shaken, but wore a determined smile. "We're not freaking out. Much."

"Here. Brought you this." Jamie tossed the Game Boy on the bed. Then he winced. "Can you play one-handed?"

"I'll figure out a way." Jamie's gesture touched him, even though there was no way he could focus on a little computer screen right now.

"You're okay?" Mila asked, her smile fading.

"I'm okay." Other than the headache, nausea, vomiting, and dizziness. The pain meds were doing their thing for the other injuries, so that was good. He drifted out again.

"What else can we get you?" Mila asked, touching his arm.

"Arden. I need Arden." Oh shit. Did he say that out loud? He kept his eyes closed. Probably he just thought it.

"Oh, Tyler," Mila whispered.

"Fuck, man, you don't look so good," Jamie muttered.

Tyler dragged his eyes open and took in Jamie's almost green pallor. "Sit. Put your head between your knees, man. You're about to pass out."

"No, I'm not." His forehead gleamed with sweat and his eyes were dark.

Mila moved over beside him and pushed Jamie's head down. "Don't be an ass." In contrast to her blunt words, she rubbed Jamie's back in a surprisingly tender gesture, biting her lip as she gazed down at him. Jesus, she looked more worried about Jamie than about him.

"Good thing you never wanted to be a doctor," Tyler quipped, using all his energy.

"We'll never speak of this again," Jamie said. He sucked in a long breath and straightened. "You scared the shit out of us, asshole."

"Yeah, that was my plan."

"What happened, Tyler?" Mila asked. "Or do you not want to talk about it?"

"I don't remember some of it. Which really pisses me off. Apparently the floor collapsed, and I fell into the basement."

"Dear God." Mila pressed a hand to her chest. "You're lucky it's not worse."

"Yep."

"The man who died…?"

Tyler blew out a breath. "Turns out he was dead before the fire started." He'd learned this from his captain and Cliff and Tremon, who'd visited him earlier. "Cops say it was a homicide. He was murdered, and then they set the house on fire." It didn't help a whole lot, but at least they knew they hadn't failed to rescue the man. It was still a traumatic thing to have seen.

"Oh wow. That's awful." Mila perched on the arm of the chair, her hand still on Jamie's back. "How long do you think you'll be in here?"

"I think they said I might be able to go home tomorrow."

"We'll be there to help."

"Thanks." A wave of dizziness swept over him, and he closed his eyes again. "But Mom said I can go to her place for a few days."

"What else do you need?" Jamie asked. "What can we do for you?"

Arden. He needed Arden. "Water."

He heard noises, then Mila said, "I'll find some ice."

He gave a tiny nod, head hurting too much to move.

Then she was back. It felt like an hour, but maybe it was a minute. Who knew? A straw touched his lips and he opened, closed them around it, and sucked down some deliciously cold water.

He dozed off and woke up, hearing low voices talking. Mom and Jamie.

"He was asking for her last night," Mom whispered. "I didn't know what to say."

Jamie gave a low growl. "I'm so pissed at her."

Tyler drifted back into a medicated sleep.

The next time he woke up, Mom was there, Mila and Jamie gone.

"Your friends will be back later," Mom told him, now calmer. "They told us to let them know if there's anything you need." She paused. "They're good friends."

"Yeah," Tyler croaked. His throat hurt. "Can I have more water?"

Mom helped him drink.

"I need to talk to Arden," Tyler said to his mom a little desperately. "I need my phone."

Mom bit her lip. "I don't think it's here, Ty."

"Oh." Probably still at the station.

"You can use mine," Mom said, digging it out of her purse.

He gazed blankly at the phone. "I can't remember her number." Pain sliced through his chest, and it wasn't from his injuries. She was gone. He couldn't call her. She didn't love him.

He drifted again. Those pain meds were really something. Too bad they didn't help a broken heart.

The sound of the front door opening and closing reached Arden's ears. She frowned and checked her watch. It was only three o'clock. Then Jamie's apartment door opened and closed. She knew the difference between his and Mila's sounds now.

What was Jamie doing home so early?

But this was good! She needed to talk to him. She dropped

the towels she was folding in her apartment and raced downstairs.

She opened Jamie's door and called out, "Hi, I'm back!"

Jamie whirled around where he was looking at mail and gaped at her. "What the hell?"

"I came back." She advanced into the apartment, closing the door behind her. "I know I screwed up. I was an idiot. I came back to…to apologize. To everyone. But mostly to Tyler." She twisted her fingers together and sucked her bottom lip briefly. "I feel terrible about how I…reacted…" Her throat squeezed. "Maybe he won't forgive me, but—"

The expression on Jamie's face stopped her.

"What?" She stepped closer, frowning. "What's wrong?"

"I didn't know you were coming back."

"I know. I didn't know myself until yesterday. I got the first flight I could." Her stomach cramped. Jamie still looked…terrible. Drawn and tired.

"Jesus, Arden." Jamie rubbed his face. "You need to know…there's been an accident."

She blinked and pressed her fingers to her throat.

"What?" She squinted at her mom. "Where?" Her first thought was a car accident. Her parents? Mila?

"Tyler."

Arden's skin went hot, then icy. Cold fingers clutched at her insides.

"Fighting a fire."

The room swirled around her, and her knees buckled. Her mind went straight to the worst-case scenario. "Is he dead?"

"No! God no. But he's in the hospital."

"Is he going to die?" She stared at Jamie, her insides squeezed in an icy grip. "He's going to die, isn't he?"

"No, he's not."

"Oh my God. Oh my God." She began to tremble. "He is. He's going to die."

This couldn't be happening. It couldn't. Remembering the day the police had come to the house to tell her... blackness enveloped her.

"Jesus, Arden."

She heard Jamie's voice faintly, felt the grip of his hands on her arms as he helped her lower to the floor. Her vision was a pinpoint of brightness, everything else was black, and her ears roared.

Moments later—or maybe hours?—her head cleared a little. She was sitting on the floor in Jamie's living room, Jamie crouched beside her. Her mouth was dry and her heart pounded.

"Put your head between your knees," Jamie ordered gruffly. "Christ."

Arden lowered her head again, breathing in shallow puffs. "I need to know...what happened. I need to know if he's okay."

"He's okay. I just came from there. Mila and I went to see him."

"I need to see him." She tried to push up, but Jamie's hand on her shoulder held her down.

"Not yet. You'll just pass out again." He paused, then muttered, "Must be a family thing."

"Sorry." She bowed her head again.

"Come on. Let's get you onto the couch." Now, he helped her rise and led her over to his sofa. She stretched out and took a few deep breaths, eyes closed.

After a while, Jamie said quietly, "Do you even give a shit how he is?"

Her eyes flew open and her head lifted to glare at him.

"That's a stupid question. I just about passed out, thinking he could be dead."

"You fucking broke his heart."

She fell back against the pillow and closed her eyes again. Her throat ached and her face burned. She wouldn't open her eyes to look at Jamie, knowing the recrimination she would see on his face. She thought she might throw up, her stomach was so tight with worry. She swallowed. "I know."

Tyler. Brave and strong, loyal and protective. He was the best man she'd ever known. She'd been so, so lucky to be with him…so lucky to be the one he wanted. Tears stung her eyes at the staggering waste of it. What had she done?

"I'm sorry," she choked out, meeting Jamie's eyes. "I messed things up."

He narrowed his eyes at her from where he sat on a nearby chair. "Seems that way."

"What did Tyler tell you?"

"He said you broke up with him."

She pulled her bottom lip between her teeth.

"He was wrecked, Arden."

She closed her eyes again. Everything inside her hurt. "I'm sorry. I was…I panicked."

"What the fuck? Why?"

"Because…because…I don't want to get lost again."

"Okay…"

"I love him. I really do." She paused. "I lost someone before."

"Yeah." Jamie's head dropped forward briefly. "Shit, Arden. I wasn't thinking about that. Are you okay?"

His sudden switch from annoyance to sympathy made her heart squeeze. "I'm not sure. I'm scared for him."

"He's gonna be okay. He—" Jamie stopped abruptly.

"I didn't handle things well. But I was scared. I didn't want to fall in love because I thought that would interfere with my plan…my goal. To figure out who I am and what I want to do with my life."

"Hell, Arden. *None* of us have it figured out. And I don't know if we're really supposed to. None of us know where we're really going in life…and even if we think we do, shit happens and it all changes. But it's not about that. It's about getting there. It's about learning and growing." He paused. "Maybe Tyler is part of figuring things out."

She nodded, her throat thick. "I think I know that now. And I realize I was also scared because…I feel guilty about what happened with Michael. I talked to Mom about it. And… maybe…it wasn't my fault he took his own life."

Jamie gaped at her. "You blame yourself?"

"I was his wife. I should have known what he was going through. I feel like…nobody should love me."

After a shocked beat, Jamie shook his head. "Lots of people love you, Arden."

One corner of her mouth lifted. "Even you?" She tried for a teasing tone, but it maybe came out a little needier than she wanted.

"Even me." He smiled.

"I love you too," she whispered. "And I'm an idiot."

"Yeah." His smile went crooked. "But at least you're smart enough to know when you screwed up. So what are you going to do to fix it?"

"I need to see him." She sucked in a breath and lifted her chin. "Take me to the hospital."

CHAPTER TWENTY-SIX

*T*yler wasn't one to lie around in bed a lot—unless he had company—but obviously he was messed up because all he did was sleep. Got up to take a leak every once in a while. Stared out the hospital window. Slept some more.

He felt marginally better than yesterday—less nausea. Still had the occasional ringing in his ears, which was annoying as fuck. Still dizzy sometimes, but that could also be the painkillers. He wanted off the drugs. They fucked with his mind and made him have weird dreams. He'd been sure Arden had been here in his hospital room last night, naked. But when he woke up, he was alone, dammit.

Mom came back of course. Couple more guys from the station had dropped by. Even his battalion chief had visited.

But not Arden. She was gone.

He was having a very pleasant dream involving a blow job…Arden's hot little mouth wrapped around him, her fingers caressing him, her hair tickling his thighs… "I don't know if I can do this," Arden whispered.

"You can do it, gorgeous." He lifted his hips. "Just open a little wider…"

A throat clearing made him open his eyes. Jamie and Arden were staring at him.

"Fuck off, Jamie." He frowned. "You can't be here." Major ick factor, since Arden was his sister. It was just a dream, but still…

"Uh…dude…"

Arden's gaze was on his dick tenting the hospital sheets. As it should be, if she was about to…

Fuck. This was real. His dick wilted.

"I'm outta here." Jamie held up his hands. "Good luck."

Tyler watched his friend's back disappear.

He swiveled his gaze back to Arden, eyes now determinedly focused on his face. "Um, hi," she said weakly.

"I'm not dreaming, am I?"

"No." She swallowed, her hands so tight on the handle of her purse her knuckles were white.

"Damn."

Her eyes widened.

"I mean…I was having a really good dream."

"I got that." Her eyes flicked to his groin, then back up. "Good to know you're not that injured."

He still wasn't totally convinced this was real. "The drugs are really good."

She lifted an eyebrow. "What are they giving you? Viagra?"

He choked out a laugh. First one in quite a few days. Then he sobered. Apparently this was in fact really happening. And he was pissed at her. "What are you doing here?"

She bit her lip, slid her gaze away from him, then back, shifting her purse from one hand to the other. "I had to make sure you were okay."

"I'm fine." He waved a bandaged hand.

Her gaze caught on the bandages, then moved to his splinted wrist. Her eyebrows drew together and one hand went to her throat. "You're not okay. You're hurt."

"You came back from Florida."

"Yes." She ran her tongue over her teeth.

He gritted his teeth at the flare of anger inside him. "What do you care if I'm okay?"

"Tyler. God." She took a step and dropped into the visitor chair, setting her purse on the floor. "Of course I care."

"That's not what you said last time I saw you."

She closed her eyes, looking like she might puke.

He was kind of feeling the same. "There's an emesis basin over there." He rolled his head toward the small table next to the bed.

"A what?"

"Emesis basin. For puking."

She grabbed it and jumped up to hold it out to him.

"Not me. You looked like *you* need it."

Her forehead creased. "I'm not going to throw up."

"Oh."

She went to set the tray back down.

"Wait. I might need it after all." He closed his eyes, willing the nausea to pass. He did not want to hurl in front of the prom queen. "Okay. I think I'm okay."

"Oh God. Tyler." She dropped the tray on the table, and sat again, leaning forward. "This is awful. What happened?"

"Eh. Don't wanna tell it again."

She blinked and nodded. "Okay. That's okay, you don't have to. Thank God you're all right. Or you will be. Right?"

"Yep." This was sucking the energy out of him, and he was so fucking confused. "So you can go now. I'm going to be all right."

Her eyes widened and her face tightened. "I didn't come

here just to make sure you're okay." Now she looked like she was facing a gang of bangers with semiautomatic machine guns aimed at her head. "I mean, I did, because I was worried stupid about you, but also because…I have to tell you something."

"Sure. Go for it."

Her forehead creased. "Are you sure you're okay?"

"Yeah. Like I said, good drugs. Hey, is that a racoon looking in the window?"

Her head jerked around, then back, eyes wide.

He gave a dry laugh. "Just messin' with you. Although I was pretty sure you were here last night. And you were pole dancing…naked."

"Oh." Her cheeks flushed pink and she bit her lip. "Okay." She inhaled a big breath. "I wanted to tell you…" Her posture stiffened, but her shoulders went back and she lifted her chin. "I want to tell you that I'm sorry. I'm sorry I hurt you. I'm sorry I was an idiot. I'm sorry I didn't realize that I…I…I love you too." Her voice trembled. "My mom helped me see how stupid I was and helped m-me…woman up and come see you and be honest with you." She met his eyes and hers shone. "You were right, Tyler. I wasn't being honest with myself."

His insides clenched.

"When it came to loving someone…I was terrified. I still am." She met his eyes. "I let Michael down. I didn't know what he was going through. I should have known. I should have been able to help him. I felt it was my fault that he died."

He couldn't speak for a moment, his throat closed up. "You feel responsible for him *dying*?"

"Yes." She closed her eyes, looking like someone was sawing off her arm. "I talked to my mom about it. I probably should have talked to someone about it a long time ago. Instead, I've been carrying this guilt around, thinking I can't be in relationship because of that."

"Christ."

"I know." She nodded. "I know I wasn't responsible for how Michael lived his life and the choices he made. I felt like I should have known, should have done something. Mom made me realize that's not what love is. You can't ever keep someone you love from hurting or making bad choices or being unhappy. You can only support them. Encourage them. I realized that's how I feel about you. I love you. And I'm sorry I hurt you."

He gazed back at her, a weird out-of-body sensation possessing him. This was Arden…the woman he loved…telling him she loved him too. What he'd always wanted, his whole fucking life. And he was afraid to believe her.

It had taken something like this for her to tell him she loved him. But did she really? Or was she just reacting to the fact that he'd been injured? It still fucking hurt that she'd rejected him and then totally bailed on everything, running away because he'd screwed up and tried too hard to control her life. Over and over she'd told him she wanted to be independent and prove she could do things on her own, and over and over he kept butting in. And then she'd told him that he was the one stopping her from figuring out who she was and what she wanted to do with her life.

Those words had felt like fire burning through every layer of his skin.

He'd been doing a lot of thinking about that. About how many times people had told him they could handle things themselves. He'd been thinking a lot about Tara, and how he'd let her and his whole family down by not being there to save her the day she'd been abducted.

And how maybe he'd been trying a little too hard ever since then to make up for that.

Exhaustion and pain and drugs made it too hard to think about things. Made it too hard to even talk right now. "'Kay, thanks," he mumbled.

After a long pause, she said, "Thanks?"

"For apologizing. 'Preciate it." He closed his eyes. "Really tired, now."

Still silence. All he could hear was distant beeping noises and chatter from outside his room. Then he heard a faint sniffle.

He cracked one eye open. Arden sat there, her face tight but stoic. Her eyes were still glossy, her lips pressed together. She gave a short nod. "I understand." She picked up her purse from the floor. "Take care, Tyler. I want…" She closed her eyes briefly. "I want the best for you. In everything. Um…you know Sorcha's in love with you, right?"

What the fuck? Sorcha? Was *Arden* on drugs?

"So maybe you should go out with her." She gave a fast swipe at one eye. "Just saying. I want you to be happy. And healthy. And…I want everything for you."

He stared at her, mind muddled, body hurting. She wanted him to go out with another woman? When she'd just told him she loved him?

"Bye, Tyler."

And then she disappeared out the door.

CHAPTER TWENTY-SEVEN

*T*yler wasn't milking it. Not really. It was nice having his mom wait on him hand and foot, though, and she actually seemed to enjoy it.

"Can I get you something else to drink?" she asked. "Another pillow?"

"Nah, I'm good." He held the remote control for the TV, pausing between binge-watching episodes of *Game of Thrones*. It wasn't really distracting him from thinking about Arden, though. He'd been a mess since she'd visited him in the hospital. Apologizing. Telling him she loved him. He was afraid to believe her, because...because he'd been hallucinating, and if that hadn't been real...and because he'd been wanting that his whole life and he'd pushed her away by trying too hard to look after her.

The doorbell rang and Mom went to answer it.

Jamie strolled in seconds later. "Hey, how's the patient?"

Tyler stopped the show. "I'm okay. How're you?"

"Not bad. Mila told me I'm supposed to bring something when I visit, so I got you this."

Tyler pushed up to sitting from his reclined position and took the gift Jamie proffered. "What is it?"

"It's a plug-n-play retro TV games arcade kit. It comes with two hundred games."

Tyler grinned, checking out the tiny handheld controller. "Retro is right."

"You just plug it into your TV."

"Cool. Thanks." It was crazy, and Tyler would bet it set Jamie back a few hundred bucks, but that was him.

"Can I get you a drink, Jamie?" Mom asked. "Beer? Scotch? Coke?"

"A Coke would be great, Mrs. Ramirez. Thanks." He threw himself down into an armchair.

Mom brought him a drink and then disappeared.

"So, how are you healing?" Jamie asked.

"Good, I guess." He held up his arm. "Got my cast on this morning."

"Uh...that's good?"

Tyler shrugged. "They just splint it until the swelling goes down. Then they put a cast on it."

"How long for the cast?"

"Six to eight weeks."

"Jesus. Are you gonna be off work that long?"

"I guess so." He sighed. "But the concussion symptoms are a lot better. Burns are healing fine."

"That's good."

"Yep." He paused and eyed Jamie, who tapped his fingers on the armrest of the chair. He waited, one eyebrow raised. "What is it?"

"Arden."

His heart bumped. "What about her?"

"She's not good."

Tyler swallowed, his heart rate quickening. "What's wrong?"

"You."

Tyler frowned.

"She came to see you in the hospital."

"Yeah."

"To tell you that she loves you."

"Yeah. Funny how it took me getting hurt for her to realize that." A burning sensation hit his gut.

"She came back before she knew you were injured, asshole!"

His tense jaw loosened. "What?"

"Yeah. I was the one who told her. She was standing in my apartment, all excited to be back and try to apologize to you and fix things, because she knew she'd messed things up, and I had to tell her you were in the hospital. She thought you were dying. I think she had a…a flashback or something." His face tightened. "She passed out on me and scared the shit out of me when she heard."

Tyler's gut clenched, remembering Arden's face when he'd opened his eyes and looked at her in the hospital room. She'd been scared, but she'd tried to be so brave. "She was already here?"

"Yeah. I guess after a talk with Mom, she realized she had to come see you. She got back the morning after your accident. She didn't even know about it."

"Shit." He closed his eyes on a wave of hot shame. "Shit."

"Yeah. And you rejected her."

"It's for the best. She…" He swallowed. "She told me I interfered in her life too much and I was stopping her from being able to start over. She kept saying she wanted to prove she could do things on her own. I screwed up."

Jamie fell back into the chair, eyes closed. "Jesus Christ."

"I'm an idiot. I'm sorry. She's your sister."

Jamie rolled his head side to side. "You do tend to be a bit overprotective of people."

"I know. I've been thinking about that, believe me. I lost…" His throat clogged up and he coughed. "I lost the best thing that ever happened to me because I just couldn't stop butting in all the time to try to help her."

"Shit." Jamie sat forward now, bowing his head.

"I knew she was trying to prove herself. But the thing is, she doesn't have to prove a goddamn thing. She's strong and determined. Even though she's been through hell, she still believes everything is going to be okay. Everyone else can see that too. In the end, she's the only person she has to prove anything to. And she needs to do that on her own. So she was right to end things between us."

Jamie heaved a sigh and pinched the bridge of his nose.

"She wants me to go out with someone else."

Jamie's eyes opened and his head jerked up. "I don't believe that."

"She said that. She told me to go out with Sorcha."

"What?"

"Yeah."

"After you told her to get lost."

"I didn't tell her that!"

"Whatever. Am I right?"

Tyler let out a breath and closed his eyes. "It's kind of fuzzy. I *was* on a lot of drugs."

"I'm right," Jamie muttered.

"She says Sorcha's in love with me."

"Everyone can see that, dickhead."

"She said she wants me to be happy."

Jamie was silent for so long, Tyler opened his eyes to peer at him.

"Wow," Jamie said. "You sure that concussion didn't cause brain damage?"

Tyler scowled.

"I never thought you were slow," Jamie said. "You told her to fuck off, and what she said was she wants you to be happy. Even if it's with another woman. Don't you get it?"

A tightness spread through Tyler's chest, and he rubbed his hand over it. "Uh…you're saying she really loves me?"

"Yes, she loves you!" Jamie pulled in a breath and lowered his voice. "She was worried about you, terrified you were going to die. She screwed up and she came to tell you that. And you fucking let her down. And here I thought you imagined yourself to be some kind of hero."

Heat swept up into Tyler's face in a hot flush.

Jamie set down his empty glass on the coffee table. "Well. I better go." He stood.

Fuck. Jamie was pissed at him.

Not as pissed as he was at himself. Jesus, he'd had another chance with Arden, and he'd fucked that up too. A sharp stabbing in his heart made him wince.

But…if she really loved him…maybe he could still fix things. Not by taking over her life. He wanted to spend the rest of his life showing her that he believed in her and believed she could do anything she set her mind to. He wanted to be her partner. Her lover. Her support when she needed it.

Could he have the chance to do that?

His muscles twitched with the need for action. His heart beat a rapid, uneven rhythm. He rubbed his mouth.

"Take care, buddy." Jamie started toward the door. "Let us know when you're coming home."

Tyler shook his head and focused on Jamie again. "Is she still here?"

Halfway across the room, Jamie turned. "Arden? Yeah."

"Tomorrow."

Jamie's head cocked.

"I'm coming home tomorrow. But…wait."

Jamie took two steps back toward him, one eyebrow cocked.

"Come back." Tyler jerked his head and swallowed. "I might need some help."

Liam's jaw dropped when he looked up from the bar and saw her standing there.

"Hi." Arden smiled tentatively at him.

"*A chara*. You're back."

She gave him a crooked smile. "I don't suppose you need a waitress? I'm looking for a job."

He smiled slowly. "As a matter of fact, we could use some help. Someone experienced. Someone beautiful who charms the customers. You'll do."

"Thank you." Her throat clogged up, and she swallowed as she climbed onto a barstool, setting her purse on the bar. "I screwed up."

"Yes. Yes, that you did. But screwups can be fixed."

"Apparently not." She sucked on her bottom lip. "That's what Jamie told me. So I went to see Tyler." Her throat squeezed shut again, and she couldn't get the words out. She bent her head.

"We went to see him last night," Liam said quietly. "He seemed a little narky."

She nodded even though she didn't know exactly what that meant.

"Probably bollucksed from the drugs," he continued, as if he knew she couldn't talk. "But it sounds like he's going to recover."

She nodded miserably.

"Did you tell him you screwed up?"

She nodded again. "He said thanks."

"Thanks?"

"For apologizing." She lifted her head, determined not to cry. "So I guess I can't fix that screwup. But..." She smiled bravely. "I can get my old job back. I'm sorry, Liam. I shouldn't have run away like that."

"No, you shouldn't have. But I think Tyler loves you, so maybe there's still hope."

"It's okay." She rubbed her mouth. "It's going to be awkward until I can find somewhere else to live, though." She'd already gone online and perused apartments in the area. Ugh. Rent was going to take nearly her whole income, and that was just for a crappy little studio apartment. But whatever. It had to be done. "I might need a raise."

Liam choked. "A raise, you say?"

She grinned. "Come on, you know I deserve it."

He shook his head, smiling. "You're something else, Arden my love."

"I'm going to put some effort into getting more catering jobs," she said. "I hope the offer to use the kitchen here stands? If I can get a few more jobs, I should be able to afford to move out."

Liam's eyes crinkled at the corners, though he still looked worried. "Yes, the offer stands. Good for you, Arden."

"Thanks. Well. When can I start?"

"Tomorrow." He turned. "Sorcha!"

Sorcha appeared from the kitchen. Her eyes widened at seeing Arden. "What's going on?"

"I just hired a new waitress.

Sorcha's lips twitched. "Seriously?"

"This is Arden. She starts tomorrow."

"You didn't even interview her, did you?" Sorcha grinned, and Arden laughed, remembering the first time she'd walked in here. "Did she fill out an application form? Did you get references?" She met Arden's eyes and opened her arms.

Arden slid off the stool and flew at her for a long hug. Coming from Sorcha, this meant a lot. "Missed you."

"Missed you too. You okay?" Sorcha pulled back to look into her eyes.

"Not really. But I will be. Thanks." She scrunched up her face, took a deep breath, then smiled. She stepped away and reached for her purse. "Thank you. Thank you both so much. I'll see you tomorrow."

She walked the familiar route back to Jamie's house. Such a lovely neighborhood. She remembered her first days there, walking these streets, Tyler worried about her walking home alone at night. She squeezed her eyes shut briefly. She'd been annoyed at him, but now she appreciated having someone who cared that much. And she'd messed it up.

At home, she climbed the beautiful staircase to the second floor and opened the door to her apartment.

She stopped. Stared. Her mouth fell open. Tyler was there.

CHAPTER TWENTY-EIGHT

$\mathcal{T}$yler stood next to the kitchen island, where a big bouquet of fall flowers glowed—sunflowers and gladioli and chrysanthemums. Also, gold and orange balloons floated above them. He looked so handsome...his arm in a cast, his face still a little pale and drawn, but God, he was beautiful and strong and brave.

She blinked. "Uh...hi. What's going on?"

"We're celebrating."

She tipped her head. "Okay. Um...what are we celebrating?" She hadn't checked her app so she had no idea what today was supposed to celebrate.

"It's National I'm an Idiot so I'm Groveling for Forgiveness Day."

Air left her lungs in a rush, her throat thickening. "Ah." She took a few steps farther into the apartment. "That sounds like something we should both be observing."

He smiled....so beautiful, his sculpted lips curving upward. "I thought so."

"So…what do we eat and drink to celebrate this important day?"

One corner of his mouth hitched up. "We eat crow."

She smiled back at him. "Ugh. Doesn't sound good at all."

"I don't think it's supposed to. That's the point…it's hard to swallow. Like being a stupid idiot is hard to swallow."

"Yeah." She sucked in a breath and let it out. "I know."

"We're also having humble pie." He gestured at a delicious-looking, golden-crusted pie on the table.

Her eyebrows flew up. "Really? Did you make that?"

"No." He grimaced.

She grinned.

"I have to warn you—you probably won't like humble pie the first time you try it. I didn't. But it kind of grows on you."

"Oh yeah?"

"Mmm. At first it kind of tastes like shit. Then it changes… to not bad…then to sweet."

"Well, I have news for you."

"What?"

"I've actually already tasted humble pie. More than once." She blinked rapidly, pressing her fist to her mouth. "But it's a good reality check and it keeps us grounded."

"I'm an idiot, Arden."

She blinked at him again, mouth still covered.

"And I'm sorry. So goddamn sorry. When you came to see me in the hospital…" He looked away briefly. "I was afraid to believe it was true. That you loved me. I was afraid you just felt sorry for me because of the accident, and that's why you came back." He met her eyes. "I thought you wanted to be on your own to figure out your life."

"I thought that too." She lowered her hand. "I was wrong."

"Yeah?"

"Yeah."

"I love you. And when you said you didn't feel the same… and you told me I was the one stopping you from proving yourself…fuck."

Her face burned. "Oh God, Tyler. I'm sorry. I was so wrong."

"I *am* an interfering idiot."

One corner of her mouth lifted.

"I've been thinking a lot about it. I'm going to do better. Especially with you…if you'll let me?"

She nodded slowly, her insides quivering, her heart slamming.

He walked toward her, lifting his arms. And then she was there, in his arms, up against him. He held onto her, tilting his head to find her mouth with his in a long, lush, desperate kiss. Her cheek was wet against his and he drew back, using his thumb to brush away the moisture. "Don't cry. Please don't cry. I don't ever want to make you cry again."

"It's okay." She blinked wet eyelashes. "I'm happy crying."

He kissed her again and she melted into him. Relief floated like bubbles in her veins, joy expanding in her chest.

He lifted his head and they smiled at each other.

"I love you, Tyler. I really, really love you."

He slid his hand into her hair. "I love you too."

He brushed his mouth across hers again in a slow, sweet kiss of regret and promise.

She drew back. "Okay, what's really in the pie?"

He chuckled. "It's an apple pie. I bought it at the farmers' market."

"I love apple pie." She swiped a hand over one wet cheek.

"And the cocktail of the day is Suck Bang and Blow."

She choked. "What?"

He nodded seriously and pointed to the blender on the counter. "Yes. Already made."

327

"Interesting. Suck Bang and Blow. Hmmm. Let's try it."

"Later. The kind of sucking and banging and blowing I want is gonna happen in the bedroom. Right now." He eased her backward, back down the hall. "I'd pick you up and carry you, but I'm a bit gimped out right now." He held up the cast.

She laughed. "I can walk."

In the bedroom, Tyler stopped next to the bed and set about undressing Arden...pulling her T-shirt over her head, unzipping her jeans while she unfastened her bra. She tugged off his T-shirt while he wrestled her snug jeans down her thighs and off, mostly one-handed, then he undid his own jeans. Looser, they dropped to the floor and he kicked them aside, then spun Arden around and fell to his back on his bed, pulling her down on top of him. He cupped her face with one hand and kissed her, trying to pour all he could into the kiss, all the emotion he felt for her, trying to show her how he felt.

She kissed him back, her mouth opening to him, her tongue stroking his. He kissed her again, bit softly at her lips, sucked her tongue into his mouth, and her hips moved against him in a needy rhythm. The soft sounds she made in the back of her throat inflamed his senses.

He kissed her over and over, tongues sliding, lips gliding, then he rolled her to her back, mouths still joined, so he could slide one hand up her body and cup one of her sweet breasts. Oh yeah...it filled his hand perfectly, so damn sweet.

She opened her thighs and he fit himself there between them. She shifted beneath him, arching her back, her fingers sliding into his hair and scraping across his scalp. Hot sizzles cascaded over his skin. He growled and sucked at the soft skin on the side of her neck.

Her moan filled his head, urging him on. He wanted her so bad, but he wanted to make her feel good. This was important. This was…everything.

He lifted his head to peer down at her, and she gazed back at him, her expression full of wonder and love. He took his weight on his elbows, arms beside her head on the pillow, hands in her hair.

Her hands lifted to his head, his face, a sweet smile curving her lips, and he swallowed hard at the love and respect and devotion he saw there. "I love you, Arden."

She caressed his hair and his rough cheek, and he turned his mouth into her palm and kissed it, closing his eyes.

"I love you too."

"Arden." He looked at her and her eyes focused on him. "I know you think you need to prove yourself. But you don't to me. I love you for who you are…I always have. I know I tease you about being a princess…the prom queen…but it's because I worship you. I want to spend the rest of my life worshipping you."

Her eyes went glossy and she blinked fast. "Thank you." Her gaze held his, her words too like a vow, a promise. "I feel the same about you. I want to worship you too. I love your courage, your honor. I love how you take care of people, and even though it made me crazy, I loved how you took care of me."

"It bugged you. I know I can be overprotective. I tried to pull back so I wouldn't smother you. I stopped walking you home from work because I knew how important it was for you to be independent. Even though I worried about you."

"I know." Her bottom lip quivered. "And I love that too."

"I promise to stop trying to rescue everyone all the time and just be smart about it. I've been thinking a lot about it since you left."

"I love that you care about people," she said. "But yes, sometimes you can overstep."

They'd done away with condoms weeks ago, thank God, so nothing was between them when she raised her knees, her hands resting on his shoulders, and he pushed inside her, a long glide of exquisite pleasure. Heat rushed through his body, emotions swirling inside him, pressure building. Their eyes connected as they moved together and he filled her again and again, lost in her, lost in love with her.

She moved beneath him, seductive and soft and welcoming, fingers playing across his shoulders. "Oh," she sighed. "Oh my God, Tyler..."

"You're so beautiful, Arden. You glow...like the sun. I just want to be in your light...always."

"Oh..."

He changed his position and she lifted her knees higher. She whimpered as he hit the right spot and they rocked together, heat building, her eyes glazing, small sighs squeezing from her throat. She cried out as her body tightened around him, pulsing. A pink flush rose over her cheeks, her teeth sinking into that lush bottom lip.

"Beautiful." He kissed her mouth, her cheek, sensation burning and twisting inside him. He pushed into her one last time and stayed there as he finished in an explosion of heat and light, pouring himself into her literally and figuratively. He made a rough, low sound, his hand tightening in her hair, then dropped his forehead to the pillow beside her. His lungs strained, his muscles quivered.

She still pulsed around him in small ripples that nearly sent him over again. "Christ, Arden. Jesus Christ."

"I love you." She kissed his shoulder. "I love you so much. And I'm so sorry I hurt you."

"I'm sorry too. Fuck." He was still trying to breathe.

"You also need to apologize for lying to me."

"What?" His head lifted to glare at her.

"You told me you didn't want a relationship."

"Oh. Uh. Yeah." He sank his teeth into his bottom lip. "Yeah, that was kind of a lie."

She pursed her lips. "And…?"

"And I'm sorry. Sort of." He hesitated. "The truth is…I've loved you forever, Arden."

She stared at him, her lips quivering. "Wh-what?"

"I guess it was more of a crush when we were younger, but…hell, I've loved you since I was fourteen years old. Getting to know you better now, as adults, it became so much more than a teenage crush."

"Oh. Oh, Tyler." She sucked her bottom lip between her teeth, her eyes bright. "I didn't know that."

"Didn't you?" He smiled wryly and brushed her hair back. "Jamie figured it out."

"Did he? Wow. He's pretty clueless about stuff like that."

Tyler snorted. "I guess I didn't hide it very well."

His pounding heart slower now, he shifted off Arden, keeping her close against him.

"Ouch!"

"Sorry, sorry." He'd bashed her with his cast.

"Are you okay?" She tipped her face up to him, concern etching a notch between her eyebrows. "You're the one with the broken arm."

"I'm okay. Damn this thing."

"It'll heal. Right?"

"Yeah, it'll heal." He got the covers arranged over them, tucking them in around Arden's beautiful naked body.

"Are you feeling better? I didn't even ask earlier."

"Much better. Still some headaches, but I can handle that.

I'm only taking Advil now, not the narcotics, so that's better too."

"Oh, good." She made a small noise. "I was so worried about you." Her voice wobbled.

"I know." He stroked a hand down her smooth back and curved it over her ass. "I'm sorry. "My mom freaked out about the accident."

"Well, yeah, I guess she would. We all did. Jamie and Mila...even Emma. And Sorcha and Liam."

"Turns out that's why she doesn't want me to be a firefighter."

"Hmm?" She gave him a puzzled look. "Because she's afraid you'll get hurt?"

"Yeah. She just about lost it. Because, you know...what happened to Tara. And then Dad dying. I'm all she has left."

"Oh God." Her eyes widened. "I see."

"Yeah." He sighed. "I felt so bad...for putting her through that."

"I understand how she feels," she said softly. "Because we both love you. I know that feeling...wanting you to be safe and happy, always. But life isn't like that."

"Jamie and Mila freaked out too."

"Because they care about you too."

Regret squeezed his lungs. He tried to make light of it. "Jamie damn near passed out in the hospital. I mean, he's my friend, but I didn't know he was such a wuss."

She gave his shoulder a light smack. "I guess I can't give him grief about that, since I nearly fainted too. But like I said, he cares about you."

"I hate that I scared the shit out of everyone."

"There are no guarantees in life," she said softly. She reached out to cup his cheek. "I know that, now. You love someone for who they are, and that's all you can do. I just wish…I should have been here for you when it happened. I hate that I wasn't. I'll never do that again."

He covered her hand with his and held it there, loving her gentle touch.

"We can be here for each other now. And for always. In all the ways we can. I know there are risks in your job…but it's who you are, and I want you to be happy."

"You said that before. When you were trying to get me to go out with Sorcha."

"Yeah, don't even think of it, dude."

He grinned. "I wasn't, believe me."

She sniffed. "I was trying to be noble. If we couldn't be together, I *would* want you to be happy with someone. I wouldn't really like it," she admitted. "But I do want you to be happy. I want you to do the job you love. I want you to move up in the fire department and maybe someday be running it."

He smiled.

"And I know your mom has to feel the same. Because she loves you too."

His chest filled with emotion, he stared back at her. "I love you."

She smiled. "I love you too."

"I love you for celebrating daiquiris and ice cream. And for baking me muffins. And for giving me blow jobs."

She let out a noise halfway between a laugh and a sob. "And I love you for walking me home at night and loving my muffins—"

"That sounds dirty."

She swatted at him. "That wasn't a euphemism. But hell… I'll just say it—I love you for loving my jay-jay."

"I really do."

"I may not know where I'm going," she said more seriously.

"But I want to figure it out with you. Loving you doesn't have to stop me from figuring it out."

"That's exactly right." He pulled her hand to his mouth and kissed it. "I want to help you figure it out. Not stop you. It fucking hurt when you said it was my fault that you couldn't do that."

"I know." Her voice wobbled. "I'm so sorry. I was wrong. It wasn't you. It was me. And you knew it. You knew I wasn't being honest with myself. And now I know…God, Tyler, you make me better. Without you…" She stopped, choking up.

He shook his head slowly. "Without me, you'd be fine. Because like I've told you…you're smart and strong. But together…we can be more than fine. We can be fucking fantastic."

The corners of her mouth lifted. "I want to be there for you too," she said earnestly. "While you make your mom proud of you and move up in the fire department. None of us have it all figured out, but maybe we're not supposed to. It's the journey where we learn the things that help us grow and prepare us for the destination…even if we're not sure what the destination is. Even if it changes along the way. If life is a journey…I want to take the journey with you."

He gathered her back into his arms. "Yeah. Hell yeah. Let's do it. Together."

EPILOGUE

"I guess I need a new wing man." Jamie morosely regarded Tyler. "Seems like you're out of the running now."

Arden laughed.

They were all seated around the fireplace at Shenanigans. Arden was working but was taking her break for a few minutes, leaning against Tyler's chair. Jamie, Mila, and Danny were there too. They were celebrating Tyler's promotion, informally since Arden was working. She and Tyler would celebrate properly some other night.

Evan Crenshaw had been off on leave since the fire where they'd found the body, getting treatment for PTSD. Tyler had been commended for how he'd taken control and had gotten Evan out of that house. There were times when his need to fix things was definitely a benefit.

Tyler was sympathetic to the guy, and felt a little guilty about being promoted ahead of him, even though he knew he was a better candidate than Evan. This wasn't how he'd wanted it to happen.

"I'll be your wing man," Mila offered. "I'm single now."

"You can't be my wing man." Jamie frowned.

"Why not?"

"Because you're not a man."

"Thank you, Captain Obvious." Mila wrinkled her nose at him as she sipped her cocktail. "I'll have you know I can wing as well as any man."

Everyone else laughed.

"No," Jamie said patiently. "The idea of a wing man is to help keep the target girl's friend occupied."

"I can do that. I can strike up a conversation with a couple of women. In fact, it might work better than another man. Less threatening." She paused. "What the hell am I even saying? This is totally obnoxious. Women aren't 'targets.' That's disgusting and predatory."

"Well, that's settled then," Jamie said dryly.

Arden shook her head. "I think Mila's the one who needs a wing man."

Mila eyebrows rose. "It's predatory whichever gender is doing it."

"True. But you said you want to meet guys and have meaningless sex."

"I did." Mila tapped her chin and narrowed her eyes at Jamie. "Oh, hey, she's right. You totally could help me with that."

Jamie choked. "What? Me? How?"

Arden felt Tyler's big body vibrating with suppressed laughter.

"We could go out together," Mila said. "Just as friends, you know. Which we are. Friends. We could help each other meet other people. I'm not looking for a boyfriend anymore. I just want some action. But I'm not very good at it. You can teach me how to do that, since you're an expert."

"I'm not helping you pick up guys," Jamie said, frowning.

"Why not?" Liam paused by their grouping at that moment.

"Because…" Jamie floundered. "Because…"

"Because it's slutty?" Mila challenged him. "It's okay for men to do it, but not women?"

"I didn't say that."

"Prove me wrong, then."

"This is stupid," he muttered.

"What do you think, Danny?" Liam asked.

Arden watched the eye contact between Danny and Liam. Danny appeared relaxed, dressed in faded jeans and fitted shirt, one ankle resting on the opposite knee. Liam on the other hand was tense and twitchy, his expression grim.

"Well, since you asked me," Danny drawled, "I think everyone needs to recognize that female sexuality exists, and women do get pleasure from sex."

"Yes!" Mila pumped a fist in the air. "Thank you, Danny."

"I also think we need to create a different definition of masculinity." He met Liam's eyes and held his gaze. Arden was pretty sure she saw sparks. "Masculine traits are typically defined by violence and brute strength. Masculinity should include being caring and nurturing as well as courageous and strong."

"That's not what we were talking about," Liam muttered. "I have to get back to work." He disappeared.

Danny sipped his drink, wearing an amused smile.

Arden glanced at Tyler and they exchanged a look of *what the hell was that?*

"I'm glad you said that, Danny," Mila announced. "See, Jamie? Women can have hookups too."

"Fine." Jamie lifted his chin. "You're on."

"Great! Let's go out Thursday night."

"Fine."

"Fine."

"I better get back to work." Arden leaned down and kissed Tyler's cheek. "I'll see you at home." She lowered her voice to a whisper. "We'll celebrate your promotion."

He made a rough noise in his throat. "Can't wait." He turned his face so their mouths met in a brief kiss. "Meanwhile, don't flirt with the customers."

She stood, grinning. "That's how I make my tips."

He shook his head, smiling, knowing she was teasing him. "Maybe I'll just sit here the rest of the evening and wait for you."

She shrugged. "That's fine."

He couldn't be there every night, but it didn't bother her anymore when he came to walk her home. She thought it was sweet. She knew she could look after herself, but having someone who cared enough to do that was lovely. She did things for Tyler too, but that didn't mean he couldn't look after himself. It just meant they cared about each other.

She was "just" a waitress at Shenanigans, but she loved her job, and she loved Liam and Sorcha. She had some new clients in her catering business, and she hoped she could grow the business. Maybe she didn't know exactly where her life was going, but that was okay. Goals were good. Working toward her goals was good. But even if she wasn't sure what her goals were, love didn't have to interfere with figuring that out. Love was part of the journey. And she and Tyler were on the journey together.

OTHER BOOKS BY KELLY JAMIESON

Heller Brothers Hockey
Breakaway

Faceoff

One Man Advantage

Hat Trick

Offside

Power Series
Power Struggle

Taming Tara

Power Shift

Rule of Three Series
Rule of Three

Rhythm of Three

Reward of Three

San Amaro Singles
With Strings Attached

How to Love

Slammed

Windy City Kink
Sweet Obsession

All Messed Up

Playing Dirty

Brew Crew
Limited Time Offer
No Obligation Required

Aces Hockey
Major Misconduct
Off Limits
Icing
Top Shelf
Back Check
Slap Shot
Playing Hurt
Big Stick
Game On

Last Shot
Body Shot
Hot Shot
Long Shot

Bayard Hockey
Shut Out
Cross Check

Wynn Hockey
Play to Win
In It To Win It

Win Big

For the Win

Stand Alone

Three of Hearts

Loving Maddie from A to Z

Dancing in the Rain

Love Me

Love Me More

Friends with Benefits

2 Hot 2 Handle

Lost and Found

One Wicked Night

Sweet Deal

Hot Ride

Crazy Ever After

All I Want for Christmas

Sexpresso Night

Irish Sex Fairy

Conference Call

Rigger

You Really Got Me

How Sweet It Is

Screwed

Firecracker

ABOUT THE AUTHOR

Kelly Jamieson is a best-selling author of over fifty romance novels and novellas. Her writing has been described as "emotionally complex", "sweet and satisfying" and "blisteringly sexy." She likes coffee (black), wine (mostly white), shoes (high heels) and hockey!

Sign up for updates about her new books and what's coming up, follow her on Twitter @KellyJamieson or on Facebook, visit her website at www.kellyjamieson.com or contact her at info@kellyjamieson.com

facebook.com/KellyJamiesonRomanceAuthor

twitter.com/KellyJamieson